MCGREGOR'S FUSES

Edward Gibson

BookPublishingWorld

A BookPublishingWorld Book

Copyright © Edward Gibson 2007

Cover design by Richard Fitt ©

All rights reserved. No part of this publication may be reproduced, stored in a retrieval system, or transmitted in any form or by any means, electronic, mechanical, photocopy, recording or otherwise, without prior written permission of the copyright owner. Nor can it be circulated in any form of binding or cover other than that in which it is published and without similar condition including this condition being imposed on a subsequent purchaser.

ISBN: 1-905553-23-4
ISBN13: 978-1-905553-23-5

*Dedicated to Alice,
without whose help I couldn't have done it!*

PREFACE

Trapped 30 feet underground by a gigantic bomb underwater. Booby-trapped, bomb dismantled seconds before it was due to explode.

Chased a future murderer over the rooftops in the middle of the night.

The murderer looked at Jock - raised the gun, and pulled the trigger.

The killer pulled the gun from under the pillow as the coppers landed on top of him.

Jock threw his weight against the door and crashed into the room where the armed men were.

The Duke glared at him.
The Dean winked at him.
Marshall Fito stared at him.
The Leading Lady said "Good Evening Darling!"

Spies, Micro Films, Micro Dots, Embassies, Legations, Royal Weddings, Funerals, Coronations, and visits by Royalty and other leaders were all extra jobs to do.

CONTENTS

CHAPTER ONE 9
   TRAPPED 10
   FRESH BLOOD 15
   ONE WEEK TO GO 23
   GOODBYE 52

CHAPTER TWO 55
   THE JOB HUNT 55
   CIVVY STREET 56
   STARTING ORDERS 59
   ROOKY COP 63
   UNWANTED 64
   NIGHTS 67
   HARDWORK 75
   BELLS 76
   WORKING ALONE 77
   EYE OPENERS 79
   STOP 81
   ATTACHMENTS 83
   ON LOAN 88
   HELP 90
   PROBATIONERS 90
   BARROW BOYS 92
   NEW IMMIGRANTS 93
   ANOTHER MEETING 94
   BOTTLED 95
   IRISH 96
   ANOTHER BOMB SCARE 98
   RANKS 100
   A HOME 103
   CASH PROBLEMS 105
   DIRTY DICK 106
   PERKS 107
   HEAVY LIFTING GEAR 112

CHAPTER THREE 115
   HOME BEAT 116
   EXTRA WORK 118
   INSTANT JUSTICE 118
   SENIOR OFFICERS 119
   ACCIDENT FOR A ROOKIE 121
   SUDDEN DEATHS 122
   MURDER 123
   EXPENSIVE TEA 123

BABY SITTING	125
MURDER	126
LOST	129
FIREWOOD	130
BICYCLES	132
CHAPTER FOUR	**135**
BOOBY TRAP	136
ON THE CARPET	141
CHAPTER FIVE	**147**
MOSLEY'S MOB	148
CLOSE SHAVE	150
BANK JOB	151
SMOG	152
TOWN JOB	154
A FORTUNE	155
A COPPER COMES TO GRIEF	156
BUSTLE PUNCHERS	158
BLOW UP	162
CHAPTER SIX	**167**
START CID	168
LONG SHIFT	172
NIGHT WORKING	175
CHAPTER SEVEN	**183**
BURGLARS	184
BREAK-INS	187
STRANGERS	188
MURDER	191
PROPERTY	195
CAR THIEVES	197
GANG FIGHT	198
CHAPTER EIGHT	**201**
THE PIG MAN	202
SETTLED IN	205
THE CIRCUS	209
FUNDS	211
CRASH	212
CHAPTER NINE	**217**
KNIFE FIGHT	218
ATTEMPTED MURDER	220
ACCIDENT	223
TIME GENTLEMEN, PLEASE!	226
DRY HUMOUR	226
CHAPTER TEN	**229**
DROWNING	230

- SUICIDE 231
- RECEIVING END 235
- HELPING HAND 238
- SPARE DRIVER 238
- PLEASURE 239
- FISH 240
- ACCIDENTS 242
- THE BELL 244

CHAPTER ELEVEN 249
- FAMILY TROUBLE 250
- MIND YOUR BACK 251
- HOSPITAL MESSAGE 252
- JUVENILE 255
- GRUB UP 256
- NO STOMACH 257
- BANK ALARM 262
- FIRE 265
- A GOOD JOB 267
- FIRST HOLIDAY 267
- WAGES 268
- CAR CHASE 269
- RIDE HIM COWBOY 274
- LAYABOUT 275

CHAPTER TWELVE 279
- BACK TO WORK 280
- BABYSITTING AGAIN 282
- NEATLY SLICED 289
- BUTTONS 290
- SAFE BLOWERS 291
- STINKERS 292
- SUSPECT 294
- POISON 295
- CRUMPET 296
- PROTECTION RACKET 297

CHAPTER THIRTEEN 299
- CHANGING TIMES 300
- UNDERCOVER CARS 300
- MOTORBIKE MUGS 307
- CANDID CAMERA 308
- TRIPLE MURDER 310

CHAPTER FOURTEEN 313
- NEW JOB 314
- SECURITY 322
- SMALL PEOPLE 324

CALL	324
BROTHERS	328
SPIES	331
HUMAN NATURE	336
CHURCH SERVICE	338
FAMILY PROBLEMS	338

A COPPER'S JOB

CHAPTER ONE

TRAPPED

"What will I do next?" he thought, as he gently raised himself out of the cold water and reached further over. He moved slowly, his fingers probing gently as he searched. It was impossible to see in the darkness of his narrow confines, and his movements were restricted. His back was touching the timber supports, whilst his face was pressed against the cold body of his sleeping companion. The reason he was careful with his movements was obvious, for his companion was a monster, unexploded bomb, weighing over 4,000 pounds.

They were lying in a hole deep under the surface of the earth, and he was trying to find the fuses. With his years of experience he could tell, just by the feel of the charging holes, exactly what type he would be dealing with. Until then, he didn't know if the slightest movement of the bomb would commence the inevitable deadly explosion, if this happened and the monster awoke, it" yawn would make a crater large enough to drop a hotel into it. It would also demolish surrounding factories and streets of houses, the number of dead could be uncountable.

There was a danger of the bomb moving for it rested on sand, water was constantly seeping into the hole, and when a nearby factory pumped water, the tunnel flooded. This happened every twenty minutes, the floods were due to a break in the system. When they arrived the man inside had to be pulled out quickly. This was done by means of a rope tied tightly around his ankles, this rope led away along the tunnel to a shaft about thirty feet away. He glanced toward the pinpoint of light which was his only connection with the civilisation, he knew that he had a good crew up there, and Corporal Soulsby would be squatting in the bottom of the shaft watching the water level like a hawk, and ready to have him hauled out at a moment's notice.

The water ran into his rubber boots as he eased himself forward further along the bomb, something brushed against his hand and he grasped it before he realised it was the rubber hosepipe which was supplying him with fresh air. The pipe was pulled forward and tucked under his chin, the air was cold but breathed in deeply and gratefully.

Time seemed endless as he continued the search for the vital organs, suddenly his fingers stopped and fastened onto a 3" locking nut. He commenced his examination and then gave a satisfied grunt before moving his hand about 20" further along the metal case. He was now looking for the secondary fuse, these were called 'Policeman Fuses' and were placed there to prevent people taking the main fuse out, a deterrent in simple words. 'A Policeman, that's an idea.' His thoughts were elsewhere as he worked, for, after spending most of his Army service on bombs, mines and explosives, he was due to retire in days. He had been considering what he would do when he took off his uniform for the last time. It had been a difficult decision, for most of his young life had been spent in uniform, but now he was certain that he had found the answer to his problem.

A sudden roar and a rush of water disturbed his thoughts and brought him back to reality. The water quickly rose, but the first flow had washed the sand from around the bomb, gently but firmly the monster moved its position. Slowly the huge metal case pressed him against the wooden uprights, he couldn't move with the tremendous weight pressing on his chest. 'Damn' he thought it rather ironic to have lasted so long in this job for this to happen, he had always expected his end would be swift, but now it looked as if a twist of fate had decided a death by drowning. 'Bugger, fancy getting drowned by a bomb', the thought amused him. The flow of air from the hose attracted his attention and he desperately held onto it with his free hand, holding it against the pressure of the water. As the seething torrent closed over his head he was breathing deeply, like a diver, with the hosepipe clamped tightly between his teeth. He realised it was only a temporary measure, for his thin cotton overalls would not be any protection against the icy cold, and he knew that he wouldn't be able to last out long.

On the surface, a group of men stood together, collars up and huddled against the bitter winter wind, with its occasional flurry of snow. They talked and joked together in typical army style as they stood in the deep mud, but each man held on tightly to the rope which went down the deep shaft and into the tunnel, this rope was attached to the man's ankles as he worked alone in the bowels of the earth.

"Cor blimey, its bloody brass monkey weather," came a remark in a typical Cockney voice.

"What are you snitching about Sparrow?" asked a small man who had been anxiously looking down the shaft.

"I only said it was brass monkey weather Serg."

"Well belt up! If this one goes up you won't have any balls to freeze" was the reply from the Sergeant.

"Yeah, but it is cold, ain't it?" the Cockney said.

"Cold. If you are cold, what about being down there in the water?" the mud splattered Sergeant asked.

"I know Serg," the man said, "but the Guvnor likes water, you know that."

"What do you mean?" one of the other men asked.

Sparrow preened himself, eager to let these men know that he had been with 'The Guv' since the war started, and knew all about him.

"Well," he said, "It started in France in 1940 at the retreat from Arras, we were blowing up bridges on the Basse Canal. One of the charges didn't go off, he just dived in and swam across the Canal to fire the charge."

"Why didn't he go over the bridge?" asked one of his audience.

"For the simple reason, Jerry was on the other side throwing all kinds of shit at us," answered Sparrow.

"Is that where he got one of his gongs?" enquired his mate.

"Naw, I don't think he even got a mention in Dispatches, same as when he jumped on a Jerry tank at the Somme, and dropped a grenade in it. If he hadn't done that we wouldn't have got away. Anyway, he's got plenty of medals now, even French and Belgium ones."

"Is that where you get the idea he likes water?"

"If you would stop interrupting me," snapped Sparrow. "I'll tell you. When we got to the beach at La Panne, that's near Dunkirk, it was bedlam, boats and ships of all sizes were there. The trouble was, they were all too far away to get to. There were loads of small boats taking the blokes from the beaches out to the bigger ships. We had to wait a couple of days in the sand dunes with Jerry giving us hell all the time, with bombs and machine guns. The Guvnor suddenly jumped up and ran into the water, we thought he had gone round the bend and was going to swim out to the big ships, or, as someone said, he was going to swim the channel. Do you know, it was one of them ship's lifeboats he was after, it had been left to drift after the swaddies had been taken on a destroyer. The Guv had about 200 yards to swim to it, he grabbed a rope and swam back to the beach with it, believe me, it was a bleedin' heavy boat."

"Did you row back to England in it?" quipped his audience.

"Don't be bleedin' stupid, do you think I'd spoil my little lily white hands." Sparrow rubbed his calloused paws on his wet muddy trousers.

"No, we got on a destroyer but Jerry sank it and we had to swim back to the beach, that is the few of us that was left."

"What happened then?" his mates were getting interested.

"We were picked up three times and each time we were put back into the drink by the Jerries. The last time was in the middle of the Channel, we were picked up by a Froggy fishing boat who brought us home."

"You'll have seen as much water as the Guv then?" he was told.

"I think I was in it more Taffy, because when we were in Blighty doing training, he used to have us on route marches, 3 days to do 100 miles, and at the end we had to swim in full marching order, rifle included."

"Well you Cockney get, you should be clean by now."

"That wasn't the last time we were heading for a watery grave. We were torpedoed when we were going abroad," the intrepid Cockney continued.

"Bloody hell, what happened?" Taffy asked.

Sparrow sucked at his cigarette and said, "It was night time and there was a hell of a crash, bodies flying in all directions, bells going like the clappers, and water rushing into our hold. We were all ordered to line up on the decks as the ship was sinking. The Guv went down into our hold, dived into the water and fastened ropes onto all of our pumps. They were pulled up, and we used them with the ship's pumps, to keep us afloat. Mind you the sea was lapping the decks before they…"

"Pull!" a frantic voice bellowed from the bottom of the shaft.

"Pull, you bastards, pull!" yelled the Sergeant as he sprang to the rope to assist. With automatic reaction the men all heaved on the rope, it tightened and then jerked to a halt.

The Sergeant shouted at the men "Pull your bloody guts out, damn you, get him out."

The men pulled and swore, rubber boots slipping in the mud. Suddenly the rope went loose and all the men fell, in an ungainly heap, in the churned up mud.

The Sergeant rose quickly and raced to the edge of the shaft.

"Are you alright down there?" he shouted as he looked down the hole, then he noticed there was no sign of the Corporal below. As he watched, a head appeared out of the muddy water.

"What's happened Corp?" shouted the worried NCO

"Bugger me Serg, you pulled his sodden boots off." The man held up a pair of rubber boots, still attached to the rope.

"Hell" groaned the Sergeant, "What a bloody way to go."

"Serg" shouted the man beside the pump, "come here." The despondent man went across to where the man stood.

"What do you want?"

"Listen" exclaimed the soldier. The Sergeant stood quite still and listened for a while.

"I can't hear anything," he said.

"Put your hand on the pipe," the man instructed. The senior NCO did as he was told.

"So what?"

"There's a bumping noise on it, like Morse code," the sapper explained. With a feeling of despair, the Sergeant once again put his hand on the pipe.

"Christ, I think you are right. Any of you idle sods know Morse code?" he shouted to the now quiet group of soldiers.

"Yeah, I do" came the Cockney's voice, as the man ran across to the Sergeant. He placed his hand on the hosepipe and concentrated on the repeated tappings, which were being repeated over and over again.

"Bomb moved-----Trapped-----using air hose-----bloody cold." He passed the message to the Sergeant who suddenly burst into action.

"Tell him we are on the way," he snapped to Sparrow. "Get one of the pumps from the other workings and an extra length of hose. Jones, get a hydraulic jack from the truck. Sparrow, two baulks of timber 3" x 3" and two feet long, quickly. Move your arses. Smithy, get another length of rope. Corporal," he yelled down the shaft "Get the boots off, have the rope ready. Hardman, get that fire built up and get a brew on."

Quickly the men accomplished their designated tasks, each knowing that speed was essential for, if any rescue was to be made, it would have to be quick, as it would be impossible to survive long in the icy water where their Guvnor was trapped.

The Sergeant quickly climbed down to the bottom of the shaft, at the water level he took off his overcoat. "Lower the jack and the timber on the spare rope" he ordered. "Corp, you wait until you feel three sharp tugs on the rope, then pull them both together." He shouted up to the man on the pump, "Chuck the end of the hose down and start the pump."

He felt the cold air coming through the pipe and wrapped it round his chest and brought the end over his shoulder and clamped it between his teeth. He waited impatiently for the Corporal to fasten the rope to his ankles and around his waist. Then, clutching his implements, he dropped into the swirling waters. He sank to the entrance of the tunnel and the ice cold water took his breath away. Making his way forward along the narrow tunnel was awkward, he moved crab-like, pushing his load forward to arms length, laying them down in the mud to lever his body along after them. He then had to repeat the operation time and time again. The thirty feet he travelled seemed more like thirty miles as he struggled against the force of the water, occasionally he caught his burden on the wooden uprights. At last his hands met with a solid block, he lowered his precious load to the ground and kept his body on them to prevent the wood from floating away, as he felt round the smooth surface of the bomb. He followed it around, looking for the widest part to enable him to pass. Soon he found the place to enter and he eased his body forward, drawing his tools with him. His outstretched hands came in contact with a soft object which wriggled when he felt it. "First time I've tickled the Boss's foot" he thought. His movements were slow and he gulped at the fresh air blowing into his mouth. "Christ but it's bloody cold, like being in a fridge. If I don't get him out soon he's had it."

He untied the rope from around his waist and fastened it to the trapped man's ankles. Then, feeling the space between the bomb and the tunnel wall he edged forward.

"Bloody good job he's twice as big as me. It'll give me a bit more room to move." He brought his load further along the tunnel and wedged them under the other man's legs. Then, slowly, he pulled his body forward, feeling with both hands and careful to avoid the life preserving hosepipe, till at last he was lying on top of his Guvnor.

As he lay there, he carefully felt past the head of the soldier whose life was in his hands. He knew that the only way to free his boss was to try and force the bomb away, this he hoped to do by using the jack. Obviously, he couldn't place the jack between the man and the tunnel entrance, for when they pulled on the rope the man would be trapped against the jack. He had to get over the body and place his material past his mate's head. First he had to transport his tools over his Guvnor and then put the wooden blocks in an upright position with the jack in between them, then by operating the jack and extending it, he hoped to gain several inches and thus release the body.

He struggled laboriously backward in the narrow space, collected the jack and then crawled forward again over the trapped man, who was in no position to object. The Sergeant was careful with the heavy jack, he didn't want to drop it on his boss's head, and at last he laid the heavy object down on the ground with a sigh of relief. Another journey back to collect his wooden blocks, pushing himself backward with his hands. He soon found that it was impossible to transport both pieces of wood at the same time, he couldn't risk losing one of them so he tucked one of them under the Guv's legs and proceeded back to where the jack lay. Once he had reached the required position, he placed the wood underneath the jack, another painfully slow journey back along the bomb was needed to get his last piece of timber. He found the constant side motion was taking its toll on his strength, which was also affected by the severe cold, but he forced himself along, using the man's clothing to assist him. After avoiding the unseen airline, he at last took hold of the length of wood and made his way to the place he would be working. At last, he lay on top of the man's head but then realised he had other problems to overcome. He had to hold both pieces of wood in an upright position to prevent them from floating away, but he also had to pick the jack up and put it in position between them and also operate it. He found it just wasn't possible to do anything in his present position. "I need another pair of hands" he muttered to himself. The only chance to use both hands was to change his position and to squeeze between the bomb and the roof of the tunnel. He squirmed around and at last slithered over the metal body, but as he moved into a working position he felt something holding him back. As it was impossible to see the cause, it was necessary to push himself backwards and as he moved he felt a jerk on his hosepipe. Tracing the pipe along, he found that it had wrapped itself around the trapped man's foot.

Quickly releasing his air pipe the Sergeant moved back to his tools. It was a tight squeeze for him and he could not use the timber supports at the sides or on the roof for this could dislodge them and the tunnel would cave in. Eventually he was back and ready to start work, he patted the man's head in sympathy before commencing. Taking hold of his first piece of wood, he pressed it against the wall of the tunnel and laid the jack beside it to hold it. The other piece of wood he stood against the bomb then he slithered forward to squeeze his head on top of the piece of timber. This way he could hold it firmly in position whilst he held the other length up against the wall. He then raised the jack and pushed it in between the two pieces of wood. The weight of the jack then held the wall piece in its correct place as he operated the jack. After a few seconds of hard graft he had extended the jack enough to wedge both lengths of wood, moving his head from out of its awkward position, he then concentrated his full strength on the jack. It seemed an endless task as the end of the jack bit deep into the wood he thought 'I don't think it's going to work', then he felt a tap on his leg and the man underneath moved slightly.

Pleasure and happiness flooded through him and he renewed his efforts to give several more turns on the jack before he slowly pushed his way backwards. All the time he worked he kept a tight grip on his hosepipe and made sure that he did not disturb the other life preserving hose. On reaching the end of the man" body, he checked to ensure that the rope was still firmly attached to the feet before attempting to drag the heavy body by the legs. He was overjoyed to find that he could pull his boss along. Another series of moving his own body backwards then pulling his Guvnor followed, as he pulled the trapped man free. Eventually, when he estimated that the man was completely clear of the bomb, he crawled forwards to verify the fact. In the darkness under the black ice cold water a hand grasped his firmly, and shook it. Satisfied that everything was OK the little Sergeant worked his way backwards, the rope around his feet was lying slack underneath him, he drew it tight and ensured that there was the same amount of spare on the other rope before he gave three sharp tugs. When the slack was pulled in he was quickly pulled towards the bottom of the shaft, arms held outstretched over his head to prevent them catching on any of the uprights. Moments later, strong arms grabbed him and pulled him to the surface of the water, he spat out the hose and a lot of sand then another head broke through beside him. The grinning face of his Guvnor turned towards him and he said,
"That's the last time you will tickle my feet, you rotten bugger, thanks all the same, I knew you'd come."
"You would have done the same for me Guv" the Sergeant shivered. "Let's go and get warm and a cup of char if those idle sods have managed to brew up."
The wet shivering Corporal handed the rubber boots to the freed man, who tipped the water out of them as he sat on one of the timber crosspieces. "Where are my socks?" he queried.
"Never seen them, do you want me to go and have a look for them?" laughed the Sergeant.
"No, let's go and get that cup of tea." He pulled the rubber boots on and together, the three wet, cold men climbed to the top of the shaft and to the welcome daylight.

FRESH BLOOD

The men were all gathered around the opening as they emerged into the bitter wind, which cut through their wet clothes. Duffel coats were quickly placed about their shoulders and the men greeted them with various remarks like "Good Show" and "Glad you are back Guv."
"Let's get some tea," the Sergeant said. "Break up lads" the last order was given quietly, knowing the strain everyone had been experiencing. The group made their way across towards the truck, where Hardman had a roaring fire going. As the men came towards him he began pouring the inevitable cuppa for each of the workers. "Glad to see you back Guv" he said as the wet men reached the fire.
"Get over to the pump Hardman and keep your eye on the water level, let us know when its down," ordered the Sergeant.

"Good show Serg," said Hardman grinning and pulling his collar up he trudged through the mud and took up his position beside the pumps which were trying to clear the water from the hole.

The men clustered together, sitting on boxes and equipment, holding their tin mugs and enjoying the hot steaming liquid. They left the space around the fire for the three cold, wet men, who squatted in front of the flames feeling the warmth penetrate their frozen bodies and clutching their hot mugs. Other groups of men came across from the other workings for their break. They had heard of the trouble and the rescue. They all left the three men to sit in silence around the fire, each knowing they'd prefer it that way, for although death was the constant companion of them all, the silent prayers of thanks were in everyone's heart.

The Corporal glanced at his two mates, "Queer couple" he thought. "Different as chalk and cheese." The Sergeant was small and middle-aged, a regular soldier who lived by the book but he was fair and got stuck into the job, he wouldn't ask anyone to do something he couldn't do himself. The boss was large, not as old as the Sergeant, and had volunteered for the Army before the war had started, same as himself. They had been together since the early days when they had joined the Bomb Disposal, why they had joined that particular branch he never knew. Both of the others looked a right pair of scruffs, sitting there covered in wet mud.

The Sergeant was happy as he sat, shivering slightly, as the wind whipped around his ears but he was constant. He looked at the Corporal sitting opposite him, he thought nothing of his vigil at the bottom of the shaft, or diving into the cold water to drag them out.

"He never complains that lad, just like the Guv." He glanced at the man he had just freed. He was sitting silent, with his old pipe clenched between his teeth, looking into the flames he never spoke much. He had one hand thrust deep into his pocket and his filthy face peeped from beneath the hood of the duffel coat. He grasped the mug of tea in his other large hand.

"Wonder what he's thinking. He was bloody lucky again, anyway it wouldn't have been right for him to go like that, undignified."

The man under scrutiny seemed oblivious to all that was going on around him, his chest and back ached where the bomb had squeezed him. His right arm had been torn against one of the timbers. He could feel the blood running down to his hand which he had inside his pocket. He knew that he was sitting there soaking up the warmth of the fire and nursing his bruises, solely because the man sitting beside him had the guts and intelligence to handle the tricky situation. Words of thanks were not really necessary to these men. They had risked their lives constantly in their hazardous profession; only the previous week he had lost two of his officers. He was deep in thought when one of the men shouted

"We've got company."

Heading across the fields towards them was a small van. They all recognised it as one of their vehicles, with its distinguishing red wings with the letters BDS in white.

"What's that bugger doing here?" muttered the Sergeant to himself. The van drew to a halt beside the truck and everyone gaped at the figure that emerged from the passenger door. The man was dressed, as a soldier said, 'Like a bloody mannequin.' He stepped daintily onto the ground as though trying to find a dry spot to place his feet, which were covered by a pair of immaculately polished riding boots. He stood still, looking at the motley crowd of mud-splattered and dishevelled men. The newcomer's jodhpurs were a good tight fit, his dress jacket neatly pressed with a gleaming Sam Browne belt and shoulder strap over it. The buttons shone like mirrors. Even the tie appeared tailor made, and upon his head the hat was placed dead square, neatly brushed, with the Royal Engineers cap badge shining like gold set dead central. He stood with a polished swagger stick in his right hand, slapping his boot with the end of it.

"Christ, its a bloody tailor's dummy," Sparrow whispered. The newcomer glared around the sea of faces all turned towards him,

"Who is in charge?" he demanded.

Speechless, one of the men indicated the fire where the three men were sitting. The officer stepped lightly through the mud towards his target. Apparently, not hearing a remark from the swaddies.

"He's a flippin ballet dancer."

As he crossed over to the fire it was noticed that he wore the treasured red flash on his sleeve which indicated that he was a member of that elite body of men. He was an officer in the Bomb Disposal. The oval red flash had a yellow bomb on it, Queen Mary had designed this badge especially for them.

"Are you in charge?" he snapped, disgusted that the person in command should grab the fire and not let the men near it. He was not sure which one of these scruffy looking individuals he should address. The Sergeant and the Corporal both looked towards their boss who had been weighing up the new arrival thin build, narrow face, narrow eyes, thin tight lips, very young in fact, possibly too young to embarrass. He looked like a schoolboy dressed up and full of his own importance, he was adopting a belligerent and bullying attitude. The Guv knew that he was probably one of the new replacement officers but, as yet, had not identified himself.

"Yes," he said. "Would you like a cup of tea?" Not getting a reply, he called.

"Charley, a cup of tea for the officer."

A battered tin mug full of steaming hot tea was placed in the newcomer's hand. Reluctantly, he accepted it but moved away from the body of men and stood beside the truck to drink it. His driver had grabbed his cup and was chatting to his mates.

"He looks a sulky bugger, doesn't he?" said the Sergeant to Soulsby who glanced at the new man and just grunted.

"Hole's clear." Hardman's voice disturbed the peace and quiet as he headed back towards the fire.

"Back to work lads." The Sergeant stood up and followed his boss back to the shaft, closely followed by the rest of the men who had dropped their mugs and raced after them. Hardman was left to wash the dishes, helped by the driver who had brought the new man.

"What's he like?" Hardman asked the transport bloke.

"Dunno, he's never spoken a word all the way here."

"I don't like the looks of him, he seems to be a bit sulky." Hardman decided, as he glanced at the man in question who was still standing beside the truck drinking his tea and glaring after the retreating body of troops.

On reaching the entrance to the hole, the Guv took off his duffel coat and hung it on a nail near the top of the shaft.

"Serg. Get my kit ready and a 'Q' coil."

"Are you going to have a go Guv?"

"Yes, it's a 35 with a No. 15, but clear the area as much as possible for quarter of an hour. I'll try and get it done before the floods come again."

The required tools were quickly delivered to him and the heavy 'Q' coil was lowered down the shaft in readiness for him to haul along the tunnel to the bomb. Corporal Soulsby was already in position at the bottom of the shaft and detached the rope from the equipment. He would use the same rope to fasten to his boss's feet before the journey along the tunnel commenced.

"Don't' tie a slip knot this time mate," he laughed at the dour Corporal as the rope was fastened. "Won't be long and we'll be back home for tea." Each man knowing in his own mind that they may not see one another again, as the big man slipped into the few inches of water, and commenced to worm his way slowly back to the bomb, pushing his required tools in front of him.

Getting alongside the cold metal case was a bit easier than before, due to the jack holding it away from the wall. He checked to see that the jack was still firmly wedged before he commenced work. He struggled and strained with the Heavy 'Q' coil to get it into position on top of the correct fuse pocket, this piece of apparatus weighed 135lb. And it was no mean piece of strength to manipulate it along the tunnel. At last he succeeded in lifting the important article into its place. This huge magnet had then to be clamped firmly to the bomb, the current was switched on and the electro-magnet was working, he then placed a neutraliser on the other fuse. Having done that, he lay back and started counting to himself. He had to work the time out properly before he started to attempt his delicate operation. The idea was simple on this type of fuse, parts of the workings in the fuse were magnetised and held still whilst he withdrew the fuse. However, if he started too early the parts would not be safe to tamper with and the result would be a sound that he wouldn't hear, that would be the explosion.

He considered all the improvements that had taken place with equipment since he had first started. 'To think we only had a hammer and chisel to take a fuse out.' No wonder they lost so many men. Jerry of course brought new and more sophisticated fuses as time progressed, but the boffins working for the Home Office were also investing gear to make the job easier and safer to defuse a bomb. At last the time was up, leaving the 'Q' coil attached, he started to remove the locking ring from the other fuse when a shout echoed along the tunnel.

"You have to come up at once."

Messages were always repeated word for word so that there could be no mistakes made as they were passed from one to another. So when he shouted back "Wait a bloody minute." The reply was relayed, by Corporal Soulsby, to the man who had given the order.

"It's an order. Get up here at once." Another interruption for him from the man at the top of the shaft.

"Sod it." The man thought things over. "I don't know if I will have time to extract the fuse before the water comes in. It could cause a short or vibration." He worked out the possible times for completing his assignment and decided to withdraw. Collecting his kit, he stuck them into his jacket, uncoupled the 'Q' coil, lay down and stretched his arms over his head.

"Pull" he shouted. He was whisked along the tunnel through the mud and water to the bottom of the shaft, where the intrepid Soulsby untied the rope from his ankles.

"What's wrong?" he asked.

The morose looking NCO indicated upwards to where the young Sub-Lieutenant was impatiently slapping his riding boots with his cane.

"Corp. pack in for the day. Bring the 'Q' coil out and fetch the gear up." He said, before pulling his duffel coat on and climbing the timbers to the surface.

As he heaved himself out of the hole onto the surface, the young newcomer was waiting for him.

"Yes," he demanded. "You wanted me?"

"You didn't salute me when I arrived," yelped the young baby face officer, who was going red with pent up rage.

"Is that what you called me up here for?" The wet man was none too happy. "For your information, we have been working for weeks trying to get this one out. It's been hard work, with water flooding in and sand shifting. Today, just when it was nearly done, you come along and stop the work just because you hadn't been saluted … Christ, some mothers do have them."

The lieutenant blanched, "Enough of that talk. I will not tolerate disobedience in any form. I'll have you on a charge. I am disgusted with what I have seen of this outfit. You are all a filthy and disobedient rabble and a disgrace to the army, with no sense of discipline. The camp is as filthy as you lot, all of you want sorting out and I am just the man to do it."

"Are you done Lieutenant? These men you are calling dirty and disobedient have all served in the Bomb Disposal right through the war. They are the few left of many who started. They have, and will again, risked their lives for their mates and others. Discipline is of two kinds, one for the Parade Ground and the other whose orders are obeyed without question regardless of danger. As regards being filthy, how can anyone work in a quagmire like this and keep clean? Alright lads, pack in." The last sentence was directed towards the men who stood quietly around, watching and listening. There was an immediate rush to load the tools back onto the truck.

"Stop!" yelled the new officer. "I am in charge here. I'll report you all for mutiny." He glared at the man beside him. "You are responsible for this, I'll see that you pay for it."

"Lieutenant, I see that you have the bomb on your sleeve, which denotes that you belong to some branch of the Bomb Disposal, however as regards these men, I am in charge and carry full responsibility for them. They always obey orders properly given, yours I'm afraid, were not. Your attitude does you no good at all."

With that last remark he walked across to the truck and climbed in. He removed his wet clothes and replaced them with clean dry ones. He then pulled his duffel coat back on, jumped from the truck and headed for a motorcycle standing nearby.

"Stop, where are you going?" demanded the youngster.

"I am going back to my camp. If you are one of us I may see you there," and he jumped onto the machine and kicked the starter. The engine burst into life, he revved it up and let the clutch out fiercely, the rear wheel spun on the wet surface, throwing a shower of water behind it. Rather unfortunately for the young officer who was in line of fire. The motorcycle quickly picked up speed and left the work site, leaving an abnormally enraged and wet officer behind. The soldiers went about their business loading the truck and trying, not too hard, to hide their amusement and pleasure at the state the new man was in.

"I am glad that I am not his batman, having to clean that mess up," said Hardman.

"Serves the bleeder right" Sparrow answered. "I wonder if the Guv did it on purpose."

"I don't know how the boss kept his temper with that little snot going on. Put us all on a fizzer for mutiny. I'd like to mutiny and stick a 500 pounder up his ..."

"Enough of that Taffy," the Corporal ordered. "You have to be careful with these young officers, keep your thoughts to yourself."

"That's the Guv all over. He thinks everyone likes water," Sparrow sniggered, "and he is trying to christen the new un."

The Guv, in the meanwhile, was speeding along the main road on the old Army Norton. Occasionally, the wheels slithered on the snow but he didn't mind for he enjoyed being out in the open and feeling the wind stinging his cheeks. The tears blew from his eyes as he sped along. "Yes this is the life, I suppose this is what a Copper's job would be like." He hadn't forgotten his decision about joining the Police Force when he retired. His journey only took about 30 minutes and he parked the old motorcycle outside the office. The Lance Corporal looked up as he strode in. All right, Hawkes?"

"Yes Guvnor, the new officer has arrived Sir."

"Good, let's get cracking on the reports." He slumped into a chair beside the fire, took out his pipe and filled it, as the office clerk got the papers ready in his typewriter. Jock filled the pipe with his strong tobacco and lit it. He puffed deeply at the smoke and then commenced his narrative of the day's work. Whilst ensuring that all details of the various sites were reported, he made no mention about the disturbance which prevented the fuse from being withdrawn. Nor did he include details of having a narrow escape. Having finished his dictation, the orderly brought him the pile of papers to sign. The door suddenly flew open and in stalked the new man he'd had words with.

"What's that motorbike parked outside the office for?" were his first words. "I will not have this camp looking like a scrap yard. There is a proper place for everything."

The Lance Corporal was startled and looked at the man who was busy signing the papers. Jock looked up and indicated with a nod of his head towards the door, and a thankful Hawkes headed outside.

"I'm bloody glad I'm not in his shoes, talking to the Guvnor like that," he thought as he slid through the door.

"I am asking again, why is that motorcycle outside this office?"

"I put it there, if you want it moved you can do it." Jock quietly continued with his paper work, trying very hard to keep his temper. The young officer strode over to him and stood glaring at the seated man. "I have never experienced such gross insolence in all my service. You have no respect for rank and no discipline whatever. I am going to report you."

"You keep saying that, but you will have to be quick about it as I only have one week to go before I leave the army."

The blustering junior officer snarled "When I'm finished with you, it will be years before you are out of the army. I'll get this camp tidied up and knock some discipline into the rest of your cronies."

"Bugger it. I'm getting fed up with you and your holier than thou attitude. Come in" he bellowed, and the Lance Corporal came in carrying two mugs of tea.

" I thought you would like a cuppa Guv."

"Thanks Hawkes, one for the Lieutenant, then get me Company HQ I want to speak to Mac."

He accepted the proffered tea and took a large drink, then settled down to smoke his pipe in silence as the NCO telephoned the required number for him. As he sat there he gazed at the new man who had just entered his life.

"Headquarters Guv," Hawkes said and handed the 'phone over. The young Lieutenant reached forward to take it but the office clerk drew it away from his outstretched hand.

"Not for you Sir" he said in a voice that showed he had little respect for this chap.

"Right, thanks for the tea, you can go now," said Jock taking the handset.

As the door closed behind him Jock spoke into the phone, "Mac?"

"Lofthouse here," came a deep voice. Hawkes had done his job right and he was connected with the Commanding Officer of his Company.

"Mac, you old bugger. Jock here, how you doing? Good, now tell me what the hell have you done to me?"

"What do you mean, you Scotch Sod?"

"Well, for your information I have been informed that this unit is the most filthy and undisciplined bunch of mutineers in the Army, and I have been put on a charge as the ring leader."

"You are joking again?" It was more of a question than an exclamation.

"No. It appears we have a young officer here who is in charge. I don't know who he is as he hasn't yet introduced himself. Now tell me what you know about him, and it had better be good, I am just about to blow my top."

"Jock, for Christ sake, control that bloody temper, don't do anything silly. I meant to tell you about him but I didn't expect him to arrive so soon. I was coming up to see you before you left us. Now remember, behave yourself and I will see you at 9am tomorrow. Now put that sod on, will you?"

The 'phone was passed over to the gaping officer, he had stood there flabbergasted. The audacity of this man to speak to anyone at Headquarters about him, and in the manner he did. He took the 'phone from the scruffy individual, with full intentions of speaking to his senior officer about the trouble he was encountering.

"Lieutenant Forbes-Jones here, who am I speaking to?" Jock smiled to himself as he put the papers into the basket for attention.

"Sir." The young officer's voice nearly disappeared into a croak. It just couldn't be possible that this monster had been talking to the Commanding Officer the way he had done. It must have been someone else.

"Yes Sir, Lieutenant Forbes-Jones Sir. I am sorry about this, Sir."

Jock left the office listening to the never-ending stream of "Yes Sir, No Sir." 'Three bags full Sir', he muttered. 'Bloody crawler'.

The small Sergeant was standing on the veranda with the office orderly when he left the office. He saluted and asked,

"Any orders, Sir?"

"Company Commander's Parade, 9am tomorrow. I want every man to be in best dress and make sure that there are no reasons for complaint. It would be appreciated if the billets were also tidy for the Major's inspection. See that the men know as soon as possible. That's all." He stopped then added, with a smile.

"Wait, no overcoats."

"Yes Sir," responded the Sergeant who caught on straight away at the last order and he couldn't resist a smile.

"Corporal see that a notice is printed and placed on the notice board at once with these orders."

"I think I'll have a bath after we've seen the wolves feed, and then we'll have ours Tom." The big man said to the Sergeant.

Together they trudged towards the hut used by the men for their meals. The soldiers had been washed, but most of them were still in their overalls, sitting and enjoying a hot meal. The Sergeant entered first and shouted

"Shun!" Instant silence settled on the room and the men sat up straight.

"Carry on." they were ordered and an immediate clattering of cutlery and chattering of voices began again.

Jock and the Sergeant moved along the hall and stopped at every table, to talk to the soldiers and to enquire if the food was satisfactory, and whether there were any complaints about the food. The visit completed, the two men went to their own quarters to get cleaned up. Jock's batman had a hot bath ready for him and clean clothes were laid out ready to wear. As he stripped off he saw the massive bruise, already showing, which covered his chest and back. The jagged tear down his arm was covered with dried blood. Feeling completely refreshed after his soak in the water. He bandaged his arm and slipped the clean clothes on, then headed for the dining room used by the Sergeants and Corporals. Normally, he would not have been allowed to use their room but it had been accepted by all the NCOs that he could, and should, dine with them. All formalities were dropped and they shared all expenses, and as they had their own bar, it was possible to sit and enjoy a few drinks after their evening meal. They were all friends together, yet the men had a mutual feeling of respect for the Guv and never took liberties with their association. The hot food was welcome, and they all had a pleasant chat, sitting around the hot stove with their drinks. The evening wore on and Jock stood up saying,

"Much as I enjoy your company, I am ready for bed. Goodnight to you all. By the way, don't forget lads, CO's Parade at 9 am. I know you won't let us down." All the Sergeants and Corporals knew about the remarks made by the young upstart who had just arrived, and a chorus of

"We won't Guv, goodnight." arose as he bade them goodnight again.

He left the mess room with Sub-Lieutenant Dobbins, who was the only other officer left since they had lost the other two section commanders, he had only been with Jock for a week but was settled in. Jock had been waiting for the replacements for his unit and the one that had arrived today was apparently one of them. The deaths were never mentioned, Jock had seen far too many of his comrades killed over the years to dwell on them. Not that he didn't feel it, but he knew that his turn was overdue, that could come at any time.

"Is he as bad as what they say Sir?"

"Don't worry Dobbo, he's young and full of his own importance, he has a lot to learn but I think he's intelligent enough."

"Will he go straight out on the diggings."

"He'll have to learn and I haven't much time, I will give him Section 2," Jock answered.

"But Sir ...,"

Jock looked quickly at the youngster, knowing what he was going to say.

"But Sir ..., that's the one you have been working on."

"I know Dobbo, but I will finish the big bastard myself one way or the other." Jock had no intentions of discussing the events of the day which nearly cost him his life. Obviously his fellow officer had been informed of the incident and was a bit worried about a novice tackling the monster bomb, especially in its dangerous position.

ONE WEEK TO GO

The next morning reveille was called at 6am and the camp was alive and buzzing. The troops bustled around and ensured that their billets and beds were spotless and ready for inspection. Before breakfast everyone was ready; best boots all spit and polished, dress uniforms were all neatly pressed. By the time the call came *On Parade* everything and everyone was ready, though the men knew that the Major wouldn't be all that bothered, they just wanted to show off for 'The Guv' and to show the new bloke up. Most of all, their pride was at stake.

The sections all stood in their lines of threes, with the Sergeants at the rear. Sub-Lieutenant Dobbins stood in front of his section but the new man didn't know which position he should take up, he marched over to the soldiers.

"Squad Shun." One of the Sergeants saw him approaching and called the men to attention. The youthful officer was surprised when he saw another officer on parade but that didn't prevent him doing his inspection. He went along the ranks examining every man with great intent. The inspection was thorough, the men's boots were checked to ensure that even the sides of the sole had been cleaned; occasionally a man had to lift his foot up so that the officer could check to see that all the studs were present and that the leather between the heel and the sole was polished. Buttons were turned to see if they had been cleaned at the back. Caps were checked to ensure they were placed correctly on the head and, once in a while, he removed a cap badge to inspect the rear for dirt. As he moved along the ranks he examined every face carefully.

He was looking for the ignorant oaf who had been a pain in the arse the day previously. Right through the ranks he went, he noticed that most of the men were about his own age group, yet the expressions on their faces and the looks in their eyes made them look much older. He couldn't help but notice that everyone had several medals on their chests, he began to feel naked when he glanced down at his own tunic. He recognised some of the medals the men wore with pride, some of them had the Military Medal and others wore the British Empire Medal. All of them had campaign medals attached to the tunics. The Section Sergeants accompanied him through each of their own sections. He had been through two of the sections and could not see the man he was looking for. 'He must be with the other Section' he thought but he couldn't very well examine them because they had their own officer. He was in a quandary because he so wanted to find that big chap; he looked along the lines of the other section trying to catch a glimpse of him. His decision was made for him when the Sergeant said,

"CO coming, Sir!"

The new man marched smartly to the front of the assembled men and called the whole unit to attention, not waiting to see whether it was the job for the other officer. He stood to strict attention, feeling very smug with himself and proud of his position. Here he was in charge of his own men and it wasn't long ago since he had left college. He had applied for a Commission in the army and had completed a course of instruction, he had then been posted to the Royal engineers. He had spent a few weeks at the headquarters, before being posted to take command of his own section. His chest was puffed out, shoulders back, he glanced out of the corners of his eyes towards his Commanding Officer. He squinted and tried to adjust his vision, there were two men approaching, the Major was one of them, he turned his head slightly and saw that the other man was a Captain. He noticed that both of the senior officers had rows and rows of medals on their chests. 'One day I will be like them', he thought as he watched the pair move towards him. Suddenly his jaw dropped, he couldn't believe it was possible. Oh God! Why did this have to happen to me? It couldn't be true, but as the two officers drew nearer he knew that he was right. It was him, in full dress uniform, the man he was admiring was the same one he had the trouble with. He wished the ground would open up and swallow him. He saluted feebly and said 'Parade ready for inspection Sir', trying not to look into their faces.

"Right, let's go," said the Major and together with the Section Sergeant they walked the ranks of men. The Major stopped several times to chat to various soldiers, most of whom he knew.

"We will do the billets now," the CO said. The officers and the Section Sergeants all accompanied the Major and the Captain on a tour of the billets. "Perfect – good show Sergeant. Carry on."

"Sergeant," Jock stopped the NCO, "Dismiss the men, they can have the rest of the day off and, seeing as it is Friday, long weekend passes for them all, except skeleton staff."

"Sir." The Sergeant saluted smartly and marched off with a clatter of hobnailed boots on the wooden floor.

"I think we will adjourn to the office," Lofthouse ordered and with Jock walking alongside him, they headed for the designated room deep in conversation. Dobbins walked behind them, followed by a luckless and fearful Forbes-Jones.

L/Corporal Hawkes was in the office when they entered and he stood up. Jock noticed another man was present. It was another 2nd Lieutenant.

"Jock, I've brought up another replacement for you." The Major indicated the new man.

"Lieutenant Hillary Sir." The young man stood at attention, Jock smiled and shook hands with the newcomer.

"Pleased to have you."

"This will bring you up to strength again Jock," the Major explained.

"On your way, you have a long weekend pass. Don't be late on Monday morning." said Jock, turning to Hawkes.

"Thank you, Sir." The NCO saluted and left the office.

Jock looked at his officers and spoke to Lt. Dobbins.

"Lt. Dobbins, would you be good enough to show Mr Hillary where his quarters are and get him settled in."

He knew that the Major had something he wanted to say to Forbes-Jones and used this chance to get the other men out of the way.

"Right Sir." The young man took the hint and they left the room.

Jock and the Major made themselves comfortable in a couple of armchairs. Lofthouse motioned to Forbes-Jones to be seated as Jock opened a drawer and took out a bottle and three glasses. He poured the drinks and sat back. Both he and the Major took their pipes from their pockets and slowly began to fill them. Not a word was spoken as they filled the pipes and lit them, then a few strong puffs to ensure that the tobacco was well and truly lit.

"Now, Mr Forbes-Jones." The Commanding Officer turned to the very quiet and extremely nervous officer, "What's your buck?"

"Sir?" queried the luckless creature.

"What are the complaints you have about this unit?"

"Sir?"

"For Christ's sake, stop stammering like a bloody clot and answer my question. You complained, I believe, about a filthy and disgusting camp. You also stated that the men were just as bad, plus the fact they were insubordinate to a point of mutiny. Am I correct?" He glared at the quiet man, who was visibly shivering. "Now, after my inspection today, I find no cause for complaint regards cleanliness. Why is this? Furthermore, where is this person who you indicated to me as being the leader, and the worst offender?"

Jock bit onto the stem of his pipe as he studied the sweating man, he puffed a cloud of smoke towards the ceiling as he awaited the reply. This lad had to be sorted out before he left the unit, that was obvious.

Forbes-Jones went pale under the direct questioning from his superior, he was hoping the question would never arise about his attitude at the work site. However, there was no getting away from the Major's question and he looked frantically towards Jock then blurted out,

"It was him, Sir, the Captain Sir."

Jock smiled inwardly at the man's predicament.

"Oh, I see. You arrived at the camp, when?"

"Yesterday, 1300 hours Sir."

"You make any attempt to check the compliment of the unit and the work in hand?"

"No Sir," came the feeble answer.

"Did you make any enquiries as to who was in charge, and what job you were supposed to do?"

"No Sir."

"You just made yourself at home in your room, unpacked your kit and found the driver to take you to the site?"

"Yes Sir."

"When you got there, the men were having a break, due to the workings being flooded."

"I didn't know about the flooding Sir," the Lieutenant answered.

"No, but it is shown in the daily works reports - if you had taken the trouble to check them you would have known."

"Yes Sir."

"Did you know that Captain MacGregor had been trapped by a bomb underneath the water for some considerable time and he had just been rescued before you arrived? Did you know that he had been injured also?"

Jock's chair dropped back onto its four legs at the last remarks.

"Hey," he exclaimed. "How do you know about that?" he interrupted.

"My driver-batman got it first hand, and by the way I don't want anything to happen to you at this stage of your service, any damage really, Jock?" The Major was worried about his mate.

"Not really, just a few bruises and scrapes." He didn't go into details about the extent of the injury.

"Right." The Major poured another round of drinks for himself and Jock, as the Lieutenant's glass was still full.

"When the men were there, did you introduce yourself upon your arrival Mr Forbes-Jones?"

"No Sir."

"Why not, you were a new arrival, nobody knew who you were."

"I'm sorry Sir."

"If you noticed, when we came into the office, Mr Hillary was new yet he introduced himself at once to the Captain. He was the newcomer, same as you were at the site."

There was no reply from the young man.

"When the water was cleared and work re-commenced, did you enquire from anyone what was happening?"

"No Sir."

"Did the men all rush to get started work at once?"

"Yes Sir."

"There was no argument from any of the men?"

"No Sir."

"Did you ask what the urgency was for the man to get back into the tunnel?"

"No Sir."

"You just finished your tea, which I presume they did give you, then went to the shaft and ordered the man out of the tunnel without knowing who he was, or what he was doing?"

"Yes Sir."

"Are you sure, in your opinion, that you are a fit and proper person to be in charge of such a dangerous operation?"

"Dangerous Sir?"

"Yes you idiot, that's what I said. That hole you were shouting down contained a 4000 pound bomb, with a vibration fuse and an anti-handling device attached. Slightest mistake and that whole bloody field would have gone up, as well as all the other bombs that the men are working on, and at least 30 men, including yourself."

Young Forbes-Jones swallowed hard.

"Listen, you young cockroach, you are just out of college, you've never tasted the cold hard world. Possibly you just joined the Army for a Commission, to avoid getting your call-up papers, but I will not allow you to be in the position to risk my men's lives. I don't think you will be needed here."

Jock sighed, "Mac, I've still got another week to go, leave it till then, and if he's no good then we can leave together."

The Major considered the offer for a while. "Well, we are getting the Jerries to come onto the sites soon, as the lads are all due for a de-mob. OK I'll leave it for a week."

"Thank you, Sir," burst out the white faced subaltern. "Thank you."

"Jock, I don't want you getting too involved this week mind you."

"Yeah. Another drink Mac. Mind you, I'm telling you one thing Mac, that big bastard's mine and nobody else is going to touch him."

"Righto, you Scotch get. Cheers."

Lieutenant Forbes-Jones stood up and asked if he was required anymore. As the two old mates wanted a short time to themselves, he was allowed to go.

After they had a few drinks together, the Major asked if it would be possible for him to join the men in their mess.

"I think they may be able to tolerate you, just for once," Jock laughed. "Come on, let's see if any of them are dining at home."

Together they headed for the Sergeant's mess, where a few of the Senior NCOs were gathering to have a drink before the meal was served. They welcomed the two officers who were plied with drinks. After lunch the Major said his good-byes to his old pal and headed back to Headquarters. Jock mounted his trusty old motorcycle and set off to spend the weekend at home.

Monday morning at 7.30am the men were all in their overalls ready to go. When young Forbes-Jones came out of the front office, he climbed into the front seat of the leading van,

"Right" he said, "Let's go."

Half an hour later the lorries pulled up in the field where the bombs lay. As the men tumbled out of the vehicles, a motorcycle roared across towards them and slowed to a halt alongside the group of men.

"Morning Guv," was the chorus from the soldiers.

"Haven't you lazy shower got started yet? Come on, let's get the whips out Sergeant." Jock laughed.

The men all treated it as a huge joke and cracked jokes as they unloaded the vehicles ready to start work.

"By the way, how did you get here so early Serg? Didn't you stop at the canteen this morning?" Jock asked the Senior NCO.

"No Sir. Lieutenant was in the lead vehicle," came the answer.

Jock turned to the new Lieutenant and said, "They always stop at a works canteen on the way to the site. They get a good filling of pies and hot tea. It puts them in a good mood for the rest of the day. In future, ensure that they always get that break in the mornings, regardless of which site they may be working on."

"Right Sir, Sorry Sir." The young man was miserable, he had dropped a clanger straight away. He looked at his Senior Officer and was hunting for words, at last he plucked up courage and said,

"I thought you were not to engage in any activities today Sir?" Jock was stripping off as the man spoke.

"Where did you get that idea?" he asked.

"What the Major said Sir." The man's voice was faint as he was unsure how to take this big man.

"Mr Forbes-Jones, just try and remember what the Major did say, and don't forget, you only have one week to prove yourself."

Jock pulled his old overalls on and slipped a pair of rubber boots over his feet.

"Anyway, how the hell are you going to learn if there is no-one to show you. I still have to get that big bastard out." He looked at the Sub-Lieutenant. "What did you intend to do today?"

The other officer looked perplexed at the question.

"I would be supervising, Sir," he answered.

"No way. The Sergeants do the supervising here, your job is to work. Where are your overalls?" the man was dressed in battle-dress.

"I'm sorry Sir, I didn't bring any," he spluttered.

"Not to worry lad, I will get you fixed up." He called over to the nearest Sergeant.

"Fix the Lieutenant up with a pair of overalls will you Spike." The Sergeant climbed into the back of one of the vehicles and soon produced an old pair.

"These should fit you Sir" he said and handed them to the young man, who looked at the shabby material in disdain.

"Get a move on lad, we haven't got all day," Jock ordered.

Forbes-Jones started to pull the overalls over his battle dress.

"What the hell are you doing. Get your uniform off first, it will get wet," Jock said to him. He waited whilst the youngster got into the back of the truck to change.

"Get the 'Q' coil and my kit ready Serg. Two ropes, Lieutenant will be going with me."

At last the newcomer was ready, not looking so resplendent in his old overalls, but he had his cap in position on his head.

"Water down" came the yell from the top of the shaft.

The two officers reached top of the shaft, Jock said

"All right Tom?" He said to the little Sergeant already in position at the top

"Yes Guv. All the gear's down waiting." He looked quizzically at the young newcomer and said to Jock

"Are you going to do it now Sir?"

"I'm taking Mr Forbes-Jones down to introduce him to our friend." The two officers climbed down the timber to the bottom of the shaft where Soulsby was waiting to fasten the ropes to their ankles. He looked as sour and dour as ever.

"Have a nice weekend Corporal?" Jock asked him.

"Yes thank you Sir," with an expression as if he had been to a funeral. "I had a smashing time." As he finished doing the ropes for his boss.

"Corporal Soulsby keeps his eye on the water level for us and has us pulled out when required, but watch him or he'll pinch your socks." Soulsby gave him a mournful look.

"I found them Sir," and handed a pair of wet woollen socks to Jock.

"See what I mean?" Jock laughed but the joke was beyond his colleague's comprehension.

The Lance Corporal looked at the new man.

"Shall I take your cap Sir?" and held his hand out. Reluctantly the article of clothing was handed over.

"It would be in the way down there Jonesey," Jock explained. "Now come on, let's go, you first." He pushed the hero into the few inches of water that still remained in the bottom. "We will take the 'Q' coil with us. You pull and I will push." The air hose was in position and a rope was attached to the huge coil. Together they moved slowly along the tunnel until Jonesey announced that he could go no further.

"Leave the coil and squeeze between the bomb and the wall," Jock ordered. As the man obeyed, Jock started to lift the heavy coil on to the top of the bomb.

"Right, now you can get the feel of it while I am busy. Put your left hand on the top and slide it along. You will feel along till you reach an obstruction about 3" in diameter." As he carried on with his task the young man searched for the designated object.

"I've found it Sir."

"Right, feel around the edge and you will be able to feel the grooves. That's where the extractor fits, you move the right ring in an anti-clockwise direction. When that's off you can ease the fuse out gently, without knocking it. First you will have to put the magnet on for 30 minutes, no more, no less. This prevents the innards moving. Now, feel inside the grooves on the surface and you will find some small holes, these are the charging holes where the electricity is supplied before the bomb leaves the plane. The position of those holes show which type of fuse you are dealing with."

The young man was still trying to accept the size of this huge monster, he never realised a bomb could be so big. His fingers examined the fuse, as directed.

"I've found them Sir," he said.

"Right, move your hand about 20" further along and you will find another one. Do the same with that."

The youngster found the second fuse and felt round it.

"Don't forget Jonesey, the slightest wrong movement or a short-out, say with water getting in, you are in trouble."

"Sir?" a weak voice came out of the darkness.

"Don't worry, if anything goes wrong nobody will be able to complain to you," was the laughing reply from his boss.

Jock kept the youngster down the hole pulling out sand from around the bomb whilst he strapped the huge coil onto the case. He was waiting for the regular deluge.

"By the way Jonesey, when the water comes and you are dragged out of the tunnel, put both your arms out straight above your head, that's essential so that they do not catch on the supporting timbers."

Hardly had he said this and the floods came in. Both men were pulled quickly to the bottom of the shaft and were helped out of the water. Jock looked at the spluttering, gasping young man.

"I forgot to tell you Jonesey, you should hold your breath under water."

The novice had been christened.

"While the water is going down we can have a cup of tea, then get a bit of practice in," said Jock

"Practice?" asked the shivering officer.

"Up on top we go, come on."

They climbed up together into the icy wind. Jock drew one of the Sergeants aside, "Stick a number 11 fuse into that last 250 pounder we took out, make sure its safe first," and the Sergeant went away to carry out his orders.

"Sergeant," Jock spoke to the little NCO at the top of the shaft, "Get another couple of pumps across from the other holes, we will have to get down as quickly as possible to do these two fuses."

"Now Jonesey, let's have that official standby for idle sods." After a quick drink, they headed across to the furthest side of the field, where a couple of bombs were lying. The sergeant was standing beside them.

"Now Jonesey, just imagine you are going back into that tunnel again, show me how you would tackle the job. There's your bomb there." The youngster walked over to the dedicated bomb and knelt down beside it. He looked at the fuse and then returned to Jock.

"Its a No. 35, I will need some tools to get it out."

"Here is the kit." Jock handed him the bag and the officer went back to his job. A few seconds after trying to take the locking nut off with his fingers, he took the hammer and chisel and started to tap the nut loose. This accomplished, he lifted the fuse out of the pocket. He then walked back to Jock holding it in his hand.

"Was that alright Sir?" Quite proud of himself after doing his first job.

Jock stared at him. "Didn't I say for you to imagine that you were going into the tunnel again, you couldn't walk in, could you? You stood on top of the bomb and decided that it was a No. 35, in the hole you had to feel for the information. You went in without any tools. You used the hammer and chisel. You never used the Crabtree, or even went through the movements of using it. Lastly, you should flap your arms now as fast as you can."

"Flap my arms Sir?" Jonesey asked "Why?"

"For the simple reason that fuse you just removed with the hammer was and still is a number 11, an anti-handling device, isn't it?" A blank forlorn look took place of smugness on the new man's face.

"Regards the hammer, treat these missiles with tenderness, don't hit them or disturb them unnecessarily, use the extractor."

"Yes Sir."

"I'll show you how to handle the policeman fuse later, and all the other fuses. So don't be despondent, we have plenty of time for recognition tests. You will be able to tell what type they are by sitting on them, by the time Tom here and myself are finished with you."

"Water's getting down," the call came.

"Right Serg. All systems go. Clear the area."

"Can I do it Sir?" Jock smiled, it was a stupid question but he admired the lad for asking.

"No way, you can ensure the area's cleared."

"I'd rather do it Sir. I will have to some day."

"No."

"Can I come with you then?" he asked.

Jock considered for a while, this was against the rules. "Well why not, as you say, you will have to do it some time, and nobody can bollock us, can they?"

"Thank you Sir."

"Don't thank me yet. We already have the coil fitted, there is just the cable to attach. You can get the feel of it, but mind you as soon as I start work, you get your arse out of that tunnel like greased lightning."

Corporal Soulsby was standing at the bottom of the shaft with the water just over his knees. He looked in astonishment when he saw the new Lieutenant climbing down with Jock.

"Is he going with you Guv?" he asked.

"Just for a few minutes, to get the feel of it, he'll be coming out before I start. As soon as you pull him out make sure he gets to the safety place, and you get away also."

Soulsby fastened the ropes to their ankles and handed the kit to Jock.

"Good Luck Guv" he said, in his usual mournful voice.

"Thanks, mind you pull him out and not me." Jock couldn't help cracking a joke with the Lance Corporal.

"Come on Jonesey, after me." He dropped down into the water and headed for the tunnel. There was a space of about 6" between the surface of the water and the roof of the tunnel. They had to crawl along with their noses just above the water, when they eventually reached the sleeping monster, the youngster said

"Christ Sir, I'm jiggered. I could do with a rest after that."

"No time Jonesey" Jock answered as he lay alongside the bomb.

"We are working against the clock."

"Is it ticking, Sir?" he asked in a terrified voice.

"Not that clock. I mean the flooding. That's why we have come down before the water is all out, it gives me a few more minutes." As he was speaking he was getting on with his task.

"I am putting the Crabtree on the front fuse, that takes 30 minutes to make it safe. Next we will switch the current on the 'Q' coil, after that I will put the extractor on the first fuse and remove it. When that is done I will start on the back fuse. I will take the locking nut off and connect the Merrylees to it. When that is done I will retire to join you and do the rest the easy way. So much for the boffins who invented it! It is the easy way, just by pulling a cord I can remove the fuse. Now then, that's finished." He reached down to take hold of the rope attached to Jonesey.

"So long! Its time for you to go." With that remark he pulled on the man's rope, next second the youngster was whisked along the tunnel through the few inches of water that remained. As soon as he estimated that the Lieutenant and the Lance Corporal had reached safety, he turned his attention to the task in hand. The Crabtree was fitted and wound up. The plungers depressed and, hopefully, the condensers were empty and the fuse would be safe in three minutes.

He waited patiently lying on his side in the ice cold water, his teeth tightly clenched on his empty pipe. He had estimated the time for the first fuse and decided *Time up*. He applied the extractor and applied full pressure onto the bar in order to release the locking nut. Once the locking nut was loose and moving freely, he discarded the tool and used his fingers. Once the nut had been removed, he wiped his hands on the piece of rag which he carried in his little kit bag. Then, slowly and gently, he eased the fuse out of the pocket. As it cleared the cavity he quickly checked it to ensure that the gain was attached to the end. Satisfied that there were no explosive picric pellets stuck to it, he unscrewed the gain and placed the fuse in his little bag. Time was the decider, as always, and he had none of this to spare.

He quickly removed the locking nut on the other fuse. He picked up his other piece of equipment, and still with the magnetic coil attached, he placed the other contraption on top of the fuse, he ensured that it was fitting squarely, then tightened two bolts. The bolts screwed into the boss of the bomb, the centre of this unit was attached to the top of the fuse and tightened on. This latest addition was attached to a worm-shaped bolt that went through a large block at the top. As the block was turned, the bolt would move upwards on its thread; due to the fact that the lower part was attached to the fuse, this action would draw the fuse upwards out of the pocket. 'Simple' he thought, considering the time spent on the manufacture. The wheel had a length of cord attached to it and as this cord was pulled, it would turn the wheel. The cord could be pulled from a safe distance, just in case of accidents, which Jock now intended to do. He collected his kit together but left them beside the bomb in the bag as he wouldn't need them. With his arms free, he pushed himself backwards along the tunnel, keeping his body straight he brought his hands under his shoulders and pushed. This movement was repeated continually until he reached the bottom of the shaft. He untied the rope from his ankles and, carrying the cord that was attached to the bomb, he quickly climbed to the surface.

The men were all standing around the fire, watching and waiting.

"Bloody cushy job you've got Corp., sitting on your arse out of the wind all the time. What's it feel like having to stand in the wind?" Sparrow couldn't resist having a dig at Lance Corporal Soulsby.

"Oh belt up, you gutless wonder," the wet NCO snarled. "If you want the job down there you can have it now. The Guv will have to be pulled out."

"Not bleedin likely. Cor, that sod could go up," the Londoner said.

Jock emerged from the hole as the good natured banter was going on. He pulled his duffel coat on and moved towards the men. He checked with the Sergeants that everyone was clear and the danger zone was also clear.

"Have all the factories been warned Serg?" he asked.

"Yes Sir, everyone is clear. The other sites have also withdrawn to their places of safety." This was essential, for the men working on other bomb holes were in danger of the bombs going off with the blast and vibration from the big one, yet he was standing only 20 feet away.

"Right Serg. I haven't got enough cord to stretch back here so I'll have to take a chance." He laid his cord along the ground.

"OK Jonesey, keep your heads down and fingers crossed." Once he had made sure that everyone had obeyed the order, he started to slowly pull on the narrow piece of cord in his hand. Checking as he did so the length, he could tell by the amount of cord drawn in exactly where the fuse was. He would be able to go as soon as the fuse had cleared the pocket. Down below, as the cord was pulled, the wheel turned, the screw bolt moved upwards and the fuse was withdrawn until it reached the maximum. A deathly silence hung over the area, everyone was literally holding their breath, and this was the telling time. Was a delay spring booby trap inserted or not?

"Well that seems OK" Jock grunted and swung over the side of the shaft as he prepared to lower himself down, he realised that the Lance Corporal was beside him.

"What are you doing here?" he asked.

"Someone has to fasten the rope to your feet and pull you out Sir," the dour man answered.

"Righto, let's hurry, we haven't much time." Jock agreed to let him stay.

"I know time is getting short Guv." The Lance Corporal knew, with the length of time he had spent at the bottom of the shaft, that the floods were due at any time. Quickly he tied the rope to his boss. Jock slid into the tunnel like greased lightning, he too knew that it was a case of touch and go.

What was waiting for him? Had it cleared? Was the clock OK? Were there any of the deadly picric pellets attached to the bottom of the fuse? Would he be in time to get the fuse disengaged before the place was flooded, with the fuse just hanging there it would be curtains for sure. He knew he was walking a tightrope at the present and seconds counted. He reached the bomb and his fingers got to work. He soon ascertained that the fuse was free, sitting right over the fuse pocket just like an apple hanging from a tree waiting to be picked. He reached over and unscrewed the gain, opened the collett and gently released the fuse, no pellets attached, thank God. He placed the gain in his bag and breathed a sigh of relief. Just then the water rushed in and he was engulfed in the torrent once again. Soulsby was just as quick, and he hauled Jock out of the narrow tunnel single-handed. As he broke surface in the shaft he looked at the miserable man who had just saved him again. Jock smiled and held the fuse up which he still held in his hand.

"There you are Corp. a present for you!" A grin creased the face of the worried NCO for a fleeting moment.

"OK Guv?" asked the Sergeant who was standing at the top of the shaft as he emerged..

"Fine Tom," he laughed. "You can get the lads to clear up down there, they can bring the coil and the Merrylees up. Then you can make arrangements to shift it."

"Right Guv. God show." The Sergeant nodded and called the gang over; he soon gave the necessary orders to the lads as Jock wandered over to where Jonesey was standing.

"I'm ready for a smoke and a cup of tea." He realised that he was actually sweating, even with the temperature below zero. "I must be getting old."

"Tea, Guv?" Hardman held a hot tin mug out for him, filled to the top with steaming tea.

" Do you want another, Sir?," he asked the Lieutenant.

After the two men had drank their tea and Jock had changed into dry overalls, they toured the various workings. The new man was shown how new shafts were sunk and how the timbers were placed in the sides. He met the men and the NCOs as they worked, altogether the day went quietly and orderly.

Back at the camp, Jock said "Right Jonesey, after tea we go to work."

"Work, Sir, I thought we had finished for the day" the man answered.

"You are never finished in this job. You never know when your valuable services will be required, but that is not what I am talking about. I mean, you are now going to school to learn a little something about bombs and fuses."

"You mean, I was going to ask you about that Sir, when do I go on the Bomb Disposal Course?" Jonesey asked.

"Course!, there are no courses. You learn the hard way in this job. However, I will show you what we have here and discuss the various fuses and the methods of dealing with them, and of course, how to remove them," Jock answered.

After their meal Jock collected the other new officer.

"Mr Hillary, I'd like you to come and join us, we are going to go over the various fuses and bombs. I'm sure you wouldn't want to miss the opportunity.." Together the three men went to a field at the rear of the camp site, the area was littered with bombs of all sizes.

"Right, make notes if you wish, so that you can identify any object you may be called on to deal with. If you have any questions, ask as you go along; we can discuss other questions you may think of later on over a drink." Jock was expecting a lot of questions.

"We start with this lot outside first; the small ones up to the big ones. 50 kilo; 112 lb. 3'6" long, with the fin. Depending whether they are SD or S.C. 500 lb. or 250 kilo, 3'3" to 3'11"; 500 kilo is 1120 pounds in weight and 5 feet long but the SD model is only 3'6" long. The 1000 kilo or 2400 pounds one is 6'3" and we call it Herman. There is another, the SD model and we call it Esau, it is only 4'10" long. Fritz here is an SD model and is 6'5" It weighs 1400 kilos or 3200 lb. The one we have on at present is called Satan and is an S.C. weighing 1800 kilos or 4000 pounds; 88'7½" without fins. Jock rattled through the figures and the two Lieutenants struggled to write them down, as if their lives depended on the figures.

"A lot of these bombs could have two fuses in them as you will have probably noticed as we have looked at them" Jock said. "One of them is always an anti-handling fuse. I'll come to them when you have finished writing."

During the conversation, they had been walking between the mounds of metal cases, each one having its own story. The only ones not amongst the pile were those which had exploded, taking with it at least one life. They entered a nearby shed and Jock informed them of its contents.

"Here are some of the little sods you will handle, but take my advice, there are no such things as a dud bomb. Never take chances. One man one bomb, and finally, if in doubt – seek advice. You must remember these points, although things have changed and improved since we first started with hammers and chisels, but don't forget the rules."

Going to a bench he picked up a fuse.

"No. 15, this is the most common, all German fuses are electric, this one is like a small electric battery. Here is a device on a telescopic arm that pumps the juice through the spring-loaded plunger terminal as the bomb leaves the plane. Once armed, the least knock or vibration will set the damned thing off. The reason they don't explode on impact is an 8 second delay before the condensers are fully charged. So, if they are dropped at low altitude they penetrate and then wait for your or me." He handed them the item to examine, and picked another fuse up.

"This one is a pure bitch, its a Type 50. Do not touch any bomb with this one fitted, not even with a pencil. This is an extremely delicate trembler switch, the resistances within the interior circuits prevent the current reaching the condensers within three to five minutes after it leaves the plane. A bomb fitted with this fuse is even too sensitive to steam out, therefore you have to use a liquid discharger which I will explain about later." He showed the item to the two men.

"Next we come to this little bugger, its a No. 17. Look at it closely. This is a clock – it looks simple doesn't it? Just stick a magnet on it and stop the clock then pull it out. However, you wouldn't be able to see this." He showed them that the fuse had been carefully cut in half for examination, and pointed out the details of the interior.

"This is the gain which contains the primary charge of Pentolite wax, this is screwed into the fuse. When the fuse is pulled out, the gain slides up here and then releases this trigger underneath. That spring forces the striker out onto that detonator. Underneath that is another gain, these gains set off these little things here." He showed them the small objects.

"These are small cylindrical pellets of picrics and are found at the bottom of the fuse pocket. If these picric went off when you had the fuse in your hand, you've had it. We have destroyed the picric these are only substitutes. So you see, even with the clock stopped the bomb still goes off when the fuse is pulled. It is not possible to tell whether an anti-handling device is attached, so we use Freddie," Jock said. "I will introduce you to Freddie." He shows them the piece of apparatus which he had used to withdraw the fuse by means of the cord.

"This is Freddie as we call it, officially the Merrylees, don't forget to use it, don't take chances. You can use it on any fuse."

He moved along the bench.

"Now here is the Liquid Discharger I mentioned, to use with the No. 50." He said and showed the two interested men a conglomeration of rubber tubes and a brass cylinder. "Suspend the case, attach the tubes, like this, use a Jubilee clip to close that one. Pump in pressure, not, and I again repeat NOT, over the red line. Let the juice run into the fuse. Wait 30 minutes then fit the Merrylees to withdraw the fuse." He looked at the worried men. "So, if you have a 17 and a 50, do the 50 first. Now here is the Crabtree discharger. Clip it on the boss and wind it up. This action depresses the plunger and causes a short, wait three minutes and that should discharge the electricity. That creature there is, of course, the 'Q'coil, Mr Jones has already met him. Very cumbersome, usually a two-man load, weighs 135 pounds and gives you muscles after a while." He smiled at their expressions and picked up another fuse.

"This is a ZUS 40 and is an anti-handling fuse, don't attempt to remove this before steaming out."

Jock covered all aspects of steaming and drilling techniques, as well as all the other items in the shed.

"Now you know where they are and what they are for, remember them. If in doubt, ask your section Sergeant, there will be times you will need his advice and assistance; and lastly, you may think you have a lousy dangerous job, but don't forget the troops."

"What do you mean, Sir?" Jonesey asked.

"Those Sappers who dig the holes, knock the timbers in and shovel the earth away around your bomb. They have to shore the baulks of wood to hold the walls and roof of the tunnels. So, when you consider all the hammering and banging and shovelling they do, they could be on top or alongside a Type 50 fuse. You and I wouldn't go near them without carpet slippers on. Every one of those lads deserve a medal, they take their lives into their hands without question, a lot more than we do."

Jonesey and Hillary listened intently to their senior officer as he praised his men.

"You think an awful lot of them, don't you Sir?" Forbes-Jones said.

"Yes Jonesey I do. We have worked together closely as a team. I have owed my life to them on more than one occasion. They are a fine bunch, although they may be a bit on the rough side. I know that most of them are due for discharge soon so I expect you to look after them properly when I've gone."

They left the shed together and headed back towards the Sergeant's mess to enjoy a few drinks before they turned in.

"I don't think I will remember all the details about the fuses and the equipment, Sir," said Young Hillary.

"Mr Jones is probably in the same frame of mind but hasn't said so. Don't worry too much, you will be going over them again and again, every night, with one of the Sergeants or me. Do not forget what I told you before, if in doubt, ask."

"Are we allowed to go in here Sir?" Hillary asked as they entered the mess.

"As a special favour, you can drink with them, don't worry, the drinks are on me. I promised the lads a drink when we got the big one out. They will be waiting for us."

The next morning, the office orderly gave the Sergeant a message indicating the fact that some unusual objects had been found in a local area. On receiving the message, Jock passed the information to Forbes-Jones.

"A job for you Jonesey. Investigate, identify and neutralise."

The youngster seemed petrified as he stared at the piece of paper. Jock noticed his consternation.

"I will come with you, seeing as it is your first job." He called for the small van to be brought round to the office.

"Come on Jonesey, get your gear." The van didn't take long before it stopped beside the veranda, Jock climbed into the front seat and gave the driver his directions, as Jonesey got into the back.

"What is it Guv?" the driver asked. "We don't know yet, call at the local Police Office and they will show us where to go."

Some time later, after they had been to the Police Station, a Police Sergeant showed them the way to some woods where the suspected bombs were. The area had been roped off and a Police Constable was standing guard.

"We have found a few here Sir," the Sergeant said.

"Right, Thank you. Now would you care to keep well away, just in case of accidents" Jock indicated to the man.

"Don't worry about us Sir, we'll keep well away" and the two coppers retreated into the distance pretty quickly.

Jock directed the Sapper to bring the reel of tape from the van. He then walked to the line of rope which had been stretched out around a fairly large area of woodland. He examined the ground very carefully as he walked along, saying when he stepped over the rope.

"We'll cover a stretch at a time, will you run the tape out Wilf?" he said to the driver. Jock moved carefully through the woods, slowly it seemed to the Lieutenant, but his boss had dealt with many similar searches, he looked at every spot where he was to place his feet. His eyes swept from side to side, both on the ground and on the trees. He restricted his search to 6 feet so that every blade of grass and every twig could be clearly seen. Behind him came Jonesey and the Sapper laying out the tape that showed the part that had been checked.

"What's this?" Forbes-Jones reached out towards a tree they had passed. The object he was attempting to get hold of was unusual, like a tin can with wings attached. "I've never seen anything like this before." The object was tangled with the branches of the tree. Before he could touch it, he was brought down by the Sapper, who had dropped the tape and took a running dive at the officer's legs. The young lieutenant was brought crashing to the ground before he could reach the mysterious object.

"What the hell do you mean by doing that – assaulting an officer?" he spluttered.

"He just saved your life, you bloody fool. Ours as well," Jock said as he came across.

"Good show Wilf, you done well, thanks," he addressed the driver.

"What is it?" asked the red-faced man sitting on the ground.

"That is a butterfly bomb, they were dropped in batches like the incendiary bombs. As they fall, the wings open out and spiral, as they turn the fuse is armed, ready to explode at the slightest touch. If that one had gone off it would probably set off any others in the area. Now search, look but do not touch anything; mark the ones you see or I will have your guts for garters. I saw that one there but we only do a marked section at a time, that was outside of the stretch we are working."

The driver, in the meanwhile, had fastened a piece of white tape to a branch near the bomb.

"Now mister, walk close beside me, not in front, we shall check the rest of the area together. Only a 6 foot width, and before you put your foot down examine the ground where it is going, we don't want you to stand on one."

They covered the whole of the roped off section and numerous missiles were marked, on the ground and in the trees. When they returned to the van, Jock collected a large ball of string.

"You stay here Wilf," Jock ordered the driver, as he took the other officer by the arm.

"Come on, I will show you how to deal with these little beauties."

They entered the woods and went from bomb to bomb, guided by the white markers fastened near each one. Then Jock gently attached the string to each one.

"Be careful, and make sure that you do not touch them," he told Jonesey as he showed him how to attach the strings and to lead them to the next one. After all the bombs had been treated correctly, the string was led away to a safe point. Jock handed the end of the string to his associate.

"Before you pull, ensure that the area is clear. Check with the Police … right, its all yours."

Jonesey obeyed his instructions before pulling on the string. He was astounded at the explosions which occurred as all the explosions were rolled into one, the sounds reverberated amongst the trees, and hundreds of fragments of shrapnel were hurled in every direction. The youngster's face was grey as he listened to the metal splattering against the trees.

"We will wait a few minutes and then check them again," Jock ordered. "Just to ensure that they all have gone."

"Is that possible Sir?" the new man asked.

"Anything is possible in this job. Never take chances."

After a five minute smoke the two men returned to the woods and examined the places where the markers were. Jonesey looked at the pitted tree trunks, he was amazed at the amount of blast damage and the number of metal slivers stuck in the trees. After they had finished their tour and returned to the van, Jonesey went up to the driver,

"I want to thank you and to apologise for the way I spoke to you before. I realise now what would have happened."

"That's OK Sir. I was thinking of myself really, all the beer I drunk last night would have ran out and been wasted," the man said.

Forbes-Jones seemed a bit puzzled by the answer; Jock saw the expression on his face.

"He meant that if we had been caught by that lot we would have punctured like colanders, holes all over." His fellow officer realised that this was true, another lesson he had learned. The two police officers approached them just then and the Sergeant asked if everything was cleared.

"Yes Sergeant, you can collect your rope now. As far as we can ascertain there are none left. If, by any chance, anything does turn up please let us know and we will attend straight away." He climbed into the van where the other two soldiers were waiting and said 'cheerio' to the men in blue.

"Right, Wilf, let's go home."

When they had returned to camp and had lunch, Jock suggested to the novice that he spend a few hours with one of the Sergeants and go over the various fuses and the bombs, whilst he got with his paper work.

The next day they were informed of a large object which had been found, it was situated apparently in a river near the bank side. Local Police had stated that the area had been closed and if they called at the Police Office, a copper would show them the location.

"Get your gear Mr Hillary," Jock said when he received the message.

"Can I come as well Sir?" asked Jonesey. Jock looked at him, they both had to learn and as quickly as possible, Lieutenant Dobbins was out on the site where the diggings were, and he wanted someone to be in charge of the camp. Well they had managed before these two came, so they can manage again.

"Right." He called the Sergeant over,

"You are in charge of the camp Larry, we shouldn't be long."

"Shall I take my gear Sir?" asked Jonesey, all excited.

"Just overalls and leave your valuables behind, Sergeant." He turned to the NCO

"Better have a block and tackle ready and a tripod, the usual lifting ear, and a squad of men just in case." The two young officers climbed into the back of the van, really apprehensive and excited at the prospect of going on their first job with a bomb.

"Right, got all your Gear?" he asked them. Having ascertained that all the required gear was aboard, they moved off towards the distant river.

An elderly policeman took them from the Police Station to the spot where the alleged bomb lay. The van was parked some distance from the river. Jock went with the others to the edge of the water.

"There it is Sir" the Policeman said, pointing to a dark object underneath the water about 3 feet from the bank.

"OK officer, leave it to us." Jock gave the man leave to disappear from the danger zone. The riverbank sloped steeply right up to the water, which was fast flowing; the height of the bank was about 6 feet. Jock stripped off, just wearing his overalls and rubber boots, he slid down the bank to the water.

"Mr Jones, what is the first job?"

"Examine and identify Sir" was the reply. 'Good' thought Jock, 'he's learnt something'.

"How would you identify Mr Hillary?" The other man thought for a few seconds.

"Size Sir, length and then try to find the fuses."

"Right, we will have a look then," Jock said as he stepped into the water with a long stick in his hand. He stepped onto the object and moved slowly along the hard slippery surface. He carefully measured the case.

"3'11" what is that Mr Jones?"

"Could be a 500 pounder Sir, S.C. model."

"Right, I will try to find the fuses." He bent down to try and feel for the fuse pocket but with his awkward position on the metal slippery surface, the fast flowing river washed him off his perch.

"Sod it" he said, with teeth chattering as he emerged from the icy water.

"Well now I'm wet, I cannot get any wetter" and he slid back under the fast flowing river to search for the fuses. His hunt was futile, he couldn't find the fuse pocket after several dives under the water he called it off.

"Waste of time, I think the fuse is underneath." He climbed the bank, with his rubber boots constantly slipping in the snow.

"OK we'll have to leave it for a while." He informed the police officer that they would be back and asked him to ensure that warning notices covered at least 200 yards each way. Jock climbed into a pair of dry overalls and pulled his duffel coat on.

"I think a telephone call is in order Mr Hillary. Will you telephone the camp and ask the Sergeant to bring the lifting gear etc."

"Where will I find a telephone round here Sir?"

"Well, I think we may as well resort to the police office, we can get a cuppa and a warm there. You can make the 'phone call from there, and the men will be able to meet us at the office when they come."

So, they all adjourned to the local cop shop whilst the necessary arrangements were made. There was a huge fire burning in the canteen and as they sat in the warmth, Jock held a casual conversation with the man who was on duty at the office.

"How long have you been in the job?"

"Nearly 23 years Sir" the man in blue answered.

"Have you been doing yours long? It's not a job I would fancy." The three soldiers were silent for a while, looking at Jock, who answered.

"It's not a job that many people would like but it is one that has to be done. You can't really force chaps into this occupation. We are all volunteers."

"It is dangerous though. You can never tell when those things are likely to go off, can you?"

"That's life officer, isn't it? No-one knows when, where, or how the end will come. It is a consolation in this job, the end is usually quick."

"How long have you been doing it?" the policeman asked.

"Since I joined the army I have been working on explosives. Now I am due to retire. How about you, what is your job like?" Jock was curious and quizzed the man incessantly regarding the duties, hours of work and everything connected with the occupation.

"You seem very interested in the Force Sir" the copper said.

"Well, I've been thinking what I will do when I leave the Army. I only have a few days to go and I have seriously considered joining the Police Force" Jock told him.

"You should get in easy enough, but you will find it a bit tame and quiet after what you do now. Discipline is hard but that shouldn't worry you. We are getting a lot of ex-service men applying at the present. Mind you the pay is lousy, only £4 a week. So good luck to you if that's what you want." Jock grinned at him,

"What, no danger money, we get six pence a day extra for doing this job."

A squeal of brakes outside attracted their attention. The PC looked out of the window and said

"There's another crowd outside who must be just as mad as you lot." Jock and his mates rose and went to join the Sergeant and his sub-section.

"OK Larry, got all the gear?" he asked.

"Yes Sir and I've brought you another dry pair of overalls, just in case" was the reply. "I need them, the other ones are wet. Follow us" he said and climbed into the van with the other officers. The little cavalcade made its way down to the river where all the ropes, block and tackle and wood were unloaded. The Sergeant accompanied the officers to the edge of the river.

"If we can lift it and swing it over to land on the bank we can have a look at the fuse. It is underneath at the present," Jock explained to the Sergeant.

"If it goes up, the angle of the bank will protect you from the blast. Fix the tripod over the bomb, face open to the bank."

Jock didn't want to try and tell the Sergeant his job, the man had brought a 3 x 2' block and tackle with him, all the necessary material for lifting a 500 pound weight. He had done the same job many a time.

"Jonesey, while the men are putting up the gin, can you check with the police and ensure that the far bank is kept clear for 200 yards. Mr Hillary, will you do the same on this side. When you are both satisfied, come back here and we will discuss the situation and I will explain to you what the Sergeant is doing. I will also tell you what we will have to do when is ready." The Sergeant was chasing the men who had been waiting beside the lorry; he told them what was required and the men got to work, swiftly the three long poles were laid out and the ends fastened together. The blocks were rived with the ropes, and in a matter of minutes they carried the apparatus to the river's edge. The Sergeant supervised the job of raising of the blocks over the bomb. One leg was placed in the water immediately behind the case, the other two were situated on either side. The bottom block was lowered almost to the level of the water and the rope led out onto the ground behind the brow of the bank, ready for the men to pull on it.

"All ready Sir," the Sergeant reported to his OC "Everything is ready Sir. The area is clear." Forbes-Jones gasped as he came running up to them.

"For God's sake Jonesey, don't run, don't ever run. This thing has been here long enough now, another few minutes wouldn't make any difference."

"Mr Hillary, is everything ready on this side of the river?"

"Yes Sir, all in order."

"Right Serg, you know the drill." He stood at the side of the river and explained to the two Lieutenants what they intended to do. Two heavy looped ropes would be placed around the bomb, one at each end, the loop would be pushed through itself so that it would tighten on the bomb as it was lifted. The bomb would be raised clear of the water and another rope attached to it, leading over the bank. Once the bomb was high enough, the last rope would be used to pull it onto the bank. Naturally, it would have to be swung a few times before it was dropped. Once on the ground they could then examine the fuse.

"As we do not know the type of fuse we will be dealing with, I will require all the gear to be placed above the bank ready for immediate use. We will need the coil as well, now then, do either of you want to do the job?"

"Yes Sir, I would like to do it, if I may," Jonesey was the first to answer.

"Right, just a word of advice, before you start to take any fuse out, or work on a bomb, go and relieve the calls of nature. You will get the feeling you want to go, and once you start work you cannot stop to go and have a run off. So, off you go."

"Ready Sir." The wet Sergeant and the Corporal climbed out of the river, they had both been under the water to fix the ropes in position. The loops had been slipped onto the hook of the lower block, ready to lift.

"Right, Larry, better get yourself changed and make sure the lads have put their dry overalls on."

A couple of minutes later the works party returned, dry and ready for action. The Sergeant detailed the men to take the rope leading to the block and tackle, whilst he and the Corporal took hold of the rope, ready to swing the missile onto the bank. The Two Lieutenants gave them a hand, Jock stood by the side of the water.

"Right Serg, bring the sod up," he shouted.

"Heave, Heave."

The steady drone of the Sergeant's voice came to Jock as he watched the sling tighten onto the bomb, then slowly began to lift it from the river bed. He wondered what the devil had in store. As it cleared the water he looked closely at it to see the fuses. At last he spotted them and moved into the river to examine them as the bomb inched its way upwards.

"Christ" he said, "Just our bloody luck."

"Stethoscope Sergeant," he shouted to the Sergeant when the bomb was raised sufficiently above the surface.

"Check."

The upward movement was halted, the men holding it suspended.

"Right, swing it." The Sergeant and his little team began to pull the missile towards the bank.

"Back," came the order from the river side. Backwards and forwards the bomb swung, each time the swing became greater. At last Jock estimated the movement was right.

"Drop it," he yelled and the soldiers automatically let the bomb drop. The judgment was just right and it dropped gently at Jock's feet.

"OK that's it," he shouted and dropped down beside the bomb and pressed his ear to it, "Damn."

"Mine Sir," a voice said in his other ear. Jonesey was there. Jock looked at him, his expression was serious.

"Do you know what it is?" The youngster examined the fuse.

"Yes Sir, No. 27."

"That's right, Clock Fuse. Time delayed," Jock said.

"I know Sir," he had learnt his fuses. Jock looked up at the Sergeant and held his hand up. The NCO threw the stethoscope down and Jock caught it and passed it to Jonesey.

"Listen to that," he ordered.

As the man pressed the instrument against the bomb, Jock climbed up the bank to collect the 'Q' coil and the Crabtree discharger.

"We will want Freddie as well Serg. We have a 15 and a 27." As he returned to his position beside Jonesey, he said, "Well?"

"It's ticking Sir." The youngster seemed to freeze. "When will it go off?"

"Your guess is as good as mine lad, shift yourself." He pushed Jonesey out of the way as he lifted the huge weight onto the case,

"Fasten that, quick."

As the Lieutenant strapped the 'Q' coil onto the bomb over the fuse, Jock placed the Crabtree over the other fuse and wound it up.

"How you doing lad?," he asked his workmate.

"I think I've got it on Sir," he said.

"Don't' think, be sure." Jock checked the apparatus. "Switch on Sergeant" he called, and the tremendous electric magnet came into action.

"Freddie, Serg" was the next order.

"Here it is Sir," the Sergeant was halfway down the bank with the gear.

"Ta" Jock muttered. "Here, Mr Jones fix this on. Serg, you stay up there and keep your eye on Mr Hillary please. Now we had better get started," he said.

"We, Sir?"

"OK you had better get started. The time is about up for the Crabtree. Don't forget, locking nut off without the hammer, lift our smoothly, check that there are no picric pellets on the bottom. Then put the fuse in a safe place. When that's done, run the cord out from the Freddie and lead it over the bank, OK?"

"Yes Sir." The lad tensed, his mind full of the instructions he head learnt from Jock, and the down-to-earth facts he had obtained from the Sergeants.

What if I mess it up, he thought. Then he remembered what Jock had told him. 'If he buggered it up, then nobody could tell him off'. He relaxed.

"All the men back Sergeant?" he called. Satisfied with the reply, he turned to Jock. "How about your Sir?"

"Oh, I'm not here" Jock said, "Carry on."

"No Sir, you only have a couple of days left to go, I don't mind if I make a mistake, but I don't see why you have to suffer. Anyway, you told us to obey the Regulations, one man one bomb." The young chap was worried as he spoke to his boss. "After all, you have taken it out of the river and done all the work, all I have to do is to take the fuse out."

"Right Jonesey, if it makes you happier, but first run through the routine."

The sub-Lieutenant went through the procedure and Jock said,

"Right, here are your tools. You should be OK be quick but steady, don't forget, we do not know how long the clock has left to run, it may be hours or seconds. The bumping it had didn't set it off but you never know. If you have any doubts, get out quick. Now don't forget what I told you about relieving your bladder. Good luck!"

He climbed to the top of the bank as the youngster settled down to place the extractor on the first fuse, he stood there looking down of the lad with his legs in the cold water, and sitting in the mud. He watched the removal procedure, and noted the trembling hands of the man as he moved the extractor.

"Steady lad," he muttered. Jones hesitated before removing the fuse, then he seemed to compose himself, wiped his hands, then continued with the removal. The hazardous job was watched carefully by Jock.

"Good lad, that's it, steady," he was talking to himself. A grunt of satisfaction came then Jonesey exhaled his breath in a long sigh as the fuse was lifted clear.

He sat for some time, gazing at it, then slowly he turned to the top of the slope and saw Jock standing there watching hi. His pallid face suddenly burst into a wreath of smiles.

"I did it Guv," he exclaimed.

"Yes Jonesey, you did it. Now move the gain from the bottom, very gently now." Jock went down the bank and took the fuse from the young sub-Lieutenant's hands.

"Now fix Freddie up, you haven't got a lot of time to waste," he advised. Jones fitted the apparatus on top of the other fuse and Jock moved to the top of the bank again. He watched closely as the lad fitted the screws in and tightened them.

"Right, lead the cord away over the top. Mind you don't pull it, just keep it loose. That's it, hang on to it so that it won't pull over the top, now pass it up to me." Jock caught hold of the end of the cord and held it until Jonesey climbed up beside him.

"OK lad, here you are, lead it over to the truck then start pulling."

They retired to the safety point where the rest of the men were, then the new man started to gently pull on the cord. It stopped moving.

"Don't jerk it" Jock stated. "The picric pellets may be attached to the bottom of the gain."

"What do I do now, Sir?," Jones asked.

"Same as the other one, ensure that there are no pellets on the bottom. Unscrew the gain gently and then disconnect the fuse," he was advised. The officer slid down the bank back to the bomb. Jock again stood at the top watching him work. The removal procedure was carried out and once more Jock smiled.

"That's it lad. Well done. You did it, now let's go home." He reached out a hand to help the officer up the bank. The lad was nearly in tears when he got to the top.

"Right Larry," Jock said to the Sergeant. "Get the gear and the case, take them back to camp. We will see you there."

"Yes, Sir. Welcome to the club Sir." He said to Forbes-Jones.

"Thank you Larry," the youngster was feeling happy. "Get your overalls changed Jonesey and we will be off," Jock said.

"Oh I haven't brought a change of clothes Sir," the smile left his face and the Sergeant laughed.

"Never mind Sir, you learn from your mistakes." Jones thought he heard that statement from someone else.

"Come on lad, its only half an hour's drive. You will have to sit in your wet clothes till you get home. In future, you will remember to always have at least one spare change of clothing to change into."

On the way back to camp they called in at the local Police Office and informed the old copper that they were leaving and the bomb was going with them. Back at camp, Jonesey went off to put on some dry clothes, Jock went into the office with Hillary.

"Message just came in Sir," and the office Corporal handed Jock a slip of paper.

"Right Mr Hillary, we can leave our wet compatriot to sort himself out, we can go and look at this one. Get some overalls, and would you get a pair for me please?" Jock requested transport to be brought round to the office. The van arrived at the same time as Jonesey.

"Going out again, are we?," he asked.

"We are, but you are not. You have your report to do. This one is for Mr Hillary," Jock answered as they climbed into the van with the driver. The other officer threw the spare clothes into the back and climbed in after them. It took them an hour to drive to the spot where a suspected bomb had been found.

On arrival at the spot, it was noticed that numerous houses surrounded the field where the object had been uncovered. The local Police, as usual, had closed the space off around the dangerous missile. Jock and Hillary were shown exactly where the suspected bomb was. They examined it together.

"Do you know what it is?" Jock asked.

"A shell Sir."

"Yes, an anti-aircraft shell. What do you propose?"

"Blow it in situ, Sir?" with a quizzical look on his face.

"Yes, we can't move this one. Get it well sandbagged and protect the surrounding property, then stick a slab of gun cotton up its behind. That'll do it."

Jock asked the driver how many sandbags they had on the van.

"Only 30 Sir" the soldier told him after he had counted them.

"It's not enough, but we will make do" Jock said as he estimated the size of the protection wall. "We will have to make it as close as possible and fill in around the wall with earth."

All of them got stuck into the job of filling the sacks with earth.

"Glad you joined?" he asked the sweating Lieutenant. "It's not all fun and games, is it?"

"I never expected this Sir," Hillary said, heaving another sack on his shoulder to carry over to the missile. All the sacks were soon filled and placed in a tight fitting wall around the object. Earth was then packed up against the outside to reinforce it.

"Satisfied Mr Hillary?" Jock was happy with the work, he just wanted the other officer to acknowledge the fact.

"Yes Sir. I will attach a detonating charge to it," was the answer. A slab of guncotton was fastened to the top end of the shell, close to the cap. A primer was inserted into the hole and then a No. 11 electrical detonator was entered into the primer. Wires were connected to the detonator and led to a spot at the edge of the field. Jock connected the two wires to the terminals on his little box.

"Right Mr Hillary, as soon as you are sure that the area is safe, you can press the plunger." Lying flat on his stomach the sub-Lieutenant depressed the handle. He was surprised at the crack which the exploding shell made as it sent a cloud of dirt and shrapnel into the sky.

"It sounds quite loud, doesn't it Sir?"

"Not as loud as a big one lad, but I hope you never have to find that out" Jock answered as he started to collect the gear together.

That evening Jock called on the two young officers.

"You have been invited to dine with the NCOs this evening. I will see you in the office and we can go down together." They were all greeted in a friendly manner when they walked in.

"Is it usual for officers to dine with the men?" Jonesey asked.

"There are no officers and ranks here, just friends doing a dangerous job together. On parade, off parade, one can never say if it will be the last time. Mind you, it doesn't happen in the best of places, but it is up to you from now on. I know some officers out on a sub-section who used to dine by themselves, a pretty lonely life."

"If it's good enough for you Sir, it's good enough for me" Jonesey said. He turned to the men in the mess.

"I have learnt a lot in a short time while I've been here, from you all. In particular," he hesitated, "from the Guvnor. I only hope that I can carry on where he left off. I doubt if I will ever be as good as he is, but with your assistance, I will try my best. That goes for Mr Hillary as well. Now I want to say Thank You all."

"Have a drink Guv," Sergeant Symonds handed the young man a beer.

"Thanks Larry" grinned Jonesey, "but I will buy the round for everyone, the drinks are on me."

"Do that Jonesey and they will keep you at it" Jock said, and everyone laughed.

Jock helped the two lads back to their billets after the night of drinking was over. Hillary wasn't too bad, but his eyes were glazed and just allowed himself to be guided along, Jock opened the door of his hut and said,

"You OK now?"

"Night Guv," the youngster mumbled as he slipped through the open door, "Thanks for everything." The other new officer was led down the path to his rooms, he never stopped talking as Jock helped him into his rooms.

"Jonesey, I have to tell you, Lieutenant Dobbins will be leaving at the end of the week, he has been posted to HQ. So, after tomorrow, you will be the boss. Look after these lads and be kind to them ….. they'll do the same for you." Forbes-Jones burped prodigiously and grinned stupidly.

"Are you married Jonesey?"

"No, too young Guv." Jock murmured quietly to himself, 'Good', then said to the other chap.

"Don't do it then, this is your family from now on, till you leave them. When you go they'll grieve for you, as they have done for all their mates they've lost. Goodnight." He gave the lad a push onto his bed, and pulled a blanket over him.

The following morning brought borders from HQ informing them that the first intake of German prisoners would be arriving about 4pm. Jock understood from the message that they were all Engineers and there would be some Bomb Disposal Experts amongst them. They would have their own officers who would be responsible for the discipline amongst the Germans. It was pointed out that the prisoners would not be used for actively defusing the bombs, but only for labour and working on shafts and tunnels. Jock made the necessary arrangements for men to remain at camp as a works party, they were to spend the day getting the billets ready for the newcomers, to light a fire in the barrack rooms and prepare them for the prisoners. Jock detailed Lieutenant Dobbins to go onto the site with two of the Sergeants and the team who were engaged on the diggings. He was pondering as to which duties to give the two new officers when a further message indicated that an unexploded bomb had been found on a beach close by. The men guessed that it was possibly a mine, as they were always turning up. A truckload of men and all the necessary gear was soon ready to go, mine detectors, tapes, shovels and other tools were all recognised as the essentials. Jock decided to take the two new officers with him, it would give them something to do and possibly a little more experience.

"Do you want me Sir?" asked the Sergeant.

"No, I don't think so Larry. You hang on in camp, keep your eyes on the lads. I'll need someone here I can rely on if anything else turns up."

"What do you think it will be Guv?" asked Jonesey as they made their way to the location.

"Apart from the strong possibility that it could be a mine, it could be anything, either British or Foreign. I'll tell you when I see it." Upon arrival at the scene, it was noted that a section of the beach had been closed, with signs displayed and local Police Officers standing around. Jock approached one of them and asked what their problem was; the local Policeman pointed to the sand.

"I think they are mines. I've seen two and marked them."

"Whereabouts are they?" asked Jock.

"Where those two sticks are," the copper answered, pointing to the stakes in the beach. Jock stood with the man in blue and surveyed the open space.

"Do you know if there were any British mines laid here during the war?"

"Yes Sir, when the scare was on about possible invasion, the army came along and laid barbed wire as well as the mines."

"I thought that was more than likely" Jock said "But do you know if they came along afterwards and cleared them away?"

"The barbed wire just seemed to fall apart with age, and the Council took it away. Regards the mines, I cannot remember ever seeing anyone coming for them," the Policeman replied.

"Damn" Jock exploded. "Jonesey, Mr Hillary, if you please." The two officers were standing beside the truck when he called and came running. "Please no, not again Mr Jones. No running."

"Sorry Sir," the demoralised Jonesey said.

"Trouble, I'm afraid," said Jock ignoring the obviously hurt feelings and indicating the stretch of beach in front of them.

"Mined in case of invasion. We don't know how many were laid, nor why they were not collected."

"Will it take long to find them Sir?" asked Hillary.

"Depends on how they have moved with the sands of time and how many were laid."

They went over to the men and Jock explained the situation to them and detailed the Sappers to the jobs they would have to do. The procedure was standard for clearing a minefield and was strictly adhered to in case of premature explosions. No man was closer than 15 feet from any other. One man with his headphones on walked in front swinging his mine detector from side to side, covering about a 10 feet wide lane with each sweep. Whenever he found reaction he halted and held the mine detector over the spot. A second man approached and laid a marker, like a hot cross bun, on the place. The first man moved on and the action was repeated each time he located any metal. A sapper came from the rear and gently searched under the marker to find the cause. If it was a mine, it was laid on the surface ready for the fuse to be removed. Once the mines were made safe another sapper took the cases back to the rear. The man who laid the markers marked the area covered by a tape. As soon as a stretch had been 'swept', the procedure was repeated on the adjacent stretch of ground alongside. It was a slow procedure, better safe that sorry; Jock's job was to take the fuses out. As it was low tide, Jock decided to sweep the beach alongside the water first then to work inland. Several such moves were going to be required before the job was done.

"Look Jonesey, its going to take hours to check this lot with only one mine detector. We have another couple in the van, I don't want you to use one, nor you Mr Hillary, it takes some time to get used to them. What I propose is that we split the whole crowd of us into three groups. One Sapper will use each minesweeper, one will mark, and we will take the fuses out. I'll show you how to do it so don't worry. As there are not enough men to remove the fuses and the mines afterwards, we will have one man to do the whole lot. If he finds it too much for him, the Sappers will have to change over and give him a break."

It was a monotonous job and the wind blew strongly from the sea, but they managed to cover the whole of the beach by lunch time.

"I think we can call it a day officer," Jock informed his interested local Policeman. "If you happen to find any more, just let us know, but as far as we can ascertain they have all been found."

Their arrival back at camp coincided with the call to the cookhouse.

"Good" said Jock, "I'm famished."

As they were sitting enjoying the hot meal, an orderly came in and approached Jock,

"Excuse me Sir, a message just came in." Jock glanced at the paper, "I suppose it could have waited for a few minutes more. Never mind, come on Mr Hillary, let's go."

"Want a squad Sir?" asked a Sergeant.

"No thanks, it's only a grenade or something similar. You get on with your meal."

"Can I come Sir?" Jonesey asked.

"If you only want a ride, you can come" he was told. The lad was like a kid going on a school outing, the way he jumped up and ran for the van. He did not even hear Jock say,

"Don't run, Jonesey."

They called at the local Police Station and an officer took them to a house on one of the new estates. Another copper was standing at the place on duty.

"I'll show you where it is Sir."

He led them through the house and down the garden, to the shed at the bottom of the garden. The object that was causing so much concern to the neighbourhood was lying on the ground covered with a bucket.

"There Sir" and Jock's informant quickly disappeared. Apparently the son of the house had been doing a bit of sorting out in the shed and had found one of his father's souvenirs which he had brought back from the war.

Jock asked for the box to be brought from the van. Jonesey started back towards the street and Jock called after him,

"Its too heavy for one man" but the youngster was already running.

"Better go and give him a hand," Jock told Mr Hillary. A few minutes later the two men came staggering down the garden path, struggling with the heavy box between them. Jock grinned as he looked at the look of strain on Jonesey's face.

"And you were going to carry it by yourself?"

While they had been away, he had checked the area around the shed and also inside of it, to ensure that there were no more relics of the war lying around. The container that the two officers were carrying was of solid metal, reinforced with bars, and it had a clamp down lid. This utensil was made special for such jobs as this; it was constructed for the carriage of explosive objects, to prevent injury to anyone in the vicinity.

He showed the pair of them what they had to dispose of.

"Know what it is?"

"A hand grenade, Sir." Hillary volunteered the information.

"Yes," Jock agreed "but do you notice that the pin has gone, and also the handle. The striker has gone down onto the detonator. The screw cap holding the detonator is still in place."

"Couldn't we just unscrew the cap?" asked Jonesey.

"A logical question. However, when you consider that the detonator consists of seven grains of fulminate of mercury, you realise that it is in an unstable condition. It could explode in your face at any time."

"You don't want me here, do you Guv?" the copper was in a hurry to go.

"No thanks officer. Just make sure that the public are kept away." The very relieved man left them.

They opened the box and gently placed the item on the ground close to the grenade,

"Can I do it Sir?" asked Jonesey.

"No, it's Mr Hillary's. Handle it very carefully, gently and slowly, put it in the box. Now clamp the lid down." Jock and Jonesey moved away from Hillary as he carried out his duty.

"What kind of grenade is it?" asked the youngster.

"A Mills 37, the general one used by the British during the war." Jock answered as he carefully watched Hilary manoeuvre the grenade.

It didn't take long for the job to be done and Hillary left the 'Box'.

"It's done Guv. Not as bad as a 500 pounder," he grinned.

"Maybe it isn't lad, but it can kill you just as quick," Jock said. "Never get too cocksure with them just because they are small."

The box was carried back to the van and Jock asked the man from the local Constabulary if there was an open field close by, where they could dispose of the missile. The Constable pointed out a convenient site for the purpose, which was unused by the public. They drove to the designated spot, checked that there was no danger to any passerby, then commenced to dig a hole, deep enough for prevention of shrapnel flying around. The grenade was placed in the bottom of the hole with a slab of guncotton tied to it. The detonator was inserted and the cables ran out. The grenade was disposed of without any trouble.

"Come on, lads. We have to get back to see the workers," Jock told them.

At 4pm prompt a convoy of lorries drove into the camp, loaded with German prisoners of War and some British Infantry who were the escorts. Jock stood on the veranda of the office with his three Lieutenants, he watched as the human load dismounted. Jock's Section

Sergeants stood at the side of the road. The newcomers were quickly herded into lines facing the officers and stood to attention. Jock noticed that there were three Sergeants and two officers amongst them. An Infantry Sergeant strode to the front of the group in true parade ground manner, stood the men at ease then brought them back to attention, made them take correct dressing, then turned to Jock and saluted.

"New detachment ready for Inspection, Sir," he yelled.

Jock acknowledged the salute.

"Jonesey, these little birds are really yours to deal with. You will have them to look after and get sorted out. Do you want to speak to them?"

Forbes-Jones was hesitant when he looked at this new burden. This was the first time he had seen real live enemy.

"I'd rather you did it Sir," he said eventually.

"Righto lad," Jock acknowledged the request.

He raised his voice so that the men on parade could hear him clearly, and to Sub-Lieutenant Forbes-Jones astonishment, in clear precise German, Jock told the men to stand easy.

"Können Sie Alles Hören?" he asked. It appeared that they could all hear him, going by the very surprised looks on their faces at being addressed in their own language.

"Gentlemen, welcome to the camp. I understand you are all volunteers for this job, and I hope you are all experienced. We will not expect any man to put his life in danger. Such work will be left to the British Officers in charge. Whilst you are here, I require strong discipline but you will be treated well and fairly. No man is to leave the camp by himself without permission. I must point out that in the event of any breaking of the camp rules, or trouble making, the persons concerned will find themselves being sent back to where they came from. I will require several men for duties in the camp. The others will be required for heavier work. Any man not doing his easy job in the camp properly will be transferred to outside work. Am I quite clear?" He did not receive any response, naturally he never expected a reply, and continued to talk to the gathered assembly.

"If anyone did not understand what I said, he can tell me or ask any questions when I come amongst you."

Jock then walked along the ranks, followed by his officers and Sergeants. He began an inspection of the German troops. Coming to the first man, he said

"Show me your hands." He checked each man's build and examined their hands as he went through the lines. Every now and then he ordered one of the Germans to stand outside of the office. Soon he had enough volunteers but finished his inspection before returning to his original position.

"Escort fall out," he ordered.

The infantry men were relieved of their job and turned smartly to the right and saluted, then marched away, no doubt to find the canteen and anything they could scrounge. The Sergeant who was in command of the guard detail marched up to the office with the necessary papers which had to be signed to relieve him of his burden. He knew the Captain would sign as soon as he was ready to do so, consequently he just waited patiently for the opportune moment. Jock once again spoke to the prisoners.

"Your billets are ready for you, blankets will be drawn by yourselves at the stores. A meal has been prepared and will be ready at 6pm, this will give you time to get cleaned up and settled in. The Sergeants here will show you to your quarters. I request that Officers and NCOs remain behind whilst their men are being seen to." He called to his Sergeants.

"Sergeants, take over." He turned to the group of Germans who were standing outside the office.

"Bleiben Sie auch." They remained as he had ordered as the rest of the men were marched away. Jock motioned the two officers to attend him. They advanced and both saluted, he acknowledged their salutes.

"You will not be expected to work but will ensure that discipline is maintained amongst your men. You will find things are easy here and your living conditions will be no different to my own officers and Sergeants. You will remember that you are all bound by your honour and trust whilst you are here. If there are any complaints made against you regards your behaviour, then I'm afraid you will be treated the same as the men and sent back to your original camp."

"From tomorrow, this officer" pointing to Forbes-Jones beside him, "will be in command and you will obey all orders given by him."

"You will both need a batman, a man to look after your uniform and billet. These men have not been used to manual work, as you can tell by the build and condition of their hands, so take your choice," he said to the officers indicating the men standing outside the office.

"Sir, you speak good German" said one of the officers smiling. "As it happens both my man and my friend's man are here, you picked them from the rest of the soldiers."

'How lucky can you get' thought Jock and he said

"The office orderly will show you and your men to your quarters."

"Thank you Sir," they both saluted and walked away towards their respective billets.

The German NCOs were still standing at attention.

"Kommen Sie hier Bitte," he requested. They advanced and stood before him. "As soon as one of my Sergeants returns, he will show you to your quarters. You will be able to wash and prepare for your meal at 6pm. It is the habit in the British Army that the men eat first and it is the duties of officers and senior NCOs to see to this. A visit to the dining room during each main meal is demanded, to ensure the men have no complaints about the food. It is also your duty, each of you, to see that your own and your men's quarters are kept clean and tidy. It is also your duty to ensure that the men are clean and presentable. You will report anything which is not correct, to your officers. Any disciplinary offences will be dealt with by them, if possible. May I remind you all again to ensure your men do not leave the camp area. You are all on parole. Regards work, you are not expected to do manual work, but will supervise your own men under the orders of the British Sergeants and other NCOs. If you, or your men, have any complaints about food or quarters, or the actions of any British Troops, then the complaints must come through your own Officers so that they can investigate. Now, here are my Sergeants who will show you to your quarters."

They all saluted and marched off with their new found colleagues. Jock turned to the waiting Infantry Sergeant.

"Sorry about being so long."

"Only too glad to get them off my hands Sir. Will you sign for them now Sir?" the man asked. Once the required papers had been signed, the Sergeant scurried off to find his mates.

"Just got rid of them before the works party gets back, Jonesey."

"Guv. Where on earth did you learn to speak like that? You took the wind out of my sails, standing there and spouting like the Fuhrer." Jock ignored the question and said, "Now, Jonesey, catch the lads when they come in. Make sure they know about the Germans, you don't want any trouble with them. Keep them apart as much as possible until they get used to the idea. Keep the Jerries quarters out of bounds and I think everything will go alright for you."

Jock went into the office to have a smoke and complete his paperwork before he went to his room to pack his gear. He heard the trucks pulling up outside the office and the orders being given for the men to fall in so that Jonesey could speak to them. He could well imagine the feelings of most of the men.

He went off to get washed and ready for his meal after he had packed. Before going to the mess room, he headed for the men's dining room and saw Forbes-Jones going in with one of the Sergeants. By the time he arrived the men were eating again and Jonesey was doing his rounds. One of the men near the door noticed him at once and immediately called the crowd to attention. Jonesey stopped at the interruption.

"Sorry Lieutenant" said Jock, "I don't want to interrupt your meal men, you know that I am a man of few words. Most of us have been together for a long time and have been through hell together. I couldn't wish for a finer and more braver group of men to serve with. Now, as you know, I leave you tomorrow in the capable hands of your new Guvnor. I'm sure that you will help him as you have helped me. From tomorrow, I will be out of the Army. I'll miss you all. Thanks for everything. Goodbye."

An uproar broke out in the dining room as the men cheered and shouted; they banged the tables with their cutlery and mugs. Jock turned and left the room with mixed feelings, leaving Jonesey to carry on with his rounds. He headed for the mess room being used by the new German intake and entered the room. The men all jumped to attention and stood rigidly at the tables.

"Carry on eating" he ordered. "In future, there is no need to stand, just sit up straight and stop eating till told to carry on. Any complaints about the food?"

As he received no reply, he turned to the nearest man and enquired as to whether their own Officers or NCOs had been in. Having been assured that they had visited, he left the Jerries to their meal and headed for his own meal. He joined the Sergeants already dining and was just starting to eat when Jonesey came in and sat down beside him.

"Jonesey, tonight I'm going to get sozzled," and then settled down to his meal. When everyone had eaten, the drinking began. The Sergeants were in the same frame of mind as Jock, they were going to have a good booze up to say goodbye to their Guv. He kept his word and the drinks flowed freely, a good night of entertainment was had, with plenty of songs and typical bawdy army songs. Then at last Jock bade his friends Goodnight, and made his lonely way back to his billet.

GOODBYE

Jock slept like a log and was up early to have a wash and a shave before he finished his packing. He was ready to go but didn't feel like breakfast. He filled his pipe and sat in his armchair surveying the room which had been his home for quite a while. Christ, but he'd miss all this. He got up and walked outside to stand on the veranda and gaze around the camp for the last time, as the memories flooded through his mind he heard a long forgotten sound. He listened, and sure enough he wasn't dreaming, it was the sound of tramping feet, the sound of men marching in step. Tramping feet, once heard, never forgotten. He looked along the road towards the sound and saw, heading towards him, all the men dressed in their best gear, headed by Jonesey. Arms swinging, shoulders back and chests out, with the medal ribbons standing out against the khaki, plenty of swagger.

Jock felt proud of the men as they marched towards him. Jonesey was in the front of the leading section.

"Eyes Right!" Lieutenant Forbes-Jones saluted, one man to another, all heads were turned smartly towards their old Guv. One body of men to the man they respected and liked. Jock raised his arm and saluted in return to this gallant breed of men.

"Eyes Front," and they were past. Then another shout of

"Eyes Right" and the second section passed by, led by Lieutenant Dobbins. The salute of respect was repeated, and then came the third call to marching troops,

"Eyes Right," young Lieutenant Hillary was engaged in his first military march past. He saluted smartly, looking at the big man he had not known very long, but had learned to respect, the soldiers marching behind him also looked upon their Guv for the last time.

"Eyes Front," and they were gone. Jock's eyes followed them down the road.

"Eyes Right" another voice bellowed, and Jock got another surprise when he saw the two German Sections marching towards him, led by their officers. The men were smart and clean and marched as if they had been trained for such an occasion, marching in precise German Military style.

"Eyes Front" came the order and they were all past, heading down the road behind the British troops.

'The cunning bastards' he thought, 'they had all this planned and never said a word to me', but he was pleased and had a lump in his throat. His van came along and pulled up in front of him.

"Ready Sir?" the driver asked. Jock nodded, he couldn't risk trying to talk, and the Sapper loaded his gear into the van. When Jock got into the passenger seat, the driver looked straight ahead and drove slowly towards the camp gate. Jock was deep in thought as he sat, looking at the different buildings as he passed them.

"Parade 'Shun," a voice bellowed, he looked up and lining the road on each side in single file were all the troops. The van drove slowly past them, Jock tried to see each face as he passed, he automatically put a name to each one, Geordie Brown, Vic Dee, Nelson Kirk, Jonny Graham, Les Geldart, Geordie Lylse, Scott, Hottun, Crinson, Harry Gordon and all the others he would never forget. As he sat in the passenger's seat he grinned constantly, he had to. The van stopped at the gate where the officers were gathered, with the Sergeants. The driver stopped the vehicle and Jonesey approached.

"You didn't think we'd let you go without saying Goodbye Guv?"

"You took me by surprise Jonesey," Jock said.

"We'll look after them and won't be hard. If possible, they will be treated as you used to treat them. Goodbye."

"Thanks, Goodbye, and be careful," Jock managed to say. He shook hands with them all before the van moved off.

His driver realised that silence was golden at that particular moment and didn't speak on the way to the railway station. When they pulled onto the forecourt of the station, Jock got out with one of his bags, the driver jumped out and collected the other but it was taken from him by the solemn faced man.

"Thanks Kenny, I'll manage." He held his hand out and said "Goodbye."

The driver was sorry to see the Guv leaving, he had been a good boss, he took the offered hand and said

"Goodbye Guvnor."

Jock stood and watched the familiar red wings of the van disappearing in the traffic, leaving a page of his life behind him he headed for the train.

At York Barracks it was chaos, thousands of men headed for civvy street. Men of all ranks and regiments were shepherded into lines. Numbers, ranks, names and regiments were all being processed and went through the various channels for clearance and papers to be stamped, signed and issued. Into another hall where all kit was handed in and checked from the Army Pay Books, which every soldier carried. Then along the counter, the line of men slowly moved, where a full issue of civilian clothing was handed to every man. The monotonous drone of voices went on.

"Shirt one, Shoes one pair, Socks one pair, Suit one (if the crumpled shapeless bag of cloth could be called a suit). One raincoat or overcoat and one hat (another shapeless piece of felt).

"Right, sign here. Next," and the soldier was no more, he was just one of the unemployed mass.

Standing outside in his crumpled suite and wearing his shapeless overcoat, with his hat making him look like a Chicago gangster. He considered his position; apart from the things he wore and the £60 in his pocket, all donated by the Government, he had nothing. He had grown out of the clothing at home.

Ah well, he was out of the Army now and he felt very, very lonely - not jumping for joy as were the usual expectations. There was nothing here like the old Army songs, how did they go?

"When this bloody war is over,
Oh how happy I will be"
he continued on with
"No more asking for a pass,
we will tell the Sergeant Major,
to stick his passes up his ...."
Oh well, home here I come.

He looked at the crowds of silent men standing at the bus stop, all quietly waiting for a bus to take them to the railway station. Gone was the friendly razza-ma-taz and the old matey, friendly feeling which was typical amongst soldiers. It was hard to credit, as he looked at the forlorn men, he was now one of them, and he didn't like it, not one little bit.

CHAPTER TWO

THE JOB HUNT

CIVVY STREET

CIVVY STREET

During the last few months of his army service, Jock had been working in an area close to his home town, where he spent most of his spare time. It was on one of his visits that he met a friend of his brother's wife, the two girls worked as nurses in the same hospital. She was a darling, a chubby brown-eyed creature with a little snub nose. Jock nicknamed her 'Puggle'. The friendship grew and when he left the army they saw each other regularly, eventually they became engaged. His courting days were restricted to the few hours she had off duty, this was due to the fact that she was compelled to live in at the hospital. She also worked split shifts, or was on night duty, starting at 7pm. Even the occasional evenings they had together were restricted as her parents retired early, they were typical Victorian type, and she was expected to be indoors for 10pm at the latest. Occasionally, they were allowed the use of the front room, but most of the time they had to spend their few hours together sharing the fire with her parents. Her dad was a good old stick, first world war soldier, and he got on well with Jock, however he had a craving for playing draughts and the checker board was out as soon as possible!

"Want a game?" he would ask, rather hopefully, "I have just thought of a good move."

Naturally Puggle was as annoyed as Jock was about this but Jock didn't want to hurt the old man's feelings by refusing. Apart from going out into the cold, there was little else they could do, even though he sometimes thought that he should have let him win more often.

Regular as clockwork, Jock wrote letters of application to various Police Forces requesting employment. One Force after another, letter after letter, each application form was carefully worded as they were sent to different Headquarters. After a while, he became despondent for all the answers were the same, he was requested to have a medical examination and then he had to pass an educational test. Once he had completed the exams, he had to wait for the results. Always the answer came back with the same message, informing him that there were no vacancies and advice was given for him to try another Force. Eventually he had to sign on at the local Unemployment Office whilst he waited for his applications to the Police being considered. He was told to report to a local firm to start work, otherwise he would not get any benefit. As he couldn't afford to go without cash, he went along to the large firm, 'I expect it will only be temporary till I get a job with the Police' he thought as he walked up to the factory gates.

He was stopped by the gateman.

"What do you want?"

"I'm from the Labour Exchange, I've come to see about a job," Jock told the brusque man.

"Are you in the Union?" the uniformed gateman asked.

"No, I've just been demobbed from the army," Jock answered.

"You can't come in here unless you are in the Union. This is a closed shop," the man told him.

"Fair enough, I'll join the Union as soon as I get the job."

"No you won't, nobody gets started here unless they are already a Union member, so don't waste my time." The gateman was getting angry.

"Look, how can I join the Union unless I start work?"

"If you come in here and get a job, the whole factory will be on strike, there are plenty of our chaps who left here to go and fight for the country. They have to come back, their job is guaranteed, so you are not getting in. That's final."

"Christ, is this the way you get treated after serving in the army?," Jock said to the Clerk at the Employment Exchange.

"Never mind. We'll see if we can find something else for you. There must be something you can do," the erstwhile civil servant answered.

The waiting began all over again and his letters had been sent to all the different City, County and Borough Police Forces, and with each one he had to have the Medical Exam and the Educational Exam. The local doctor said that he knew every wrinkle on Jock's face and the local Police Inspector, who had to sit with him during the time he answered the question papers, was getting a bit fed up.

"Why don't you give up and try for something else?" Jock refused, although he was becoming annoyed and perplexed as each application proved negative.

In desperation and as a final resort, he wrote off to the Big City, where, he thought, there must be some possibility of starting. Sure enough, after his letter of request, he received the usual application form sent back, but the Medical and Educational Exams were not to be taken at the local Police Office. He had to use some of his dwindling funds to travel all the way to the Big City. One day was to be used for medical and the second day for the written exams. They would put him up for the night. If he failed the medical or written tests then they would refund his cash outlay. If, however, he were accepted then he would not be reimbursed.

Eventually, the day came when a letter landed on the doormat. It was the one he'd been waiting for, indicating the day, the time and place he was to present himself for scrutiny, mentally and physically.

"About time too," he said, and packed an overnight bag in preparation. Then he waited impatiently for the day to arrive. The local Police Inspector advised him to study up on English Geography as they were very strict on that subject. He did as advised and before he had finished he knew every County, their location, size in square miles, all the rivers, cities and towns, and their population; the produce from each County and general businesses. The ground layout wasn't missed and he knew all about the various strata. He was sure that if any question was asked on English Geography, he would answer it.

The train pulled in on time and, swinging out onto the platform, he marched along quickly before the train had stopped. Once he had threaded his way through the crowds gathered on the platform, he headed for the newsagents shop which he could see. As this was his first visit to the city, he required a map in order to find his way around. The newsagent suggested the A to Z which was a comprehensive book showing all the roads and places of interest in the City. Each street was entered in the back of the book in alphabetical order, a number alongside showed exactly where the road was on the map. The underground stations were also included in the book and the various stations were shown on the map. This was the ideal thing for Jock, it would help him to find the place he had to attend for the examinations and also, if he was lucky enough to be accepted, he would need it when he was posted onto a station. He perused the contents and soon found the location of the exams, sticking the book into his pocket he headed for the underground station. It didn't take him long to reach his destination and as he walked along the street from the station, he checked the names of the streets as he went.

Eventually, as he came to the road that he wanted, he noticed several other men headed in the same direction; he was not alone as he headed for the dirty grey building. Crowds of men, all around his age were gathered outside the offices, all awaiting their turn to enter the front doors. A queue was formed up on the inside in the passageway. As each man produced his papers his name was ticked off a sheet by a Police Sergeant, the men were then directed to wait in a large hall.

Jock took his place in one of the seats and looked around the sea of faces, a quick count of the number of men proved that there were well over three hundred hopefuls!

"Bloody hell, you'll have to be lucky to be picked out of this lot," Jock said to the chap sitting next to him.

"I've been trying for six months to get a job, since I left the Commandos. This is my last resort, if I don't get in, I'll have to go back into the army I suppose," answered the stranger.

"I have tried all over the country to join the Police, since I left school. This is the last one, both in England and Scotland. If I fail this time then I'm afraid I have had it," said a tall man sitting beside him. Jock thought to himself, 'Me too'.

A Police Sergeant started calling out a string of names, ten at a time. The men stood up as their names were called, he motioned them through a door. Quarter of an hour later another ten names were called, these men followed the first lot out. This slow procession carried on for hour after hour, until eventually Jock heard his own name called. He joined the other solemn faced chaps and headed after the Sergeant. They were led along a passage, a door opened and they were pushed inside.

"Strip off, put your clothes in a locker. There is a towel each for you to wear," the Sergeant instructed the applicants. They were then pushed, ushered and prodded from room to room, with different doctors and different examinations, tests and inspections. Weight; height; build; eyesight; teeth; hearing; breathing; colour-blindness and physical movements. The formidable check included x-rays and, eventually, finished off in a large room. On opening the door, there were several people inside, behind the lights, two towels laid on the floor about a foot apart.

"Stand on the towels, one foot on each" came a voice from the distance. "Drop your towel." The owner of the voice seemed vague and disinterested.

Then the visual examinations took place; squeeze, cough, turn round and bend down, and a more personal examination took place.

"Right, get dressed and wait in the other room" he was ordered.

A few minutes later all ten waited, the Sergeant came in and called two names out.

"The rest of you can go." Jock and another chap were ordered to wait in the hall again.

By the end of the day, the hopefuls were all though with their medical checks, they had been weeded out. Only ten men remained in the hall from the original 347. Jock had spoken to his two former acquaintances of a few hours previously, the Commando Sergeant had failed because his teeth hadn't clenched evenly at the back, (Sorry, it could lead to digestive problems later). The lad from University had failed once again, and had been told the reason (he had lost his appendix when he had been 12 years of age and this could cause some stomach problems later).

The ten men were taken to a local Police Hostel to spend the night. Next day at 9 am they once again entered the same building, ready for the Educational Examinations. The hall had been prepared for the exam, with desks and seats all spaced out with a few feet between each candidate. The room was packed once again by men who had apparently passed their medical examinations on previous occasions. The exam was to be held under strict Civil Service conditions and under their auspices and was broken up into different subjects which were to last all day.

During the lunch break, Jock and the others mingled together and chatted as men with a common purpose, that was to join the Police Force. He was quietly confident with his attempts but noted that in the geography questions, he did not get any about England. When the afternoon session was over they were allowed to leave and find their own way home.

"You will be notified of the results," they were told.

STARTING ORDERS

A brown envelope arrived with orders for him to attend at 9am for entrance arrangements and training. He was informed that he had passed the Education Exam and obtained such a high result that he would not have to take any further exams for promotion. At that time there was a standard of education needed to join, before promotion to Sergeant, and another one for reaching the rank of Inspector and above. Of course there were Police exams to pass as well before those ranks could be reached.

One week later he said his good-byes to his family and Puggle and then he was on his way once again to the Big City. He easily found his way to the building this time, 'Getting an old hand', he thought as he threaded his way through the crowds. Thirty men were assembled in the great hall, Jock looked around just to see if he could find anyone he could recognise from the previous visit and he soon spotted the other nine who had passed with him. As they waited the men chatted together about their future prospects and the past difficulties they had each experienced to reach their present position. It transpired that the other members of the little crowd were ones who had been on previous Education exams; one of Jock's associates worked the figures out.

"Bleedin' hell, that means that only 30 of us have got through from about 1,000."

The astonishment was obvious in his shrill Cockney voice. A Sergeant who had entered the room at that moment called them all to attention; they were requested to be seated, the Sergeant stood quietly beside a desk on a platform and waited until they were all settled.

"Right Gentlemen, I did happen to overhear the last remark made by our budding mathematician and I must say that he is not far out in his calculations. I must, however, point out that it is not the only weeding out that you have to face. You will attend an intensive course of training at the Police College. This will last for three months, you will have an exam at the end of each month and then a final exam. Failing to pass the exams will put you back one week and then you have a second chance. If you fail on the second occasion, you will be discharged. Every week you will be tested on the work you have done. If your demeanour; behaviour; intellect; dress; deportment; attitude and your general knowledge of law and police duties is reasonable enough to allow the Force to employ you, then you will be posted onto

Divisions. Whilst there, you are on probation for two years, you will continue studies and classes, with an exam every six months.

If at any time you fail to carry out your duties correctly, fail to pass any exam, disobey orders, or do anything which makes you unwanted, then you will be discharged. The reason quoted will be that you will not be likely to become a good and efficient Police Officer. Do I make myself clear?"

During the next hour, general instructions were given and they were introduced to the Commandant of the Training School. All the men were registered and listed and names were checked. The Oath of Allegiance was sworn and the copies of the Official Act were signed.

"Right, you have a long break, two hours for lunch, and I would advise each and every one of you to take advantage of this break, to treat yourselves to a visit to the hairdressers, and that is an order, you look like a lot of tramps. When we assemble after you have been fed we will go and get you all kitted out and bedded down," said the Sergeant at lunch time.

Jock left with a couple of the chaps and they found a gents' hairdressers close by, but when they entered the shop they got the sock of their lives for the place was crammed full with newly sworn rookies. One barber was working like a man bewitched, judging by the speed that the hair was being removed from each scalp; the finished results were standard and each looked the same, bare from the neck up to the ears and then very short.

"Hell, we used to get our hair cropped like that when we were in the desert." Said on of Jock's friends.

The other one remarked that the barber must be half Red Indian, "He's scalping everyone."

"I'm not waiting to be given a short back and sides like that," Jock said, "I'm going to find another one, anyone coming?" The three of them left the premises together and started the search for another barber's shop. They hunted all over the area without seeing another place, time was getting on for their return.

"Look there's a one," said one of the lads suddenly. A feeling of relief passed through them as they entered the shop, it was empty. They stopped dead as Sweeny Todd smiled at them.

"You will have to hurry, you haven't got much time" he said. "Never mind, I will be quick." He motioned them towards the empty chair.

"Who is first?" They had no option but to take turns and sit in the chair and be scalped like the rest of the gang had been, and three minutes later they were all out on the pavement heading for the assembly hall with the cold wind cutting into the newly bared flesh. A quick rush down the road and they managed to scrape into the hall before the roll call began.

"Right, everyone here? There's a bus outside so if you would be good enough to take your seats on the transport, we will head for the stores and get some sort of uniform for you all … Go." A short while later the hopefuls were all seated in the coach and headed for the depot.

Down at the stores each man was measured and fitted with their new uniforms. Any alterations that were required were marked on the garments which were to be delivered after alterations had been made. Each man was fitted with one suit, helmet and overcoat, numerals to be worn at the Training School were also issued. Each recruit was asked which medals he was entitled to wear, and the required ribbons and bars were given to them.

"What medals have you got, or were you stuck at home right through the war?" the pompous civvy who worked in the stores asked Jock when it was his turn

"Why, were you?" Jock couldn't resist an answer to the snide remark.

"Enough of your buck, what medals have you got?" the man snarled.

Jock rattled through the list of decorations that he was entitled to wear.

"Just a minute, give me a chance," the man was visibly shaken. Jock repeated the list, slower. At the mention of some of them, he asked

"What's that, which country is that from?" he asked at various times. "I'll have to order some for you," or "We don't have any demand for that one." As he carried on writing the list of decorations down on his list he said, "I'm running out of space, are there any more? You have more flaming gongs that Montgomery."

Boots had to be bought by each individual officer. There is always a good selection in the Police Canteen they were informed, the Latchet type were recommended, only £5, which was more than a week's wages.

Once every man had collected his uniform, they were taken by bus to the Training College. They were shown to their rooms and welcomed by the Inspector in charge, who gave them a detailed run down on the Regulations whilst in residence. A charge was to be made for food and laundry.

The next three months were hectic, the work was hard both physically and mentally. All aspects of police work had to be learned. Law and Regulations to be learned, word perfect, that was the only accepted way, right down to the Section and Sub-section, including the commas and full stops! The real work was obviously the mental strain trying to learn so much in so short a time. As the men all concentrated on learning the day's work, they gathered in the huge lounge to learn the given pieces. Apart from the law there were set incidents, which officers had to deal with, ranging from accidents to burglary. First aid classes, self defence, drills and swimming (each man was expected to obtain the Bronze Medallion at least). The drill Sergeant was typical of his profession, a bully with no soul, he was a little horror. On one occasion it was a bitterly cold day and during the hour's marching drill, he noticed that some of the ex navy type were swinging their arms in the way they had been used to. The arms were not swung back to front, shoulder high at the front and as far back as possible. No, these ex matelots were swinging their arms forwards across their chests and outwards, instead of backward. The little Hitler, as he was nicknamed, kept on yelling for a while then he said.

"I'll put a stop to that slovenly way of marching. Until you do it right, you will all march with your arms straight down at your sides." For a full hour he marched the company back and forwards, hands soon became frozen and fingers numb, it didn't help anyone for him to adopt that attitude. The men all felt the cold because they had never been issued with any gloves. It was a childish and petty punishment, making all the other persons suffer for a few. When the parade was over he yelled

"If you have any complaints you can take it out of the ones who wouldn't do as they were told. In future, if they swing their arms sideways, you will be treated the same way."

As the ex navy chaps did not want the rest of the College trainees to be punished for their mistakes, they ensured that future marches were all in order. The system had won.

Jock found that he couldn't concentrate in the communal hall, the babble of voices as each man repeated out loud to himself (and everyone else within hearing) the piece that had to be learned. Consequently, with so many different classes and men learning different things, it was bedlam. The new starters were learning such preliminary pieces as

"The word police means generally the arrangements made .," this was blended with

"An assault is the intentional application of force upon another .," or sections from Homicide, Road Traffic Acts, which would be mixed with parts from the Licensing Act, Diplomatic Privileges. Jock just couldn't concentrate, so, each night after the evening meal he settled in his bedroom to study. Coming towards the end of training, having passed the examination satisfactorily, everyone was on edge for the Finals. There was all kinds of skulduggery going on by people who were not too sure of their knowledge. Crib notes were written, for any problem pieces, on scraps of paper, shirt cuffs or inside the arms. Sergeants discussed the possible problems and also questions which might arise. Old exam papers were obtained and had a thorough going over as the men tried to find if there was some regular system for questions. They tried to perm the subjects, hoping to find the answer to their problems, so that they could concentrate all the time left available to learning the questions that could come up in the exam papers. Other chaps tried to read over and over again all the work that they had been taught over the past three months.

The day of the exams was a blow to the cribbers for the desks were laid out as the civil service exams had been. Also, a Sergeant was posted at the back of the classroom, another at the front and another supervising officer patrolled up and down each aisle. The ones who had tried to perm the old papers were also out of luck because none of the questions had previously been asked. The exams took most of the day and a lot of fingernails were chewed as the trainees tried to dig down into their brain boxes for the correct answers. When the torture was over, everyone gathered in the hall discussing the papers.

"What did you put for such and such question?" seemed to be the general question that was being asked, and very often the remark came,

"Cor, I never put that, I forgot about that," or

"I really buggered that one up." The instructors were present, asking men who had been in their squads how they managed. Obviously it was in their own interests that all the members of his class passed with high marks.

Eventually, the results came through and there was a rush to the notice board to read the papers avidly; cries rent the air as various men found that they had been successful, regardless of how far down the list they were. Also on the board was the list of postings; the men who had passed were all delegated to different Police Stations throughout the City. Jock noticed that only two men were above him on the list and that he had been posted to a Station with three of the lucky ones. The Sergeants were all engaged with their own little groups, discussing the area to which they had to report for work.

"You did well Jock," his instructor said.

"The luck of the Irish," Jock said.

"Irish?," I thought you were Scottish?" The Sergeant was perplexed.

"Just in a manner of speaking Skipper," Jock explained. When he asked which Station he had been posted to and Jock enlightened him.

"I know it well, it's a bleedin tough area but you should be alright."

Jock used to have wrestling matches with this strong Sergeant, both during training and in the evenings.

"One thing you will have to remember though, they don't have rules in a punch up. It's a case of first in and get in hard. Find the leader of the local mob and sort him out. I guarantee that you will not get and more trouble with his mob." The Sergeant went on to give further details about the ground that surrounded Jock's intended Station, 'His Patch' as it was called.

"There are a lot of Toms, Blacks, drunks and plenty of traffic work. The main roads have plenty of shops, including big ones. There is a market as well, where you are likely to get all sorts, from pickpockets to indecency, barrow boys, to keep you on the run. The whole of the area is predominantly covered with houses, a semi-rural atmosphere on the outsides of the patch as well. Your main troubles will be with the heavy mobs, they hate coppers and will get you if they can. Jock remembered his Sergeant's advice right through his service.

ROOKY COP

He and his three mates reported to the designated Station and, after giving their names to the Sub-Division Inspector's clerk, they were posted onto a shift and given a leave party. One day off every week, alternating days, Monday one week then Tuesday the following week and so on; one weekend in six weeks. Two of them had to go on late shift and two on early days. They were then issued with their beat books, which showed the layout of each beat and its boundaries. It also showed the various times and places a PC had to make a ring (that was to telephone the Station in case a copper was requested to answer a call, do a message, or attend some non urgent request). Beats had to be worked according to a system, the direction of patrol being alternated each day, this was to ensure that the copper on the beat did not appear at the same place at the same time; baffle the villains was the idea. Shifts were to be worked on an eight hour basis, day shift was broken into early, and late, these covered a period of eight weeks and then it was four weeks on nights. The instructions all seemed complicated to the four newcomers but the clerk told them they would soon get used to the workings and that the duty list would be put up in the charge room each week, any variations of duty would also be shown.

After all the details had been crammed into their heads, they were taken to the stores by Police van to collect all the uniform they would require to do the job - three jackets with button-up neck in different materials for the change of weather. The old-fashioned ceremonial dress jacket with no front pockets, skirted at the back, with buttons and pockets in the flaps; top coats, capes, truncheons and helmets, the enormous pile slowly mounted up, then it came to the point of issuing letters and numerals for all the jackets and overcoats, including the cape. Further medal ribbons were issued, going by the list previously taken by the store-keeper.

Eventually they were fully loaded and staggered back to the van with their new possessions and were taken to the Police Section House which was to be their homes until such time that other accommodation was found by themselves. Each man had his own room with all facilities provided, a canteen was provided downstairs where meals could be bought at any hour.

A warden was on duty at the door for 24 hours; it was this man who called officers from their sleep to get ready for work. Jock and his colleagues found this was one of the problems they had to face; due to the distance between the Section House and the Police Office, they had to work out how long it took to get to work. The only transport available was the tramcar and that would take a full half-hour. As they had to be on parade 15 minutes before the official starting time, Jock and his mates made a habit of getting up at 4.30 am and they found that was enough time to get off the tram and walk to the parade shed. Without any overtime they had a long day and were ready for forty winks when they returned to the Section House. Getting up and leaving the building and standing waiting for a tram at that time of the morning on a cold wet winter morning is soul destroying, 'if anyone doesn't agree, they want to try it' Jock thought as he stood shivering on the stop one morning.

UNWANTED

Jock's first tour of duty was on such a morning; he and his mate arrived in time and consequently had a full quarter of an hour to wait in the parade shed for the Sergeant and the other coppers to appear. At 5.45am a Sergeant and five PCs left the room where the telephones were and headed for the shed. They had been drinking tea and keeping warm in front of a big fire (this was not for rookies) as the room was out of bounds, it was the nerve centre of the station. As they had been told they had to keep out of the room, it appeared obvious that there were rules for some and rules for the rest. The newcomers soon found that, apart from these rules, strangers were not welcome and as time went on these facts became more obvious.

The Sergeant detailed the men to their different beats but when it came to Jock and his mate, he had to put them on a beat with one of the old coppers. There was a lot of grumbling and complaints from the two men who had been unlucky enough to have the rookies for company, they were supposed to show them the beats and how to work them. Jock's first 'teacher' was a very large Welshman who made no bones about being lumbered with the 'sprog' and vented his feelings very loudly to the Sergeant.

"Look Taffy, someone has to take them out, don't get onto me." The man was really apologising to the big PC.

"There's all the others, isn't there?" Taffy retorted.

"There's all week to go, someone will have them a few times."

The Sergeant then read out a list of stolen cars and items from the 'Rough Book'. This was a book kept for any item that may be of any importance to the chaps at the station.

"Produce your appointments," the Sergeant ordered, and every man showed the various items he was supposed to carry with him. The Sergeant checked these and he then ordered them to put them away. He left the shed and later returned with an inspector, who examined the men's dress.

"Right, no skiving. Shun, Right turn, quick march," and Jock headed for his first day on the beat.

He felt strange, even though there were very few people around in this dark wet morning, they all stared at him (at least that's what he thought). The Welshman strode along without a word, as if to show by his sullen attitude and silence that he strongly objected to being a wet nurse to a rookie. It became obvious to Jock that his very presence was causing concern to this man, he must have had something planned that he wanted to do and now he can't because I'm here. Although he appreciated the man's feelings, he couldn't do anything about the situation. The morning was really cold and the occasional rain came in the strong wind. They wore their overcoats and carried their capes over their left shoulders as they moved through the darkened streets. After about 30 minutes walking the Welshman suddenly stopped and turned to Jock,

"You wait here, I won't be long. Just keep out of the way till I get back," he ordered and walked away.

Jock stood in the doorway of a shop out of the wind, he took out his beat book and studied it for a while. Rather perplexed, he took out his map book, the A to Z which he had bought. He looked at the names of the streets where he was standing and checked them on the map. After a bit of a search, he at last found the place where he was standing. 'That's queer, according to the map and the beat book we are off the beat', he muttered to himself. 'If my reckoning is right, we came in the wrong direction from the station'. As the rain began to come down heavier, he unfolded his cape and slipped it over his shoulders in preparation for his morning's walking. About an hour had elapsed before his erstwhile companion decided to return.

"Come on" he said, and together they walked back the way they had just come.

"I though we were on 6, 7 and 8 beats?" Jock spoke to the man.

"Yeh."

"Surely, this is a bit off the beats we were detailed to?" Jock insisted.

"Look lad, where we go and what I do is no concern of yours." The Welshman stated, and immediately lapsed into silence once again.

They returned to the Police Station.

"I'm going to make a ring, you just hang around out of sight." With that remark the Welshman went into the building. Jock saw him enter the Communications Room and through the window Jock saw him take his helmet off and sit down. He then passed a packet of cigarettes round to the several coppers who were gathered there. 'Looks like I'm in for another long wait' he decided, and turned at the sound which came from the canteen. 'Sounds like a cup of tea being made'. A light was on in the canteen and he could see a fat old copper engaged in the process of brewing up. He headed for the doorway, having decided that he may just as well sit and have a cuppa as stand in the rain.

"What are you doing in here?" Fatty asked.

"Me, I'm going to have a cup of tea," Jock told him.

"Not this, this is for the Sergeants and the Inspector."

"By the look of it, there are a hell of lot of Sergeants and Inspectors," Jock said indicating the tray which was loaded with cups.

"If it's good enough for you lot to drink tea, then it's good enough for me." He found himself a cup and proceeded to pour a cup of tea out for himself as the old chap went out complaining,

"Bloody young upstarts."

It was 8.30am before the Welshman eventually showed himself and directed Jock to follow him as they had a school crossing to do. In actual fact, it was Jock that was engaged with the job of taking kids across the road. His instructor was engaged in deep conversation with a nearby shopkeeper. After this detail they went back to the office for breakfast, which lasted a full 30 minutes. Taffy sat with some of his old pals eating a colossal meal. Jock's meagre cash flow restricted the amount he could buy. He had worked his finances out, considering transport, laundry and meals, and he knew that he had to be careful with his spending.

The rest of the day was taken up with walking to the school crossing for another two periods. When 2pm came and he booked off to the Sergeant, he felt heartily sick of the whole procedure. Was this man an exception, or had he always been so morose and lazy during the war. It became clear to Jock that this big man had a huge appetite and that he had been for a breakfast when he left Jock standing in the doorway.

The next morning he was directed to go with a different PC He noted that the Welshman had a look of pleasure and relief on his face. This new instructor was also getting on in years but was cheerful and quite affable. They left the Police Station and he was told where the beat started and how far they had to go. The different types of shops and security points to observe, trouble spots and school crossings were indicated, and also the times that they had to be done. His new tutor indicated that all rings for that beat had to be made at the station as it was actually on their beat. As they ambled along talking, the man suddenly stopped at a shop, he took out a key and opened the door of the premises and went inside.

"Come on," he told the very surprised junior. Jock followed him into the shop, his mate went into the back of the premises and took off his helmet and jacket and placed an apron around his waist.

"Sit down and take your hat off." The lights were switched on.

"What do you want for breakfast?" Before Jock could answer, the first customer came in and soon the shop was full. The speed that the meals were cooked and served proved that this old copper was no slouch at the job. Jock had been served with a full breakfast, bacon, egg, tomatoes, bread and butter, and a pot of tea. Bob greeted two men who entered the shop about half an hour later.

"Bloody late again." A mild exchange of banter was returned, the two newcomers went into the kitchen and put aprons on. Bob came and sat beside Jock to eat the meal he had prepared.

"They are a couple of good lads, the trouble is they live at the other side of the city and this is the earliest they can get here. They would lose a lot of trade if I didn't open up for them and get the cookers going."

Jock didn't answer.

"I pack in shortly and I'm going to start my own business, making caravans." Bob continued. The conversation proved that he was looking forward to his new life.

The rest of the day, however, was more or less a dull repetition of the previous day's working, school crossings and tea at the station. His third day of introduction to the policeman's life was with a man younger than the others, apparently he had joined just before the war and did not volunteer to join the armed forces.

"I think we will have a cup of tea. Fancy one?" he said, about 10 minutes after leaving the station, and promptly turned into a café. There were already three uniformed officers sitting inside, including Jock's mate from Training School.

"Tea and toast for two, Bill," he said to the man behind the counter. Customers came and went as the men sat there, they seemed to accept the situation as being normal. Johnny, his associate, eventually said "We'll have to get cracking, we have a ring to make." He stubbed his cigarette out, "Come on."

It took a good half hour to reach the police box where they had to make a ring and enter it into the book. After the entry had been made they sat in the box and had another smoke.

"Can't stay long, the Inspector might call in," Johnny indicated.

They stepped out into the now busy streets and stood beside the wall watching the early morning traffic tearing past and the crowds of people rushing to work.

"Just think, they are just starting work and we have nearly done half a shift; by the time we get down to the nick it will be breakfast time. After breakfast we will just have enough time to walk back here for our next ring," Jock's mate had just made a long speech.

"Don't you ever get any time to do any work?" asked Jock. "As far as I have seen, this job consists of tea and more tea, between skiving."

"Our job is just to be there in case we are needed" was the reply.

The following day he had to attend instruction classes so he had only a couple of hours to go before breakfast time and then all the rookie coppers had to go to Instruction Classes to learn more about law, order and traffic offences.

Friday and Saturday were normally days when the young coppers were posted onto the market area. The early part of the days started quiet and by 9 am all the shops and arcades were open and quite a few shoppers on the move. Jock noticed some barrows being loaded with fruit and vegetables, the normal flat-tops had been altered and replaced by a large slope. The angles of the slopes were unbelievable and it was on these slopes that the produce was arranged, but how on earth they managed to push these things was a mystery. As soon as they were loaded, the famous barrow boys started work, they would push their colossal loads along the streets until they found a convenient spot to park. The old PC who had been delegated to take Jock out ambled along, stopping to chat with everyone, he seemed to know them all. Jock wasn't interested, he was looking forward to Sunday which was his day off. After that he would be posted on nights for a week before being allowed out by himself.

NIGHTS

"Shun, Right turn, quick march." The Night duty Sergeant gave the orders to the small group of men. They turned quietly and headed for the various beats they had been allocated, and each man had at least three beats due to the manpower shortage. Jock felt the weight of the large 'Wooton' lantern pulling on his belt; these lamps were large and heavy, powered by an accumulator, somewhat similar to a car battery. The two handles folded over the sides so that the lamp could be clipped on the belt.

A large leather patch protected the uniform from the acid. The men wore their capes over their overcoats as protection against the rain which was falling heavily; their oilskin leggings slapped and scraped as they walked along.

Another 'unlucky' old timer had been 'lumbered' with Jock's company; at least he seemed more conscientious than the others had been. Jock thought it had been bad enough on day shift when there had been people and traffic about and he expected night shift to be deadly with monotony. His elderly companion informed him where the beat started and they commenced to check the property, just to ensure that everything was locked securely.

"Check everything when you start and again before you book off," his old instructor told him. "Better you find a break in than the owner when he comes to work."

All shops, factories, stores and other premises were checked thoroughly by the two men. At 11pm they had only covered one side of one of the beats when Jock called to his mate to inform him of an open door he had found; the back door of a chemist's shop was open.

"Right lad, you go down to the Station and get the key holder out," Spud told him. "I'll hang on here and look after the place." Typical old timer, he was to sit in the dry and warm whilst Jock had to plod his way back in the rain to the Police Office; he turned and trudged back towards the Nick.

An unusual sound came to his ears before he had gone half a mile; he stopped and listened. The streets were deserted and the sound seemed to have come from across the road; it had been faint but was a distinct sound of metal striking something. He waited, standing still in the rain, but the noise was not repeated. He decided to investigate and unclipped his lamp from his belt and carried it in his left hand as he headed across the road. He entered the garden of a large house, the grounds were filled with bushes and trees at the sides; the house was being used for business purposes. Walking quietly and listening, he moved slowly through the garden heading towards the spot where he believed the sound came from. It was difficult to concentrate with the sound of rain splattering down on the trees. The wind didn't help any as it whistled around his ears. He tried to see through the rain which was coming down in torrents but with the dim light from the street lamps and the cover afforded by the trees, it was difficult. He checked the doors and windows as he moved along, conscious of the noise made by his leggings. At last he stood in front of the point where he thought the sound had come from. A slithering noise became evident for a few seconds. Action at last, this is what he had joined the police force for, the blood coursed quicker through his veins. This was it, he looked at the line of bushes in front of him but couldn't see a thing. Right, he decided, and took a running jump into the bushes beside the wall and switched his lamp on at the same time. Branches snapped under his weight and suddenly a voice cracked out,

"Christ, my bleedin' back, you've broken it."

"Let's get him, he's by himself," another voice came from beside Jock. He swung his light round towards the sound of the voice - what a pity, for the owner of the voice had decided to attack at the same time. He received the heavy lamp right in the face and crashed down in agony beside his mate who was still complaining about the 15 stone that was resting on his back. The struggle didn't even start; the man that tried to eat the big lamp dropped a jemmy and the man on the bottom was out of luck - poor sod, got hit on the head with it.

"I'm arresting you both as suspected persons loitering with intent to commit a felony and being in possession of housebreaking instruments." He cautioned them as he had been taught to at the College.

"I'm going to take you to the Police Station and you'd better behave yourselves till you get there." He marched them down to the Nick and placed them in the Charge Room.

"Sit down there" Jock ordered, and indicated the seats he required the men to take. The Duty Sergeant looked up from the desk in the front office and saw Jock standing in the adjacent room; from his position, he couldn't see the two prisoners.

"What the blazes are you doing there? You are supposed to be on the beat" he yelled. The reply came quietly from the charge room.

"Two prisoners, Sergeant." The bewildered Sergeant dragged himself from the comfort of his armchair to see what this new rookie was babbling on about. As he entered the room he saw the two large wet and bloody captives, sitting forlornly in their seats.

"On your feet, please," Jock said to the men.

"Stand in front of the Sergeant at the desk." The men did as he ordered them and the Skipper examined their damaged faces from where he stood.

"Where is the PC you were posted with?" he asked Jock. "Did he arrest these two?",

"I found a chemist's shop open Sergeant; he is looking after the place whilst I got a keyholder; I arrested these two men on the way back to the office." Jock explained.

"Well, where did you arrest them and why, if he wasn't with you? The poor old man was anticipating all sorts of miscarriage of justice. Jock rattled off the details of evidence and arrest as he had been taught in the training school.

"I just don't believe it," the Sergeant muttered. "How did these men get the injuries?"

"That one smashed his face against my lantern and he hit his mate in the face with this jemmy." Jock held the jemmy up.

"It's unbelievable but it's true Skip." Obviously the Sergeant didn't believe him.

"Is that correct?" he asked the men. He got the shock of his life when he was told that the statement was correct.

"Right, put them down in the cells, different ones," the Sergeant instructed Jock.

"Don't you think we should search them first?" Jock asked. The Sergeant tried to save face, he had made a mistake.

"Of course, I expected you would have done that automatically. You never put anyone down before they are searched." He spoke as if it had been a mistake on Jock's part.

"Right, turn out your pockets," he told the prisoners. When they had emptied their pockets, he then searched them. The table was soon littered with their belongings, which included several housebreaking implements.

"Now, put them in the cells then go and see about that key holder" he ordered Jock.

"I'll get in touch with the CID about these two."

The two hapless prisoners were tucked away in their separate rooms and Jock went into the Holy of Holies (The Communication Room) to make the required arrangements for someone to attend the Chemist's shop.

"It will take some time before we will know if the key holder has been warned and will attend; you might as well wait in the Canteen and have a cup of tea." Before going into the Canteen, Jock went into the front office to see about the prisoners.

"The CID have had a chat with them and they have gone round to examine the premises. You might as well have a cup of tea while you wait." The Sergeant was being generous, giving permission for him to have a cuppa.

The fire was blazing in the canteen; he poured a cup of the hot refreshing liquid out and sat in front of the fire to enjoy this unexpected pleasure. An hour later the men were charged and Jock signed the Charge Sheet.

"You had better wait in the Canteen for your mate; if you go out, you might miss him and get yourself lost," said the Duty Sergeant. So Jock, willing as usual, accepted the order without argument and went into the warm Canteen to wait for the old copper to return.

He had his meal as he waited and various PCs came and went after finishing their meals. At 3am the tired looking wet copper at last showed his face. He divested himself of his wet clothes and looked at Jock.

"I've been worrying my inside out about you, I was wondering what had happened to you. Why the hell I should worry, I don't know. Here you are sitting on your arse in the warm and I've been out in the rain. I leave you for a couple of minutes and you go and arrest a couple of villains. The CID would give their right arms to get them on their books, they tell me they are wanted in Liverpool, is that right?"

"Yes, that's right" answered Jock. "Look here, I'm sorry I couldn't get back to you but the Sergeant wouldn't let me go in case I got lost."

"Never mind" the oldster replied. "When I've had my grub we can go and check the rest of the property. If you get any more prisoners I'd like to be there. They told me that they both have broken noses, you learn quick." The man had the impression that Jock had done the damage on purpose. Jock noticed that the ice seemed to have been broken with this man and he seemed more friendly.

The rain eased off and the rest of the beats were duly checked, to ensure that no shops had been left open by their owners, or had been broken into.

The following night Jock was on with a younger chap, he had left the College only the month before and he was still trying to digest the various beats and the boundaries. He told Jock that two of them had come to the Station together, his friend was in actual fact taking Jock's mate around. He kept referring to the beat book, to make sure he was on the correct beat. It came as a surprise when they bumped into the other two Rookies, the books were under great scrutiny by them all. Here they were, four coppers on the beat and all lost.

During the tour of duty, Jock quizzed his companion regarding the Station and the other men's attitude.

"Oh, you have noticed as well have you?" Well, you will find that they all have their own fiddles and devious ways. The Sergeants and the Inspectors are just as bad and they don't like newcomers at the Station, just in case they are reported. They don't like work, that is obvious, Summons are unheard of as far as they are concerned. Arrests are made only if they have to, or if they suit. There are a lot of backhanders going on as far as I can see. Don't forget they have spent all their War service at this Nick. There are a lot of them who get their heads down at night, to do a spare time job the next day. As you know, we have the coffee stalls and there is always trouble at one of them, we always double up on them until midnight but you can bet your last dollar that if an old timer is posted to any of the stalls, they keep well out of the way of any trouble. Normally if anyone does interfere, he is bound to finish off in hospital."

"How's that?" asked Jock.

"The mob, they always turn up at one of the stalls and whoever is on that stall must keep out of the way, that is when the old timers disappear till the mob has gone," his mate replied.

"Who is the leader of the mob?" asked Jock; he remembered his instructor's advice.

"That's the bloke you will have to watch, he causes the trouble and has often been inside for assault on coppers. That's why the old ones are frightened of him. They have good reason mind, for he gets in quick with the boot, straight to the balls. So watch him, he is a big coloured chap, called Pete," his mate advised.

TROUBLE

The rest of the week passed quietly, apart from a couple of drunks who insisted upon making a nuisance of themselves. On Saturday night the old timers all seemed to be on edge as they waited to find out which beat they had been posted to. They were also in a sweat in case they got lumbered onto a coffee stall, as this would hamper their movements, as well as putting them in the line of danger. Jock was attached to an elderly Scotsman for the night and, as it happened, they had a stall to look after. The man complained bitterly as they approached the stall.

"Just my bloody luck. Why he had to put me on this stall I will never know," he moaned on. "I've other things to do," looking at the crowd who were gathered.

"Look at that, the buggers are there already. There's a right crowd there, we will have trouble tonight, I feel it in my bones." A few minutes later they stopped opposite the stall.

"Yes, I thought so," he muttered. "The black bastard's there."

"Who are you referring to? Who is that?," Jock asked.

"The big chap, Pete. He's the leader of the local mob." The old man was worried, and it showed in his face and his voice as he answered.

"Well, we can soon shift them out of it," Jock stated.

"No way. It's been tried before and nobody has succeeded. He has put more coppers in hospital than I can remember. They are all as bad as one another; they hate coppers. They are vicious and they have all their gear with them," Jock's accomplice said.

"What gear is that?" Jock was still innocent.

"Knives; razors; razor blades in their hats; knuckle dusters; coshes; chains and hammers, in fact they have everything that can be used to inflict injury. Believe me, they do use them." The old-timer told him. "I don't know why they don't have a law to prevent them carrying weapons like that."

"Is that the big bloke who is always putting coppers in hospital. I've heard he does one a week," Jock stated.

"That's him, and his favourite weapon is his boots, he's very quick with them. I think we'll just hang around out of the way until they've gone."

Not a very helpful keeper of the law, Jock thought.

"Why isn't he arrested then?" Jock quizzed him.

"He has been a couple of times but the CID and the rest of the lads find it easier to just keep out of his way, if possible."

"That's bloody marvellous" snorted Jock. "He runs the villains and the coppers are frightened of him. Which one is he?"

"Him there, the chap with the fancy jacket on, and those are some of his mob with him" said the older man indicating a huge coloured man sitting on the guard rails beside the coffee stall.

"Right, you stay here and hold my coat and cape, and you'd better hang onto my lamp as well," said Jock handing his gear to the copper who said,

"Good luck lad, be careful."

Jock crossed the road and pushed his way through the crowd of villains and teenage hooligans. The pavement was completely blocked by them. He fixed his eyes on the face of the man he was after as he pushed through the others. As the crowd noticed the look on his face and the obvious purpose of his movements, they slowly parted to let him pass. They left a clear path right through to the leader of the mob. A silence fell over the throng as he steadily closed the gap on his quarry. He stopped in front of the mobster who was chewing his gum and staring fixedly at the new copper. He saw the rows of medals on his tunic and smirked to himself.

"Here's a new guy to sort out, standing there with all his lovely new medals. I'll soon have them off his back and kick his face in." His gang closed tight around the boss as Jock said

"Are you the yellow bastard they call Pete? Are you the one who can't fight his own battles and needs a crowd of lunatics to do it for him? Because he can't do it himself?"

A gasp ran through the crowd as Jock went on "They say you have a yellow streak right down your back, is that true?"

The gangs gasped, surely this bloke had signed his death warrant, and Pete would kill him for that. Pete stopped chewing, his jaw dropped for a moment.

"You've got yours coming copper. I'll kill you for that," he snarled.

"As I said, you are a yellow bastard, you couldn't do it yourself. You have to have the help of this crowd of layabouts to do it, everyone will know that what I said was true, you are too spineless to do it alone."

"I will do it myself and I don't need anyone to help me." The enraged man had been shown up, not only in front of his mob but also a lot of the other people. If he used his gang to attack Jock then everyone would say he was too frightened to do it himself. He couldn't resist the bait. Jock rubbed it in a bit more, get your opponent mad and he doesn't think straight.

"You would like to do the same to me as you have to the other coppers, wouldn't you? It won't work, for I've heard all about you and your boots. Let me tell you that I can fight your way, because I was brought up on it, I will slaughter you son."

The frenzied man jumped down from his perch to face his antagonist who, he noticed, was about his own size.

"Right, you've asked for it" he screamed.

"Not in the street son, we don't want to cause a breach of the peace," Jock informed him. "We'll go up the back alley."

"Right, makes no difference to me." The villain agreed and together they headed for the alley.

The old PC stood in a doorway watching them as they headed for the lane.

"I knew you couldn't do it yourself," Jock indicated the crowd who were following them.

Pete turned on the pack and shouted

"Keep out of this. This one's mine. If anyone sticks his neb in, I'll stitch him." The old copper heard these words as he thought that officially he was supposed to be looking after this stupid rookie but somehow he had a feeling that the rookie wasn't as stupid as all that, he didn't need a nursemaid.

Into the unlit back street the pair of them went, followed closely by the mob. Jock took his old pipe out of his pocket and then put it in his mouth, and as he stopped with his back to the wall he took out his tobacco. The two men stood facing each other, the copper with his back to the wall and his adversary backed by his gang who now stood in a half circle around the two intended contestants.

"Right," Pete said, and slipped his lovely jacket off his shoulders - he didn't want to get it torn or covered with the copper's blood. He looked at the insolent bobby who was in the process of filling his pipe.

"I'll teach you, you sod," he said.

As soon as the lovely jacket reached his elbows, Jock's foot came up hard and fast. Pete felt the tremendous pain in his crutch and automatically doubled up, grabbing at the tender point between his legs. The scream he let out couldn't be stopped as he bent forwards. As his face came downwards it came in contact with Jock's knee which was travelling in the opposite direction. His head was jerked upwards with the sudden blow which had broken his nose by the sound and the amount of blood that spurted out. As his head jerked backwards away from this sudden pain, his neck came in contact with Jock's arm and he received a tremendous chop on the back of the neck, which pole-axed him. With his hands still clutching his extremely tender private parts, he couldn't stop his face hitting the concrete road surface. As the unlucky wretch dropped face down into the gutter, a solid leather boot was dropped down hard on it. If he could have seen, he would have noticed the shining metal studs on the sole and the steel tips on the front and heel. Jock stood in that position with his foot on the big man's face and finished filling his pipe.

"Who's next?" asked Jock looking round at them as their boss lay motionless in the gutter.

No movement came from the mob, the bewildered thugs had just seen the impossible. The toughest man in town, lying in front of them and he'd been put there by a rookie copper who had been filling his pipe at the time. They'd all seen it happen, but still couldn't believe it. There was neither comment nor movement from the silent men.

Jock took his pipe from his mouth and spoke to the man lying in agony under his foot.

"See them boots Nig, steel plates on heel and toes. I told you that I fight your way, just try and imagine what your balls are like. If you want your face to be the same way, just say the word."

"I've had enough Guvnor. You're the boss," the words were mumbled through split lips and broken teeth.

"Right then, if none of you want to try your hand" Jock said to the mob.

"Match," he addressed the man nearest him, who quickly produced a box of matches for Jock - who selected a match and slowly started to light his pipe. As he did so, he examined the vicious crowd who were gathered around. All right when they're in a crowd but no good and no guts by themselves. Once the pipe had been lit he returned the box.

"Thanks," he said "and now gentlemen, from now on I don't want any trouble with you. Just remember that I am on the beat here. If you see me coming, then I would advise you to move somewhere else, fast. Now I want you six," as he pointed to the ones in the front line, "to pick this man up, face upper most, three on each side and carry him away from here, straight past the coffee stall and up the road. Get the idea? Now move," the last words were snapped at them.

Without any arguments, the allocated men did as they had been bid and face showing for all the crowds at the stall to see, they emerged from the lane, led by the disconsolate mob carrying their boss, with the rest tailing along behind. Jock came at the rear, smoking his pipe.

"Straight through" he ordered the bearers as they hesitated. The crowd around the stall parted to allow the procession to go past. The locals all gazed at the battered face of the local leader. They also looked at the young copper, without a mark on him and he was contentedly puffing at his pipe as he strolled along.

The old copper stood in his deep doorway and gazed at the scene, it was like a funeral procession. He noticed that Jock appeared unmarked but the mob leader was like a dead man as he was carried along! What the hell happened down there? No doubt he'd never find out, but at least there was one copper in town who could look after himself. Slowly, the bearers carried Pete through the crowd; they were all transfixed at the sight.

"Look at him" one man said, "there's not a mark on him." The remark caused numerous faces to turn in Jock's direction.

"Straight on gentlemen. Take him home," he ordered as he stopped beside the coffee stall. As he stood there, he gazed at the motley collection of men who were gathered there, slowly turning his head looking at the sea of faces. Stare into their eyes, they are shifty, they have something to hide or fear. He weighed each one up that he could see clearly, before he spoke.

"For a long time, you have all been getting your own way around here. I'm afraid that is all over now. We do not want you or your friends to gather around the stalls and block the pavements. So now, if you have finished your tea, I would request that you all go home. If you haven't drunk your tea, now is the time to do so. Drink up and shove off. I'll give you a couple of minutes."

The crowd broke up and the men all made their respective ways home, or to find another coffee stall. They didn't fancy staying where this bloke was, after they'd seen what he could do.

When the last one had gone, Jock crossed the road to his partner and stood in the doorway beside him.

"I think I'd better put my coat on, it's getting a bit chilly," he said, and took his overcoat from the old copper.

"What the hell happened round there?" asked the old-timer helping him on with his overcoat.

"We came to an understanding. From now on, they will do as I tell them."

"Understanding?" Mac said. "He looked as if he was dead they way they carried him round there, his face was a bloody mess."

"Ah yes, he fell down and hit his face in the gutter" Jock answered.

"Whatever happened, you certainly cleared the worst trouble spot up in the town." The old man didn't believe him.

Jock smiled, "Has that type of thing always gone on around here?"

"As long as I can remember, but I can see that things are going to change with the likes of you around here. You nicked a couple of blokes the other night and didn't you give them a good hiding as well?"

"You got it wrong Mac, one of them hit his face accidentally and dropped a jemmy onto his friend," Jock corrected the man.

"Well, if that's your story, look out Jock here's the Inspector." The talk came to an end as the Inspector and the Sergeant arrived. They stepped out of the doorway and the old-timer saluted.

"All correct Sir."

The Inspector acknowledged the salute and said,

"All quiet Mac. I see that you have shifted the crowds on." He indicated the coffee stall. Mac glanced at his young companion and said,

"Yes Sir, all quiet, no trouble."

"That's the way it should be." The Inspector turned to Jock.

"Just take a few hints from your seniors, Mac will show you what to do and we might be able to make a copper out of you."

Jock slipped his truncheon from his coat sleeve down into the trouser pocket where it should have been.

"Yes Sir, I certainly will learn a lot from them," he answered.

HARDWORK

At midnight, they started to check the shops on their beats before going into the Station for breakfast. There were two other elderly PCs in the canteen when they entered, and the question

"Want a game?" was directed at Jock.

Obviously he was being required to make a foursome and the other two chaps looked surprised for they must have been waiting for one of their mates to come in. Jock accepted the offer,

"OK, though I haven't played for a long time, and I haven't much money."

"Typical Scotsman," grunted one of the others. "Come on then, we only play for half-pennies."

It transpired that cribbage and solo were the favourite games with the men at this Station and as they played, they ate their sandwiches and conversed. Old Mac told the other two about the evening's work and the two old-timers looked at Jock with some admiration.

"You mean to tell us that you actually offered Pete out? Then went round the back lane with him and his whole mob? You must be bloody mad," one of them said.

"Mad or not, you should have seen the way they carried him out," Mac chuckled. "And this young sod, just walking along behind them smoking his pipe."

The two coppers tried to get further details of the punch-up, but Jock didn't expand any further on the subject. By the time came for the game to end, several more men had entered the room for their meals and Mac soon spread the news to each one about the leader of the mob being beaten.

"What were you in during the War lad?" asked one of the coppers. "Were you in the Commandos or something?"

"No" answered Jock, "I was in the Royal Engineers."

"What were you in the army lad?" asked a Sergeant who was waiting to play. Jock spoke with his mouth full of food as he tried to finish before going out, he didn't enlarge on his rank, just said,

"I was in Bomb Disposal."

"Bomb Disposal," the Sergeant said, "Does that mean you used to dig them out?"

"That's right Serg," Jock answered as he pulled his overcoat on. He had done alright with the cards and now had quite a bit of spare cash.

"You'll have to give us a chance to win some of it back lad, you lucky sod," one of the old-timers told him.

"Righto, anytime," Jock didn't realise exactly how soon they would be after it.

Together he and Mac headed out into the cold darkened and quiet streets and back onto the beat.

"It's bloody cold Jock," Mac told him after they had walked around for a while. "I think it's time for a cuppa," he said. "Fancy one?"

He led Jock through the back streets and into the darkened railway station; he pushed a door open which led into an unlit passageway - at the end of the passage Jock noticed another door. As they pushed it open he blinked at the sudden light, the smoke caught his breath, and the heat was terrific. There was a roaring fire in the grate and the cigarettes from the four other coppers already sitting in the room were the cause of the smoke. They were playing cards and had cups of tea standing in front of them.

"Come on Mac, we've been waiting for you." They pushed along and made room for the two new-comers.

"Come on Jock, we want our money back," one of them said.

Mac took off his overcoat and sat down as the railway porter went to get another couple of cups; he soon placed a fresh cup of tea in front of both of them, as the cards were dealt for a game of pontoon.

Not to be outdone, Jock lit his pipe and settled down into the game, as the clock ticked round he was soon quite a bit into pocket. Suddenly Mac stood up.

"We'll go out first, I'm broke incidentally, we'll see you later," he said to the other coppers. To Jock he said

"Now don't forget lad, Mum's the word. Don't let on to anyone that you were in here," he said to Jock.

BELLS

The bell started ringing at the most inopportune moment. The shrill clamour broke the silence in the parade room as the Inspector was inspecting the night shift. The men were all prepared for going out, it was Sunday, the last night shift for six weeks. Every eye turned towards the sound of the ringing, and the old copper looked really sorry for himself as he became the focus of such attention. Desperately, he fumbled in his pockets as he tried to cut off the source of the sound. The Inspector couldn't ignore the bell any longer and had to pass some comment.

"What the hell is that Jenkins?" he asked, in a voice which suggested that he knew what it was and that the old copper was a blithering idiot. Lamely, the chap tried to find an explanation.

"Er, my watch is broken Sir, and this is the only way I can tell the time for my rings." He pulled a small alarm watch out of his pocket.

"Switch the bloody thing off for God's sake, and get your watch mended as soon as you can."

No more was said, but everyone knew that the clock was to make sure that he would be awakened from his nightly kip, in time for him to book off from his tour of night work. As they marched out from the parade shed, the rest of the relief all took the Mickey out of the miserable suffering man. Jock found out that Sunday was a deadly day. Early days were bad enough, but night duty was worse. There were very few people about and no coffee stalls. 'Everyone must go to bed early on a Sunday night, to get up for work on Monday' were Jock's thoughts on this subject. Not that it made much difference to the older set. Jock had been accepted, to a certain degree, he was not invited to join in with their card games, regardless of where they were held, and Sundays was no exception.

His two weeks training on the streets with a qualified officer was over.

"You are posted to this relief for nights tonight. Same as your mate," said the Sergeant when he booked off duty at 6am.

"Just my blooming luck. I thought I would be able to see what the town looked like during the hours of daylight," Jock complained.

"That's alright lad. Another posting on night duty will give you a bit of experience," he was told.

WORKING ALONE

So, the start of working the beats by himself commenced on the Monday night; Jock was just a wee bit apprehensive as he swung his cape over his shoulders. He checked his lantern and found the light was rather dim, or as a soldier would have said 'bloody useless'. He headed out towards the property that he had been delegated to cover that night and, according to his beat book and the map, it appeared that the two beats were on the outside border of the station and had very little on them in the way of shops. The times for his ringing in were noted and the boxes from which they had to be made. 'Damn' he thought, 'It will take me all my time to get from one box to the other to make a ring. It must be more than two hours walk; it will be a bit of a rush to get back to the station for breakfast'.

On the way to the first box he constantly checked the shops and offices; conscientiously turning every door handle and every window which needed checking - they were all examined. The rain started to pour down and as he swung his cape into position over his overcoat he noticed the wind had risen as well. All seemed to be in order, everything locked up and secure, until suddenly a door opened under his pressure. He froze, 'what the hell do I do now?' he thought as he stood listening intently. He could hear nothing except the rain pattering down on his cape and the wind howling through the trees. He opened the door very gently and quietly just in case there was someone there - he didn't want to alarm them. Gently he closed the door behind him and entered the passageway. He pushed his cape over the back of his shoulders and drew his truncheon; moving quietly along the passage, shining the dim lantern which didn't help much, he began to check the different doors leading from the passage, everything seemed alright.

Suddenly as he turned a corner, he found himself face to face with a massive figure of indescribable shape. The massive misshapen figure raised one arm in a threatening manner, just as Jock did automatically. Seconds seemed to race, the thoughts flew through his brain and time seemed to have no meaning as he waited for this creature to act. Then it dawned upon him that he was looking at his own reflection in a full length mirror, 'bloody hell, fancy being frightened of your own shadow' he muttered as he carried on with his search. There were no signs of any intruders but there was ample evidence of a recent party; he acknowledged the fact that after the fun and games had been completed, the crowd had gone and left the door open accidentally. Closing the door correctly behind him he left the hall and carried on with his patrol, saying nothing to anyone about his recent scare.

As he was making his entry in the book at the box, after making the ring, the door of the box opened and another PC stood there.

"What time's your ring mate?" he asked.

"I've just made it" answered Jock "but it will take me all my time to get back to the nick for breakfast."

"What do you have to go back there for, just get your grub outside" the newcomer said.

"Are you joking? Sit outside in the rain instead of getting a few minutes warm in the canteen. Anyway, I haven't brought any sandwiches with me tonight."

The other chap made his entry in the book and rang his station.

"How long have you been in the job?"

Jock admitted that this was his first night out by himself.

"Well look. I'm off the next Division and we use the same box, I'll show you where we go."

He took Jock along the road and down a back alley; as he entered a yard and opened a door leading into one of the buildings.

"Come on," he said.

Jock found himself in a kitchen where a man was sitting.

"What time is your breakfast?" the other copper asked.

"Two o'clock."

"Well you have time to get your breakfast here, then go back to the box and ring in, tell them you're having your breakfast out in the box."

A man had been sitting down when they entered the room, he had jumped to his feet and started to prepare a meal for the two of them. He already had the usual selection of food semi-prepared and in a short space of time, he laid a hot meal in front of them. All the time he worked he held a conversation with the other copper who he appeared to know quite well.

"I'll have a big mug of tea as well Alf, and one for my mate here," Jock's new-found friend stated.

The meal was lovely and they both enjoyed it.

"How much?" asked Jock wiping his mouth.

"Forget it Guv, I'm only too pleased to see you about here." He refused to take payment for the food.

When they left the premises the other bobby told Jock.

"He gets a lot of trouble around here with the Teddy Boys and we try to keep an eye on the place for him, to help him out. He's quite a good chap really."

"I wouldn't want to take advantage of his gratitude" Jock remarked.

"Yes, I know how you feel but it's his way of saying thank you," the other chap told him. "You would probably hurt his feelings if you refused and insisted on paying."

As they parted company Jock went along to the box and telephoned the station, he informed them of his location and then settled down to have a smoke until he was due out. He watched the clock carefully and as soon as he was due to go out he pulled his cape on, put his pipe in his pocket. The thirty minutes were nearly up and he scrawled the necessary line in the book; he was half way through doing this when the door of the box flew open and the Inspector stood there glaring at him. Jock continued writing in the book, put his pen away, then swung the cape over his shoulder.

"All correct Sir," he stated.

"What are you doing here?" the little man snarled.

"Having my breakfast Sir. I'm just going out" was the reply. "I didn't think I would have time to get back to the station, so I had my break here."

The Inspector snatched the book up and examined it.

"You are nearly due out. I don't want any fiddling or skiving on my relief. Finish your break and get out." With that final remark he slammed the door. Jock grinned to himself.

"I bet the sod is hanging around waiting to see if I do go." He fastened his cape and left the cold comfort of the box. He hunched his shoulders up against the bitter wind, hands pushed right down into his pockets to keep them warm as he turned along the lonely stretch of road which would take him to his next batch of shops. He had to walk in that direction according to his beat book. As he started walking, he caught sight of the Police car parked in a side street further along the road. There was a terrible sound of gear grinding as the engine revved up, the Inspector had been watching but didn't want Jock to know - but in his hurry to get the car out of sight, he made a proper hash of it. Jock couldn't help laughing to himself when he considered the feelings of the little Irish man. The vehicle was out of vision when Jock reached the junction.

EYE OPENERS

The following night was just as cold and wet as he moved through the darkened streets. He had been given a change of beat and was covering some of the built-up area where there were a lot of shops. A howling dog attracted his attention and he traced the sound to a lock-up shed beneath the railway. Smoke was pouring from a broken window and the dog's pitiful call echoed from the inside. Across the road Jock noticed the Fire Station, doors closed and all lights out, except for a little room where a man dozed in a dim light.

"Excuse me," he said to the fireman. "That shed over the road, it's a lock-up, there's smoke coming out of the window and there's a dog barking inside. Is that usual?"

"Ring the bell." The man didn't even look up.

"I don't want to call the fire engine out if that's a regular thing. Surely you must know if it's always like that," Jock insisted.

"Nothing to do with me lad. If there's smoke and you are worried, ring the bell, it's on the door post." He indicated the general direction.

"Sod you," Jock muttered. "If that's the way you want it."

"That's the way I want it, just press the button," was the final instruction.

Jock pressed the large brass bell and a tremendous clanging noise rent the night air, lights flashed on as all over the place the building came to life. Men came sliding down poles and seconds later the engine was running. One of the firemen came over to the office where Jock stood and the night attendant gave him a slip of paper,

"The usual one across the road."

The chaps in the engine had the cheek to start sounding the fire bell on the engine and the deafening clanging noise died away as it left the station and stopped on the opposite side of the street. The man with the paper in his hand strolled across to where it was standing and spoke to one of the firemen.

"Report, Stop. False alarm with good intent. Fish curers." The wireless crackled briefly as the message was transmitted. Engine still running the machine started off and drove round to the back of the station and into the garage. A few seconds later the building was in darkness, the men had gone to sleep to await another call.

"Bugger that for a job, it's enough to give anyone a heart attack getting wakened up like that." Apparently, he had done the same as every new copper during his first night on the beat.

Nearly 2am, so he headed back to the office. The rain was coming down in torrents; the streets were deserted, well very nearly. As he clung close to the buildings to get some slight protection from the downpour, he saw a man coming towards him on the opposite side of the road. 'Christ, but he's had a right skinful, he's drunk as a Lord'. The oncoming man was staggering from one side of the pavement to the other, between the wall and the pedestrian guard rails. Occasionally he fell to the ground, his legs seemed to be like jelly as they quavered and then gave way underneath him. Without having the rails to prevent his movement, the drunk staggered onto the roadway, trying to get his balance. He wasn't successful and fell in an ungainly heap in the middle of the road.

'Bloody good job there's no traffic about' thought Jock as he watched the man slipping and sliding on his wobbly legs. He eventually managed to get onto his feet on Jock's side of the road and there he made his own erratic fashionable movement along the pavement towards Jock. Jock stood in a doorway, watching the painful struggle in the rain as the man made his apparent way home. Suddenly he saw the man's face, he recognised him as being one of the old coppers from the nick. His helmet was missing and he didn't have a raincoat or overcoat on. His tunic must have been saturated with the rain and mud. He weaved his way past Jock with unseeing eyes. 'If I take him back to the nick he'll be in trouble'. Jock considered the prospects of dealing with this creature who was bringing disgrace on the uniform. He decided in the end just to let the drunken bum make his own way through the lonely streets to wherever he was going, and he continued his walk back to the canteen for his meal.

After breakfast he reached his beat and started to check the shops once more, each door handle was turned and pushed. As he came to one deep doorway, he was already in the entrance when he realised someone else was already there. He switched his torch on and saw a very active man and a female inside the doorway. He said to himself 'we have a right flaming crowd at this station' as he looked at them. He spoke to the man before he left.

"Try the door for me Pat." A hand came out of the clutch, with the thumb uppermost, as if to signify that his request would be dealt with. The nocturnal activities did not slow down. Jock went on his way, shaking his head sadly. 'Is there nothing else they can get up to at this nick?'

As he continued working his beat he saw a light flashing in one of the side streets; as he drew closer he recognised one of the Sergeants and it appeared as though he was looking for something.

"What have you lost, Skipper?" he asked. "Can I help you?"

"Oh" the embarrassed Sergeant answered. "It was nothing," he hadn't heard Jock come along.

"You must have been looking for something Serg," Jock persisted.

"Well, it's like this young'un. These rich people what come to the shows, they have plenty of cash and when they climb into their cars the money falls out of their trouser pockets. The old saying is finders keepers." He went on with his search for wealth, or a few coppers that someone had dropped out of their clothing. Jock carried on with his patrol but next night, as he passed the spot, he remembered what the Sergeant had said. He checked the road as he walked along and luck must have been on his side for he found a ten shilling note. 'A full day's wages'.

When he was in for refreshments the Sergeant came up to him and asked him if he had been past the place, Jock acknowledged the fact that he had.

"Find 'owt?" the Sergeant asked.

"As a matter of fact I did Sergeant. Ten bob," Jock said.

"Well where is it, I want my share, after all it was me that told you about the place," said the Sergeant holding out his hand.

"Oh it's in the office Sergeant if you want it. I handed it in, property found. Here's my pocket book," Jock smiled.

"You bloody fool, that was one of the perks on that beat." The senior officer swore under his breath and snarled at Jock as he walked away, still cursing these young coppers under his breath.

STOP

"Excuse me Sir." Jock was over a mile from the Station when he decided to stop this chap in the early hours of the morning, carrying a sack on his cycle.

"What have you got in your sack?" It was a reasonable enough question as any Constable was allowed to stop, search and detain any suspicious person, and as far as he was concerned this chap was suspicious when he was carrying a sack on his bike in the middle of the night.

"It's my business" was the terse reply. The man was angry and refused to state who he was nor would he say what the contents of the sack were. Despite several attempts by Jock, the man still refused.

"I'll report you to your Inspector," he said. Jock agreed with him.

"Of course Sir, I will give you the chance to do that because I am going to take you down to the Police Station for further enquiries, owing to the fact that you will not divulge the contents of the sack."

"I keep telling you, that is my business," the man said, but he willingly went with Jock.

He was taken down to the Station but cursed and shouted all the way about coppers; he was really a nasty piece of work. Even at the Station when the Sergeant and the Inspector tried to reason with him

"You are a lot of bloody idiots. I keep telling you that is my business," the man just shouted.

Eventually, he was pushed so hard that he said,

"Sod you, sod the lot of you," and tipped his bag out on the charge room floor. "See, I told you that it was my business." A load of shoes landed on the floor. "I am a cobbler by trade and I take some work home with me."

Apart from being an awkward man, he was also innocent and was allowed to go.

"If you had explained this at the time it would have saved you a lot of inconvenience Sir" the Inspector told him. "Now just be careful in future." Not long after that, as Jock walked from the nick, he heard the sound of metal, it appeared to come from around the corner. As he rounded the corner he saw two men and one of them was in the process of straightening up. Black overcoats and white silk scarves; they looked like real gentlemen going down town, after all it was only 2am, the night was young for them.

"Excuse me Sir," Jock was polite with his request. "Do you mind showing me what it was you just picked up?"

"Nothing officer," came the deep University brogue, "I didn't pick anything up." The explanation was quite bland and it was made from the chap that Jock suspected.

"I saw you bend down and pick something off the pavement."

"I'm sorry Officer but you are very mistaken," the man insisted. Jock had a feeling they had something to hide, he noticed that the chap had not put his hand inside his pocket since straightening up and so decided to play a bit of bluff.

"I saw you slip something up your sleeve, so if you don't mind I'll have a look" he said.

"Oh that," the man was effuse with his apologies. "I'm an engineer and a friend asked me to make this for him for his business." He opened his hand and allowed a long slender case opener (Jemmy) to slide down his sleeve into his palm. It was about 12" long and three eighths of an inch in diameter; Jock took it from him.

"How about you Sir," he asked the other man. "Have you anything that you have made for a friend?"

"I'm not with him, I don't know him," the chap answered. Jock thought the statement stank, for two chaps dressed like this at this time of the night, they must know one another; his thoughts were broken by an obnoxious voice, the sound he normally hated, the Patrolling Officer.

"Are you OK there?"

He knew he had trouble here and inwardly was pleased to hear the Sergeant who was squeezing himself out of the patrol car and coming across.

"Is everything alright?" he asked again.

"Yes, thanks for coming Sergeant, I was just arresting these two men for possessing housebreaking implements."

The Skipper gazed goggle eyed at this young copper. He had just brought a chap in for questioning and now he was trying it on with these two men; these blokes weren't housebreakers, they were all dressed up, probably going down town.

"Are you sure?" he asked Jock.

"Yes Serg." The skipper wouldn't argue with him in the street.

"Right sonny, get in the car," the Skipper told the two men. "We'll soon get this mess sorted out."

Looking at Jock he muttered "You too."

They all climbed into the ancient Wolseley and soon arrived at the Station. The Station Officer and his assistant came out into the charge room.

"Right, empty your pockets," Jock ordered them. The two strangers did as he ordered without complaint, then the Station Officer and the PC searched the men. Soon a mountain of housebreaking goodies appeared on the table, the collection included lock picks, jemmies, keys, torches, gloves and wire cutters.

"Check the car," the Station Officer ordered his assistant "in case they have hidden anything behind the seat."

The gentlemen thieves were charged and placed in the cells ready for Court in the morning. They asked for numerous other offences to be taken into consideration, with the air of a regular thief, indicating that they may as well get rid of them all as he charged later, as this would increase the sentences. This caused the Patrolling Officer to gaze with a curious expression on his face at this new copper standing beside him, wondering no doubt how he did it.

ATTACHMENTS

All probationers had attachment periods. Occasionally, they were on the area cars, river police, CID, or Town Office; one week with each department, just to get to know how they operated. Jock's first attachment was in the front office as assistant to the Station Officer, in simple words he was tea boy, stoke the fire up to keep them warm and deal with any small problem that may arrive at the office desk. He was amazed at the amount of tea consumed in the office. Normally he was left to his own resources in the front office whilst the Sergeants went into the Inspector's room until needed.

The door of the office suddenly banged open and a hysterical female charged into the office. The Sergeant heard the noise and came in to see what the trouble was about. Eventually the facts became clear, her husband had assaulted her and thrown her out of the house. Apparently this was a regular thing as he she was known to the Sergeant.

"Go round with her and get it sorted out, they only live a couple of streets away," he ordered Jock.

Upon reaching the terraced house she went down to the basement door and rang the bell, a man answered the door and Jock noticed that he was bleeding profusely from a wound to the head.

"Come in" the woman said.

"Bastard's not coming in here," said the man as Jock went to enter. Jock indicated the lady in question and replied,

"This woman states that you assaulted her, she invited me in." He indicated that he wanted to get the matter sorted out as she had been beaten up.

"Me, assault her? Who the bloody hell do you think did this then?" the man started to get annoyed with Jock.

"Now look, don't start shouting at me or you'll find yourself in real trouble" Jock pointed out to him.

"Just quieten down."

"Don't you threaten my husband and talk to him like that" the female shrieked at him.

"You lot are all the same, you take advantage of your uniform." The very loving lady just started on the custodian of the law. Jock just turned and left them to their matrimonial bliss; they were the best of pals and united against the common enemy, the copper.

"All right Jock?" asked the Station Sergeant as he went in. Jock had just learnt another lesson about husband and wife problems. They will fight like cat and dog, nearly kill one another, but just let anyone else stick their noses in and they will gang up united against the intruder. A commotion started in the charge room and attracted attention. Only a drunk being brought in - the Sergeant went in to see about the charge. Jock observed the proceedings from the front office, the man was searched and before long the desk was covered with a large quantity of notes. All the cash was in different currencies and the arresting officer assisted the Sergeant to place them in the piles for each different country. During this procedure the drunk was allowed to sit on a form - he was forgotten as the coppers began to count the enormous amount of cash.

"Where the hell did he get all this from?" asked the Sergeant.

The drunk haphazardly ignored everyone, he sat there with a look of contentment on his face, Jock smiled at the look of extreme happiness and then he noticed the man lift a bottle up to his lips and begin to drink. Without hesitation Jock flung himself through the door and knocked the bottle of Lysol from the man's hands. The others looked round at the interruption, when the Sergeant saw what the drunk had been doing he said,

"Right, get an ambulance at once and you'd better have your stories right, he drank that on the way to the Station before he was searched. I don't want any trouble at this nick."

The man was soon taken to hospital and apart from burning to his lips and gullet he soon recovered.

"Nip over to the café and get my sandwiches. They are ordered, just tell him who they are for. By the way, use the back door to the café," was the order given by the Station Sergeant. Jock entered the kitchen of the all-night café and the owner, who was sweating away at the cooker and serving as well by himself, was trying to cope with a dozen orders. He looked across when Jock entered.

"Help yourself," and he nodded towards the large teapot on the range. Jock poured himself a cuppa and sat down to wait for the rush to die down, the sweating man eventually sat down.

"I've come for the Station Sergeant's sandwiches, he told me they had been ordered."

"Yes, it's a standing order. I'll knock some up for him," and a half loaf was soon made into sandwiches with different fillings. The pile was placed in front of Jock. "You're new here aren't you?" the cook said. "Do you want any done?"

"No thanks, I've brought my sandwiches with me." Jock thanked him.

"Well, if ever you want a cuppa or any grub, just drop in, use the back door though just in case you frighten my customers away."

It was obvious that this man was working himself to the ground, the café was open all day and night, it was only shut between 3am and 4am for cleaning purposes. He worked by himself, cooking, serving and cleaning; the only sleep he got was when he managed to get a few minutes sitting on a chair. How the hell the human body could stand it made Jock wonder, it just seemed impossible for him to exist.

The front door of the office opened, the Sergeant was in the midst of devouring his huge meal and Jock was in the office.

"Can you tell me where I can find digs for the night?" he asked. Jock took up the book which had lists of addresses of such places. "There's a slight problem," explained the man. "I've been to quite a few places but they can't put the two of us up."

"Two of you?" Jock asked. "Is it your wife or a mate?"

"No, it's an elephant." Jock smiled and looked over the counter, "I see, that makes a difference, it would be hard to find digs for an elephant."

"It isn't there, it's outside," said the man looking at him in sympathy.

"What's the problem?" - the words could just be understood as the Sergeant decided to see who was disturbing his breakfast - his request came just after he had taken a large bite of a bacon butty.

"This chap is looking for bed and breakfast for himself and an elephant," Jock

explained and just managed to dodge a splatter of greasy breadcrumbs and slivers of bacon which shot out of the gaping orifice.

"Elephant!" he spluttered. "Where is it?" he asked as he peered over the counter. The little man must have thought all coppers were bonkers, as if he would bring the elephant into the building.

"It's outside."

"Go and have a look Jock," the Sergeant decided to humour the man. Sure enough, outside the office was a low loader and inside the box was an elephant and as it swayed from side to side, the whole truck moved.

"Well?" asked the Skipper when he returned.

"There is an elephant there Skip" agreed Jock. The Sergeant was not sure whether they were ganging up on him and taking the Mickey, but the little man explained.

"We're starting a show at the Theatre next week and the elephant is part of the act." The explanation seemed to satisfy the Sergeant and with his vast local knowledge he directed the midnight circus to a guest house which had a large space at the rear.

"They often get people from the theatre staying there." He informed Jock for his future reference.

A week on the river in winter is not advocated for a holiday, especially on night shift. It was a freezing cold time of the year, the river police were dressed for the cruise but Jock wasn't. It was dull, cruising up and down the reaches, checking different wharfs and ships at anchor. Nothing happened during that attachment period to convince Jock that he should apply for the job.

CID, now that could be a different proposition, one assumed. There was always one CID officer on reserve duty at each station to handle any questions or problems, or to handle any cases which were brought in. This duty changed daily as well as each shift, all CID had their turn. Any reported crimes were then put down to the officer on duty. Any other influx were designated by the Detective Inspector to various members of the department to investigate. Attachments spent most of their time in the office, or running errands with files. On one occasion, Jock was requested to take a file to Headquarters - he had never been there - it was in a different part of the City. He caught a tramcar outside the office which took him all the way. Crossing the road he reached the centre island, he checked the movement of the traffic and the lights before crossing to the other side. The traffic drew to a halt and the traffic lights changed to red, Jock glanced up the road, nothing coming, a quick and unnecessary glance to the right and he stepped off the island. A car came driving fast round the corner, straight past the red light - its front wing grazed his leg and his hand was struck by the wing mirror. Due to the stationary traffic, the car had to stop.

"Bloody drivers, no consideration, he should be done for jumping the lights," Jock cursed the driver. He stepped back and looked at the driver, who was in uniform, the man was looking straight ahead with a wooden expression on his face. His companion also adopted a similar pose, sitting like a pair of dummies. He was just about to give the chauffeur a piece of his mind and tell him off about his driving, when he saw the two female passengers sitting quietly in the back of the car. They sat, stern faced, and appeared to be ignoring everything that was going on around. The four of them must have seen Jock stepping out and they must also have known that he had been hit, however slightly. As he looked down at them he said to himself, 'Christ, I very nearly dropped a clanger there'. The chocolate coloured Rolls Royce slid quietly away; the fact that it had no registration plates on was not noticed in the bustle of the traffic, as the Royal Car sped on its way!

"Jock, the boss wants to see your," said the Desk Sergeant back at the Station.

"What for?" replied Jock.

"Couldn't tell you, but there's a panic on" the Sergeant answered. The Sub-Divisional Inspector was in the yard waiting for him.

"I have been told that you were in the Bomb Disposal. Is that right?" he asked.

"Yes Sir," Jock wondered what was on the mind of the worried looking man.

"The cinema across the road is full and they've found a bomb in the toilets. Could you have a look at it. We don't want to cause a panic."

"Don't worry Sir, I'll see to it," Jock smiled at the worried man, this was something he was used to and could handle. He crossed the road to the local picture house and saw a very frightened attendant at the entrance. The doorman directed him to the place where the object was.

"We put a closed notice on the door," he explained.

"I'd go for a walk if I were you," Jock told him - he was happy doing this job, back in his own element. He cautiously checked the door to the small room and entered. Examination of the interior disclosed a cardboard box with two wires protruding from a hole in one end. The lid of the box was taped down. He took out his knife and slowly but carefully he cut a hole in the top so that he could examine the contents. He ran his fingers round the inside of the hole then enlarged it until he could see the whole of the interior. He eased the lid off and checked under the metal cylinder that lay inside. Once he was satisfied, he lifted the object out of the container and examined it closely. He grinned, put it back in the box, tucked the box under his arm and walked out of the cinema

"It's OK you can go back inside" Jock commented to the worried doorman and he headed for the Station. The Inspector was waiting for him.

"Have you sorted it out?" he asked.

"Yes Sir. The cinema is OK I brought it over with me" and he held out the box.

"What? What is it? What are you going to do with it?" asked his boss.

"I'll show you," Jock took the metal cylinder from the box.

"Be careful with that, I have my chickens and rabbits here." The boss had kept several livestock at the back of the offices during the war.

"It's OK Sir" as Jock held one end of the tube and struck the other end hard on the ground. A shower of broken cement fell out. "See Sir, it's only a metal pipe filled with cement and a couple of bits of wire stuck in" he explained, be he was talking to himself because the Inspector had broken all records and disappeared. The yard was empty.

The best attachment period was on the cars. Each Station had an area patrol car; a driver, wireless operator and a plain clothes observer manned these cars. The observers were all uniform men who got ten shillings a week for the wear and tear of their clothes. When Jock was doing his attachment, he received the ten shillings for being in plain clothes.

The first night was fairly busy, with stolen cars, alarms and suspects all mixed up with accident calls. Calls were constantly erupting over the wireless and neighbouring Stations were also checked in case they became involved in a job which may require assistance. Night crawling was a regular thing, with the cars slowly moving along as they checked shops and other property. These slow drives compensated for the high speed drives when they went on calls or chases. Witching hour was between 2am and 3am when the car had to cover a nearby ground during refreshments. They just stayed in a central position so that they could attend either ground quickly. The drivers used to pull into a quiet cul-de-sac, however as soon as a call came over for that car, it was action stations. The engine would be switched on and the car ready to go as the operator wrote the message down.

Jock's driver was naturally a first class driver and all the time he was driving he gave a commentary, which proved useful for Jock later as he listened to the man. The CID had their own car for attending wherever their services were required on nights. The WPC, there was always one on each Division on night duty but she had to get the spare driver or the van driver to take her to the Station which may have required her services. Otherwise she spent the time sleeping in the women's room, knitting, or she found something else to do to pass the time away. It was one of the latter desires that came to Jock's notice, under rather unusual circumstances.

"Hello Darling. I haven't seen you for a long time. Where are you going?" The sultry sexy voice came to Jock's ears as they prepared to leave the Station yard. "Give me a ride to pass the time away." He noticed a very attractive female leaning in the driver's window, her arms were wrapped around him.

"Come on then, jump in, we're just going for a short drive," the lucky man said.

Without another word the beauty got in the back beside Jock, she sat behind the wireless operator.

"I'll be leaving you soon darling" she said to the driver. "I'm going abroad to work." It was not surprising that she should leave the job as women police only got a small wage, it was less than a copper's wage and that was bad enough.

"I'll miss you" laughed the driver as he drove along. He stopped shortly afterwards in an open field where he switched off the lights, he left the engine running to keep the car warm. The flighty female leaned forwards over the seat to wrap her arms round his neck, pushing between him and the wireless man.

"Here, hang on, I'll get out and you can have my seat," said the wireless man and he got out from behind his wireless and got into the back seat. The WPC was wedged between him and Jock.

"Let me out then," she said.

"No go gal, if you want to get in the front seat you can climb over." He was generous for he gave her a hand to get over the back of the seat, in fact he gave her two hands. She didn't move, she was stuck there, but her skirt did as her assistant pushed.

"Cor look at that, lovely black stockings and suspenders. What a lovely rump you have," he said. The female did not acknowledge, she was too busy kissing the driver and was quite content to be straddled over the seat. She appeared ignorant and unconcerned about the other end of her torso.

"This is too good to miss," the operator said, and proceeded to say goodbye in the nicest possible way to the lady. However, they do have other uses such as dealing with children and young persons, and women who are in need of assistance. Also, for the searching of female prisoners. However, they are not physically suited to the ordinary police work.

ON LOAN

Six men stood at attention, showing their appointments to the Inspector in preparation for their tour of duty.

"Right, put them away" he ordered.

Before they could be marched out, a breathless PC came in and handed the Inspector a message. Apparently the neighbouring Police Station did not have any men available for doing beat duty and the Inspector there had asked for a loan of some men to patrol the ground. Three volunteers were required.

"You end three, right turn, quick march" the Inspector ordered. "You are on attachment for the night." Jock and Ernie, both new recruits, left the shed with old Mac.

"I've got my bike here, I'll see you over there," the old Scotsman told them as they headed for the front office to arrange some form of transport. The three of them paraded again, for the second time they were inspected.

"Have any of you been here before?" asked the section Sergeant

Mac agreed that he had been there several times and that he knew the area. He was then detailed to go to the sub-station.

"There is nobody down there, you will have the whole ground to yourself." He turned his attention to Jock and Ernie.

"Do you know the area at all?" and as the answer was negative in both cases, he directed Ernie to his six beats.

"Turn right when you get outside the office, keep walking till you reach the river, that's your limit, grub at 1.30." Ernie went out to patrol and wasn't seen again that night, he couldn't be found - apparently he had got lost and couldn't find his way back to the Station.

"Your patch is bigger than his, I'll come with you and show you the boundaries," the Sergeant said to Jock. They wandered along chatting, he was quite a pleasant chap, different from the crowd at his own Station. Everything seemed quiet on the beats, and suddenly the Sergeant disappeared from Jock's side. He showed his face, about half an hour later, from a crowded café.

"I thought you were coming in with me for breakfast" he said. He left the young copper to patrol the huge area of shops and houses alone, and returned to the office.

Eventually, Jock decided to head back to the nick for his grub and as he didn't have a beat book, he had no idea where he was. All he knew was that the Station was in the middle of a large complex of Council flats, all he had to do was find the flats. On the way he came across a couple lying on the pavement, the man and woman were in a right old state, happy as kings as they lay in the rain, trying to get to their feet. Obviously they couldn't be left in that position so Jock decided that he would have to take them in for their own good. He struggled with them, first he got the man up and stood the weaving torso against the wall. Next he levered the lady to her feet as she giggled and laughed.

"Eeh lad, mind where you put your hands."

Eventually he had both of them standing up, they had to be supported all the time. He had one on each side of him as they staggered along, it was just impossible to walk in a straight line and the three of them wobbled and staggered along, the two drunks were constantly singing and laughing. As they moved along, Jock kept looking for the Station, but he never saw it. At long last they reached the road beside the river and he had to admit, he was lost.

"Bugger it, I must have missed the turning" he said.

The man broke off his rendering of 'The Lambeth Walk' and asked,

"Wassa marra Guvnor?" in a slurred Cockney voice.

"I was looking for the Nick, we must have passed it." Jock had to admit.

"Thas right Guvnor, ish up there." The man waved his arm airily around him. Having received the general direction of where his grub was Jock considered the situation. He'd had a hell of a job to get the two of them so far, he certainly didn't relish having to cart them all the way back up. He stood them up against one another, balanced now, yes but still a bit shaky. He made his mind up.

"Right now, are you two OK? Do you think you can manage the rest of they way by yourselves?" he asked.

"Yes Guvnor, you're an angel," the man wept. "Nobody else would have helped us." "I hope the hell you are OK and can find your way home. Now off you go."

Arms around one another the couple staggered along, singing at the tops of their voices. As they went one way he retraced his steps, hoping to find his own way. He was lucky, for he eventually found the Police Station and had his grub, poor Ernie didn't. As he was the only one available he was asked to join in for a game of cards. They went into the communications room and they all played as they ate their meals. There was the Inspector, the Sergeant and the chap from the communications. Eventually Jock had to go, leaving the three of them to continue.

HELP

Next night, a worried man stopped Jock when he was back on his own beats.

"I have a pub across the road and I have some real trouble there Guv. There's a crowd of drunks in there who will not leave, I have called time, but they won't go."

"You shouldn't have drunks on your premises" Jock informed him as he accompanied him across the road. There was an argument going on, it was the usual friendly affair although very lively. It was being carried on between three men who were obviously mates. Jock gently ushered them outside whilst they still argued, they were well under the influence of drink. Out on the pavement, they still didn't realize that they had been put out of the pub, until the publican slammed the door behind them.

"Hey Charlie. What have you done? You've locked us out."

"It's after hours," shouted the publican. "Maybe so, but you shouldn't have thrown us out Charlie" one of the enraged men yelled.

"I didn't throw you out" the owner shouted back, "It was him." His voice came clearly through the glass. The general attitude of the drunks changed at once from their friendly discussion to a concentrated aggression against their united enemy, the man in blue. This was the bugger that had thrown them out of their own pub. The verbal abuse soon turned into violence and physical force was used against Jock, who had his hands full dealing with the three men. He didn't want to hurt them after the dirty trick their friend, the publican, had played on them. The owner of the pub had however telephoned for the Police before he had stopped Jock and the Police van turned up with a couple of coppers inside. The trio were whipped off to the nick to sleep it off and appeared at the Magistrates' Court next morning to receive a fine of five shillings each. Jock had learnt another lesson, in future when called to licensed premises let the owner eject the people, or tell them he wants them out. The copper only assists him to prevent a Breach of Peace.

PROBATIONERS

Instruction classes - all probation officers had to attend them, regardless of what shift they happened to be on. Travelling expenses were not paid. Classes for First Aid Instruction were also held; all PCs had to pass the exams and obtain the Bronze Medallion at least. The Instructor on First Aid had a cushy job as that was his sole duty. Small wonder that he obtained the black ribbon of the Order of Jerusalem, he did his best to ensure that all his protégés passed the tests. Pay Day was on each Friday, the PCs had to approach the desk where the Inspector sat with the pay clerk and, in typical army style, he collected his weekly crumbs, march to the table smartly, stop, salute, one pace forward, collect the pay in the right hand and transfer it to the left hand, one pace back, salute once again, turn smartly, and march off. There was usually a Sergeant sitting at a table collecting for coppers who were in hospital; they bought fags for them. Sometimes the collection was for a wreath. Outside the Station one could always see the wives of the Policemen gathered, waiting for the week's wages to buy food for the children. So much for a well paid job.

Each probationer had a Sergeant who had to submit a monthly report on his work, attitude and behaviour. One of the men, who had joined with Jock, received his marching orders and was sacked. He had got married but very rarely went home, his wife complained that he never had a day off and during the course of the enquiry it transpired that he had made friends with a local female. He had been spending his free time with his lady-love. The trouble arose because of the rent book. Rent was paid up to £1 per week and the book had to be signed by the landlady. In this case the PC just signed the book for his landlady and kept the money. Forgery was the official verdict and the sack was the result. The bosses kept a tight eye on all probationers.

A Policeman had been shot dead when he had challenged a man one night. A full description was circulated and photographs were put in the papers of the suspect, who was armed and dangerous; the orders were 'Do not approach'. One day shortly afterwards, Jock was just leaving the Station yard and the area car came screeching in.

"Quick Jock. Get the boss, we've got him in a bedsitter." Jock quickly informed the Inspector and the three of them were soon standing in the kitchen of a small terraced house.

"How do you know it's him?" the Inspector asked the landlady.

"They didn't have any luggage, which I thought funny. Then I saw the paper today." She showed them the picture in the paper.

"It's them, I'm sure of it."

The Inspector asked the landlady what she normally did in the mornings.

"I take their breakfast up on a tray, I knock at the door and tell them that their breakfast is there and put it on the floor outside the door, they collect it afterwards."

"Why do you do that?"

"They have always been like that since they arrived. When I first took it up to them, they just shouted out for me to leave it as they were still in bed and I've done the same each day."

"Righto lady, do the same thing and go straight downstairs after you leave the breakfast," the Inspector instructed.

The meal was taken up to the room; the landlady knocked on the door and informed the occupants that their breakfast was served. She then went back down to her kitchen. Shortly afterwards, the latch clicked on the bedroom door and as it did so the woodwork was struck by 45 stones of human flesh from the outside. The door crashed inwards and hit the man on the other side. He had just been in the process of unlocking the door, he staggered backwards and landed on the bed and the three big coppers landed on top of him. There was an almighty struggle as they fought together. The man had got his hand under the pillow and grabbed a gun, which was loaded.

A female voice came from under the pile of bodies as they squirmed around,

"Let me out, I can't breathe."

"Get out then" snapped the Inspector as the man was held down. A female crawled out of the scrum, clad only in her birthday suit.

"Get some clothes on" the Inspector told her (spoilsport). They had the murderer under control now. "Take her downstairs Jock."

Another killer arrested but the Inspector was on the carpet for not obeying instructions regarding the approach to an armed and dangerous man, but then that's what coppers are paid for, even if they did get a medal afterwards.

BARROW BOYS

Jock had saved enough cash to pay for a trip home and during his visit, arrangements were made for the Wedding Day. All his halfpennies and pennies had to be accounted for, due to the lack of sufficient remuneration from his employers for his services, or as the man in the street would say 'Bloody Poor Pay'. He kept his records diligently regarding his expenditure and everything that was not necessary was cut out. Even his smoking, which he really enjoyed, was stopped. The old pipe was only used to bite on, a small comfort when on night duty.

Temptation was often placed before him, as no doubt it was before other coppers. He often thought about the reported backhanders, no wonder they take the cash when they get such poor wages. On one occasion he was posted, like all the young coppers were, on the market. The reason, of course, was to chase the barrow boys and to get summonses and arrests. These were really required for their monthly reports, it showed that they had been working and the Sergeants had something to write about. The streets were narrow and it didn't take much to block them, one car parked opposite a barrow would stop all movement of traffic. The costermongers prepared their barrows on an open space near the market area. How they managed to get such huge pyramids of fruit and veg. onto the barrows was a work of art. They were also fixed so that all the good stuff was on show to the public but anyone who made a purchase was served with the rotten stuff which they cleverly stacked in the boxes under the display at the rear. These chaps also had the gift of working the scales. They could drop the goods on the scales hard enough to make the tray drop and before they had a chance to swing back up, they would whip the bag off the scales before the customer could see it. As he walked past the waste ground Jock noticed that all the barrows had gone and as he strolled past he saw piles of silver on a window sill. There was no sign of anyone who could claim ownership to the money; to Jock it seemed like a little fortune. He decided to take it into the Station for safe-keeping. He counted the piles; it was an easy matter, 20 piles of half crowns, eight in each pile. £20 was over a month's pay to him. He entered the facts into his pocket book and headed for the office. He handed the cash to the Station Sergeant in the office.

"Where did you say you found it?" he asked Jock. Jock explained the exact location, the Sergeant turned and looked at the Inspector who was sitting at the desk and the Inspector dropped his eyes to the book in front of him.

"Right lad, back to work," he was ordered after his pocket book had been signed.

A couple of hours later a PC came up to him and said

"You up the lane?"

"Yes, why?" asked Jock.

"Where's my money?"

"Your money. I haven't got any money belonging to you."

"It was on the window sill," the man snarled.

"Oh, was that your money? I didn't know. That was a queer place to leave a month's wages."

"Come on, don't feck about, I want that money, if you like I'll give you half." The man was enraged.

"Halve it with me. No thanks, you can have it all seeing that it's yours. I don't want any of your cash," Jock said. "After all, it's yours you say." The man looked a little bit happier.

"Come on, we'll get it."

The man asked where it was.

"In the front office, I handed it in when I found it, aren't you lucky," Jock told him. The man went purple.

"Sod off!" was the angry retort as he made his way back to the market to explain to the barrow boys that they would still be getting arrested or summonsed, even though they had paid.

The barrow boys got their usual deserts that day, a couple of summonses each and one or two were nicked. There were twenty of them working that day, it cost them an average of £5 each time they were nicked, so it's obvious that if they all paid £1 as a backhander, they were saving a lot of cash. Those days were finished for them, no more backhanders were allowed, Jock had put a stop to it. At firs, when they got arrested, the barrow boys tried to leave somebody else to look after the stall. By doing this the barrow was still causing obstruction, as the caretaker carried on selling goods. However, it seems that there is an art in pushing one of these grossly overloaded barrows, one had to get just the right balance to prevent them overturning. The coppers insisted that when arrested, the costermongers must remove their barrows as well. It was funny seeing the station yard crammed full with barrows covered with all types of fruit and veg. One or two of these hard working lads decided that they would not push the barrows all the way to the station, it was rather unfortunate for them that the two coppers who tried to push the barrows had no experience whatsoever, the results were not laughable as far as the barrow boys were concerned. As soon as the copper picked up the shafts he found that it was not possible to balance the cargo, the whole lot tipped up and a tremendous river of apples, oranges, tomatoes, pears and numerous other types of greens rolled down the street. That was the last time a barrow boy requested a copper to push his barrow if he wanted it moved.

NEW IMMIGRANTS

"I don't feel well," came a plaintiff voice from the throngs on the crowded pavement.

"No, you do look a bit pale dearie," came a reply. Jock glanced round at the two females who were chatting and he smiled for they were both as black as coal. How on earth could anyone say that one of them looked pale! The coloured population did not create any problems for the police, although they were on the increase. He found them to be a very pleasant crowd and were generally happy; he had made friends with several coloured people when he had served in the merchant navy and had worked in the Leeward and Windward Islands. Occasional raids had to be on certain houses which seemed to thrive on card games and parties, smoking hash. A couple of vans had to be used to run a shuttle service to collect the crowds of prisoners from the one flat.

Their living quarters were the problem. Apparently one enterprising Jamaican ran a business providing them with rooms; he had an office in Jamaica and another in this country. He used to advertise in local papers offering accommodation and prospects of a job, for only Fifty Pounds; naturally with massive unemployment in Jamaica, he had plenty of applicants. They came across in their droves, paid the £50 and he gave them a key to one of his houses; three floors and a semi basement, plenty of rooms. Of course the newcomers would have to share a room with several other people. Regarding employment, he gave them the address of the local Employment Office. One youngster thought that he had been conned when he found out the truth, he took his money back, and the old man complained to the police that he had been robbed. The youngster was arrested and charged; it was found that the money had belonged to the elderly conman at that particular time and the lad was guilty. This episode did bring the facts of the fiddle to public notice and it was halted.

It was obvious that all these people couldn't carry on living in such circumstances so they soon devised a system to benefit them all. They got together in groups of twenty and each member paid the sum of Five Pounds into a kitty; they then drew lots and in order of the draw, each member collected the cash and put it down as a deposit on a house. They then let the rooms to other immigrants. They carried on drawing the dole money and still paid the £5 each week into the kitty, until all twenty members had a house. The same system carried on and each of these people put their £5 into another kitty and drew lots to see who would have one of the cars which they would buy when they came out on the list. The first lucky man used his money to buy a car and, consequently, each and every one of them owned a house and a car within forty weeks, and they still drew dole. Some of the more enterprising members carried on this system and bought another house, letting the first one out to some of the newcomers to this country. Ones who had left their own country with a job and whose lives soon changed for the better, for they too were soon to be rich getting rent from the houses and money from the Government.

ANOTHER MEETING

Moseley's mob were on the move again 'England for the English' and 'Keep Britain White' were the two most used war cries. A large box van was his rostrum with a Union Jack flying from the top, the whole lot lit by a spotlight from each corner. This is where the speaker stood as he bellowed out his words of knowledge to the throngs who used to gather to heckle them. He could see the mobs from where he stood and he was generally out of the way of any missiles which were thrown. This movement had a lot of opposition from the various political and religious bodies. Jewish, Communists, Blacks from all parts of the world all mixed together with hordes of others, all with one common purpose, that was to attack and try to prevent these meetings taking place. All the political parties tried their best, or worst, to prevent Moseley's Mob from holding a meeting. As soon as it was known that they were going to meet at a certain place the opposition would be there beforehand. Little groups of two or three would congregate on each corner with one person talking. This was officially a meeting and no other could be held there. The big van would drive around until a convenient spot was selected, the van would park, spotlights switched on and the loudspeakers would crackle. The little meetings would break up and the men with thousands of others would be potential adversaries towards the big van.

On nights such as this, police were drafted in from all over the City and hundreds of coppers were walking the streets supplemented by busloads of reserves. Special Constables, who very rarely show their faces, were also available. At one such meeting, Jock was standing on the edge of the crowd and about ten feet away from him were two of these Specials, a couple of drunks began a boisterous battle with one another close to the part-timers, they began gesturing frantically to Jock. The nodding and waving went on for some time before Jock went over to them.

"What's the matter?" he asked.

"There's a fight there," they indicated, as if Jock couldn't see it.

"Well, deal with it, there are two of you" he said.

"We can't. We were told if any trouble started we had to get a real Policeman to deal with it," was the reply.

"You've got a bloody uniform on for Christ's sake. What the hell do you want to parade like coppers for, if you can't keep the law?" Jock was fuming, he turned round and grabbed the two troublemakers by the scruffs of their necks and pushed them out of the crowd into a back alley.

"Right, if you want to kick hell out of one another and have a fight, you can do it down here. Don't disturb the meeting." They went and were not seen again. The two Specials returned to their position in the shop doorway, with their thumbs stuck inside the top pockets of their tunics, trying to look impressive.

"Bloody Specials," Jock muttered as he returned to his post with the young PC who

had been drafted in from outside to assist with the meeting. Jock wasn't the only one who didn't like Specials, the ones there were a right shower, booked on for a couple of hours each week, they generally finished up in the billiard room, otherwise they would go to the pictures and stand at the rear until it was time to book off. They used to be up to all kinds of tricks, such as when they attended football or cricket matches. Their job was to keep the main roads clear and prevent cars parking. One chap used to patrol and chase the drivers, he directed them to a convenient side street, where his companion was directing the cars onto a convenient car park (a bombsite) and collecting the parking fees. They were disliked by the coppers in general, after all, what other job would allow men to do their jobs for them without pay. The Police Authority however stated that they were the mainstay of law and order and were depended on for emergencies.

BOTTLED

"Help." Jock and his mate were walking towards the Station just after midnight;

"I want a Doctor." A blood-covered hand was thrust between their faces from the rear. The hand belonged to a man who was bleeding profusely from ghastly wounds to his face and neck.

"Get an ambulance Jack!" he told his mate, then he ordered the injured man to lie down so that he could stop the bleeding.

"No, I want a Doctor," the man gasped. He refused to get down so that First Aid could be carried out and Jock had to use force to pin him to the ground. He had to use both his thumbs to apply the required pressure on the artery which had been severed. The man was bleeding to death and that was the only way to save his life. The Station was not far from the spot where he struggled in the pool of blood and an ambulance was soon on the scene. He accompanied the case to hospital.

"Here I'll give you a spell," the ambulance man said, "By the looks of him though, he's a goner."

The patient was stiff and white as a sheet. When they reached the hospital the casualty doctor soon turned the flesh inside out, to look for any pieces of glass left behind, then soon stitched the wound up and placed him on a blood drip. He lived, but wouldn't say who had done it to him.

"That's my business. I'll sort it out myself," was his answer. Jock and his mate had followed the trail of blood back along the pavement and had found a broken milk bottle at the spot where the assault had taken place. They had carefully collected all the pieces for evidence and to obtain fingerprints, just in case the man had died. They then made enquiries all around the area. The searching soon disclosed all the persons who had been concerned in the bottle party but the CID stated later that it was up to the injured party, and if he didn't want to sign the complaint then they couldn't do anything. If the man had died it would have been different.

IRISH

"Officer. I have a woman in my restaurant who is refusing to pay for her meal, she is causing trouble." A small Chinaman whispered the complaint into Jock's ear, it was just after closing time and anything could happen at that hour. The café was full when Jock entered the premises, he saw a very well built woman who only stood about 5' high, she was giving vent to her feelings in a loud manner; she was engaged in giving an obscene description of all Chinamen and their Honourable Ancestors. One of her massive hands had a poor little Chink by the back of the neck and she was giving emphasis about his parents wrongdoings by banging his head on the counter. Every time she stated that his parents should have been married, brought forth another bump.

"Here, hold on Luv. What's the trouble? These gents tell me you haven't paid your bill," Jock said as he detached the bag of bones from her colossal paw.

"Do you think I'm going to pay for the shit they gave me, not feckin' likely," and she grabbed once again at the battered Chinaman. Jock dragged him away.

"Sorry madam but you will have to pay. How much does she owe?" he asked the proprietor. When he received the information Jock took the money from the woman's purse, a receipt was obtained and that was placed in the purse and given back to the gigantic female.

"Come on ducks, you don't want to stay in here do you?" She was as drunk as anyone could get and still stay on their feet; she was willing to walk but couldn't travel in a straight line without assistance.

"Cor, she's got some bloody strength," Jock said as he assisted her out of the café. He muttered to the proprietor that he would probably need someone to assist him. The little man sped off to the nick to get another copper. It was obvious that she'd have to go inside and he levered her in the general direction of the Police Station. Before they got there she began to get really naughty with him and he was half expecting her to start banging his head against a brick wall. The Chinaman returned with a mountain of a man, the section Sergeant, 6'6" and built like a tank - but even with one on each side of her the woman managed to make a progress from one side of the road to the other. They could just hold her and no more, her feet were on the go as well as her arms and tongue! Eventually, they reached sanctuary and she was bedded down into a convenient cell.

"Do you know who she is?" said Big Bill, the Sergeant.

"Never seen her before skipper" Jock truthfully answered.

"Elizabeth. She lives with an Irishman. He is a ganger on the railway and he keeps his men in check with his fists and feet. You nicked her, so you can have the job of informing him that she has been arrested. I'm bloody sure that I'm not. So, good luck." Jock went to the address given, which wasn't too far from the Station. The door was opened by a huge figure which reminded him of the body he had met in the passageway the night he found the premises open.

"What the hell do you want?" said the big Irishman said in a very surly brogue.

"Liz has been nicked. Drunk."

"Who is it?" a female voice sounded from the bedroom.

"It's Liz, she's pissed again and has been knocked off," the man shouted back. "Well let the cow stay there."

As the obscenities flew from the front door to the bedroom and back, Jock interrupted and asked the man if he was coming to collect her.

"We'll see," was the only reply he could get from him. When the Irishman eventually arrived the fun began in earnest. The Station Sergeant wanted the female out of the place but she started to fight with her man friend. So at first he was willing to take her but she wouldn't go with him, next thing it was the other way round, she wanted to go but he was refusing.

"Let the cow stay here, we are well shot of the likes of her," he argued

The Sergeant tried all ways to persuade him to sign the bail forms and take her home with him; eventually they reached a mutual agreement, if only for a short spell, and the Skipper breathed a sigh of relief when they left.

Turning to Jock and the Sergeant said

"You had better follow them Jock, just to see that they get away from the Station." Jock got his helmet on and followed the couple. He found them having a right old 'ding dong' battle right outside the back entrance of the Station. The Patrolling Inspector sat in his car patiently waiting to drive; the couple wouldn't move and no way was he going to get out of his car to sort them out. When he saw Jock coming along, he called him over.

"Those two should be locked up." Jock knew that the man was afraid to get out to talk to them so he told the Inspector that she had just been arrested.

"I have just arrested her Guv, he's bailing her out. If you wish, I can take them both in and put them down to you."

The Supervising Officer didn't answer, he just waited for Jock to push the pair of them onto the pavement and start them on their way home so that he could drive in. The female didn't turn up at Court the next morning and Jock had to take a warrant out for her. He went back to the Station and left his bike in the yard before he walked round to her house. Several loud knocks on the door were required before she eventually answered.

"Who is it?" she asked.

"The copper that nicked you last night" Jock answered. "You didn't turn up at Court so they have issued a warrant and I have to take you down there myself now."

"How the hell could I go?" she asked, "I can't see a bloody thing." The statement was true, for both her eyes were tightly closed, the whole of her face was bruised and swollen. Jock asked who had done it, even though he knew the answer.

"Mick, of course, but I will deny it if anyone else asks." This was their way of life; the Irishman ruled the two women in his life the same way that he ran his workmen but they would all stick together against the law.

She was taken to Court in the Police van, fined five shillings, the usual, and taken back home again.

"Thanks Guv, you are a gent" she said as she fumbled her way back into the pigsty which she called home.

Jock booked off duty at 3pm after 17 hours work; he had to cycle back home to get a few hours sleep, then he was back at work at 10pm, ready for another tour of night duty.

He turned up, as fresh as ever, the weather was just as bad as one could expect, rain and wind didn't help and the cold bit into the bones. As he entered the shed an old copper came out of the Communication Room and called him over.

"Jock, you are wanted in the front office, I've been waiting for you coming."

"What for, do you know?" Jock wondered what on earth he had done wrong this time, as he headed for the front office.

ANOTHER BOMB SCARE

When he arrived, he found all the Sergeants and the Inspectors from the night shift and late turn were gathered in a conference. One of the Inspectors turned to Jock as he entered.

"I've been told that you were in Bomb Disposal, and know something about bombs." Jock noticed the Sergeant there who had asked him about his job in the Army.

"We have found an object which is believed to be a bomb. At present, we are not sure and want you to have a look at it before we send for the Disposal Squad. Will you have a look?"

Jock didn't mind, this was something he knew about and said so.

"I don't mind, so I might even save you a 'phone call."

He was taken by the Inspector to the location, which was a factory with oil storage tanks. A Police Constable from the late turn shift stood at the entrance with a couple of civvies. The PC took them to an oil tank and pointed to a cylindrical object.

"There it is. Not one of those things like the cinema. Jock looked at the object beside his feet and his face was serious as he answered.

"No Taffy, it's not another one of those things, as you call it. This one isn't funny, as a matter of fact I haven't seen one of these for a very long time."

"Do you mean it could go off?" the young Welshman asked.

Jock got down on his knees and examined the missile more closely.

"Just my bloody luck" he exclaimed. "If I were you Taffy, I would scarper and tell the Inspector I want him." The youngster went over to where the Inspector was standing and passed the message on, at the same time he indicated that he was on late turn and should be off duty. The PC was allowed to go on his way most gratefully, the Inspector crossed to where Jock was.

"What's the problem?" he asked. "Is it a bomb or not?" He gazed down at the object which looked like a couple of tin cans joined together.

"This is an Italian hand grenade, Sir. How the hell it got here I couldn't tell you. The lads used to call them 'Yellow Perils'. It's made with the two outer cases being screwed together in the centre, here." as he pointed to the join. "There's another container inside which holds the explosive, and between the two cases there are hundreds of ball bearings and bits of shrapnel. The device which sets it off is situated in the top, it is a striker over a detonator; this is normally held back by a bit of wire which goes through a hole in it. When the wire is removed, the striker is forced down onto a finely balanced plate by means of a strong spring. As soon as the plate is tilted, the spring forces the striker onwards onto the detonator, and Bingo."

"Where's this striker you were talking about, and the bit of wire?" the curious Inspector asked, "I cannot see them."

"They are usually found at the top here" Jock pointed, "You can just see the top where that hole is, and the striker is just inside."

"Could it go off then?" asked his boss.

"Sir, I would rather face that chap on the bed again with his gun, he was a damn site safer than this thing," Jock said.

"Do you mean that the slightest movement could set it off?" The Inspector was worried. "If it went off, would it do any damage to the oil tank?"

"I think there's always a chance Guv, otherwise we could just yank it with a bit of string, but I think it's too close to take a chance." The boss was quick with making decisions.

"Right, we'll get the Bomb Squad out."

"I've done one of these before Guv. The chances of the new men in BDS having even seen one is remote, so I'll just do it myself. So I would like you to leave now Inspector, I won't be long." As Jock was speaking he lay down on the ground, settled in the mud and rested his arms to steady them. He waited until the Inspector was safely out of the way before he commenced the delicate operation.

He held the grenade about a foot in front of his face as he lay there, this position gave him full control of his arms and hands with elbows rested. He could also see quite clearly what he was doing and he could also ensure that the missile was held up straight and did not shake. He rubbed his hands on his overcoat to dry them, before gripping the bottom portion with his left hand, to force the base down into the earth. Then, grasping the top piece with his rough hand, he commenced the long slow job of concentrating on the unscrewing. Gently and slowly, a lot of pressure was needed to start the movement off, eventually he was at the point of decision, the top was just off but still held firmly. If the top was jerked, even now, the striker could still hit the detonator. Slowly he lifted the dangerous object upwards, then with a quick flick of his wrist he turned it. The plate stayed in a horizontal position and the spring forced the striker onwards causing the object to fly harmlessly into the ground. He breathed a sigh of relief, collected the parts together and walked across to where the crowd of men stood.

"It's OK Inspector," he said. "Right, jump in and I'll give you a run back to the Station" his boss told him. As they drove along, the Inspector asked what Jock had done with the grenade.

"Where is it now then?"

"In my pocket" Jock replied. "But don't worry Sir, it's in the other side. I am between you and that. It cannot go off."

The car reached the Station in record time due to the fact that the Inspector wanted to get rid of this madman and his lethal cargo as soon as possible. The local Bomb Disposal Unit were called and they removed the grenade; as Jock had forecast, none of the men had seen one of the Italian Grenades before.

RANKS

Recruits were coming into the job in a steady stream, more ex-Service men seeking their fortunes and hoping to reach the top positions. However, they were in for a surprise because of the Trenchard Scheme. In 1931, Lord Trenchard, Marshall of the RAF was made Commissioner of Police in place of Lord Byng of Vimy. He reorganised the Metropolitan Police by importing officers of varying ranks from the Armed Forces into key posts in the Police. To ensure a constant succession of such men, he encouraged University Graduates to join; he also introduced these men into the Civil Services Branch of the Secretariat at New Scotland Yard. These men attended a 15 month training course before going on the streets for 8 months as a PC and 4 months as a Sergeant. They were then promoted to Junior Station Inspectors. After the war they were all promoted quickly through the ranks and with their contacts in high places, a lot reached the rank of Chief Constable and similar positions. The basic idea was that only men of great integrity and high educational standards controlled the Police. Not that any of them would be any good as coppers, they were good at management and attending functions and parties. Quite a lot of them attained the aptitude to travel and attend Foreign Conferences to advise and discuss various methods.

As these men moved the ladder, the other ranks were changed to accommodate them. A lowly Sub-Divisional Inspector had to pips and one clerk to help him and he soon became a Superintendent with a Crown on his shoulder and two Chief Inspectors and a whole bevy of office staff to run the same station. These variations of ranks made no difference to the lowly PC, it was only the higher ranks which moved to command the new rookies who were coming in. The recruits came from all walks of life, apart from the Forces, and there was also a right mixture of personalities. Strangers came from Ireland, Wales and Scotland, they came from places as far apart as Aberdeen to Penzance and brogues and accents had to be translated. The men all rubbed shoulders together with one aim in life, to be a good copper. They concentrated on learning as much as they could about this bit city until they were all virtually walking encyclopaedias. There was one great fault, all of these chaps were subject to persecution mania, and Jock had already sampled this from the Sergeants and certain Inspectors.

One unfortunate rookie was soon classed as a nutter, he just ignored the Inspector's orders and the Sergeant's yells; he went his own sweet way and got up to some queer tricks. Apart from his reports looking like a kid's comic, he used to sit in the canteen for his meals and ignore everyone, and by the expressions on his face he was working problems out in his mind. On one occasion, he took his week's holiday but after the fifth day he was on parade at 5.45am. When the Section Sergeant had completed detailing the men onto their beats he automatically asked,

"Is there anyone I've missed?" He got a shock when a plaintiff voice said,

"Yes Sir, Sergeant, Me." After the perplexed skipper had checked the duty rota, without success, he said "according to this, you are on holiday."

"I was Sergeant but I got fed up, I had nothing to do at home." The Probationer explained. Despairingly, the Sergeant changed the beats round to fit the newcomer in, it was easier than trying to argue with him. He was detailed to two beats which ran alongside Jock's patch.

"Just my luck" he said, not that he minded taking the new lads out. Even though he was a probationer himself, he often had the job of taking the new lads around, this was to save the oldsters from complaining. The other PCs all grinned because they knew that the coppers on those beats walked to the end of the ground together, so Jock was well and truly lumbered with the nutter.

On the way to the box where his first ring was due, Jock tried to engage the chap in conversation without a great deal of success.

"Why don't you talk to anyone at the Station?" His outright question was answered at once. "For the simple reason, they cannot teach me anything, they're all ignorant. I would be wasting my time entering into any form of conversation with them," was the answer.

"Surely you would be able to learn something from them?"

"No, I know everything. Those ignorant peasants don't interest me." The lad was full of his own importance, really big-headed. The conversation was carried on in similar tones, interrupted only occasionally by some member of the public who required assistance. At long last they reached the box, Jock opened the door and went inside to make his ring.

"Have you got a ring to make?" he asked.

"No" the lad said as he followed Jock into the box. Jock telephoned the office and was just making the entry in the book when the door was flung open and standing there glowering at them, was the Patrolling Sergeant.

"What are you doing in here?"

"Talking to my friend" the lad said and promptly shut the door in the face of the Supervising Officer. Jock reached across and opened the door again promptly and pushed the miscreant.

"Out" he said. The Sergeant pushed past him and picked up the book, he noticed that Jock still held his pencil and his entry was only half completed.

"This sod is a nut case, I'm sure of it. Finish your entry and get on your beat, I'll attend to him." Thankfully, he completed this task and left the Sergeant wondering what to do with the other chap.

The following day the man was posted onto their shift, which was early days. He should have booked off at 2pm but he didn't show his face, as he was posted on the market area, he couldn't be far away from the office. As it was the whole of the late turn, relief were detailed to look for him. He was found rambling along the busy streets with a happy smile on his face as he twisted his fingers together, he was talking away to himself when he was stopped. He told the Sergeant that he didn't want to book off as he was quite content walking round the streets. There seemed to be no way that they could penetrate the Probationer's ego, or deflate him.

Till one night, the other PCs were getting a wee bit fed up with him and decided to play a prank on him just to see the reactions. As soon as they found out which beat he was on, the rest of the relief got cracking. Four of them made a point of meeting one another near the main road where he would be passing on the way to make his ring. The cyclist was going to let them know when the object of the exercise was approaching. Sure enough, he came ambling slowly along the road towards the rest of the men.

"Come on Smudge, hurry up." Smithy was ordered.

"Get it off." Smithy whipped his topcoat off and gave it to one of the others to hold, then he took his tunic off and turned it inside out. A rope was fastened around his chest and he put the tunic on again, the rope came out of the top beside his neck when it was buttoned up. The rookie could be seen walking towards them. Quickly Smithy climbed up one of the tall street lights, assisted with the rope which had been thrown over the crossbar. Once he reached the top, the rope was fastened to the base of the post, Smudger left his hold on the lamp and hung limply in the wind, head inclined to the side. The rest of the crowd made themselves scarce to a point where they could observe the results.

They didn't have long to wait for the object of their affections was rapidly closing the distance, before long he would be able to see the body hanging by the neck from a street lamp.

"Do you think he'll see him?" Charley asked. "

The bugger always walks along with his head down." Robbo answered in a whisper, "He is bound to see him, unless he's blind."

"I think he's just sleep walking," Taffy suggested.

"In all the years I've been in the job, I've never seen anything like this happen," replied Old Mac, the cyclist.

They all waited with baited breath as closer and closer the rookie approached, until at last he was underneath the hanging man. He glanced up and carried on walking.

"I don't believe it" Mac said. "He sees a bloke strung up from a lamp standard and ignores it." The probationer strolled a bit further along the road and then stopped. He seemed to be considering something, then eventually he turned back and stopped beside the lamp.

"Are you alright up there?" he called. Getting no reply, he walked in a circle around the post, as though trying to make up his mind why the chap was hanging around in the middle of the night. He suddenly decided that something was terribly wrong for he took to his heels and ran. He ran all the way back to the Station to describe the hanging to the Sergeant, the Supervising Officer was only half convinced, but had to send the car to investigate, just to be on the safe side. Naturally when the car arrived, the body had gone. Things got worse for this particular PC, he wasn't allowed to carry on as a Policeman but whether he was promoted or got the sack, none of the coppers ever found out.

He wasn't the only nutter at the Station because some of the chaps seemed to regard the job as one huge joke, as if they had joined for fun and games, a cops and robbers situation. Naturally, some of the PCs were prone to accidents as Jock soon found out. One particular copper was wending his way quietly back to the station for breakfast on one fine summer's night; as he passed under the railway bridge he was saturated with torrents of water as someone emptied all the fire buckets onto him from the railway station. Mad as hell and wet to the skin, he stalked to the Police Station. As it was a warm night all the windows of the canteen were open; sounds of frivolity and joyous laughter reached his ears, he was sure that his name was mentioned.

Without further ado, he took the hosepipe which was used for washing the cars, turned the water on and aimed the jet directly into the canteen. Come heaven and high water he was going to get his own back on the ones who had soaked him. Jock was sitting between the two windows at the time, with his back to the wall, and consequently he was the only dry one in the nick that night and there were a lot of soggy, uneaten sandwiches.

The same man wasn't above handing out a joke though, as he called it. Such as one winter's night when several inches of snow lay around, he climbed up onto the roof and dropped handfuls down a chimney which was belching out black smoke. It wasn't the Inspector who got it, but the foul smelling sooty water belched out into the communications room, everything and everyone was covered. They never caught him but his cycle, which he had left padlocked to the rails, was later found hanging over the Blue Light at the front of the nick. Whilst these things were going on, some chaps could get away with it but just let a Probationer step out of line, even being on the wrong side of the road meant he would be off his beat. To talk to another copper could be classed as being idle and gossiping, or failing to work the beat correctly.

A HOME

Up till now Jock had lived in the Police Section House, saving his pennies and looking for a place for himself to live in. With the wedding day arranged, he had applied for permission to get married just to be on the safe side. The police authorities had checked and vetted his wife and her family before they gave permission. Now he was living like a hermit, apart from going to work he spent all his spare time at the hostel. With the prospects of married life looming close he had began to search for the house in his spare time.

Early days, this shift made him feel despondent at the best of times but now he believed that the only people getting houses these days were the coloured gentry fresh from Jamaica. He had completed his day's work and search but before preparing for bed he went down to see the warden to arrange an early call for the following day.

"Hey Jock, are you still looking for a flat?" A PC from his Station came in the door, he had just taken four hours time off from his late turn shift.

"Yes I am" admitted Jock "but I don't think there's much hope."

"Didn't you see that one in the rough book today?"

"There wasn't anything in the roof book this morning about any houses," Jock stated.

"Well, there was one in this afternoon" the man told him. Jock asked the warden if he could use the telephone and got in touch with the communication room at his station.

"Is that place in the rough book still going?" "Well cross it out now, I want it. What's the address?" he said when told that the property was still shown and hadn't been crossed out. As soon as the address was given he went upstairs and got dressed, shortly afterwards he was running to catch a tram to take him to his destination.

The property lay about half a mile from his station, it was a house built in the early Victorian style. When first built, it had been used by a large family and set in a semi-rural residential area, however as the city slowly expanded the sprawling slums soon surrounded this estate, which was made up of similar type houses. The gentry left their homes and went further afield to live and the houses were left to decay or let to several families.

They became part of the city's slums. The average accommodation for each family was one complete floor, usually consisting of two rooms. It was one of these flats which was to become Jock's first home. The first floor flat was in a deplorable condition due to the fact that it had never been used since the original owners had left. The only surviving member of the family had kept the rooms for her visits to the city when she called to collect the rents. There were several pieces of antique furniture in both rooms, the lady declined to sell them for sentimental reasons but told Jock he could use them until he arranged to get some furniture of his own.

A Scottish lady lived on the top floor with her son, his wife and two children; the ground floor and basement flats were both occupied by elderly spinsters. Apparently there had been a long standing feud between the Scottish family and the old lady who lived on the ground floor so the landlady had decided to get a copper as tenant for the middle floor to try and keep the peace. This was how Jock managed to get the chance of a flat. Obviously there would have to be a lot of work done on the flat to make it habitable, plus the fact a cooker was needed and other bits and pieces.

Furniture, sheets and other linen were all rationed and only obtained with dockets. Naturally the linen had to be new, therefore the dockets were used, and the furniture had to be secondhand. As soon as things had been sorted out with the landlady Jock wrote to Puggle who insisted upon coming down to give him a hand with the work and to help sort the place out. Although Jock tried to persuade her to wait until the flat was clean and more like a home, she declined and started to pack her cases, after all it was to be her first home as well. She believed that they should work together through all the difficulties, so their married life began in earnest. The fact that she didn't have a cooker did not deter her, all the meals were properly prepared on time, the only form of cooking was a small two-ringed paraffin heater which rested on the floor. She managed that with the utmost dexterity for over a week until their own cooker arrived. They went into great detail about living expenses, the rent was taking a fifth of his wages so they were left with just over three pounds to pay for everything, light, heat and food. Clothes were out of the question, as was smoking or sweets etc. They worked the housekeeping money out to a fine art so that they could just afford to live.

The only thing that Jock insisted on was that he should purchase a small dog to keep her company whilst he was at work. It was five shillings well spent on a lovable bundle of cuddle, bought at the market. The 'Big City' was a lonely place and the hours that Jock had to be away from home were often long. It must have been purgatory for her waiting alone, not knowing when, or if, he would be coming home. Mrs. Mac, the lady on the top floor, was quite friendly and took Puggle under her wing but she couldn't be around all the time. Apart from her age and the invalid daughter she was looking after, they entertained quite a lot due to the fact that her son was on the stage and his friends visited a lot. Jock met quite a few well-known celebrities when they called at the house. One day the family upstairs were getting ready for a dinner party and, for some reason, the dinner was laid on the floor after it had been cooked and a lovely rabbit, which lay cooling on a plate, somehow disappeared. Judy, the pup, must have been off colour that day for she didn't want any dinner!

The pup did prove to be a Godsend for Puggle; she was often driven to distraction because of the worry when Jock was late home, especially with the troubles that prevailed in that area. One day, as they were walking through the market, she was struck by the fact that a huge coloured man always lifted his hat saying,

"Good Morning Sir, Good Morning Madam." Curious, she asked Jock who the man was and upon being told the identity of the man.

"Do you mean he is the one that is always assaulting the police?" she had heard of the mob.

"That's him" Jock admitted.

"The one who is always putting Coppers in hospital?" she asked.

"That's him."

"Then why does he always lift his hat and say 'Good Morning Sir and Good Morning Madam'?" she asked, "he seems a nice man."

'I'll have to see him about that' Jock thought, and later he did correct Pete and insisted that in future he must acknowledge the ladies first. He did.

CASH PROBLEMS

Money was always a constant problem. The fact that neither of them could afford any luxuries or Insurances was accepted but when their child was due they were charged for the hospital services, it took two weeks wages which they desperately needed.

"Your husband is a Policeman, you can afford to pay" Puggle was told. The National Health Act came into force later. The pram was also needed and a second-hand one cost another two weeks wages. Jock was in a corner financially and was compelled to ask for financial assistance from the Police Funds; this was eventually granted to pay those two bills but the loan had to be repaid at the rate of £1 per week. So it was a case of clothe and feed a baby, feed themselves, pay for gas and electricity and the gas cooker, all out of less than £3 (three pounds).

It was two years later that Jock bought a second-hand jacket from the market for one pound, he always used his police trousers for wearing when he was off duty, just the same as the rest of the coppers. It was a hard cruel world but they were happy together, even though all their friends and relations were hundreds of miles away. The Big City is a lonely place at the best of times and a copper is a lonely man because of his profession but it must have been hell for the wives sitting at home waiting for the husbands to return.

As money was a vital factor in their existence, it was quite apparent that something had to be done to supplement their income. Jock spoke to the owner of a local factory about the financial problems raging at the time and the man was good enough to realise that the coppers pay was not a fortune. He suggested to Jock that if at any time he could help he just had to ask and if it was possible he would assist. Not many people in this world like that, Jock contemplated the suggestion and appreciated the offer.

"If your wife wouldn't mind doing a small job, I think we could fit her in with some outside work. It wouldn't be a lot but at least it would help you out." The owner of the business considered the state of the country when the police force were so underpaid that the coppers and their families were nearly on the bread line.

"I have a few ladies who sew buttons on cards for me, the pay varies with the type and size of buttons. I try to save the big buttons for the elderly who have bad eyesight. So if your wife is interested let me know."

Jock mentioned the fact to Puggle upon his return home.

"The pay wouldn't be a lot but I can help you with the work when I'm at home." So it was arranged and he called at the factory to get the instructions and the materials. Five large boxes of buttons just like shirt buttons, a couple of cartons of cards and spools of thread. When Jock finished work he used to sit with Puggle, doing the buttons, and chatting together. They had no wireless at that time and hadn't been able to afford one; Television was still in its infancy. Jock and Puggle were one of the numerous families who had yet to experience the pleasure of TV so they had no option but to while away the long hours with conversation. Jock's fingers were like huge puddings when it came to threading the needle and sew the small objects on the cards, the point of the needle usually found it's way into his fingers as he valiantly strove to keep up with his wife. There had to be one dozen buttons sewn onto each card; 12 cards were then fastened together with elastic bands and placed in one of the boxes supplied. Each box contained 12 gross of buttons, all neatly sewn onto cards. To manage this took hours of work, the payment for each 12 gross was five shillings. Between them they managed to complete the full quota of five boxes which had been allotted to them. For their labours they were paid the full amount of twenty-five shillings; it used to take all their spare time and every day was a working day, but it was well worth while. It required two very large suitcases to carry the week's work to the factory about two miles walk away.

With this huge supplement to their income it was decided that some form of transport would be handy. Apart from carrying the cases, they could probably get away from the city for an outing. It was decided that they should buy a second-hand motorcycle and sidecar, which could be obtained for only twenty pounds and this was purchased for only £1 a week. The remaining five shillings paid for the running costs. When the bike had been paid for they were experts at placing buttons cards and even managed to get some extra work. After five months, their transport had been paid for and had even enjoyed several trips to the country and the coast. With the cash coming in from the spare time job they decided to splash out and use their extra income and bought a television; a real 17" black and white telly, such luxury. That's the way life is, if you want anything you have to work for it, that is if it is to be obtained honestly.

DIRTY DICK

Flat changing had become a regular thing, Jock had always been on the lookout for a bigger and better place for his family to live in; he had found several flats, each better than the other, until he had a whole house with a large garden. The family were quite happy in this place and he was content to stay there. However, the landlady had other ideas, the lady was a Jewess and had a business like head; she bought old properties, let them out, then offered these houses to her tenants. They paid weekly, all done official through the Solicitors and Jock was offered the house at market value.

"You can pay weekly, I'll sign your rent book for you, that way you can get rent allowance which will pay for the house. The attics can be let out and the cash you get from that will pay your rates, with some left over."

Real business-like. Her capital was in property, guaranteed weekly return and as she wasn't the owner, she wouldn't be liable for the rates and the upkeep.

"I'll think it over," Jock said. It was very tempting, his family would at last have a decent home and they would be able to afford it. He decided to do a bit of checking first before committing himself. A call at the local Council offices soon disclosed the fact that all the houses in that street were scheduled to be demolished over various periods of time; the property was to be pulled down to make way for a new school and playing fields.

"I wouldn't touch it if I were you," the man at the Council advised. Jock took his advice and called at the landlady's house to put her in the picture.

"Good God. I didn't know that. It's the first time I've heard of this. I'll have to sell the house."

"Sorry, but I couldn't afford to take the chance. I don't want it," Jock told her.

The landlady wanted to get rid of the house as soon as possible and put pressure on Jock to get out as quickly as he could. She could get more for the place if it was empty, so Jock had to apply for Police accommodation. His Application was considered and processed and eventually, much to the gratification of the Jewess, he was offered a small cottage attached to a Police Station, over the stables. All the bedrooms except one were over the stables themselves, with concrete floors. The sitting cum dining room was at the rear and looked out onto a high wall with the main railway line running along the top. At the side of the house was a school, with the inevitable banging of balls, whilst on the other were the piggeries with it's smell and swarms of flies. This was owned and run by PCs and Sergeants who had worked them right through the war years. When Jock arrived he was offered a share in them, this was to prevent him complaining about the smell and the flies. £50 was asked but this was well outside of his capabilities. They had to contend with the receipt of the occasional leg of pork which, of course, was bribery. The kitchen was the only room with an outlook, it faced the station yard; all activities could be seen, washing cars, grooming horses, or bringing in stray dogs. Above all, the movement of coppers was the most interesting. One man, a Sergeant, was a regular visitor and soon acquired the nickname of Dirty Dick. He had another piggery close by the station and every day he would turn up in uniform and go down into the basement to get changed into his working clothes which were a raggy old pair of overalls. Once he was dressed for his labours he collected a handcart from the piggery then went around the shops collecting swill for his pigs. Apparently this had gone on right through the war years as well. Once the pigs had received their fill, he returned to the station and, after a quick change, he was back on the streets chasing the young coppers. His nickname came from his association with the pigs and the fact that he never wore socks or underwear.

PERKS

"Excuse me Officer." A young woman stopped Jock as he walked through the market. It was Saturday and he was posted late turn and had not been right round the area yet.

"I was trying to get past that greengrocers shop on the main road but the pavement is completely blocked. I had to push my pram into the middle of the road to get past their lorry and was nearly hit by a bus. I think it's disgusting." Jock knew the shop she was referring to and promised to look into the matter for her.

The pavement was only about three feet wide at this point; the owner of the shop which had an open front had placed boxes outside on the pavement and this reduced the space by half. As soon as his customers started to queue, the pavement was blocked. This man had parked his lorry outside the shop; on the lorry, he kept all his stock for replenishing his counters. Pedestrians just could not get past this blockage, they were compelled to face the traffic to go their way. The traffic also had problems with this man's lorry; it reduced the width of the roadway by half and as there was a tremendous amount of traffic in that road it could only pass this point with difficulty. Jock had several words of advice for the owner of the shop and the driver of the lorry before he reported them for various offences. That put the cat amongst the pigeons; from tea time until he booked off duty, he was badgered by various Sergeants and old coppers about his actions. They all told him he was banging his head against a brick wall and advised to forget all about a summons. At 10pm when he booked off duty, the boss was waiting to see him - he had him in the middle of the Station yard where they could not be overhead - as the old man bared his heart. He pleaded, cajoled and threatened Jock about his report.

"They were very good to us during the war years," he said.

"I wasn't in this country during the war Sir, you had all the perks here, I don't owe them anything."

"We were never allowed to go without, it's the least we can do for them. Let's forget about the trouble," the Inspector said.

"Sir," Jock answered. "That place is on my beat and there are offences being committed and complaints being made about this man. If there are any offences being committed when I go past, then I will report the people concerned."

So the answer was obvious - he was taken off that beat and never allowed to patrol it again. The following day, as he headed for his new beat he saw the boss coming from the back entrance of the same shop carrying several bags of fruit and vegetables. Jock couldn't resist the temptation to pass comment about shopping on Sundays as he passed. A sheepish smile was all the boss could muster in reply.

Jock continued his stroll in the Winter sunshine, only three beats to work. He noticed a crowd had gathered near a large junction, not far from where he lived 'another accident' he thought as he made his way to the scene of interest. A rope had been placed around a building site and he noticed a small van which brought back memories. Red wings and white letters 'BDS' He saw a group of swaddies close to the vehicle with all their gear.

"What have you got?" he enquired.

The soldiers glanced at him without interest, 'Another bloody Nosey Parker'. One of them decided to answer,

"Just a bomb."

"Any problems?" Jock enquired.

"None for us, bonny lad, all the worries are his." A Sergeant indicated a lonely young Lieutenant who was crouched in the middle of the site. Jock decided to go across to speak to the officer and just out of interest, to have a look at the bomb.

"Shouldn't go over there lad. It's a dangerous," a voice followed him.

"Good morning, Lieutenant, I hear you have problems." Jock spoke to the young officer as he gazed at the metal case in front of him. The startled man looked up from the 500 pound bomb that he had been meditating upon.

"You shouldn't be here, this is a bomb" he said.

"I know, I used to work with them" Jock explained.

"Did you really. When?"

"Right through the war." He strolled over to the excavation and looked at the black metal case which had been unearthed by workmen. "Hmm. No. 11 and a 35" he murmured.

"You certainly do know about them then. That's the problem, I haven't dealt with those two fuses together," the Officer stated.

"No problem Lieutenant. I'll give you a hand," Jock volunteered.

"Should you, won't you get into trouble?" the young chap asked.

"We can sort that problem out afterwards. There used to be a saying in my old mob - 'If you bugger it up then nobody can bollock you'." Jock brought back memories. "Now, first things first, we'll do this." The Army Officer was in a proper state; he mentally considered all rules and regulations, none of them said anything about a civvy helping.

"I'm not so sure that we should."

"Lieutenant. If you have never dealt with these two fuses before, it means a long wait till someone else arrives. It will be possible that they have never handled them, so don't waste time. Have you got all the necessary gear. Clamps, drills, magnet, extractor, a length of stiff wire, and a steel rule?"

"We have all the stuff, except the wire and a rule," the man told him.

"Right, let's go and see what we can dig up," Jock suggested. Together they returned to the squad of soldiers who had been watching with curiosity. As the officers ordered the gear to be prepared Jock went across to the local shops and borrowed the tape measure and also managed to scrounge a length of wire.

"Right Lieutenant, I've managed to get the stuff we want, let's go" he said as he
returned to the group of soldiers

He nodded greetings towards the soldiers and proceeded to remove his overcoat so that his movements wouldn't be hampered. A gasp came from one of them and he nudged his mud-splattered colleague, who had also noticed the rows of medals on Jock's tunic. The eldest of the soldiers had recognised some of the various ribbons on Jock's chest and he looked at him with great respect. The two men walked over to the bomb and Jock sat, legs astride, over the case and began to get the tape measure out.

"Right, this is what we have to do." He then went into detail for the interested Officer about the attempts they were about to make. So the operation commenced. Patiently drilling after the correct position had been re-checked.

"We have to drill exactly nine inches down the edge of the fuse pocket of the number 11. We must break into the pocket but not touch the fuse itself. It must also penetrate the bottom tube which contains the two wires where they lead to the policeman fuse, without breaking them or making any disturbance - otherwise we've had it," said Jock.

"We have an automatic drill now, we just attach it to the case and then operate it by remote control." The Officer put Jock's mind at rest over the drilling operations.

"Marvellous. What will they think of next? They'll be bringing out a robot next to do the work for us" laughed Jock. "Talking of automation, let's get the 'Q' coil fitted then we can put the drill on." Between them they hoisted the heavy coil into position and fastened it into place.

"Switch on" the Officer shouted, and the electric magnet was thrown into action at once.

"Let's put the other sod out of action now," Jock suggested as he placed the required apparatus on the other fuse so that the electricity would be drawn from it's batteries. The drill was then clamped onto the bomb and the position of the drill was re-checked.

"Well, let's try our luck. I think we are ready to drill," Jock said. Together both men returned to the safety point and the drill was set in motion. No words were spoken and everyone held their breath as the sharp bit penetrated the metal case. The actual operation didn't take very long and the army officer eventually.

"Well, I think we should see whether your measurements were correct Officer." Nine inches had been drilled and no explosion.

"Right, shall we go and have a look then?" asked Jock.

The two Bomb Disposal Officers, young and old, returned to their task with the common enemy. Together they examined the hole made by the drill; the cut was clean, exactly one-eighth of an inch, had been removed from the edge of the fuse pocket. At the bottom, they could see quite clearly the two wires which had been exposed, leading to the other fuse. Jock once again explained the situation to the army man.

"When you have these two fuse numbers, you must deal first with the 35, but if you withdraw it you could break the contact by breaking these two wires. So leave that in after it has been made inert, as we have done. We then keep the circuit in contact with this piece of wire, ensure that it's in contact at all times. Short them out by making a spring loop in the wire, like this, push it down here." He pushed the wire down the newly drilled hole towards the exposed wires.

"Push the wire past the top one and under the other, hook it up - like this - and hook it into position. Fold the wire over the top of the fuse as it is being withdrawn, this ensures that it will remain in contact all the time until we need it."

The contact was made, the demagnetiser had worked it's time out on the other fuse, so Jock placed the extractor on it.

"Now for the moment of truth" he said as he slowly withdrew the fuse from its pocket. Once the dangerous object had been removed he placed it to one side.

"Right Lieutenant, if you haven't done one before, now is your chance." The youngster was quite game to have a go. "Unscrew the locking nut, extractor on, OK? Now, lift, slowly, keeping the wire over the top of the fuse. Let the wire slide through the cut that was made in the side of the fuse pocket. That's right, hold it firm and never slacken off. You are doing fine, it's coming nicely, another couple of inches. When it is clear, keep the wire in position, till the fuse is well away from the bomb - just in case there are any grains of picric sticking on the bottom. Fine, that's nice and it is clean, you have done it, Congratulations Lieutenant."

The bomb was safe and Jock walked back with the officer towards the mob who had been watching this most unusual operation with some considerable concern. Who had ever heard of a copper helping to disarm a bomb. The Sergeant was waiting anxiously.

"A copper sitting on a booby trapped bomb and making it safe. Who would ever believe him, it's not natural." He watched as Jock slipped his overcoat on.

"It's alright Serg. He's one of us," the Lieutenant told him.

"One of us?" the Sergeant muttered. He was perplexed.

"He's a copper."

"Well he used to be in the mob," the officer explained.

"Oh!" The penny dropped. "What company?" The rest of the Sappers were all listening to this conversation and when Jock told the Sergeant which company he'd been in, he said,

"They had a 4,000 pounder up there didn't they, a Captain MacGregor did it - I hear it was a dodgy one."

"Yes, that's right and it was a bit awkward," Jock admitted as he recalled the time he had nearly died.

"Did you know Captain MacGregor then?" the officer asked.

Jock smiled, "Yes, all my life."

The Sergeant gaped, "Do you mean that you are ... Sorry Sir, I thought you were just a nosey parker ... Are you really him?"

"Yes Sergeant and you were right on both counts, I was just a nosey parker for after all, this had nothing to do with me."

"Would you like a cuppa Guv?" one of the soldiers asked. Jock was just going to accept the offer when a voice boomed out.

"What are you doing? You are off your beat. Report back to the Inspector at the office." It was the Section Sergeant who stood glowering at him.

"Righto, Sergeant," Jock answered as the Sergeant walked away.

"Bloody little Hitler. Who the hell does he think he is, talking to you like that?" asked the Lieutenant as the Sergeant walked away.

"He is my Section Sergeant, times change you know," Jock answered as he prepared to leave.

"Will you get into trouble?" The man was worried.

"More than likely but I'm getting used to it now," Jock told him. "Now I must go. Good luck." He shook hands with the officer and headed back to the Station for another session with the Sub-Division Inspector.

On the carpet, Jock stood to attention before the Inspector. The Sergeant had reported him and the list of complaints were being read out - they had been written down quickly and the forms lay on the desk in front of the boss. The Sergeant had gone to town and had thrown the book at Jock; off his beat, failing to work his beat correctly, idle and gossiping and boots covered with mud. In simple words, he was a proper scruff. The list of charges was read out.

"These are serious offences, have you anything to say?" asked the senior officer. As he did not get any reply from Jock he continued.

"The Sergeant reminds me that this is not the first time he has had occasion to talk to you about your work - is that correct?"

"Yes Sir," Jock had to admit this, as he had been chased and spoken to by the Sergeant on numerous occasions for some piddling little thing.

"Well, I'm afraid we'll have to do something about this, you could be finished in the job, you realise this? You are still on probation you know."

A knock at the door interrupted them and in walked the young Army Officer.

"Sorry, I hope I haven't disturbed you but we have another job we have to go to Inspector. I didn't want to leave without saying goodbye to Captain MacGregor here for all his help, advice and assistance with this very difficult job that we had to do." He looked towards Jock and smiled. The Inspector sat in a daze, trying to look intelligent and take all this in. He hadn't the faintest idea what was going on. He looked at the Sergeant for assistance, the Sergeant said,

"We had an unexploded bomb Sir and we had to call the Bomb Disposal out."

"Yes Inspector, that's right. As you know, we had this 500 pound bomb to deal with - the fuses were of a type that I had no working knowledge of. It was Captain MacGregor here who defused it. It had an anti-handling device attached - that is a booby trap. Now, thanks to him, I know how to deal with any more that I may come across and I will be able to handle the situation. My Sergeant and men also asked me to pass their best wishes to him. They were very pleased to meet him after all that they had heard about his work in the past. I am sure that you must be very pleased to have such a brave and capable man in your force."

The Inspector sat, with his mouth open, as he listened to the glowing praise for the man who stood in front of him and who was actually in danger of getting the sack. The army officer turned to Jock and held out his hand.

"Goodbye Sir, and thank you for your assistance and good luck to you in your new career." As he shook hands he gave a sly wink before he left the room.

'Crafty young bugger' thought Jock. 'He knew I was in trouble and he has done this to get me off the hook'. When the door closed behind his newfound friend, he realised that the Sergeant and the Inspector were looking at him with curious expressions on their faces.

"Is that correct what he said, did you actually take the fuse out of that bomb?" the boss asked.

"That's right Sir. It was booby-trapped with an unusual type of fuse - there was a good chance it would have exploded. The Officer had not dealt with this combination before and I had, so it was only common sense that I should assist."

"But it's not a copper's job" the Sergeant said.

"Protection of life and property is, I believe, a part of a copper's job Serg. At least that is what I was taught at training school," Jock answered. "I was only trying to help."

The Sub-Divisional Inspector was trying to assess this young copper; he looked at his file which he seemed to know by heart these days. There were plenty of arrests for crime and numerous summonses. He has done his work well and was high up in marks for examinations; he had passed the exams for promotion as well. The praise from the Army Officer was good enough for him but somehow he always seemed to fall into trouble with the Section Sergeant and the Inspector on his shift. Finally, he made his decision.

"Right, MacGregor, you can go and get yourself cleaned up but you'll have to smarten your ideas up. Stay on your own beat in future. Now go and get some work done." He had to say something to satisfy the Sergeant but Jock was sure there was a twinkle in his eyes.

"Right, Sir. Thank you." Jock saluted and left the office.

HEAVY LIFTING GEAR

Whenever an event occurred that required extra police, the old timers were never given these jobs and Jock was always amongst the ones chosen, regardless of which shift he was on at the time. Town jobs such as funerals, weddings, Trooping the Colour, Lord Mayor's Show, Rehearsals and political meetings. On all of these jobs, except the political meetings, one had to wear the old fashioned heavy ceremonial dress tunic, with all medals polished. These coats were really hot in summer, the only consolation was that with having them buttoned up to the neck a copper could get away with only a vest underneath. Nearly all of these details required a very early start, usually between three thirty and four o'clock in the morning the men would arrive at their Stations for parade and inspection. They would then be transported to the desired location where they would be inspected again and detailed to their exact positions. They were always in place before the crowds and the army arrived to line the routes. On some occasions the coppers returned to their stations before the eight hours were up and if they had any overtime due, the lucky ones could take time off and go home. If however there was no overtime due, the unlucky policeman was detailed to walk the streets for the remainder of his tour of duty, dressed in the ceremonial dress with all their medals, they would be posted onto the market area more often than not. The sight used to give the barrow boys a good laugh, even if the sweating coppers didn't see the joke.

Other occasions that required extra police were the usual political meeting or demonstration, with the inevitable fighting which arose afterwards; actually these fights were more like blood-curdling riots. There was one demonstration when all the men who were detailed to attend were issued with a sheaf of papers showing exactly what was happening and where every copper was posted. This was most unusual as the general thing was to get down town where they were posted. A separate list of names was also attached, denoting those posted onto special duties and Jock's name was amongst these. The type of duty was not specified but, according to the papers, he and another eleven lucky men would be just sitting in a bus whilst everyone else was working. The dossier was fairly comprehensive but nobody could fathom out what the special duty was. Till the day came the lucky dozen sat and smoked, watching all the other chaps lining the streets, one line along the pavement and another along the centre of the road. A long line of protesters came along with their usual escort of coppers, they were marched between the two lines of PCs lining the route but were halted by a solid block of blue uniforms. Upon reaching this obstruction they all sat down in the roadway. No noise, shouting, fights or disturbances but they refused to move when the Riot Act was read out to them by a very senior copper.

The call was sent out for the heavy lifting gear, then Jock and his friends soon found out what their cushy job was. They were turned out of the bus and marched along the sitting crowds to the front of the line. They were the labourers and their job was to shift the pile of human flesh that sprawled across the roadway.

"Move them. They are all under arrest," the Senior Officer stated. This was the first peaceful sit down demonstration - the ladies had not learnt that trousers should be worn. Buses and coaches drove alongside the line of squatters and stopped at the head of the queue. The heavy lifting gear then began to sweat and strain, filling the transport vehicles. The bodies were lifted and placed in the first truck and when it was full a copper stood on the running board, it would be his job to delivery the forty bodies to one of the many special stations and ensure that they were charged. At these stations, several Inspectors and Sergeants sat in a line doing all the necessary paperwork; each coach load that arrived was placed in front of one of the charging officers. It was to be expected however that whilst the charge sheets were being typed out, the prisoners all sat down again, this time in the station yard. Some of them tended to play 'silly buggers' and refused to move up to the tables; one enterprising young Sergeant decided that the best way to move them was to turn the water taps on. He did this and water flowed down the yard and a lot of wet bottoms was the result, apart from moving the squatters he also lost his stripes at a later hearing.

In the meanwhile, the sweating slaves were slowly picking their way through the pile of bodies and filling another bus or lorry. It had been found, by trial and error, that the best way to pick the creatures off the road was to bend down behind them, place the arms round the front of the squatter, clasp the hands and then straighten up. The squatter's knees were pressed against their chests and their backs were pressed against the copper's chest, it was easy for the lifter and a pleasure for the onlookers who all got a thrill at the sight of bare bottoms or stocking tops (tights were not worn in those days).

Eventually, the line of vehicles ended and Jock and his mates were ready for their well-earned break, but they were out of luck. Surrounded by bowler-hatted types and crowds of senior officers who had watched the proceedings with blank expressions on their faces, they stretched their aching limbs and wiped the sweat from the red gleaming features, enjoying the brief relief.

"Right, shift those people off the road. Put them onto the grass verge." A Chief Superintendent shouted - apparently he did not want to miss his lunch.

So it began once more, bend, lift, walk, bend and release, walk back for another load. The trouble was, as soon as the person was dropped onto the grass at the side of the road, they got up and walked back to where they had been previously. The Senior Officers could not see that the coppers were wasting their time but insisted that the heavy lifting gear keep on the move till the coaches returned. Eventually their labours ceased, worn out and weary they had cleared the obstruction and as the Senior Officers all went back to their offices, patting each other on the back and saying 'what a good job we did'. Jock and his mates made their own individual ways back to the home stations, to be met by the Station Sergeants with the old familiar saying,

"All these cushy town jobs. It'll do you good to get some work done." Then the inevitable posting onto the beat would come, until the eight hours were up.

CHAPTER THREE

HOME BEAT

HOME BEAT

Life has its problems and everyone suffers from them at some time or other; whether they are financial, social or health. Jock suddenly found himself facing difficulties when Puggle became seriously ill; she was taken to hospital and her condition was such that she had to remain there for several weeks. The home had to be run and the youngsters looked after till she came out. He took his holidays but it became obvious that he would have to make other arrangements also. He managed to get the elderly lady upstairs to help until Puggle came out. However, the Hospital Authorities refused to discharge her unless she had a home help. Jock knew that he could not afford a home help, who would not be available at all times, so he approached the Sub-Divisional Inspector and explained the situation. His boss told him in no uncertain terms that he could not afford a home help on his wages. After some discussion he eventually asked

"Do you have a pedal cycle?" Jock wondered what a pushbike had to do with his quandary but agreed that he did possess an old one.

"I'm not an authorised cyclist though," he said.

"Not to worry about that, I'll put your name on the list. Now, can you manage to look after the youngsters and your wife without any assistance?"

Jock agreed that he could do the washing, cleaning and cooking but was not able to be there all the while.

"OK lad, I'll tell you what we'll do. I'll post you onto the beat where you live; you can then check your property on your bike when you start and again before you book off. As long as the property has been checked and is alright, you can spend the rest of the time looking after the family. Would that suit you?"

"It would be the answer to all my problems Sir, Jock answered, but I wouldn't want to take the Mickey; if I could drop in occasionally that would be OK."

"You do as I have told you, the beat will still be there when you have gone. You just look after your family. Let me know how things are going each week. If you don't see me, you can let my clerk know when you come for your pay."

"Thanks very much Sir," Jock was indeed grateful.

"Nonsense lad. You have shown me you are not afraid to work, you have done more work than any of the other chaps. It's the least I can do for you. So, good luck, and I hope everything turns out satisfactory."

"Thanks again Gu,v" Jock said as he left the office. It was a load off his mind.

The duty sheet was altered and his name was placed in the required place, so it looked as though his troubles were indeed over. However, the very next day he was reminded that the Sergeant and the two Inspectors lurked in the background, they never relented on their chasing of the Probationers. They were constantly looking for trouble.

He was posted onto a local function, along with another young copper. Their job was to stand at the door of the Town Hall and look pretty for all the various Mayors who were attending for a banquet.

"Relieve one another for your refreshments" was the last order from the Sergeant when he visited them at their post. After he had gone, the pair of them began to negotiate for their meal break.

"If you don't mind Bob, I would like to go first. My wife was expecting me to call in. I'll see that everything is OK then I'll come back and let you get away; I won't bother about any grub." As his mate agreed to this arrangement, Jock left him. He walked down to the Nick and collected his cycle and rode home to put Puggle's mind at rest and to see that all was in order. He told her that he had been lumbered on the Town Hall job but not to worry.

"I'm going straight back up there, I'll see you when it's finished." Just then a loud banging at the front door attracted their attention. When Jock looked out he saw the Section Sergeant standing there.

"It's alright, it's only the Sergeant. I'll see you later." Jock wasn't worried, after all he had permission from the boss.

"What are you doing here?" The man was beside himself with glee, after all he had just caught this Scots get at last. Without waiting for an explanation, he ordered Jock to return to the Station and to report to the Inspector.

"And leave that cycle. You are not an authorised cyclist."

The Inspector was waiting with the Sergeant when Jock eventually walked into the office. The pair of them were obviously overjoyed at this chance to sort him out; there was no way he could wriggle out of this - after all the Sergeant had actually caught him at home. Jock received a brief tirade of abuse from them both before he was taken before the boss; the old man looked sadly at the scene in front of him. 'What had the lad been up to now'? It seemed to be getting a regular thing having him standing on the carpet with the Inspector and the Sergeant reporting him. He looked at the expressions on the faces of the supervising officers and then back to Jock, who was gazing quietly at a point over his head.

"Alright, what's wrong this time?" he asked.

The Inspector started by giving the relevant details and then left it to the Sergeant to complete his statement with all the facts. Jock saw the worried expression change on the Sub-Divisional Inspector's face. The worried look seemed to disappear and a look of pleasure took its place.

"Is that all?" he said. "I gave this man permission to go home whenever he pleased, to see that his family were alright. I also posted him onto the beat, with strict instructions that he was not to be taken off it for any reason. I also placed his name on the list of authorised cyclists myself so that he could check his beat quicker. Under the circumstances, I cannot see that he has done anything wrong."

The Sergeant explained that he was totally ignorant of these orders. The old man turned to Jock and asked if he had informed the Sergeant and the Inspector of the arrangements.

"I tried to Sir, but I couldn't get a word in. I was told I could do all my explaining to you."

"Right lad, off you go, we don't need you any more just now." The SD Inspector dismissed him but requested the other two men to remain behind.

Jock left the office and went home to put Puggle's mind at rest; from then on he carried on working his beat and only calling at the Station once a week - to collect his wages and to report to the old man.

EXTRA WORK

Through the numerous actors and actresses with whom Jock had become acquainted, he got to know a man who ran a boarding house for stage people. He asked Jock if he could help him by doing a few odd jobs around the place.

"I'm useless with my hands and I want so much done."

Jock agreed to help him out with the work. It started with the garden and once that had been sorted out the owner asked him to build some huts around the perimeter to house hens and rabbits. A new tap was then fitted into an outside toilet to attach a hosepipe to. Joinery, painting and decorating was followed by electrical work, and more plumbing followed. The owner was quite satisfied with the results.

"I have a problem in the kitchen" he said one day. "They cannot reach the cooker." He indicated his new quests. These people were all small folk, midgets as some people called them. They were of all heights, the smallest of them could not even see the top of the cooker and as all tenants had to do their own meals, they were in trouble. Jock quickly solved the problem by making a unit which consisted of steps set at various heights. As the unit was moved along, the little men and women could set it at the position which suited them to do their cooking. When all these jobs had been done, each week Jock was paid a Ten Dollar note by the owner who said,

"My parents live in America and have plenty of cash; they send me an allowance every week. I make plenty out of this place so this is the least I can do for the help you have given me." The money came in very handy for helping out the family budget.

Sometimes long hours were caused by incidents not related to his part-time work. Occasionally, a normal tour of duty could be twelve hours a day - caused by rail strikes, football matches or even prison riots. They did not get paid for the extra hours worked, these hours went into the Time Off Card which meant that they could take the overtime off at a later date, provided that it suited the Force.

INSTANT JUSTICE

It was during one of his twelve-hour shifts - Jock had just been relieved on the picket line and was on his way back to the Station for his meal. As he cycled along the typical back street of the slum area he saw that the residents were all out in their usual positions, sitting on the steps that led up to the front door of the tenements. As he rode along he noticed three youngsters, all on one cycle. There was one on the crossbar doing the steering, another sat on the saddle trying to pedal whilst the third lad sat on his shoulders. As the bike wobbled and weaved along the road the one on the top was enjoying himself, waving madly towards the people sitting on the steps. The onlookers were all waving and shouting at the trio, who thought the locals were congratulating them on their achievement; they didn't know that the adults were only trying to warn them that a copper was right behind them. The lad on the top suddenly glanced behind and saw Jock and in his hurry to get down, he brought the whole circus act down with him into a heap. They sat in an ungainly pile around the bike as Jock approached.

"Are you alright?" Jock asked them. "Have you hurt yourselves?" The urchins looked at the figure in blue.

"No, we aren't hurt Guv."

"Right then, what do you want. Do you want to go to Court, or do you want your backsides kicked?" Jock tried to look grim.

A quick discussion with the tousled heads together then, in unison, they answered "We'll have our arses kicked Guv."

"OK stand in the gutter and bend over to touch the pavement," he instructed them. He stood his own cycle against the kerbstone and proceeded to untie his cape from the handlebars. The watching crowds had grown quiet - not a sound was heard in that small back street as the locals watched. Everyone was curious and full of expectancy, the rumps of the offenders faced the heavens as they waited patiently for their punishment. Jock dispensed justice quickly, with a good hard smack across the buttocks of each one with his cape.

"Right Guv. Thanks very much Guv." Three grins on three cheeky faces, as they lay on the pavement.

"Just be careful in future. You can get yourself killed messing around on your bike like that." Jock told them as he fastened his cape back onto the handlebars. The crowds were all laughing - this was the life they lived and knew. Instant punishment.

As Jock rode away a man stepped out in front of him.

"Just a minute Guv," he said "one of them kids was mine."

"Yes."

"Well, I want to shake your hand. I know you could have taken him to Court but you are a man after me own heart. I'll kill the little bleeder when I get me hands on him."

"Why?" Jock asked him. "He's been punished already. It wouldn't be fair to punish him twice."

"OK Guv - if you say so - and thanks again."

SENIOR OFFICERS

As Jock found out during his service, Sergeants and Inspectors were made up of various qualities but, in general, although they were quick to chase the young coppers, they were always on their best behaviour whenever a person with higher rank than themselves appeared. One of the best jobs during the rail strike was to be posted to a large junction where a police box stood. The man on this duty just sat in the box and flicked a switch to stop or start the traffic. With a twelve-hour shift to do, everyone found this was a cushy job. Although at rush hours the roads were packed, all the copper on duty could do was to give each road a few minutes running - this way the traffic did keep moving. It was easy to read a book, read one page and then change the lights and allow the cars to crawl another few hundred yards.

Occasionally, a Sergeant came along to watch the cars moving and to see that the copper hadn't gone to sleep. One such Sergeant who stood on the corner watching the desperate cursing drivers crash their gears as they prepared to move another few yards, was never too particular in his own appearance. He always wore the flat cap which were only worn by drivers and Inspectors; the headgear was old and crumpled, dirty and covered with grease stains. His uniform jacket was not much different and it was obvious that his trousers had never been pressed and, instead of the official boots, he wore soft black shoes. He stood at his favourite corner beside the traffic lights and observed the movement of the traffic; in this position he was in an ideal location to observe the legs of the female occupants of the cars. One day though he was out of luck - a car pulled alongside and was halted by the red light, the passenger sitting in the back of the great black limousine examined the Sergeant and was not too pleased with what he saw. It was rather unfortunate for the Skipper that this was a very senior officer on his way to work and, in particular, this man cast terror into the hearts of all his subordinate officers. He was so impressed that upon reaching his office, he made a telephone call and arranged for the Sergeant to be on duty at the same place and time every day for a month. His instructions were that he would be properly dressed as per regulations so that the senior officer could inspect him.

Whenever this boss visited the Stations in his area, it was a case of panic for all concerned. He went through the books with a small toothed comb - if there were any faults he would find them and woe betide the person responsible. His eyes were always on the go as he travelled the patch and one day he saw a young probationer going into a motorcycle shop. The car was stopped and the boss followed the youngster into the premises. He demanded to know what the lad was doing in the shop. Young Taffy looked at this well dressed civilian.

"That's my business Sir," he said,

He had no idea that he should be on bended knees, or shaking in his shoes before this great man. The officer told him who he was but that did not help any for the Welshman was not long out of training school and he had been instructed that all High Ranking Officers carried a Silver Token which showed their name and rank.

"I have never seen you before Sir. How do I know that you are what you say? Have you got your identification please."

Now, all coppers had to carry their Warrant Cards with them at all times, otherwise they were in trouble. The same order was in force regarding the Silver Token; the reason, of course, is to prevent any person passing themselves as coppers. The Lord was on Taffy's side that day because the great man was embarrassed. He had been caught without his official identity. Taffy told him that anyone could say they were policemen and that it was an offence to pose as one; he suggested that this well-spoken gentleman get lost, before he was arrested. The boss went quietly away, after noting the number on Taffy's shoulder.

Taffy booked in for refreshments at the same time as Jock; there was a deathly hush in the office. The Sergeants and Inspector stood stiffly to one side as the great man sat and signed the books - as one page was checked, the Inspector swiftly turned the page. As this robot like movement was disturbed by the entry of the two PCs, the chap looked up from his paper work.

"Hold on a minute Constable." At this order, Jock and Taffy stood still at the counter.

The officer arose from his seat at the desk and came over to them. He looked at Taffy and smiled.

"Remember - is this what you wanted me to produce?"

"Yes Sir, Sorry Sir!" Taffy nodded as the Silver Token was handed to him.

"Why should you be sorry? You were doing your job. As you say, anyone could pass themselves off as policemen. You did the right thing. I'm glad you didn't arrest me though, for both our sakes. Now have a good look at it, you too officer," he said to Jock "for I don't think you are likely to see another one under such circumstances. Now away you go and enjoy your breakfasts," and he returned to his pile of books.

ACCIDENT FOR A ROOKIE

One of the worst jobs to get lumbered with was a point; a junction which required the presence of a Policeman or two to direct traffic. On hot days the body oozed sweat from every pore, the moisture ran down from the tight leather band around the forehead. Every move became a great strain and the pressure on the bladder didn't help the agony; it was a recognised thing that a chap posted on an adjacent beat should take over a point occasionally so that the point duty man could relieve himself. More often than not the poor chap wouldn't see another copper until he was finished work. The old-timers had it worked out to a fine art in avoiding the junctions.

However, traffic lights were becoming a craze and slowly the area was getting covered with them. The men were pleased as the torment of standing in the torrential rain was nearly over; no more standing like idiots as the drivers splashed through the puddles, sending up showers of dirty water over the copper. No more standing in the snow and ice, slowly freezing to death, and swinging the arms in frantic gyrations to keep the body warm. So, the traffic lights were a welcome sight.

One set of lights had been installed at a 'T' junction on the main road where a never-ending stream of traffic passed. Jock was on the beat and had just walked past the junction when a terrific crash was heard. He looked round in time to see one of the local dust carts travelling at speed - these carts were just huge boxes on wheels, a horse was attached to the shafts which led directly to the base of the cart. The driver of these monstrosities had to stand on the shafts to handle the horses. The contraption had just emerged from the side street, the beast travelling fact. It swung into the main stream of traffic and as it did so the cart struck a window cleaner's barrow. The barrow struck the guard-rails but the ladders continued on over the top, closely followed by the window cleaner himself. The ladders flew over the heads of the crowds on the pavement and shattered a huge plate glass window. The terrified horse ploughed its way along the outside lane of cars, the swaying cart hitting nearly every vehicle. The driver had not only lost control of the beast, he had also lost his reins and his foothold and the unlucky man was stretched across the shafts just out of reach of the horse's hooves.

Jock jumped over the guard-rails into the line of moving cars. He shot between two vehicles to get in front of the thrashing hooves of the terrified horse. The drivers realised something was wrong and slowed down, only to be hit by the cart as it passed. As the animal drew close, Jock began to run to match the speed of the horse as it came past. Desperately he grabbed at the harness beside the horse's mouth. He clutched the leather and was immediately pulled off his feet. He eventually got his balance back and heaved at the bit in an attempt to stop the runaway and slowly the vehicle began to move over to the side of the road. Jock was getting squeezed between the cars and the horse. At last the line of cars was passed and the horse moved towards the kerb. Jock realised he was in a dangerous position for right ahead of him, stopped at the next lights, was a double decker bus. The horse swung to miss the big red monster, it squeezed between a wall and the lights just as the cart hit the bus. Jock was thrown clear of the thudding metal shoes; the horse became jammed as the shafts had snapped off.

The cart was stationary after hitting the bus, the driver was thrown onto the road. The bus had lurched forward, throwing the conductor from the platform onto the ground and then the bus hit a loaded taxi which had just been passing.

Twelve cars; one bus; one taxi; one window cleaner's barrow; one refuse collector's cart and one shop window damaged. Nobody was killed but a lot of people were injured. Jock picked himself up, nursing his bruises, and looked back along the trail of havoc caused by the runaway. He saw the window cleaner standing beside the remnants of his cart and the line of cars which had been thrown against the pedestrian guard-rails. 'First things first' he thought as he fastened the frightened horse up to prevent another similar episode. He then began to check the injured people and arranged for ambulances to attend.

The bus driver and his conductor were injured, together with five of their passengers and the bus company had to be informed to remove the vehicle. The taxi driver and both of his passengers accompanied the others to hospital. As the poor old dustman couldn't get up, he was allowed to remain there until the ambulance men saw to him. None of the people in the line of cars had been hurt so that made his job a bit easier.

The Sergeant came along after some eager citizen had told him about the horror along the road.

"You OK Mac?" he asked, and carried on his way, leaving Jock to get on with it. After all it didn't need two Policemen to report an accident.

This, of course, was an accident that had to be reported - most of the other incidents which occurred were just damage only. If the touch was slight they were classed as error on the part of the driver and what could be expected with so many cars close together. The drivers exchanged names etc. and informed their insurance companies.

SUDDEN DEATHS

Death comes in a multitude of ways from the normal old age variety, to the fierce and brutal termination of life. The people concerned did not know when they were going to be involved, no more than the copper walking the streets who was called to deal with the results.

'I could do with a smoke now' - and having completed the report on the multi-accident, Jock headed for the nearest Public Convenience. These places were a Godsend, handy for all types of things, from the call of nature to cups of tea, sit down and rest awhile, smoke, or even have a game of cards during night duty. Going down the steps he was met by the attendant.

"Bloody hell Guv, it didn't take you long to get here" he exclaimed.

"What do you mean?" asked Jock.

"I have just sent a bloke out to find a copper."

"Why, what's wrong?"

"There's a client in number one. He's been there a long time and I can't get any reply from him. I cannot open the door either." The worried man pushed the offending door to prove his statement.

"Here, hang onto these." Jock gave his overcoat and helmet to the man to hold. He climbed up to look over the partition and saw the body of a man lying on the floor, wedged between the basin and the door. He climbed over and dropped down onto the seat; from that position he had to bend over and grasp the man and lift him up so that the door could be opened. However, the space was so small he had to wrap his arms right round the body and hold it upright to allow the door to open fully. Willing hands grasped the man and heaved him into the room beyond.

Unfortunately, the man's foot got caught under the door and the performance had to be repeated in reverse so that the offending obstruction could be moved. Jock again struggled with the dead weight against him until the door was opened once more - on this occasion he saw the Sergeant and an old PC standing there.

"Right Mac, we have him" the Sergeant said. When Jock emerged from the cubicle he said, "Johnny will report this, you go and get yourself cleaned up, you've done enough." He held his nose, "You stink more than this one does."

Sure enough his diagnosis was correct for Jock was covered from top to bottom with a thick foul smelling substance which was the discharge from the corpse.

MURDER

Other termination of life became a regular thing in Jock's life in the years to follow. Babies found dead in bed (cot deaths), children suffocated in bed (occasionally by drunken parents). Natural deaths, accidents, suicides and, of course, deaths caused by other people. One of the latter involved a young schoolgirl, slashed and mutilated with an open razor. A man, who was suspected of interfering with young girls, heard that the police were trying to contact him. He blamed the girl for grassing (informing) on him, so he went after her with a cut-throat razor. When Jock found the results of the meeting he was appalled, the girl lay in a dark back street with severe slashes to both sides of the neck and face. Her hands were both cut to pieces as she had tried to defend herself from the assailant when he hacked and chopped at her with the deadly weapon.

Enquiries were commenced and the man concerned was arrested. Numerous witnesses were obtained and the case seemed watertight - Jock had the job of picking the prisoner up at the prison and taking him to Court. He stayed in the cells with him and put the handcuffs on to take the man into the dock. After the hearing was over he returned the man to prison. During the time he was in his company, the killer stated that he was going to plead guilty - he admitted doing it. However, his Solicitor pleaded 'Not Guilty' and the case was thrown out on a technical point.

EXPENSIVE TEA

"I'm getting fed up with all these reports I'm getting" shouted the Station Sergeant. "I have been informed that some of you are in the habit of going into cafes for cups of tea in the mornings. This practice will cease at once."

The Governing bodies tried all ways to get the men out onto their beats in an attempt to stop the morning tea. They started marching them out in single file, each copper breaking off as he reached his beat. This did not work, the station was in the middle of the patch and the beats too far spread out. Anyway, a Sergeant had to go with them and this meant he had to walk so he missed his tea in the office. They tried taking them out in the van and the driver had his orders where to drop each copper.

The dropping places were always on the outskirts of the beats and as soon as they were dropped off, a beeline was made for the nearest café. So that system didn't last long either. Just after the Sergeant had given vent to his feelings about the idle coppers and their tea, Jock and Ernie were in the kitchen of a local café.

"Morning Bill" standard greeting; "How's tricks?" another needless question.

"I wouldn't hang around too long, the Sergeant hasn't been in yet Jock - he'll be coming in for his sandwiches." He had hardly got the words out of his mouth when the hinges on the back gate screeched.

"That'll be him now, you'd better hide in here." The proprietor pushed the pair of them into the pantry and closed the door behind them.

"I hope he doesn't come in here for some jam," Jock muttered - they could see through a crack into the kitchen and watched the Station Sergeant and his mate as they entered.

"Hi Bill, got any grub ready?"

"It's there waiting for you," the proprietor said, pointing to a large parcel.

"Bloody cold outside, I think I'll have a cuppa," the big man said, "and knock up a bacon butty as well, just to keep me going."

The meal was quickly prepared - and consumed by the two supervising officers who were totally unaware that they were under scrutiny by the couple of scroungers hiding in the pantry. Eventually the feast was over and the Sergeants continued their patrol.

"Hells bells!" said Ernie, "To think that he was yelling his head off at us only a few minutes ago about cups of tea."

This was only the start of the pressure for as soon as the Sergeants and the Inspector had consumed their own tea in the mornings, they were out in force checking every possible place where a copper might be having his tea. They did have some success in the witch-hunt, on night shift; the all night café was raided during the hour the door was closed. An Inspector went in the back door and five PCs ran out the front door, only to find a couple of Sergeants waiting for them. They were all charged and fined one full week's pay, which made their cup of tea a very expensive one. One week later, as the men lined up to salute for their pay they were stopped by a Sergeant, sitting at the next table.

"Collection," he said.

It was a recognised thing for a collection to be made at the pay table - it could be for someone in hospital, or to purchase a wreath. Jock paid his sixpence automatically and casually asked who it was for.

"The Inspector!" was the retort.

"I didn't know he'd died," Jock said.

"He hasn't, he's in hospital," the Sergeant said, "This is for cigarettes for him."

"Not my bloody money, I want that back. I think it's a bloody liberty asking us for him." Jock got his tanner back and the Sergeant turned to the pay clerk.

"Another one - we haven't collected anything yet."

Every week there was a collection and the men all gave willingly even though their pay was small; that is except for this man - he was hated.

BABY SITTING

Taking a new recruit out at night to commence the regular monotonous checking of property - Jock had become a regular nursemaid for the other newcomers to the Station - he didn't mind showing them the ropes and in fact enjoyed their company. The regular checking of property began, it was part and parcel of the job, and quite often property was left open. A push on a door and it flew inwards, the bell jangled loudly. The place was an off-licence, a large case of cigarettes lay opened on the floor and hundreds of fags were scattered around the shop. The place was in darkness - only lit by their torches the shop and the shelves seemed undisturbed so Jock decided to check the back room. Just as he reached out to grasp hold of the handle it started to turn slowly. When he had first entered the shop he believed that thieves had been disturbed, now he was certain. As the handle continued to turn he withdrew his truncheon and prepared to meet the intruder, suddenly the door flew open. Jock was just about to greet the burglars with his stick when, by the light from his torch, he noticed that the man who rushed out was wearing carpet slippers. It eventually proved to be the owner of the off-licence, drunk as a newt and it took a lot of convincing the man that the door of the shop had been left open by him and that he must lock it when they left.

Just across the road another shop door was found ajar, it was a dry cleaners and row after row of clothing hung from the rails just waiting for some light fingered person to come along. He telephoned the Police Station from the premises and ascertained that the key holder actually lived above the shop. She was knocked out of bed and advised to lock the door properly. Ten minutes later, on the edge of his beat, he found a door leading into a bank, standing wide open. ,

"Do you think it's a robbery?" whispered his new colleague, aghast at what he saw.

They could hear noises coming from the inside and slowly made their way in.

"Hit first and ask questions after if they are doing the place," Jock told him. The sound appeared to be coming from the manager's section. Jock indicated to his mate that he would go over the counter and enter the office by the staff door. His mate was to use the public doorway. Together, they opened the doors and rushed inside where they were greeted with a terrific crash and a man screamed - with terror as it turned out to be. The 'villain' turned out to be the caretaker who lived in the flat above with his family. He had come round to check the premises for the last time and had noticed a window slightly open. He had to climb onto the windowsill to ease the heavy window up and then push a couple of bolts in. It was during the lifting of the window that the two coppers had rushed in. The sudden noise and the lights from the torches had made him panic - he lost his grip on the window and the heavy sash fell down, and so did he, with a crash - that was when he had yelled. It wasn't a bank robber after all, just the very shaken and thankful caretaker who insisted upon providing the inevitable cup of tea for the night walkers.

A stroll down the other side of the beats proved uneventful but the new chap couldn't help remarking upon the number of shops etc. left open. The midnight ring was made at the box before heading for the station. They approached one of the all-night coffee stalls and the sickly sweet smell of fried onions came to greet them, it was enough to make the mouth water but above that came the indescribable aroma of fried bacon.

"There should be a law against making smells like that," the rookie remarked, "I have a cheese sandwich for breakfast today."

Every night when Jock was on this beat he checked this stall, there was never any trouble - whether it was with his expected presence or not, but the clients were better. This may also be due to the regular visit of one of Jock's friends who was a famous heavyweight boxer. He was there when they arrived at the stall.

"Hallo Jock, want a cuppa?" he said. "I see you have company tonight, how's the wife and kids?"

"They are fine thanks. This young chap is keeping his eye on me." Jock introduced the new chap to the boxer.

"I'm very pleased to meet you Sir. I have taken a great interest in your career, I think that you are one of the best."

"One of the best" Jock said, "He *is* the best."

"Hey, cut that out you two or I'll think that you're after a job."

"Oh I don't want a job Sir. I'll be quite happy in the police," the lad replied.

"I may be a little pissed Jock, but I'm not joking. I think I'll need someone to guard my back just now."

"You're joking of course. I thought the Club was doing OK?"

"The Club is doing quite well, probably that's the trouble. The Mob have decided to move in."

"What? The protection racket?" asked Jock - thinking it incredible that this man should be threatened.

"Well I have had several threats recently. Apart from slinging them out, I've told them to get stuffed and that anyone else who comes the heavy hand with me will get trouble." A smile lit up his battered face; his broken nose, split eyebrows and cauliflower ears didn't mar his genial expression. "It's a long time since I had a good punch-up and enjoyed myself," he grinned continually at the thought.

"Come on have a cup of coffee."

He always bought Jock a cuppa but wouldn't listen when he was asked to have another himself.

"No, I must be off, otherwise the wife will give me a good hiding! Goodnight." He waived merrily as he went. Jock never saw him again - the following night he was found dead in his car at the rear of his Club. Suicide? No way, thought Jock who had just lost a good friend.

MURDER

Although Jock was still doing his probation, he was getting to know quite a lot of the local thieves and though boys. He was always getting the new coppers to take out, to train them and to show the youngsters how to handle various situations. Naturally, the Sergeants were always looking for a good return of summonses and it was a waste of time expecting one of the old timers to take a rookie out and prosecute anyone (they wouldn't know where to start). So, once more Jock was walking around the market area with another sprog looking for work for him.

It wasn't long before they ran into a large coloured man who was working in the main road with his barrow. He started getting quite naughty, refused to shift and became aggressive - using language that was never taught in a classroom, nor heard in a church. The inevitable happened, he was arrested - on the way to the Station, he decided to buy some cigarettes but Jock informed him that would not be possible.

"Just you try and stop me," the huge man said and headed into the doorway of a shop. He got half way in, his head and shoulders lay over the threshold, his feet and legs spread across the pavement.

"You bastard, I'll get you for that," he yelled.

"Right lad, any time you like," answered Jock. "But now you go inside my way. You had your chance to walk in properly." He pulled the big man to his feet and locked his arm up his back. With one hand he walked the belligerent troublemaker to the Nick. The man was bent double with his arm held by Jock.

"You are taking advantage of your uniform."

"I can easily take it off but I don't think it would make any difference to you. It certainly doesn't worry your brother." Jock knew that this man was related to the chap who led the local mob.

"I'll get Pete to sort you out when he comes out. He'll kill you." The man was in a frenzy. Pete was inside for three months - for assault on police.

The story went around, obviously spread by this awkward person, that Pete was scheduled for a job as soon as he was released. Everyone knew, the locals, the barrow boys and the coppers.

"I hear you're in for it Constable," one of the Sergeants said to him in confidence. "You slipped up. You sorted Pete's brother out the other day, didn't you?"

"Yes," admitted Jock, "but he asked for it."

"May be so lad but you are in for trouble soon. I'd watch myself if I were you. Pete has been released and they tell me he is looking for revenge. He's mad that chap and he'll kill somebody some day."

"Thanks for the warning Sergeant," Jock said.

Saturday night and the usual trouble spots had to be covered, Jock was on the coffee stall on the main road, with a rookie to assist him. The crowds had gathered early and as they approached the stall Jock saw Big Pete, sitting as brazen as brass on the guard rails drinking his coffee, surrounded by his mob, and beside him was a local thief who Jock had recently arrested. The thief was out on licence but couldn't resist going out with his old crowd. Jock marched straight through the crowd and before Pete knew what was happening, he was grabbed by the arm and pulled from his perch.

"Piss off," Jock told him, "you too," the other man was ordered as he landed on the pavement.

"Yes Sir, sorry Sir." The joint reply came from both of the men in unison. They put their cups on the flap of the stall and walked away. Jock looked after them as they left.

"That's funny. He's supposed to be looking for me. He must not have recognised me otherwise he wouldn't have gone quietly - he would have had a go. Very strange." He decided to clear the rest of the people away from the pavement before going after the terrible duo. About half an hour later he saw them standing on a bus stop. Pete was unmistakable, he wore a large white Stetson and carried a walking stick; the stick was at least three feet long and two inches thick, with a large silver knob. He told the youngster to keep out of sight and not to interfere under any circumstances as he approached the two villains.

"I hear you're looking for me Pete," he said. The man looked worried.

"No Sir, why should I be looking for you?" He was, as usual, very polite.

"I had trouble with your eldest brother and he told me that you were going to sort me out. Well, here I am."

"Look Sir," the man was really frightened. "We have an understanding - you are the boss. I've never given you any trouble, have I Guv?" Jock admitted that the man had always behaved himself when he was there. "Well, I don't intend to have another go, not after the last time."

"There are two of you now, if you fancy your chances."

"Guvnor, there were ten of us the night you nearly killed me. No thanks, my brother can fight his own battles."

"Fair enough," Jock said.

"Here's my bus coming Sir, may we go please?"

"Where are you going?"

"West, for a bit of crumpet!" answered the man.

"Righto, off you go, but behave yourselves," Jock said as he let the men get on the bus and watched them drive off.

"Who was that Jock?" The youngster's voice brought him back to the work in hand. "People you had best avoid."

Next day, a Police Circular indicated that a murder had been committed. A description of the murdered man was given and Jock recognised the details at once, and went into the front office.

"I know that man, the one who was killed," he stated. The CID Inspector and his team were gathered in the office at the time, he told them that he had arrested the man himself and that he was out on licence. The whole crowd suddenly became intelligent, of course they had known all the time who he was.

"I saw him last night with Pete."

"Are you sure?"

"Yes, I was speaking to them. They were going over West, they told me."

"Why were you speaking to them?" asked the Inspector and Jock explained the situation to him.

"You mean you were looking for a fight with them?"

"Put it like that, yes," said Jock.

"You must be out of your little mind to look for a fight with Pete. If you fancy yourself that much, you can go and bring him in. If you can find him - because I'm bloody sure that I'm not going to tangle with him," said the Detective Inspector.

So Jock was detailed to go and arrest the toughest villain in the district for murder. He went straight to the mother's house and she opened the door.

"Is Pete in?" he asked.

"Yes."

"Pete," she shouted, "here's one of your mates to see you." She yelled the information along the passage.

"He's in the bath, just go through" she said to Jock. Jock went along to the bathroom, Pete was just getting out of the water.

"Right, Pete. You know why I've come, don't you."

"Yes Guvnor. I hit him too hard. I'll just get dried, won't take a second." He quickly towelled himself dry and pulled his trousers on and then slipped a shirt on.

"Right Guv, I'm ready."

"You want some shoes on Pete, and I want the clothes you were wearing last night and also the stick. Is that what you hit him with?"

"Yes Guv. We had an argument about some filly."

"Ready?" Jock enquired.

"Yes Guv." The man was quite unperturbed as they headed for the Station.

"Aren't you going to have a go?" Jock had expected some attempt to run.

"Waste of time Guv. That's why they sent you to nick me." What a fool, to lose his temper over women and kill one of his mates. At the Station there was a great crowd of Detectives, all ranks, they swiftly surrounded the prisoner and he was whipped away to the CID quarters. Naturally, he was officially arrested by the Detective Inspector. Jock never saw him again - he was found guilty - and hung.

"Well done lad. Now let's have you outside and get some work done," the Station Sergeant said with a smile on his face.

LOST

"Excuse me Sir." Jock recognised the accent of the man who spoke to him from the driver's seat of an old battered Ford Popular. "Can you tell me how to get to the Great North Road?" The car's springs were creaking under the weight of its passengers, plus all the luggage stacked on the roof rack. The driver sounded, and looked, frustrated as he asked for directions.

"It's the Edgeware Road you want, Jock replied "but I'm afraid you have a long way to go to get to it."

"Just my bloody luck. I've asked dozens of people the way and they have had me driving round in circles, it's obvious they don't know the way," the driver groaned.

"Never mind Sir," Jock tried to soothe the man. "I'll show you the way, give me a piece of paper and I'll draw a map with the directions on it. I'll put the names of the roads on where you have to turn so you shouldn't get lost this time." He marked on the paper all the junctions where the man had to turn, with all the traffic lights indicated and the names of the streets, the man couldn't go wrong. "It's about fifteen miles but follow the directions and you'll be alright."

The driver went over the instructions with Jock just to verify that he had grasped them.

"I don't know how you can remember all that," he said. Jock quizzed him with regard to his home town and was given the general area of his domicile.

"I know the area, just whereabouts exactly do you live?"

"It's only a small place, you wouldna ken it."

"Try me," Jock suggested, and when the man told him the name of the town he asked,

"Which end of the High Street do you live, beside the Catholic Church or down beside the Whitewashed Cottages?" The poor driver just gaped for a while and eventually he asked Jock.

"How on earth do you do it? You can draw a map of this place for me, then describe my home town which is hundreds of miles away."

"Simple," Jock said "I was born and bred there."

"Och man, awa with ye. If ya cum frae there, what are you talking all posh like that fae?" He was referring to the fact that Jock was talking like a Southerner, without the slightest sign of accent.

FIREWOOD

"We will have to get some firewood," Puggle informed him, "it's getting down."

"Right pet, I'll get some later." Jock was on his way to work so he would have to see to the timber problem the following day, when he was off. During the afternoon, as he strolled along his beats, he saw clouds of smoke billowing up; he went to investigate the cause of the fire and saw it came from a large compound and as he entered the yard he saw three men engaged with a large fire. They were throwing boxes and crates on as fast as they could.

"Alright Guv?" A small elderly man approached him.

"Yes, I saw the smoke and wondered what it was, I had to check to see if everything was OK."

"Oh the fire? We're just getting rid of a load of boxes because we need room to move and they are cluttering the place up."

"That's funny" Jock said, "I was asked to get some wood for the fire as we are running out, and here you are complain that you can't move for it."

"We're burning tons of it Guv, you can have some if you want it." The man offered the answer to his problem.

"Fine if you are going to burn it anyway, but I can't take it now. I'll call in on the way home - I'll be able to put it in my saddle bag."

"Where do you live Guv, I'll drop some in for you - it'll be no trouble as I'll be going out on the truck." Jock thanked the man and told him where he lived.

"Are you sure it's no trouble?" The man insisted that it was no problem and told Jock he would just drop it in the front garden for him.

When he booked off duty and went home, he got the shock of his life because the front garden was piled up high with boxes of all shapes and sizes. They had cleaned the yard out and transferred all the timber down to Jock's house. It took him hours to carry all the boxes from the front garden and stack them neatly at the back of the premises. The next day he hunted the donor up and got on to him about the load.

"I only wanted a few pieces to light a fire, not a load like that."

"Well Guv, it was in my way and I had to keep at least one lad in the yard to burn it and business is lost when I'm a man short."

"What is your business?" Jock asked.

"I run a few barras Guv." Hells bells, a barrow boy

"I hope you're not getting the idea that you can get any favours for a bit of firewood? I'd rather pay for it," Jock told the little man.

"Nonsense Guv, I wouldn't want you to and I don't want paid for it. In fact you've done me a favour by taking it off my hands."

"As long as you realise that if you or any of your barrows are caught breaking the law, I will do them just the same as the others."

"OK Guv. No favours asked, you just do your job and if any of my lads get caught, it's their lookout. I've already told them that by the way because I know you are strict on the streets."

Jock walked down the main road later and saw two barrows in the restricted area. One of the men moved as soon as he recognised Jock but the other carried on serving. He grinned at Jock when he stopped beside the barrow.

"Morning Guv, enough wood for you yesterday - it nearly broke my bleeding back loading and unloading that lot."

"You know the facts about trading and you have been told by your boss that it makes no difference that you got rid of the old boxes. I'll give you the benefit of the doubt and tell you myself now. The fact that a load of boxes were placed in my garden will make no difference to your work around here - when you see me, you'll move, otherwise you get done. If you don't' move after I have reported you, then I will nick you."

"Look Guv, I'm only trying to make a living." The man was shaken by the ultimatum.

"Move, for the last time." The order was given but the barrow boy decided to be awkward and refused to shift the obstruction. Instead he served another customer, just to how his defiance. As he was obviously 'taking the Mickey' out of Jock he was reported, and visibly shaken when Jock did report him.

"Are you satisfied now?" he asked, as Jock put his pocket book away.

"No. Move, or you'll be arrested for wilful obstruction."

"You wouldn't bloody dare," the belligerent man said. On the way to the Police Station, he cursed the big copper who had just arrested him. He wasn't cursing for being arrested, these men accepted the fact that they would be nicked quite often. He was cursing because Jock was making him push the heavily laden barrow all the way to the Station. He was bailed out ten minutes later and Jock saw him several times in the distance but the chap was like a greyhound whenever he spotted the blue uniform.

During his rounds Jock saw the old chap who owned the barrows - the news had been spread around and he already knew about the sortie. He stopped the policeman and apologised for the barrow boy's behaviour.

"He came and complained about you nicking him Guv," the man said.

"I told him he had been warned that you were straight and wouldn't be bought, especially for a bit of firewood. Anyway, he doesn't work for me now, I fired him for causing aggro with the law - I don't want that because when one of my barrows are off the road, I am losing money."

Jock had learnt a lesson as well about different people who inhabit the area and work the streets and also their mannerisms and expectations; he also learnt to be cautious. Particularly, he found out early in his service that everything had to be paid for, otherwise people would take advantage of any favours which had been granted. A copper couldn't do his job properly if he accepted backhanders of any form.

BICYCLES

It didn't take long to find out that the lowly cycle was a veritable Godsend to the copper on the beat. It was essential for getting to and from work during unsociable hours because a quicker and more direct route could be taken than the buses or tramcars. They were also handy for doing school-crossings which seemed to blend in with refreshment times. Some of the crossings were on the very edge of the ground and as the last of the kids trooped into school at 2pm but the copper on that crossing had too book off at 2pm, it was difficult as the policeman had to hand his reports in to be checked by the Section Sergeant - and the trusty steed came in handy. Official Cyclists were paid ten shillings each week. They were posted on cycle duty but their name had to be on the official register before being considered for posting on to that duty. It was a cushy job, standing by at the office just drinking tea and playing cards, waiting for any messages that had to be done (unless there was a copper walking that beat as the message came in). Jock, of course, never rose to such dizzy heights of authorised cyclist, nor did any of the other young coppers. These jobs were all kept for the older men.

Another task where the bike came in handy was for the Magistrates' Courts because his station was in between two Courts and this meant that he could have cases on at both of them at the same time. That was when he had to make some arrangements with one Court to have his case brought forward, then he would get on to the other Court and request that his other cases be put back. Once the first case was over, he would have to jump on his bike and pedal like hell for several miles to the other Court. The trouble was though that the general public does not know when a copper is on duty or not - in any case when they were in trouble - they would stop the poor copper to help him out. That left the Policeman to do some explaining about being late for Court. Yes, the cycle was certainly a great help and everyone knew how valuable they were - that's why everyone had some type of cycle.

One day, he had just collected his bike from the station yard and was checking his beat for the last time before he went to do his last crossing. He found that he could get right round this beat in the half hour he had to wait between the schools coming out and going back in. During the journey he noticed another copper riding along on his beat. 'Poaching' was not allowed - so he stopped the man.

"Hello Johnny, what beat are you on?"

"I've just been to get my bike from the station Jock, I'm on my way back to do my last crossing now," the man explained. This explanation was satisfactory due to the fact that Knock knew the other man's beat was adjacent to his and he had to cross Jock's patch to reach his school crossing.

"Look out Jock, the bastard's on the prowl." He had noticed the duty officer's car going past the end of the road.

"He's just gone past, he'll swing round and try to catch us." He jumped onto his cycle and rode away towards his school. Jock did the same, travelling in the opposite direction. It wasn't that he was unduly worried about the patrolling officer but he was nearly due at the crossing. As he rode along, a car suddenly passed him and swung towards the pavement. The driver cut in so sharply that Jock was forced to brake and swing to the side. In doing so, he struck the kerb and was thrown onto the pavement. He picked himself up and strode round to the driver's window.

"What the hell do you think you are doing," he snapped at the driver. The Inspector was driving. He rose quickly to the occasion - he was not going to be spoken to by a young copper like that and he promptly started to use his rank, demanding to know what beat Jock was on and who he had been talking to along the street. Jock was not going to be put off and said,

"If you carry on driving like that, you are going to be reported for dangerous driving." The Inspector was furious.

"What beat are you on?"

The Inspector was trying to change the subject by asking Jock what his duties were.

"You know what beat I am posted to - this one," he retorted.

"Why have you got your cycle out?" the supervising officer asked.

"I've done my first school and collected the bike so that I can check my beat again before doing the last crossing," Jock replied. He still did not intend the Inspector to get away with his driving error.

"Who was that you were talking to?" his boss asked. Jock informed him who the copper was and also why he had stopped the man.

"You were not doing your beat properly, you were idle and gossiping." The Inspector had to have a dig in, he knew he had done wrong when he cut in front of Jock and was trying to make it look as though the PC was at fault.

"I've told you why I stopped him. Now I must inform you that I am cautioning you for your manner of driving. I consider it disgusting and dangerous for a person in your position to handle a motor vehicle the way you did. I shall be entering a report on the matter." Jock spoke to the Inspector as though he was just another naughty driver.

"Now, you will have to excuse me, I have a school crossing to do." With that remark, he got onto his cycle and rode away. As he stood at the kerbside waiting for the youngsters to come along, a man stopped beside him.

"Have you been in trouble?" he asked Jock. "Because if you haven't, I had better let you know that the Inspector and Sergeant are sitting in a car around the corner watching you."

"I know," Jock said, "They are probably watching me the same way as I can see them - through the reflection in the shop window at the corner." He thanked the stranger and carried on with his duties, but the heat was on. Although he knew it was a waste of time, he still put a report in about the incident involving the push bike - he never heard any more about it but knew that things would have to come to a head between himself and the Inspector before long. He carried on doing his job properly and obeying all lawful orders - but he was conscious of the Sergeant and Inspector waiting to pounce.

CHAPTER FOUR

BOOBY TRAP

BOOBY TRAP

It was a dirty wet night, the rain was coming down in torrents making everyone wet and miserable. Jock was glad when his refreshments were due and he could go into the station to dry off a bit and get warm. He was posted to two of the largest beats and they consisted of very few shops but an awful lot of houses. Consequently, life was a bit dull and lonely in his neck of the woods and the rain didn't help to cheer him up. He booked in for breakfast at the same time as another young copper.

"We might be alright for a game of cards Jock, if there's anyone else in," the chap said.

When they entered the canteen they were soon roped in for a foursome.

"Come on Jock, make a four."

"Hang on, till I pour a cuppa. You deal the cards and I'll be with you in a second" Jock said as he poured tea for himself and the other chap. He placed the tea on the table and collected his packet of sandwiches then sat with the others. He had just started to eat his food when the canteen door flew open and there stood the Section Sergeant.

"MacGregor," he yelled. "Get out. You are overdue. Now move." After giving the order he went out and slammed the door behind him.

"What the hell was that all about?" one of the players asked, breaking the heavy silence which now hung over the canteen. You've just come in." Jock looked at his watch and began to drink his tea.

"I'm going to have my half hour, to hell with him," and he carried on eating and playing until his official refreshments were over. He left the canteen with the same man that he had entered with, leaving the same men in the canteen who had been there when they had started their meal break.

"Why the hell should he pick on you Jock? You went in there with me and yet all those other lazy sods are still sitting there, he didn't chase them out."

They entered the front office together and booked out. The other lad nudged him.

"That's where he got mixed up" and he indicated in the book where another PC, whose number was practically the same as Jock's, had been due out when the Sergeant had burst into the canteen. "The skipper has got mixed up with the numbers and he is still in the canteen."

"MacGregor." That hated voice disturbed their conversation. "There's a message to be done and it's on your beat." He handed Jock a piece of paper with the message on. Jock looked at the message as he left the office and said to his colleague.

"Christ, this is nowhere near my beat, it's at the other end of the patch."

"Where is it for?" the other lad asked. Jock handed him the message to read and the copper laughed.

"Bloody hell, he's certainly got his knickers in a twist tonight." The message was for the PC whose number was similar to Jock's and he was still fiddling in the canteen. The cyclist should have done it by rights but one couldn't expect him to go out and get wet, especially when he was in the communication room playing cards with the Sergeant.

"Are you going to do it then?" Jock's mate asked.

"Why not, I was ordered to it and it will be a change from 12 and 13 beats" Jock answered.

"I'm going down that way, I'll walk down with you," the other chap offered and together they headed off into the rain towards the distant location. Half an hour's walk brought them to the large block of flats mentioned in the message.

"So long Jock, see you later." His partner bade farewell and proceeded to check his property, leaving Jock to take care of his message.

He had just completed his task and was returning to the office to inform them that the message had been done when the wireless car went tearing past him. He huddled down into his cape, head down against the driving rain and muttered to himself,

"Lucky sods, sitting in comfort in this weather. They must be on a call." He noticed the brake lights coming on and the car drew to a halt about two hundred yards in front of him. Wondering if they required any assistance, Jock increased his speed. The car was stationary outside a works depot, the gateway was open so he went in. He followed the sound of voices and flashing torches and came across the men from the police car and two security men. They were standing in a semi-circle near the base of a gas tank.

"What the hell is it?" the voice came quite clearly to him as he approached.

"What's wrong Sid?" Jock asked one of the coppers.

"A chap was disturbed by one of the security men, he ran off and they've lost him but he left these cases here against the tank." The driver of the car looked round when he heard Jock's voice.

"Hey Jock, just the man we want. You were in Bomb Disposal weren't you?"

Jock admitted that he had.

"Did you have anything to do with booby traps or things like this? Have a look at them will you and tell me what you think," the driver asked him.

"It doesn't look right to me." Jock knelt on the ground beside the cases which had been neatly placed one on top of the other. He checked the locks and hinges and noticed the narrow gap between them.

"Dodgy," he muttered as he continued his examination.

"Got a sharp knife?" he asked, and a jack-knife was passed to him. He opened the blade out and gently started to cut a hole in the lid of the uppermost case. Once he had made it large enough he put a finger inside and felt underneath, and satisfied he cut another portion away and repeated the process. Eventually, he had made a hole large enough to examine the contents of the case.

"You have a right one here Johnny," he said to the driver as he continued to cut away at the lid. When the hole was large enough he placed his hand inside and checked right round the inside edges of the lid until he was satisfied that it would be safe to open it. He undid the locks and swung the lid open gently, disclosing the contents to the little group of men who stood there. They looked with some disbelief.

"What the hell is it?" one of the security men eventually asked.

"A bomb, believe it or not," Jock said as he worked on.

"Bloody hell, could it go off?" the other guard asked.

"I think that's why it was put there and if I'm not mistaken, it's due to explode in about five minutes from now," Jock told him.

"You're not joking are you Jock?" the driver asked.

"I never joke about bombs Johnny."

"I'd better get the Bomb Squad out then," the wireless operator had found a convenient way to get out of the blast and made himself scarce.

"Have you got a pair of wire cutters or pliers handy?" Jock asked the security men and one of them suddenly came to life when he realised that Jock had spoken to him.

"There's a pair in the hut I can get!" he said.

"How long will it take you to get them and get back here?"

"Only a few minutes," the man answered

"If you can't get back here in two minutes I would advise you not to bother coming back at all because it'll be too late," Jock told him. The man was already running towards his hut. Jock advised that the other men should also make themselves scarce and the plain clothes observer and the wireless operator took his advice. Only the driver remained beside Jock.

"Hadn't you better join your mates Johnny?" he asked the man. "You'll have a lot of reports to write if your car gets damaged."

"You're a cool sod Jock. Sitting on your arse in the mud beside that thing, which you said could go off at any time. Why don't you leave it for the Army Bomb Disposal Squad. It's their job isn't it?"

"Agreed, it is their job, but don't you think it's a waste of time even trying to get them here. This thing will go up in three minutes, how long do you think it would take to get through on the 'phone?" Jock said. "This would have gone up before they even got the message and when you consider what will happen if this gas tank goes up as well ..." he didn't finish his sentence.

"I'll stay and give you a hand," and he knelt down beside Jock.

"That is if you need it." He looked closely at the contraption inside the case.

"What do you make of it really Jock, joking aside?"

"I've told you, I don't joke about things like this. That is about two pounds of industrial explosive at least. That is a clock, a wire attached to the winder and into the detonator. Another wire comes from here," and he pointed to the face of the clock. "From there it goes to a battery and the other end of the battery is connected to the detonator. Once this pointer here comes into contact by reaching this point, it completes the circuit from the battery to the detonator. Then whump, up it goes."

"Bloody fanatics to put that here. It puts the shits up me."

"Me too," answered Jock.

"You could fool me, just sitting there looking at it, have you ever had any bombs go up on you?" The man was sweating and just talking to cover his fear.

"Yes."

"Any petrol ones, like this could be?"

"Only once with petrol. I lost all my clothes, hair and exposed skin. Do you know, I never felt a thing at the time. I saw flames shooting past me then the blast hit me. It was nearly ten minutes later before I felt anything."

"Here you are mate!" panted the security man as he handed the wire cutters to Jock.

"Thanks pal. You'd better make yourself scarce, go and join your mate." He was talking to himself again for the security man was already out of hearing.

"I've got a habit of doing that Johnny, always talking to myself. By the way, there's no sense you staying here just now. We don't know where all the other wires lead to, possibly they could be attached to something in the bottom case. I'll have to cut the wires, so why don't you just back off a bit to be on the safe side, you can always come back once I've done that. If anything goes wrong, you'll be in a position to explain what happened."

Johnny accepted the logic of Jock's statement and moved further away from the bomb, he stopped at a distance where he could see what was happening, and watch this young rookie cop sitting in the mud with death at his finger tips.

"Good Luck Jock" he muttered as the youngster bent over the contraption.

Jock, in the meanwhile, was again considering the layout of the various wires which lay in a jumble around the clock. He checked each one out separately before making the final decision.

"Right, here goes nothing." He grasped the first wire, held his breath and cut it.

"Is there another one underneath which I can't see?" he wondered as he grasped hold of the next wire and repeated the procedure. Still nothing happened and he quickly cut all the other wires in sequence and lifted the clock out, wires dangling.

"Is it OK now Jock?" Johnny, who was quickly back at his side asked. "Do you think it would have gone off?" Jock eased the detonator out of the explosive and put it in his pocket, he laid the battery down alongside the clock on the ground and pulled the primary charge away from it.

"Do you think it would have gone off?" Johnny again asked him. Jock grinned, the rain running down his face, he looked at the clock and picked it up. He passed the object over to Johnny, the driver took hold of it and looked at it, as he did so the bell sounded. Poor bugger, he nearly filled his pants with shock as he dropped the timepiece on the ground.

"Sod you!" he exclaimed, but soon recovered from his terrifying experience and said, "That's it then, it's all over?"

"I don't know, I'm still dubious of this one," and Jock indicated the second case. "I think that the first one was too easy to disarm, possibly to put anyone off their guard. I don't like it." The driver looked at the two cases, they looked safe enough to him.

"What makes you think that Jock?" He was shown the narrow space between the cases and said "What do you think is wrong then?"

"If I'm right, there could be another wire attaching the two cases, or there could be a release type mechanism there. If the top case was moved or lifted, it could set off a charge in the bottom case."

"You must be joking Jock. Alright, alright, I know, you aren't joking but are you sure?" Johnny asked.

"No, I'm not sure, I'm just careful." Jock stood up.

"Where are you going then?" the driver asked.

"I'm not going anywhere, I'm only getting a bit of string out of my pocket and stretching my legs for a bit." He fumbled in his pockets for a length of string.

"Stop!" he said suddenly as the driver bent down beside the cases and grasped hold of the top one. The man froze at the tone in Jock's voice.

"Wait till I check it Johnny, just to be on the safe side." Jock once again took up his position beside the cases and, stretching the string out tight, he slowly inserted it in the gap between the cases. Gently he slid it along until the movement was checked. He marked the position and then repeated the same movement at the other side of the cases. Once again the string stopped and the position was marked - the whole operation was done again from the other edges and the places marked where the string had stopped.

"That's it. There's something right there!" and he pointed to the centre of the case. He started stripping the paper lining out from the uppermost case.

"What are you doing now Jock?" the driver asked.

"Just making sure that there's nothing fastened through the case, and the paper stuck down over it. If they had used a pull igniter, it would have to be fastened securely to the top case and they could only do that by drilling a hole to connect it - the join would be hidden by the paper lining," replied Jock, carrying on with the job. His examination proved that there were no wires or break in the case.

"That leaves us with a release type," he said to the driver. Slowly, he started to slide the uppermost case along, keeping even pressure on it as he did so and watching the marks that he had made on the fabric. Taking his piece of string from his pocket again, he slid it along the gap to check the position of the obstruction.

"Half an inch to go," he said, and gently moved the container along a little further until the cause of concern could just be seen. "Right Johnny, can you slide the case along very slowly, keeping the pressure on this end here, and don't forget ... very slowly, until I tell you to stop. When you stop, you must still keep the weight on, don't, whatever you do, lift the case up or let it tilt." His companion gripped the suitcase and obeyed the instructions.

"Easy does it Johnny, just a little bit more." Jock was waiting for the chance to place his fingers on the metal object which he had seen. At last, he considered he could place enough pressure on it with his fingertips.

"Stop." The painfully slow movement ceased. Jock shone his torch on the metal and, satisfied that he had a good grip, he breathed a sigh of relief, his suspicions had been correct.

"OK Johnny, keep moving." The case was once more slid along and Jock increased his grip.

"Right, it's clear. You can take the case away, lay it down gently over there." He nodded towards the ground away from the tank.

"Is that it?" breathed the driver.

"Just one thing more Johnny. If I take my finger off this, we'll be taking early retirement. Have a look around and you'll probably find a pin with a length of wire attached, or a nail will do."

The driver searched around and eventually handed the item that Jock had described.

"This it?"

"Thanks, yes" and Jock slipped the pin into a hole and stood up after detaching the igniter from the bottom fuse.

"What's that then Jock?"

"We used to call them book release because they open like a book and a strong spring sends the striker across onto the detonator."

Jock opened the catch and showed the simple workings to his mate, the striker was held firmly in place by the pin. He removed the detonator from the appliance and put it in his pocket.

"There, that's better, you can see how it works now. This pin holds the striker back but when the pin is out, it's held back by this little catch in the lid of the book. As the lid is forced back by this spring when the weight is lifted off, the pin flies over like this." He demonstrated the action.

"This pin hits the end of the detonator and that's it. Simple isn't it? They are only a quarter of an inch thick. They were used on booby traps during the war, Jerries placed them under bodies, souvenirs, or anything else that would have to be moved."

"We won't have any trouble with this one now," he said as he began to open the second case after checking it. "About ten pounds of Nitro and a gallon of petrol - enough to give you a warm send-off."

He placed the two cases together and gave the driver the two detonators.

"These are dangerous, even a dead battery can set them off, keep them away from your wireless set, even the static can do it. Give them to the Bomb chaps when they arrive and tell them how it was fixed up." The driver handled the detonators very carefully as he received them.

"I think I'll just leave them down here Jock."

Jock remembered that he still had a message to reply to.

"OK now Johnny - I have just been doing a message - the Sergeant will do his nut."

"I'd give you a lift Jock but we'll have to hang on till the squad arrives. Thanks for the lesson though."

Jock headed for the Police Station, wet and muddy, but happy. Not for long as it turned out though, for he hadn't got very far along the road before the duty officer's car pulled in alongside.

"What beat are you posted to?" the man with the pipe asked.

"Twelve and Thirteen, Sir" answered Jock.

"You're off your beat, what are you doing down here. Report to me at the station."

"Yes, Sir," Jock was in trouble once again.

ON THE CARPET

The Inspector stared at the condition of Jock's uniform as he entered the office.

"Where the bloody hell have you been? What have you been up to? Why is your uniform in such a filthy condition? Why were you off your beats? Your beats are at the other end of the patch, so you'd better have a bloody good explanation ready!" he yelled.

"I had to caution him at breakfast time Inspector, he had overstayed his time for his refreshments," said the Sergeant having a little dig.

"Is that so? Right, MacGregor. What have you got to say?"

Jock tried to explain that the Sergeant had been mixed up with another PC who had been due out and that he had given him a message to do which the other copper should have had. The Sergeant denied being responsible for sending him off his beat.

"Well, you may have some explanation for your uniform." The Inspector came to the rescue of his Sergeant. "Why is it in such a filthy condition, did the Sergeant do that as well?"

"No Sir, the Sergeant had nothing to do with that" Jock answered.

"Oh, that's nice, the nasty old Sergeant hasn't been blamed for all the mud on your clothes. Go and get yourself cleaned up, you are disgusting. Report back to me here. This matter is not finished by a long chalk." The Inspector's voice was loaded with sarcasm.

"Yes Sir," Jock saluted before going into the communications Room where he handed in the reply to the message he had just done, then headed for the canteen for a cuppa. He later sponged the mud off his uniform and had a good wash. He felt much better when he returned to the front office to face his persecutors again.

'I suppose their little minds need something to work on, just to show they are alive', he thought as he entered the office.

The Inspector was sitting at the desk drinking his tea as Jock went in, he indicated with a nod of his head where he wanted Jock to stand until he decided to resume his barrage of abuse. Eventually he placed his cup down and turned to the subject of his pleasure.

"Right MacGregor, now you have some explaining to do. Let me hear your latest fairy tale."

Before Jock started speaking, the telephone rang. The Assistant Station officer answered the call and then passed the handpiece to the Inspector, who listened carefully. He replaced the receiver and turned to the Sergeant.

"Come on Sergeant we have some work to do. They've found an unexploded bomb and the Bomb Disposal Squad have been called out, we'd better get down there." He turned to Jock as he was leaving the office.

"I'll see you later about this, you haven't heard the last of it. Now get round your beat and get some work done instead of hanging around the office."

"Yes Sir." Jock went to have another cup of tea before he went back onto his beat.

The following night the relief had just been detailed to their respective beats.

"MacGregor, I'll see you in the office," the Inspector ordered.

"Well, here we go again, the bugger never lets up." Jock muttered to the copper standing next to him in the line as they marched out of the parade shed. When he entered the front office he found the Sub-Divisional Inspector was present - he sat at the desk checking the books and looked up as Jock entered.

"Hello MacGregor, just on or going off?"

"Just starting Sir," Jock said as he took up his position on the mat in front of the desk to wait for the Inspector's arrival. It soon became obvious that he and the Sergeant had decided to pay a visit to the Wet Canteen downstairs where the beer etc. was sold. Jock was still waiting in the same position, till the Sub-Divisional Inspector gave him a quizzical look and said.

"Waiting for someone?"

"The Inspector wants to see me again Sir" Jock answered.

"Trouble again?"

"Afraid so Sir - I'm getting used to it now." Jock smiled.

The door of the office opened but Jock didn't bother to look to see who had come in, he expected it to be the Inspector. 'Here we go', he thought.

"Hey Jock, I was talking to some old mates of yours last night after you left." It was the driver of the police car.

"They had a look at the bomb. The Lieutenant was as mad as hell when he saw it. He wanted to know who had been messing about with it. When I told him it had been a copper who had done it, he nearly blew up himself. When I told him your name, he said he knew you and it was OK, I had to give you his thanks and best wishes. After I told him how it had been fitted up, he told me he had never had to deal with anything like that before and when I told him that you had just beaten the clock, he said it would be just like you to have a go."

"What's this all about" asked the SDI. who had been listening intently to the driver.

The driver told him all about the incident. The Guvnor read the entry in the Occurrence Book.

"I can't see your name mentioned MacGregor."

"No Sir," Jock said.

"The Inspector only states that the Bomb Disposal Squad were called and the bomb was made safe," the boss stated. "Now then, how did you come to be involved?"

Jock told him about the Sergeant's mix up with the other copper's number and the message and this explained why he was off his beat when he came upon the incident.

"Is that why the Inspector wants to see you? the boss asked, "because you were off your beat?"

"Well, my uniform got in a bit of a state - I was all muddy, clothes as well as my boots."

"Guvnor," the driver interrupted, "It was pissing down with rain all the time, and the bomb only had a couple of minutes to go before it went off. It would have blown the gas tank up. Jock came along and calmly sat on the ground and took it to pieces, it was booby trapped as well. There was just no way he could wait for the Bomb Squad to arrive, and the thing couldn't be moved. I think it's bloody disgusting if Jock gets into trouble for that. As regards the mud, I was covered with it myself." Old Johnny was livid with rage as he addressed his boss. The old man looked at the entry.

"Short and sweet, doesn't take long to read and obviously a lot missing." He looked at Jock and said, "Get a bollocking last night, did you?"

"Correct Sir," answered Jock.

"This is the second time isn't it?" the SDI. asked.

"What's that Sir. The second time for what?"

"The second time you've dealt with bombs since you came to the station."

"No Sir, the fourth time." Jock reminded him of the various incidents.

"That big one. You were on the carpet for that one as well weren't you?"

"Yes Sir."

"You're not in a hurry are you?" the boss asked the driver.

"Well Sir, we are booked off the air at this station so that we can catch up with the stolen cars," Johnny told him.

"Good, have a look around for the Inspector and tell him that Mr MacGregor is waiting for him in the office, inform him that he is keen to get out on his beat. If he argues, tell him that I am here also," the SDI told him, "and come back here as well, will you?"

The Inspector and the Sergeant arrived shortly afterwards, closely followed by the driver, and as they entered the room the stink of beer became very evident. The SDI appeared to be deeply engrossed in the various books and was ignoring the rest of the coppers who were in the office. The old ritual commenced and the Inspector began to use his rank, no doubt to try and impress his boss.

"Last night, MacGregor, you were found off your beat, your uniform was a disgrace - it was covered with mud. You made a feeble explanation last night, now I want the whole story because I am not satisfied."

. "Inspector, before you go any further, are you sure of all your facts in this case?" said the SDI looking up.

"I found MacGregor about 3 miles from his allocated beat when I was out on patrol. I am sure of my facts," the Inspector said.

"I have been checking the books and the messages and I notice that Mr MacGregor was given a message to do. I also note that the address shown was not on his beat. Where exactly did you see him when he was off his beat?" The old man was playing with the Inspector, who became alert at this questioning and informed the Station Boss where the alleged offence took place.

"That is between the office and the place where the message was done." A statement, not a question.

"Who gave you the message to do?"

"Him," replied Jock pointing at the Sergeant.

"Is that correct Sergeant?" the Boss asked.

"Yes Sir," he said as he hurriedly went on to explain. "It was a mix up."

"Nevertheless you did give him a direct order, which he obeyed by doing the message?"

"Yes Sir." The poor Sergeant regretted ever having heard of MacGregor.

"You were aware of this message were you Inspector?"

The tight-lipped Irish Inspector couldn't deny that he knew about the message, for Jock had told him when he explained the previous night. He had also checked the message pad and signed them himself.

"Well, how the hell can you say he was off his beat when he was lawfully obeying an order?"

"He'd had ample time to do the message and get back to the office." The Inspector was wriggling at the end of the hook. Jock was really enjoying himself as he watched him sweat.

"And when I stopped him, I noticed that his clothing was covered with mud. Obviously he had been doing something which he shouldn't have."

"I was just looking at the times Inspector. It seems that you had a busy night, there was an entry about the Bomb Disposal Squad coming out, wasn't there?" The boss had his head bent over the book. "There isn't much in the OB about it, surely an unexploded bomb beside a gas tank deserves more explanation."

"The missile had been made safe when I arrived Sir. Everything was in order." The Inspector believed that his statement covered him.

"I would think that the times are very relevant, don't you Inspector?" The boss turned the book around so the Inspector could see them. "If you care to check the time on the message form with the time of reply - insert the time you stopped Mr MacGregor and the time of the call to the bomb, and then work out the facts. This place was on the route back to the office for Mr MacGregor and somehow the bomb had been defused before you got there. Use your head Inspector."

The Inspector didn't reply - slowly he was remembering the last time that he had Jock on the carpet, that was when he had disarmed a 500 pound bomb when he had been on duty.

"Would you tell the Sergeant and the Inspector what happened when you were called to this job last night?" said the Sub-Divisional Inspector turning to the driver.

The driver went into great detail, missing nothing out, and including the fact that death had been so close that the contact had been made as Jock had passed the clock over to him to hold. He also included in his narrative that the rain had never stopped whilst Jock had knelt beside the bomb to render it safe.

"It appears that under such circumstances Inspector, that it would be possible for Mr MacGregor to get some mud on his uniform, don't you think?" He paused a moment before continuing. "Now, if he had been drinking on duty I would be inclined to take a very different view of the matter for in my opinion <u>that</u> is a serious offence. Don't you agree Inspector?"

The silence from the Inspector and the Sergeant proved that they were feeling far from being comfortable.

"Is there anything else you want this Constable for?" the SDI. asked. He received assurance from the Officer in charge of night duty that Jock was no longer needed.

"Right, Goodnight Mr MacGregor, watch yourself. Now Inspector, you and I have something to discuss, you as well Sergeant. If you would be kind enough to step in here."

The three men were just going into the Inspector's office as Jock left the room, in company with the driver.

"I'd watch your back if I were you Jock. I believe the Inspector and the Sergeant have got it in for you," was the advice given by Johnny before they parted company.

CHAPTER FIVE

HOME BEAT

MOSLEY'S MOB

Booking on duty at 2pm Jock found that everyone had been detailed to take an early meal. Reinforcements were coming in from other stations at 6pm and each PC would be doubled up with one of these strangers. Shifts had been changed for some coppers and all days off had been cancelled. There were so many police on duty that afternoon that Jock found he only had one beat to work and that was close to the office, covering sections of two main roads. The main roads also had several coppers who had nothing else to do but walk along those streets. By the time he had finished his school crossing it was time for his tea break. He went in early because he knew that it would be bedlam in the canteen with all the strangers on the patch. He knew that with so many bodies around the nick he would be able to have a longer break, at least until they were all paraded again. He was right in his estimation of the conditions which prevailed on the station premises, the place was packed, apparently all the other coppers had the same idea and had come in early. Reinforcements drifted in to increase the station to bursting point. Parade at 5.45pm was chaos as the newcomers were paired off with the local bobbies, instructions were given so that every man knew exactly where he had to work and what to do when the call came for their services. A tremendous reserve of manpower was held at the station, whilst the other chaps patrolled the town centre. At every street corner one could see a small meeting being held, only one man on a box talking to another two, but legally it was a meeting. No other meeting could be set up anywhere near them, it was the joint efforts of various parties to prevent Mosley's men starting their advertised meeting in the town. All the coppers on reserve were waiting to be loaded into coaches to be driven to the meeting, if indeed Mosley's men succeeded in starting a meeting.

Eventually, the speakers were all getting sore throats and they just stood waiting for the big coach to come, with the unwanted people on board. Everyone was waiting, the whole of the area was a tinder box, one spark - that's all that was needed. Suddenly it came, driving slowly along the main road, Union Jacks flying, floodlights on the four top corners of the vehicle, a large box truck with the National Anthem blaring out loud from it's loudspeakers. This was the spark that began the blood-curdling bloodbath and evening of vicious violence, for as this monster moved along the streets, the mobs began to gather, waiting for it to become stationary. The driver moved slowly, checking each side street looking for a suitable place to park his vehicle and start the meeting. When he succeeded in finding a place, a group of men immediately climbed onto the roof of the truck, others poured out of the back of the vehicle and promptly surrounded the truck, these were the bully boys, strong-arm men who would stop anyone getting near the truck and hand out hard knocks to anyone who attempted to interfere with the meeting.

As soon as the brakes were applied and the engine was switched off, all the other little meetings broke up, hundreds of people headed for the big truck and converged on the intruder, all creeds, nationalities and all various political parties joined in common cause. There were also numerous people who went to the meeting with one intent, that was to have a fight - with anyone - but preferably with the police. All patrolling officers obeyed their instructions and made their way towards the big vehicle which was still playing the music. News was also relayed to the station so that the extra coppers could be taken to their vantage points, in readiness for the expected trouble and the riots which always followed one of Mosley's meetings.

The speakers blared, insults flew, tempers became short, insulted parties, religions, nationalities, Jews, coloured people, Communists and Labour supporters all joined together and pushed forward with one united intention. Bottles began to fly, bricks were thrown, blood began to flow and heaving fighting bodies were everywhere. The truck rocked as the mob tried to overturn it, things had reached such a pitch that lives could be at risk, so the Officer in charge of the Police ordered the meeting to be closed down. With a struggle, the road was cleared yard by yard by the outnumbered Police, to allow the vehicle to be driven away through the thousands who surrounded it. Some of the bully boys were unable to gain entry before the lorry drove off, they had to fight their way towards public transport. Whenever any of them were recognised by the crowd as they sought to escape, the wrath of the mob was then turned upon the various tramcars and buses which were then attacked, regardless of the many innocent people who were passengers at the time. Eventually, the crowds slowly dispersed after their antagonists had left, leaving the police to an area littered with broken bottles, bricks and lengths of wood. Several fights were taken to local pubs, where the various elements engaged in combat once again, until the coppers cleared them all out.

One of Jock's orders had been to keep an eye on his property which was close to the meeting place. It had been quite possible for a shop window to be broken, either accidentally by a missile, or even by a body being thrown through it. Then again, it was a marvellous opportunity for any criminal to take his chance whilst the noise of the crowds drowned the sound of his entry. His attachment left him and headed for the Police Station to get transport back to his own Division as Jock walked along his shops. He reached a huge multiple store which had several showcases between the shop and the pavement. The inside of the arcade was dark and Jock didn't have a torch - due to the fact that it had been daylight when he had left the Station. He moved slowly through the arcade, feeling the windows with his hand as he moved along. If there had been a broken window, he would have found it straight away. There were no lights on in the shop so he couldn't see anything till suddenly he saw a light, the trouble was it was coming from the street. He couldn't understand this at first, here he was looking through a window into the street, then the penny dropped - he must be inside the shop! 'How the hell did that happen?' he thought. He struck a match and confirmed the situation, here he was inside one of the largest stores in the town, but how had he managed it? He worked his way back sadly, he was no use in this situation without a torch. Eventually he found the reason, leading from the arcade into the shop was a huge roller shutter which hadn't been lowered. It seemed impossible for the staff to vacate the premises without realising the fact, but the shutter could only be operated from inside the store. He walked out onto the pavement and waited patiently for another copper to come along and assist, night shift would be making their way to work shortly and he would get one of them to pass the information on. Sure enough, an old PC trundled his cycle along in the direction of the nick, he seemed reluctant to face another night out of bed and he was more than reluctant to stop and assist Jock.

"I don't start work till ten o'clock," he moaned.

"Well when you do start work, will you let someone know that I have found this place wide open?" Jock indicated the large store behind him.

A quarter of an hour passed before the whole of the night shift arrived, complete with torches and with one wild rush they disappeared inside the departmental store and dispersed amongst the various departments. Jock shrugged his shoulders and left them to it and made his way back towards the station to book off.

CLOSE SHAVE

"Hey, Jock - going my way?" an old copper asked him.
"Yes, for the first mile at least" was the reply. "It's a cold one tonight isn't it?"
The two coppers walked side by side along the darkened streets towards their beats.
"Yes, I expect we'll have some ice before the morning," the old man replied, "but I'm ready for it."
"How?" Jock enquired.
"Always wear my pyjamas under my uniform - and two pairs of socks and two pairs of gloves in this weather." The oldster grinned. "You won't catch me getting cold."
"Pyjamas?" asked Jock in astonishment.
"Of course, I can't get away with these long johns that a lot of them wear, so I wear the pyjamas. I just tuck the bottoms inside my socks."
"Good God, what next?"
"Any trick you can use to keep warm on a winter's night lad is worth trying. Now come on, let's have a quick one to help keep the chill out."
The old timer pushed a back gate open and entered a back yard, he opened a door which led into a passage and Jock followed him inside. At the end of the passage he saw a glass door which stood open at an angle - reflected in the glass he noticed a man who came to meet them, when he saw them he just held two fingers up and then disappeared from view again. A few moments later he came back holding two glasses of beer.
"Let's stand round here" the old copper said as he indicated the alcove at the end of the passage. "We're out of sight here."
From their position, they could see the passage reflected in the glass door. They had just started to enjoy their drink when the back door opened - they saw the barman look round and then he held two fingers up and nodded. Two pints were quickly produced and he walked passed Jock and his mate with the drinks. A quick glance in the glass doorway showed who the two newcomers were - it was the Inspector and the section Sergeant who were enjoying a quick pint. Jock and his mate were stuck in their niche, hardly daring to breathe or move with the two supervising officers just around the corner. Eventually, the barman came out, collected two empty glasses.
"Goodnight Sir," he said returning to his duties behind the bar. Jock and his mate looked at one another as the door closed behind the boss.
"That was bloody close lad," the old-timer said.
"Aye," said Jock as he finished off his drink, "Let's get out of here." The barman collected their glasses.

"Is he always like that?" Jock asked.

"Yes, he is only too pleased to see a copper because they get a hell of a lot of trouble at this pub."

They parted company outside the premises. Jock carried on his way to check his property, leaving the old chap to keep his pyjamas up. Breakfast was a welcome break from the icy cold - as he booked in at the station the Inspector looked up from his paperwork.

"Tomorrow night MacGregor, you will work in an anti-clockwise direction."

"Why Sir? According to my beat book it's clockwise," Jock responded.

"Why. You may ask. It is to ensure that you are in different places at different times. In simple words, it's to make sure that you are not in the same place at the same time as you were tonight. Understand?"

"My beat book ..." began Jock.

"Never mind your bloody beat book, you silly sod. Just remember that you can see a reflection both ways through a glass door." The supervising officers had seen the pair of them having a drink in the passage but couldn't do anything about it as they were doing the same thing. So Jock did as he was advised and worked his beat the opposite way the following night. Trouble was, by the time he had got around the ground, the pub was closed - crafty bloody Inspector - but Jock never went back to that pub again in any case.

BANK JOB

This is a bloody monotonous job, Jock thought, as he held his head down against the cold wind. Constantly trying stop doors, his eyes and ears on the alert for anything unusual. A dog barking, a rattle of metal, indeed anything out of the ordinary. Grab, twist, push, another door checked. Never a thought that such a place would be OK or that the contents of the building would be of any use to a thief. Each and every door received the same treatment and windows were also checked. Then it happened, it always comes unexpectedly, yet it was always anticipated. The handle turned and the door opened. Jock stood back to see which building was open. Oh no, another bank. Feint noises came to his ears - someone was inside - he stopped a late night traveller.

"Excuse me Sir. Could you stop at that 'phone box and tell them that I have found this Bank open and that there is someone inside?" Jock indicated a Police 'phone box a couple of hundred yards away and then returned to a position just inside the door of the Bank, and waited. It wasn't that he minded having a go, but seeing it was a Bank he decided to go by the book and call for assistance.

After a while, having convinced himself that he could still hear feint voices coming from the darkened interior, he returned to the pavement to see if the man had made the 'phone call. There was no sign of him at the Police Box, surely he couldn't have made the call already. A glance in the opposite direction showed the midnight traveller running like hell, back the way he had come. Apparently he didn't want to get mixed up with any possible shoot-out during a Bank raid - couldn't blame him really - after all, he didn't get paid for risking his life. So, back inside Jock went, he didn't want to leave the premises in case the persons inside escaped. No lights were showing as he moved into the eerie darkness and moving slowly, he checked the public sector before sliding over the counter. Everything appeared to be in order but the door leading to the manager's office was open. Jock quietly entered the room, listening intently, the voices could still be heard. The office was undisturbed when he checked it but another door led into a passage and this was also open - it was from this direction that the voices were coming. As he listened, he was conscious of a soft padding noise which seemed to be coming nearer and as he watched the open doorway, he saw a shadowy figure go slowly past the opening. Quick as a flash, Jock returned to the office and jumped over the counter, he had noticed that the stranger was dressed in rough clothing and he was headed for the public sector. As the door opened, Jock switched his torch on and raised his stick, the light shone straight into the intruder's eyes. The man screamed as he saw the raised truncheon and he raised his arms in terror.

"Don't hit me please."

"Who are you, and what are you doing here?" asked Jock.

The man stuttered as he tried to regain control of his vocal chords.

"Who are you?" Jock asked again.

"I'm the manager." The man at last managed to speak, still unable to see who was talking to him behind the bright light.

"The manager?" Jock swung his light over the dirty overalls and torn plimsolls that the man was wearing. "Who are you trying to kid?"

"I am, I am, I can prove it." The man was terrified.

"It's the middle of the night and I find you creeping around the inside of a Bank, dressed in overalls and sandshoes, and you expect me to believe you are the Bank manager.

"I am," the man said as he raised his voice and shouted, "Maggie, ain't I the manager of this Bank?" A female voice came floating down the stairs.

"Of course you are you silly old bugger, now hurry up and lock that door, I want to get to bed."

Apparently, when the Bank staff left the premises at the end of the day's work, they slipped the Yale lock on the door behind them. The manager, who lived above the Bank, double locked the door after they had all gone. This day it hadn't been done due to the fact that he had been engaged with some painting and decorating and this was the reason he had the overalls on. He was a greatly relieved man when he found that his interrogator was a local copper.

"It's the first time that I have left the door open and believe me, it will be the last," he said.

"Goodnight, make sure you lock it behind me," Jock said as he went on his way. Next time he might be lucky.

SMOG

Smog, one had really to experience it to appreciate the filthy stuff; the nose was blocked with dirt, it found its way down the throat causing fits of coughing and choking. Huge black blobs of sticky phlegm were constantly being ejected by the men who had to walk around in it during the night. Traffic crawled along with headlights blazing, sometimes the flow of traffic came to a standstill as the drivers couldn't see. Car after car followed the one in front, hoping that the man could see and was going their way. Houses and shops had to keep their lights on during daytime it was so dark. Nights, of course, was much worse. Many a time Jock found a double decker bus in the back streets where the driver had finished up after getting lost.

It was on one such night, only a week after the 'Craig and Bentley' job, that was a bloody farce - a couple of villains went out on a job one night, it was a screwing job and they had a gun with them. The result was obvious, a copper got in the way, he was shot, and died. Public feeling was stirred up by a few 'goodie goodies', nobody seemed worried that a wife had lost her husband and the children had lost their dad, everyone seemed more bothered about the 'poor little innocent boy' who had been caught on the job. The public seemed more concerned about the fact that the eldest man was hung and, because the villain who had the gun was under age to die, he was sentenced to life. Poor little innocents, chased and persecuted by the coppers, forget about the dead copper and his family.

The smog was dense, a thick yellow unbreathable air, torches were of no use, they could not penetrate the gloom. It was only local knowledge that allowed anyone to walk around the streets without getting lost. Nothing could be seen, a crash of broken glass indicated that a window had been broken, this noise continued through the night as thieves took advantage of the murk and broke into the different shops. Alarms were going off all over the place, muted by the fog. Coppers walked along, touching the walls and windows as they went - this was the only way they could find a broken window. As Jock walked along a narrow back lane he heard an unusual sound, it was different from the other noises which prevailed and seemed to come from a higher level. He focused on the approximate position that the sound came from and headed towards it. He entered a doorway leading into a covered passage, he knew that this led to a flat over the shops and access to the roofs was possible. Inside the passage he stopped and listened, the sound came again, he waited, the sound seemed to be coming nearer. Someone was coming down from the rooftops and headed for the passage. He waited patiently as the unseen person or persons came nearer. When he had estimated the intruders were almost upon him, he switched on his torch and only a couple of feet from him stood two huge men.

A quick battle ensued, it was everyone for himself and as only one man could face him at a time Jock was happy in the confined space. He pulled no punches using his lantern and stick in a devastating manner. One battered opponent down and he started on the second, he didn't know whether these two men had any friends coming along behind them so he couldn't take any chances. He did not want another 'Craig and Bentley' case. Blood began to flow and the second man gave up the fight and sank on the ground beside his colleague. As it happened, they were by themselves. They gave no trouble as he walked them down to the Station, possibly the warning he gave them may have had something to do with it.

"Try to get away and I'll split both your heads wide open." Just a friendly bit of advice which he gave, holding both of them tightly in arm locks.

The men were strangers to him and as he was of the opinion that he knew all the local thieves, he believed they had either just moved onto the toby, or were working off their own patch. The CID took them upstairs for a cosy chat and after they had finished quizzing the villains, they had admitted breaking into the bookies shop, possessing housebreaking gear and resisting arrest - apart from the assault on Police and having numerous other jobs taken into consideration - which they admitted.

They appeared at Court the same morning, at 10am, and pleaded 'Guilty' on all counts. The Magistrate listened patiently to the evidence and looked closely at the two men before pronouncing sentence.

"Fined £1 each. Next case."

A gasp arose from the body of the Court, the Police Inspector in charge of the Court Cards stood up and looked at Jock. He was awaiting him to appeal against the sentence. The Magistrate saw him and he looked at Jock, he had a slight smile on his face and when Jock shook his head at the Inspector, the old man nodded.

"Thank you officer." Nothing had been said but he knew as well as Jock that the men had been punished and would not work that area again.

The next case in was a little Jew boy who had been selling silk stockings on the pavement, his case didn't take long as he also pleaded 'Guilty'.

"Fined £5. Next case."

The Court Inspector started having a go at Jock when he collected his court card.

"Why didn't you appeal against the sentence. They only got fined a pound for all those offences?" Just then he heard the result of the little Jew Boy.

"Christ, he got fined five times as much as those two villains."

"Guv, I only arrest them - I'm not worried what the sentence is. They were done for assault on me but anyone can see that they came off worse. The old man probably thinks the same and that's why he gave them a nominal sentence. I don't think they will hang around our patch any more and that's all we want."

TOWN JOB

Town jobs came with great regularity, they were a change from normal beat duties but could be boring after a while. Once again the young coppers were always chosen for these duties and it was on one of these very early morning starts that found Jock standing at the side of the Mall.

As usual, they were in position hours before the show was scheduled to start and a couple of yards away from him stood one of the chaps who had been in the training school with him. As the crowds began to gather, his colleague approached him.

"I'm just going to phone my fiancé, if anyone wants to know where I've gone just say I've gone to the toilet."

"Righto" answered Jock.

The lovelorn copper wasn't away long but about ten minutes later Jock saw him engaged in conversation with a really beautiful, well-dressed female. He moved towards this intrepid man - he was going to question him regarding his companion - when the copper introduced him to the lady. It was his girlfriend who had made arrangements to come and stand with him whilst he was on duty. Jock eyed her up and down, Christ she was really a beauty, lucky bugger. They got married a few weeks later and the copper was called into the old man's office, the conversation was apparently short and non too sweet.

"Your wife is a prostitute. You can not be allowed to remain in the Police Force."

He had to resign and as he told Jock later, he did not know that his wife was on the game. She was high class and did not walk the streets, she waited for her clients to come to her.

Anyway, it didn't make any difference to him, he still lived with her as Jock found out later when he was working for another Department. He saw the man, late at night, mincing along with two little poodles on leads. He had been kicked out whilst his wife did her exercises at home.

The postings came up for another town job and Jock's name was there as usual. He had time available on his card so he asked for the day off and was granted it - anything to avoid that bloody melee.

"I've got the day off," he told Puggle.

"Good, we can go and see the Trooping of the Colour," was her reply. Jock never thought of these things because he was so used to being present during all the ceremonial proceedings that he forgot about Puggle and the youngster. She never got away from the stress and strain of home very much so Jock took them both down to Horse Guards parade to see the show - it was a change for them all. His wife and youngster hadn't seen the show before and he was squeezed in at the back of the crowds who were pushing and shoving in their attempts to see the soldiers.

"To think, I could be standing in comfort in the front," he thought. However, the day out did bring a bit of light relief. They also began to make visits to the Zoo and, as they were Honorary Members of the Zoological Society, they didn't have to pay to get in, otherwise they could never have afforded the visits.

A FORTUNE

A sudden clatter disrupted his thoughts as he plodded along his beat, he was worried about the financial state of affairs because things were not getting any better. The noise that distracted him was caused by a large black leather bank bag.

"Where the hell did that come from?" he wondered as he glanced around, he was the only person on the pavement at that moment so nobody could have thrown or dropped it. Puzzled, he picked it up and examined it, it was locked but had the name of the Bank on it. By the feel of it there must be a lot of cash inside his newly obtained load. He decided to take it straight into the Police Office and as he entered the front office, he noticed there was a man talking to the Station Officer. The chap was in a very distressed state and was struggling to get his words out. Jock laid his find on the counter and waited for the bloke to finish with his complaint, the Sergeant just glanced at him as he listened to his customer.

"How much was in it?" he asked.

"Nearly five thousand pounds," the man whispered.

"Can you give me a description of it?" the Sergeant asked.

"Well, it was an ordinary Bank bag, black leather with a brass lock."

"Something like this?" and the skipper picked up the bag that Jock had laid on the desk.

The customer was exalted with joy.

"That's it," he screamed. "How did you do it." He must have thought it was a miracle.

"Not so fast bonny lad, you'll have to prove it's yours - describe the contents etc. before I hand it over." He turned to Jock and held his hand out for his pocket book, as he signed the entry he told Jock how the chap had lost the bag.

"He was putting some stuff in his car and laid the bag on the roof - he drove away forgetting all about it."

"Did he say there was 5,000 nicker in there? That's ten years pay for me, I don't think I could forget where I put it."

"On your way lad, go and get some work done, I'll see to this" the Sergeant ordered. No doubt he would see to it and any free drinks that came along later.

"Call at the pie shop on your way in for Breakfast Jock and collect the pies." Jock received the orders as he stepped into the cold night air, ready for another boring tour of night duty.

"Where's this pie shop that I'm supposed to go to?" he asked one of the old coppers.

"It's the bakery on your beat, they'll have them ready for you," he was informed. "Meet me on the corner and I'll go with you at about one o'clock."

Jock met the man as planned and together they entered the building. It was lovely and warm and the smell was really delicious, compared with the atmosphere outside, this was sheer bliss.

"I'll be with you in a second Guv." A little man passed them carrying a dirty black bucket filled with a dark steaming greasy mixture.

"I'll just finish this row."

Long benches were covered with pies of all shapes and sizes, a quick punch with his finger in the corner of the pies was quickly followed by the insertion of a funnel, nearly as black as the bucket. The greasy substance was poured from the bucket into the funnel until it showed itself at the other corner of the pie. The same procedure was repeated with every pie along the row. As the mixture cooled, the baker returned it to stand in front of a furnace where he collected another similar container and then carried on filling his pies. As soon as the jelly had been inserted into all the cases he returned his bucket to its place beside the fire.

"Right, that's ready for the next lot, now then I haven't had a chance to put yours up yet. You'd better just help yourself from that load beside the door," he indicated trays full of pies that stood beside the doorway, apparently awaiting collection. Jock's associate produced a large bag from his deep pocket and proceeded to fill it.

"I'll take them down for you lad, just help yourself to any you want."

"Sorry, I don't think I fancy one just now," Jock graciously declined his suggestion, the very sight of the preparation had put him off such thoughts.

"Well, take some home for the family," the old man said.

'I wonder what they put into them?' Jock murmured to himself. It seemed the coppers had been looked after by the baker all during the war years and they hadn't died from food poisoning but Jock wasn't going to take any chances. His elderly companion took his bundle down to the Communication Room where the regular consumers of the ghastly concoction would no doubt devour them.

A COPPER COMES TO GRIEF

Jock sat in the canteen having his sandwiches and warming himself. He was the only one present until a young chap came in - he was the last one of the crowd who joined the station with Jock. He looked really out of sorts as he took off his overcoat and poured a cup of tea. He slumped in a chair opposite Jock.

"What's the matter Steve?"

The lad looked across at him and said, "I'm sick."

"Go and see the duty officer and tell him that you are going off duty due to the fact that you're sick."

"Not sick in that sense Jock, I'm just fed up with this job and the way people go on."

"You're not the only one Steve, I've had my belly full of them as well but I look at this way, in a year or so all the old coppers will be out and these bloody Inspectors and Sergeants will also be finished - and then things will change."

"It's not only them Jock but the public as well. Tonight was the final straw for me, I'm packing the job in, I've had enough."

Jock realized that the copper was in a pretty bad state and asked him why he intended chucking the Force in.

"You may think I'm being bloody silly but, as you know, I was posted on the outside beat tonight and you know that lonely stretch along the top where there are no street lights."

"I know the place, but you're not frightened of the dark, are you?"

"No kidding Jock, you know I'm not, but tonight I was just starting to go down there when a girl came up to me. She asked me to escort her along that dark part as she was afraid."

"Well, what's wrong with that?" Jock asked, wondering what had happened to influence the lad to such an extent that he was willing to resign because of it.

"There's nothing wrong with the request, except for one thing. When we reached the middle of that dark section, she told me that her parents were always on to her to be careful, they had told her that she could always trust a Policeman."

"Well, that's sound advice - so what happened?"

"That's what I told her, you can always trust a copper. The next thing I knew she had hold of my arm and was pushing me into the field."

"I knew that I could trust you, you'll be careful won't you?" she told me.

I asked her what she meant, although it was becoming obvious to me. She told me that she had led a very sheltered life but was only human and had normal instincts - she told me that she had heard and read about sex but wanted to experience it but she didn't want to have a baby - and as she could trust a policeman, she couldn't think of anyone better to have it with.

"Good God, and did you keep her happy?" Jock didn't know whether his mate was pulling his leg or not.

"No, I told her to beat it and not to try that line with me."

"And?"

"She started shouting and told me that if I didn't do what she asked then she would complain - she would say that I had attacked her and tried to rape her." The young copper sobbed quietly.

"What did you do then?" asked Jock, certain now that he wasn't having his leg pulled.

"I ran like hell Jock, I ran like hell and as far as I know she is still there."

"Look Steve, I think the best thing you can do is to report this to the duty officer."

The young copper left the job. He resigned, not because of the fear of violence or death but because of the actions of a silly young girl who wanted to have her way with him. There are some queer perverts walking the streets of this country.

BUSTLE PUNCHERS

"Officer, Officer, there's a man down there," the middle aged female gasped.

"Yes Madam, which one, where?" Jock looked at the crowded market street.

"Along there," she pointed in the general direction. The lady was in a very distressed state and couldn't give a logical explanation.

"Madam, you'll have to show me." He knew that if a man was involved in some incident in the market then the offence was most likely to be indecent, although there was a chance that the man was light fingered and stealing purses. He took the woman's arm and pushed through the crowds, she was reluctant but allowed Jock to propel her along, when suddenly she stopped and refused to go any further.

"Him," she said, pointing towards a stall selling ladies lingerie. A cluster of interested females were gathered around the stall, all looking for bargains. On the fringe of the crowd stood several men, because, as usual, the husbands stood at the back waiting for their wives to make their purchases. As the complainant was not in any condition to assist Jock any further in the identification, nor able to pinpoint him, then he had to make the decision by himself.

The woman had been unable to inform him about the man's activities which had made her so distressed. If it had been a pickpocket she wouldn't have known about it, unless she had seen another person's purse being stolen - in which case, Jock considered the act shouldn't have disturbed her so much. He decided therefore that the man must have been a 'Bustle Puncher' and this lady had been one of his rubs. He went around the stall and examined all the men very closely, most of them wore loose fitting raincoats and all of them had their hands in their pockets. They all stood at the back of the crowd and were in close proximity of the women. They could have been with their wives but, as Jock knew, it was a habit for strangers to tangle with the women in such circumstances. Husbands generally were disinterested and would be awaiting the chance to break free from the scrum, as soon as their spouse had grabbed some alleged bargain. One of these men was a mental case, but all Jock had to go on was their attitude or the expression on their face, he watched each one before making his decision and he had to be right for he wouldn't get a second chance.

Mind made up, he saw a man pressing very close to a woman, apparently trying to look interested at the goods on offer - this was not natural. He made his way through the crowds until he was behind the man and then he grabbed him by the arm and swung him round. The woman noticed that the pressure had been removed from the rear portion of her anatomy and she glanced round, probably to see who had been pushing against her. Then she saw the man being held by Jock, she also saw the open raincoat which couldn't cover the exposed pulsating flesh. She screamed and this attracted the attention of other customers who also saw the man's nakedness and they converged on the copper and the quaking bustle puncher. Jock pulled the man along away from the enraged mob, eventually a more open part of the road was reached and a full sprint was needed to keep his prisoner away from the hostile crowd. Luckily they didn't have far to go to the Police Station and Jock ushered the breathless man into the Charge Room, the Station Sergeant came in to meet them.

"Indecent Exposure?" he asked, looking down at the man's pride and joy. This type of offence was typical of those which occur regularly in crowded streets, particularly markets. Normally, any woman who receives the unwanted attention from these morons either moves away, or stays and enjoys the contact. Very rarely do they complain. The other kind of offence committed by these mentally sick people is indecent exposure and most of these cases are reported to the police but, surprisingly enough, very few of the women can describe the man's face! I wonder why? Not all of them are reported at the time either because when one lady complained about a man exposing himself, she stated that every morning the man rode past on his cycle, whipped open his raincoat and, after exposing himself, rode around the block and gave a repeat performance further along the street. When asked how long this had been going on.

"About three years," the lady replied. The name and address of the man was obtained by Jock who gave it to the woman so that she could do whatever she liked with it - she could even sue him if she so wanted.

It was around this time that Jock decided to go to Evening Classes, he wanted to ensure that when the time came, his knowledge of languages would be such that he would be able to pass any examination required. He decided to concentrate on just five languages and brush up on grammar. He found it was a problem at times to fit the classes in with his work, especially when he was on late turn.

In the meanwhile he continued working his beat and as he had a law exam coming soon, he made a habit of studying as he walked along the quiet streets. One day he was doing this when his thoughts were disturbed.

"Guv, come quick, there's a bloody murder going on." A man panted and indicated along the street where a crowd stood outside a house.

As he approached the premises he could hear screams and sounds of splintering wood, further shouts followed and then sounds of breaking glass came as he entered the house. As he entered the front room he saw the cause and realised that this was the best free for all he had witnessed for a long time. Two men and two women were having the time of their lives. Unable to make himself heard over the noise, he drew his stick and hit the table - the sound served its purpose and the row ceased as the contestants gaped at the intruder. Secretly Jock had hoped that the table would not disintegrate when he hit it for he had seen that happen on one similar occasion during a fight at a coloured man's house - this time he was in luck because the table remained in one piece.

As the quartet quietened down he asked what the row was about and an explanation came automatically from the blood-covered fighters. They all tried to talk at the same time and, as a result, they were at one another's throats again! Jock realised from the few words spoken that they were all foreign nationals. 'What's the use?' he sighed and was just about to hit the table again when a fresh voice was heard.

"Right, what the bloody hell is going on here?" It was the Section Sergeant - the one that was always after Jock's blood. Naturally the crowd carried on fighting until the Sergeant drew his stick and brought it crashing down on the table. The table shattered and Jock couldn't help but grin - the noise stopped the foreigners once more.

"What the hell do you lot think you're doing?" the Sergeant asked. One would have thought this was an invitation for them to carry on fighting because, once again, they threw themselves into the fray.

"Right. Let's have them outside. I'm going to arrest them." He ordered Jock to take the troublemakers outside and place them in the Police Van which had brought him to the scene.

The physical violence stopped but the verbal abuse continued as they were driven to the Nick. Leaving them in the Charge Room, the skipper ordered Jock to remain with them; he went into the front office to discuss the situation with the Station Officer who was the Inspector that hated the sight of Jock. A few minutes later they both came out with the Charge Sheets.

The Inspector took up his position behind the desk and pointed at one of the men.

"You, as he indicated to the front of the desk, Here." The man accepted the order and took up his place that had been indicated.

"Name?" the Station Officer asked.

"Che?" said the man, looking blank.

"Name?" the Inspector demanded again, "and don't piss me about."

Jock decided to give a little assistance at this point.

"Inspector, he said, I don't think he knows what you are talking about."

"You keep your nose out of this Constable. This has nothing to do with you," the Senior Officer barked.

"Now you, I'll ask you only once again, what is your name?"

Jock spoke to the unlucky prisoner as he stood looking blank,

"Volere dire votre nom?"

"Ah, Si. Io sono Julio Minello," the man answered.

"What the hell did you say?" bellowed the enraged Inspector.

"These people are Italians Sir, they do not speak English," Jock told him.

"But you can speak to them, in their language, so you can stay here and tell them what it is all about," his boss told him. At this point, Jock decided to be bloody awkward and work according to the book. His decision was based purely on the Inspector's attitude.

"Now look here, I am ordering you," showing his rank once again.

"You can order till you are blue in the face Inspector. You know that an official interpreter is required in these circumstances - you cannot order me to do something that is not official." His back was up against this man.

The argument was brought to a halt when the Sub-Divisional Inspector walked in,

"What's going on Inspector?" he asked.

The Inspector was enraged because Jock was adopting a stubborn attitude over these foreigners and he couldn't resist another attempt to have a go.

"This Constable has refused to obey an order, Sir."

"It wasn't an official order, that's why I refused," came Jock's reply.

"Alright Inspector, what did you tell him to do?" The old man was getting used to these two now and when the reason of disobedience was explained to him, he said,

"He's right you know, you should have an Official Interpreter."

"Jock," said the Inspector as he turned to the young copper. "Can you really speak their language?" Jock was still mad with the little Irish Inspector and gave his views about the incident before answering the question.

"The Sergeant arrested them, I have nothing to do with the case, I was only detailed to stay with them. Regarding their language, yes I do understand them."

"Well, look Mr MacGregor, do me a favour. I don't want you to get mixed up in any long-winded Court case because I know that you're not paid as an interpreter. All I want you to do is to explain to them the reason why they are being charged. I will make arrangements for proper representation for them at Court. Will you do that for me, just to get them off the premises?" He pleaded with Jock and, at the same time, he was drawing him into the front office as he spoke.

"I know that you don't get on with the Inspector, but don't lower your standards to his level, it doesn't suit you." The old Inspector remembered the respect the Army Officer had shown for this ex-army chap.

Jock agreed to assist with the four Italians and the boss stayed with them all the time, listening to a language that he had never heard before.

The following day Jock was called back to the Station, the wireless car pulled in alongside of him as he strolled along.

"The Inspector wants to see you back at the Nick, Jock, looks like you're in trouble again," said the driver grinning, "I'll give you a lift back."

When he entered the front office, Jock saw the Inspector and the Section Sergeant standing talking to the elderly Assistant Station Officer and they all looked up as he entered. Without any preliminaries, the Inspector ordered Jock to find out what an old lady was wanting and he indicated the woman sitting in a chair. Jock noticed that she was crying.

"She's one of that crowd that was in here last night. At least she speaks the same as they did, so ask her what she wants."

"I've told you Inspector that I'm not an official interpreter" Jock responded.

"You'll do as you are bloody well told to, you're just trying to be bloody awkward, aren't you?"

"No, Inspector, I am not the awkward one. I work according to the book - I thought that had already been explained. Last night the Sub-Divisional Inspector told me that I would not be needed any more with the crowd who were arrested last night."

Even as he was speaking, the Inspector was reaching for the telephone. He asked to be put through to the Guvnor's office - cursing Jock as he waited.

"Sir!" he said as he made contact with the only man who could get this stupid copper to do anything. "Sir, we have a foreigner in the front office and I believe she is connected with the same ones arrested last night because she speaks the same language. MacGregor has been called for and is at present in the office. No Sir, he refuses to talk with the woman. Right Sir." Jock gathered by the one-sided conversation that the boss was on his way down. Sure enough, a few seconds later, the weary gaffer walked into another clash of temperaments.

"Again!" he growled. "Look, Mr MacGregor, is this lady connected with the four prisoners last night?"

Jock shrugged his shoulders, at least that would be easy enough to prove and he spoke to the woman but she just looked blank.

"Tu Italiano?" he then asked.

The old lady still gazed at Jock, as if waiting to be helped from her predicament but she never answered his question.

"She isn't Italian, Sir." Jock then spoke to the woman in various other languages before getting an answer - once she realised that someone could speak her own language, she began to expound all her worries.

"Just a moment madam," said Jock as he stopped the flow of words. He turned to his boss and informed him that the old lady was a German and was in no way connected with the four fighters of the previous day.

"Christ, what a bloody dozy lot of nits I've got to help me run this place. What are you going to do about her Inspector?" The boss just got a blank stare in return to his question.

"Shall I deal with her Guv?" said Jock, embarrassed at the scene.

"Can you speak German as well?" his boss swung round upon him.

"I make out quite well with it Guv," answered Jock as he turned to the old lady.

"Entschuldigen Sie Mich Gnadige Frau, was ist loss?"

After several minutes conversation with the woman, Jock took a half-crown from his pocket and gave it to her and he then wrote several instructions down and handed them to her to read. She left the office, full of smiles and thanks.

"Full of surprises you great Scotch get" said the SD Inspector.

"Scots, Sir" Jock corrected him, "Not Scotch."

"Bugger it lad, whichever way you say it, you seem to be able to say it in any language. You surprise me, how many foreign languages can you speak?"

"Seven, Sir." The answer brought every head up in the office because they had all been listening as they tried to make out what the woman's trouble was.

"Seven?" the boss exploded. "Then what the hell are you doing walking the beat? You should be in Special Branch, not pushing doors and mixing with this ignorant lot." He waved his arm generally to include very one in the room.

"We may be dozy but we're not silly enough to fall for the old sob story and hand money over. He'll never see that again." The Inspector beamed at the thought that Jock had dropped a clanger when he gave the old lady the money, little did he know that it was all the cash that Jock possessed.

"I intend to Sir, as soon as I finish my probation," Jock ignored the remark and answered his boss, then turned, left the office and returned to his beats.

BLOW UP

As he walked the beat the following day, he knew that things would come to a head with the Irish Inspector. He couldn't tolerate the man who was constantly looking for faults and as he walked around he was turning things over in his mind, wondering whether it was worth sticking it. Bob had left the job just after he had joined, now he had set himself up in business making caravans and he had asked Jock to join him. It was the lack of capital that held him back. An old American Officer pal of his now lived in California, they corresponded with one another and he had suggested that Jock bring his wife and family to live in America. Once again, the lack of cash prevented it; it looked as though he had no other option but to carry on being a copper and to put up with all the little niggles and problems. Like all young probationers, he was getting his share of beat work. 'Get some summonses' was a regular request from the Sergeants. Obviously someone had to sort the traffic out and who better to do this than the new men, the amount of work done could be shown on their weekly reports by the Sergeants.

Weekends always created problems around the town centre because of the amount of traffic using the area. The pocket books were always out and, naturally, the motorists who received the attention of the coppers got annoyed. Every copper was used to the old sayings of 'Why don't you go and catch some burglars' or, 'I know your boss - he's a friend of mine'. It was only a man with a small mind that took any notice of them as they swore and threatened, but their statements were always entered in the reports. On this particular day, Jock and a dour Cockney worked the market area conscientiously and a lot of people were reported, including a couple of nasty types who swore and threatened to get them the sack.

When he booked off duty, he handed his reports in to the Sergeant and then made his way up to the Sub-Divisional Inspector's office. He had made his mind up to request a transfer and if he couldn't get it he was going to pack the job in. He discussed the situation with his boss who finally agreed with him and told Jock to collect the forms required from the front office and he would help him fill them in.

As he entered the front office he saw the Inspector sitting at the desk, he looked up at Jock, eyes bulging with rage and his face red with pent-up anger which he couldn't hide. He had been checking the reports handed to him by the Sergeant and he had come across a couple he didn't like. It had been a couple of his mates who had been reported for obstruction by Jock and the other copper. Well naturally, it was to be expected, he was annoyed and he blew his top. It didn't help matters when one of the coppers involved had walked in upon him; the Inspector was ready to strike anyone who came near him and he went for this particular recruit with all his venom.

"What the bloody hell do you mean by putting such shit in your report?" he bellowed. "That's what I think of your sodding lousy report."

He slipped up in a number of ways; first, when he shouted, second when he swore and thirdly when he threw the book in question at Jock.

Sensing trouble, the Section Sergeants and the office staff slipped into the Inspector's office and closed the door, but they all looked through the glass panel so that they could enjoy the sight of the young copper getting his trousers taken down.

Jock was not in a particularly bright and friendly mood himself and relations with this particular man were very strained so, naturally, when the shouting began his own anger exploded. When the pocket book was hurled at him, he grabbed it and returned it with such force that the unexpected missile struck the Inspector in the face.

"You stupid bastard," the Inspector yelled. "What the hell do you think you're doing?" The look of hatred on his face towards this young copper was quite evident.

Jock didn't hesitate when the Inspector started shouting abuse at him in such a manner; in one swift movement, he swung his legs over the counter and was in front of the desk. He reached across and grabbed the now terrified Inspector by the collar, he pulled the man straight across the desk until he was lying on top of his papers. He stuck his nose close up to the Officer's face and said to the bewildered man

"Listen to me, you little Irish sod. I had better men under me in the Army than you will ever be. I cam down here to get a transfer form to get away from you but now I've changed mind, I've had enough, I'm packing the job in."

He dropped the unlucky man on top of his papers and walked out of the room but not before he saw all the grinning faces at the little glass window of the Inspector's office. Mad as hell, he stalked up the stairs to the Boss's room and barged in.

"Come in" said the surprised man, looking up at his visitor. "What's wrong?"

"I've changed my mind Guv, I'm packing the job in" Jock stated. I've had enough of that Irish sod downstairs."

"Been having words with the Inspector again, Jock?" asked the boss.

"I've taken as much as I can Guv. I'd be better off in another job," Jock answered. The old man picked the telephone up.

"Front office please," he said. "Oh, Inspector, would you mind stepping up to my office a moment?"

Shortly afterwards a knock at the door signified the fact that he had dropped everything and had ran up the stairs as quickly as he could.

"Come in Inspector. Now would you tell me what the hell is going on?" the Guvnor requested.

Jock glowered at the little Irishman as he started complaining about the way he was attacked by the young copper. As the snide remarks dripped from the Inspector's mouth Jock started to interrupt the pack of lies and eventually, another shouting match was taking place between them.

"Alright Inspector, you'd better go. You're like a red rag to a bull, I'll see to this." The gaffer had to stop the affray before it got out of hand. 'Christ, he must have certainly been riding MacGregor for him to react like this' he thought.

"Now Mr MacGregor, let's quieten down and discuss this in a sensible manner." he said. "I was beginning to worry about the Inspector's safety for a while."

"It's no good Guv, I'm packing the job in, otherwise I would be sorting that bloke out" Jock answered.

"Now look Jock. Have you anything against me? Would you want to see me getting into trouble?"

"No Sir, you have always been a good boss."

"Well, it's like this. Everyone that packs the job in are asked the reason why. A report would have to be submitted and if there was any suggestion that the cause of resignation was due to persecution by the Inspector or the Sergeant, then I would carry the can for it."

"I wouldn't want to get you into any bother Guv" and Jock meant what he said.

"Right, now how about that transfer?"

They sat together for a long time discussing all possibilities.

"You should apply for Special Branch, with your qualifications Jock it's the only job for you."

"No vacancies at present Guv, I've made enquiries," Jock responded.

"Well, I could arrange for you to start at another Nick but with the manpower shortage as it stands, we just couldn't guarantee that either of you would not be sent on loan and that would certainly put the cat amongst the pigeons. No, I think the best thing for you would be to go into another department, such as CID until you can get into Special Branch, what do you think?"

"As long as I have nothing to do with him Sir, I don't mind." Jock agreed with the SD Inspector, although he knew that he would only be attached to the Criminal Investigation Department as an Aide. This meant a 'General Dogsbody' because Aides to CID were used to do all the odd jobs to save the detectives for the investigation work, at least that was the general idea. Delivering the Daily Pawn Sheets to Pawnbrokers and the jewellers which contained lists of stolen property and this was only one of the dirty jobs. Long uncomfortable hours of observation were another. Having these facts in mind, plus the fact that it would only be a temporary job, Jock believed it would be the answer to the situation. He would also be entitled to the ten bob a week for plain clothes allowance, that would come in handy for Puggle.

"Well, if you think it can be arranged, I'll lose nothing by giving it a try," he said.

The next morning when he booked on for Early Turn, he was informed that he had to see the Detective Inspector at 9 am and, prompt as usual, he knocked on the door.

"Right lad, sit down." The man was abrupt as he indicated a chair whilst his attention was on a pile of papers in front of him. He did eventually look up.

"Right, sorry about that, I've been reading your records. I understand that you wish to be considered for the CID. Your record is extremely good and you have the talent for work, you also have quite a number of arrests for crime. Why haven't you applied before?"

Jock explained that he had his eyes on a job with the elite and that it had been the SD Inspector's idea that he apply for the CID.

CHAPTER SIX

START CID

START CID

"Ah well now that's sorted out, you're in the CID now so go home and change into civvy clothes - you won't be needing your uniform again," he was instructed.

So began the trials and tribulations of his new appointment as an Aide to the CID. The work was demanding, the official hours were not always adhered to because overtime was constantly required, unpaid of course. Jock was delegated to work with another newcomer to the Department, their job was more or less to do the leg work for the permanent members of the Branch. Enquiry work and messages blended in with observations on premises for the Detectives. A daily round had to be made of all jewellers and pawnshops with the lists of stolen property. Apart from all the menial jobs, they were expected to bring in the villains as well. There was always strong competition between the aides; there were six of them altogether in the office and the hunt for criminals was constant as each group tried to arrest more than the others did. These arrests were required to prove their position in the Department so that when they went on a Board of Selection, their records could show how good they were.

Vigilance and constant patrolling accounted for most of the arrests but naturally, each Aide soon realised it was essential to use the many informants available. This is the way the regular members of the Department operated, so the newcomers had to do the same. It became a regular thing to hold secret meetings with different villains so that they could obtain information. Naturally, these men required payment for their services and it depended on the value of the information and the goods involved how much they got, if anything. Many of these villains worked as 'double agents', that is to say they would arrange a job to be done, sometimes taking part in it, or collect their share of the takings later. Then they would 'grass' on the others. The other crooks would be arrested and some of the stolen goods recovered; the informant would then request his payment from the law or the Insurance. These greedy people had to have the palms of their hands greased and would be quick to complain if they were shortchanged.

Discipline was more relaxed than the uniform branch but every man had to keep a diary showing his movements each day. Every place he visited and persons he contacted were entered in the book. It was in this missive that each officer kept his records of stops, arrests and out-of-pocket expenses. The Detective Inspector, who would not allow any obvious 'fiddling' with expenses, checked these diaries every week. He turned down an application by two Aides for a two-penny bus ride that they had included on their expense sheets. He insisted that their job was on the streets where the crime was being committed. Yet the same man held no reservations for paying out large sums for information from 'Grasses', provided that arrests were made and property recovered.

The 'Postman' round could prove a bit soul destroying because it meant that the Aides who were delivering the Pawn sheets had to walk right round the Sub-Division to visit every shop, and God help them if any Pawnbroker didn't get his daily copy. All the time they walked the prospective Detectives had to keep their eyes and ears peeled, in the hope of increasing their weekly totals. Winter was a killer, the rain and snow made the villains stay at home during the daytime but Summertime brought them out in force.

They came for car thefts and cycle stealing but the best time for the Aides were the weekends - around the shops and markets. These places always proved satisfactory because shoplifters were always spotted by the Store Detectives and arrested. The CID Officer on reserve duty always got those bodies to add to his weekly total. The Store Detectives worked in harmony, if one of them was suspicious of any member of the public or, if no crime was seen to have been committed, they would follow them and pass the information onto another store sleuth. Sometimes as many as three different Store Detectives followed one person; they would not detain them until they actually saw an offence being committed, in which case they would contact the Police.

One day, Jock was approached by one of the Security Officers who explained that a man and woman with a teenage girl were working in the shops. "We haven't seen them actually take anything yet but they are up to something" the Store Detective said.

"Where are they now?" asked Jock.

"In Woollies. The Branch Manager and three of his floor walkers have been watching them besides our crowd" the man answered.

"That's them over there." He indicated the persons under suspicion.

Jock and his pal joined the small army of peace keepers and watched the antics of the suspects. It soon became obvious that the trio were experts at the game.

"We'll stop them when they reach the pavement," Jock said.

As the group came out of the store they were surrounded by their opposition. Jock confronted them and said,

"Excuse me. We are Police Officers." Nothing else was said but the man bolted through the crowds. Jock left the woman and the girl in the care of Charlie and the store detectives and gave chase. Through the crowded streets, in and out of traffic, pushing individuals aside, the thief ran. As he went he occasionally threw a wallet or a purse away. Jock ignored the items being discarded and kept up close on the man's heels. The run was bad enough but the hazard of dodging cars and weaving past slow-moving pedestrians didn't help; the quarry was obviously a very fit man, apart from being panic stricken for he kept ahead of Jock in his desperate need to escape. For over half an hour the chase continued, they turned towards the nick but, as usual, there were no coppers around when they were needed. As they passed the gate of the back yard Jock glimpsed a cycle resting against the wall and thought to himself 'Christ, I'm knackered'.

The villain turned right and went straight past the front door of the Police Station so Jock stopped and ran back to the yard and collected the cycle. He had no idea whose bike it was - anyway he would return it after he'd arrested the fleeing man. He rode out of the yard and soon caught up with the panting man - as he rode alongside, the villain suddenly gave him a sweeping blow. The vicious swipe caught him the stomach and, apart from catching him unawares, it knocked what little wind he had right out of him. He was sent flying in a heap, along with the cycle.

"You bastard, I'll get you for that!" he gasped as he sat on the road. As he sat there, he saw the girl who had been with the man, running for a bus which was coming along. The man got his sights on the same bus and made to climb aboard. Jock decided otherwise and jumped back on the bike and, travelling as fast as he could he drove straight into the running man and hit him just as he was reaching for the handrail. As he struck the crook he left go of the handlebars and threw his arms around the gasping man. Together they went down in a heap, the cycle was forgotten and a proper 'free for all' began. Jock soon realised that although the man was out of breath like himself, he was a fighter that knew how to use himself. No punches were pulled and no quarter asked, or expected. Jock gave the chap a good hiding before getting an arm lock on him.

"Here Guv. Let me have a go," a voice said. Jock looked up and saw a prison warder standing over them with his truncheon raised. "I'll soon quieten him down."

"That won't be needed, but if you want to help you can take the cycle down to the office." The officer grudgingly put his stick back into his trousers.

"Alright Guv, I'll go quietly" Jock's prisoner said.

"No way lad" he was told. "I've given you two chances, this time you go in my way" and with his arm tucked right up his back the man was marched into the station.

Charlie was in the Charge Room with the woman when he entered and he appeared pleased when he saw Jock walk in with the man.

"The woman threw her arms around me, she pinned my hands down and told the girl to run," he explained the reason of the absent prisoner, before Jock enquired.

"That's alright. I saw her get on a number 25 for the City." The prisoners were searched and questioned; they would not give any information as regards the girl, or their address. A whole pile of ration books were recovered from the prisoner's bags.

"Fifty two different names, some of them are repeated several times." The Station Sergeant finished listing the property. "It looks like these people have had a good day's shopping."

There were still a large number of purses and wallets in their possession which the couple had been unable to dispose of. The amount of goods found was far in excess of the amount allowed to any family, by virtue of the ration books - all clothes and linen were rationed very strictly. As Jock waded through the pile of books checking the names and addresses, he suddenly stopped and said

"Look here Charlie and note the address, it's on the route that the number 25 was going. I bet that the girl was headed there and that's where they have been living."

A message was sent at once to the police that covered that particular area, requesting them to watch the premises, arrest the girl and then search the house. It proved to be an Aladdin's cave, crammed full of stolen property from furs to foodstuffs.

The woman and the man agreed to plead guilty and assist in all matters, provided that the girl wasn't charged. As it turned out, she was an escapee from a remand home so she could only be returned in any case. The man was a deserter from the Commandos, he had been adrift for a few years but was still a very fit man.

"You're a good fighter Guv - I wouldn't want to meet you again in a punch-up," he said to Jock.

The 'Guilty' plea was accepted and the lady got five years for her part in the crime, the man received two years - then to be returned to the Army for punishment for desertion. A total of sixty three crimes were written off.

It was surprising how one could pick out these light fingered people in a crowd. After numerous such arrests, Jock was out with a young chap who was on attachment. They were sitting in a café having a cuppa and watching the shoppers going by.

"Come on Lofty, we've got a couple of workers." Jock got up and was leaving the premises when the other copper called after him.

"I haven't started my tea yet." But he was talking to himself because Jock was away after his suspects. The chap reluctantly left his cup of tea and followed him.

"Who are you after, what's the matter?" he asked.

"See those two women over there" - Jock indicated the two females in question who were blending with the crowds, "They are after that old woman and her friend over there."

The young chap couldn't understand how Jock could make such a statement and said,

"How do you know?"

"Just a hunch" Jock answered. "Stay close by me and if any of them run, you grab her and hang on, take no notice if she screams rape."

The elderly lady and her companion stopped at a toy shop in the market and looked at the display. Mingling with the surrounding crowds, the two suspects walked straight up to the victims and stopped behind them. One of them bent down and opened the clasp of the old woman's handbag, put her hand inside and withdrew a purse. Greased lightning and very, very smooth - a matter of seconds and very discreet. They believed that they had got away with it until suddenly the hand that held the purse was grasped very tightly, by Jock.

"You're nicked" he said.

The woman threw her coat over Jock's head and fought hard to escape - they finished off on the ground. He pulled her to her feet and disentangled himself from the coat. Her accomplice had turned to run when she witnessed the arrest, only to run straight into Lofty's arms.

"Excuse me, madam," Jock spoke to the old lady. "Have you lost your purse?"

The old dear went straight to her handbag to check but when she found it open and the purse missing, she cried out.

"Oh no, my purse is missing."

"Is this it?" said Jock as he held the item up.

"Oh yes, thank you very much" she said and held her hand out to take her property back.

"I'm sorry madam but if you want it you'll have to come down to the Police Station. This woman has just stolen your purse out of your handbag."

The prisoner started to plead and cry, begging the victim not to charge her - gallons of tears, dozens of starving kids at home, up to the eyes in debt - this was the first time she'd ever done anything like this.

"Oh I won't press charges, just give me my purse back and let her go." The old woman had been swayed but Jock indicated that he was the person who would be doing the charge. All the victim had to do was to attend the Station to collect her purse.

The two thieves were charged and pleaded 'Guilty'. They just looked like two ordinary women out shopping but their criminal history was like a fairy story because they were hardened criminals. They both got five years for this offence and countless others which they had taken into consideration.

Pickpockets were not limited to men and women, the offspring of thieves were good learners and often supplemented their pocket money by 'working the markets', and they used some hard working woman's housekeeping money for that purpose. Their general way of working was in a group of three, one on each side squeezed and pushed against some unlucky lady who was laden with shopping. Her bags were slowly pushed to the rear where the third member of the gang could open the handbag and take the purse as she pushed and swore at the two who were bustling her. Naturally if the purse was laid on the top of the shopping, the thieves wouldn't take more than a few seconds to relieve the women of their cash. When these little perishers were caught and taken to Court, it was always the coppers who were made to look like villains, chasing and persecuting the little darlings - who were only playing. Dear little children - who would willingly use a knife to slash some victim - just for the fun of it.

LONG SHIFT

The trouble with 'Plain Clothes Duty' was that no overtime could be claimed, regardless of how many hours were worked or who had detailed the men to work. Jock and his mate were on day shift, they had completed the delivery of the pawn lists and arrested two cycle thieves. All the paperwork had been completed and they were ready for another patrol of the town - but as they were leaving the station yard, a voice bellowed after them.

"Mac, the DI wants you." The Detective Sergeant waved to him from the upstairs window.

"What have we done wrong now, I wonder?" Jock muttered.

When they entered the office the boss said,

"I've got a job for you two tonight. I've got info that a mob are going to have a go at the main Post Office and I have arranged with the shop owner next door to the Post Office for you to use his shop to keep observation. He'll be waiting for you now to let you in so you'd better get round there straight away."

"How long will we have to go before we are relieved Guv?" asked Jock.

"It will be an all night job I should think, unless the bodies start work early. Why?" the boss asked.

"Just that we have been on since nine this morning and we haven't had any refreshment break yet, Jock said.

"Just your luck isn't it? I expect you've been sitting on your arses all day. Never mind, you might get a few collars felt if you're lucky." The Guv was not interested in their welfare.

Jock and his mate made their way to the observation point, which turned out to be a pawnbroker' shop. The owner showed them the room they could use, which gave good vision of the front and rear of the Post Office. He then bade them goodnight and left them to the soul destroying job. Jock's mate had a walk around the premises as Jock kept watch amongst all the stale smelling bundles of clothing.

"Hey Jock, we're in shit street, the other copper said. "We're locked in, even if the blighters did come to do the job, we couldn't get to them."

His statement proved correct - they were well and truly locked inside the pawnshop. At nine the next morning the owner arrived and opened his premises and released the two weary and bleary eyed coppers.

"What the hell do you mean by locking us in? How could we get out to catch the burglars with all the doors locked"? Jock asked.

"Not my problem. I couldn't leave the shop open all night, I have too many valuables in there." The little Jewish man said.

Jock and his mate called in at the Station and had a go at the Detective Sergeant who had made the arrangements for the observation. The man couldn't give an answer when asked what they should do if the villains did turn up.

"I don't know, the Guv made the arrangements, and he said that the obo has to be done every night." His discussion was broken off when the Guvnor shouted out from his room.

"Which aides are on duty this morning"?

"They're in here Guv, the CID Sergeant answered. The Detective Inspector came in with a handful of papers.

"Right, you two can get started on these enquiries. I want them done at once," and he held the papers out to Jock.

"Not me Guv." Jock had had enough. "I started work yesterday morning at 9 am and I have been on duty for 24 hours without a meal or a break. I don't mind doing extra work, but there is a limit."

"Right, go and get a shave and a meal and I'll see you later.

Jock gratefully got on his cycle and rode home to put Puggle's mind at rest - she had been worrying all night. He had made arrangements to meet his mate just before 5pm at the nick and, together, they walked into the office.

"Oh there you are," the Guvnor spotted them at once. "Here are the papers."

"Sorry, Guv. We can't do them. You have detailed us on night duty observation and we have to be there at five o'clock."

They left him standing with his pile of bumf in his hand, wondering what to do with them. The shopkeeper was waiting for them and escorted them to the upstairs room again.

"Goodnight, see you in the morning."

These duties continued for a whole week and eventually the Detective Inspector was pressed by his Sergeants to call off the night duty. This was due to the fact that they had to do all their own errands and enquiries - they wouldn't admit the fact but the Aides were priceless.

Jock and his colleague were not allowed to settle down on day shift for long; after their week's rest in the pawnshop, they had grown lazy. The long days caused by extra duties were a regular thing and as soon as they came off the Post Office observation they were given another job to do. Starting at 9 am, they faithfully did the day's work, not knowing that another cold night was ahead of them.

A local taxi proprietor owned several cabs; he employed a Scotsman as a cleaner and it was his job to clean all the taxis and fill them up with petrol ready for the following day's run. The owner of the business noticed that the petrol consumption of the vehicles varied considerably and he was losing quite a lot of money. It seemed that someone was nicking his petrol and Jock and his mate were delegated the job of sorting it out for him.

As it appeared quite obvious that the cleaner was the prime suspect, it was arranged that the two coppers would enter the premises early and take up their positions. They needed places where they could see all around the yard and it didn't take long to find out that the only place they could be out of sight was on the top of a container lorry. As the night drew on the darkness fell with the increasing cold.

"I'm sure that Scots get isn't going to do anything," muttered Charlie.

He was wrong - for at four o'clock, after all the cabs had been washed, the cleaner collected a length of rubber hose and a two-gallon petrol tin and he siphoned one cab after the other, transferring the petrol into the tanks of private cars. The cars were garaged on the premises and the owners had been dropping a few bob each week for the juice. This was a regular habit of his and this precious rationed liquid, which was only obtainable with ration books, found new owners during the night.

The cleaner was a very surprised man when he was confronted by two men who seemed to appear from out of space; he was speechless at first but after a while he admitted he had been asked by several drivers to supply them with petrol. The names and addresses of the other persons concerned were obtained from him and Jock and his mate took the prisoners to the local nick where he was held, whilst they went out to collect the unlucky drivers from their warm beds. Together they were all charged and the owner of the taxis was a happy man. In fact, he was the only happy man for the two weary coppers had all the charge sheets and fingerprints to do - the cases had to be ready for Court at 10am. By the time this paperwork was done and the prisoners had been bailed out, it was time for them to go to the Court. The cases were not heard until just before lunch so the two tired coppers went back to the Station to complete the files, before going home for a few hours well-earned rest. They had been on duty continuously for nearly thirty hours - why did any sane person want to be in the CID?

As they always worked in pairs, they shared the arrests; stops in the street often produced good results. Jock had accomplished an uncanny knack of spotting a baddy and rarely a day went by without some success in this field. Cycle thieves were a common occurrence; swimming baths and library cycle parks were the most regular places for cycles to suddenly find a new owner. A good 'tealeaf' would just walk past the lines of unattended bikes, pick the one he wanted and ensure that it wasn't locked, A natural approach to the machine was made, the thief would pull it from the rack, mount it and just pedal slowly away. Jock and his mates were experienced and very conversant with these methods and they spotted a villain at once. They would split up, one on each side of the line of bikes so that when the bike was stolen the thief would be riding towards one of them, the thief had probably seen them either sleeping on the grass, or lounging against a wall reading a newspaper.

One of these cycle thieves made a good living nicking bikes and selling them; he slipped up one day though by stealing a real posh chrome-plated one. He took a liking to the machine and decided to keep it. He had a sideline also, he used to break into houses and steal from them and he also broke into the gas meters for quick cash. One of the householders spotted him and described him and his chrome-plated cycle - and he also mentioned the fact that the villain had a glass eye. Armed with all the details, it didn't take long to pin the villain down. He was on the dole, so Jock and his mate waited outside the 'Exchange' on the day he was due to collect his cash. The gleaming cycle came along, the quick gleaming eye of the rider scanning the streets for a copper. He spotted Charlie straight away and turned the bike to ride in the opposite direction, straight into Jock's waiting arms.

"You're nicked" he said.

"Fair enough Guv. It's a fair cop." The man offered no violence and, at the Police Station when he was question, he admitted over one hundred similar offences.

With their luck and skill, Jock and Charlie were leaving all the other Aides behind with their number of arrests, so the great man in charge decided to split them up so that they could pass their talents onto their new partners. This way he hoped to clear up more crimes on his patch and put a feather in his own cap.

NIGHT WORKING

Jock's new mate was a suave Lancashire lad whose wife had a good job; they had no children and consequently were pretty well off compared to Jock. This chap lived in the Police Canteen for his meals - all he seemed to be interested in was women, talking to them, talking about them, looking at them or cracking dirty jokes with them. He was hoping to get into the Department permanently and had been informed that the only way to get on was to join the Freemasons. Whether he succeeded or not in his attempts Jock never knew but to his knowledge, the man was never made up as a CID Officer, nor was he promoted.

As the usual night duty for the Department meant that a fully qualified CID Officer had to be on duty to cover the whole Division, a couple of Aides had to be on duty also to assist with the work. They spent the night at one of the several stations and awaited telephone calls requiring their attention. This waiting business proved to be a soul-destroying process, especially when things were quiet; the Sergeant managed to play cards in the canteen but there was no room for Jock and Jack. They played snooker till they were sick of the sight of the balls and they drank tea till there was no room for any more.

"I'm sick of this, let's go for a walk round the town!" Jack complained.

"OK We'll have to ask the Skipper first though," Jock answered.

They made their way down to the Canteen where the air was thick with cigarette and cigar smoke, made worse each second as the four card players puffed away.

"Will it be alright if we have a walk around the town Skipper, just to get a bit of fresh air and check the shops?" Jack asked the Sergeant, who appeared to be on a winning streak judging by the pile of cash in front of him.

"Righto lad, but don't be long just in case we're needed."

Gratefully the two Aides slipped away into the darkness and the cold clear night air. The streets appeared to be quiet as they strolled along.

"Seems quiet Jock."

"Yeh but the villains don't keep to the main streets do they? Let's get round the back of the shops and check them," Jock answered. "Move quietly and keep out of sight and when we get there, no talking out loud." Jock always believed in going where the uniformed copper wouldn't, or couldn't, go but where the crooks did.

His luck was in once again, his instincts sharp as a razor, he motioned Jack towards him and whispered in his ear.

"The basement of the furniture shop - someone is having a go - take it easy and quiet till we're right on top of them."

Slowly they made their way to the rails which surrounded the basement door and looking over the top they saw three men engaged in business - trying to force the back door of the shop. The torches were switched on and at once there was panic amongst the group, they even tried to hide in the outside toilet, dropping housebreaking implements as they scampered. Jock had recognised the three men and called on them by their names to climb up and bring their gear with them.

"You have to come up this way, so you might as well come up now, you're all nicked." One of them he noted was an escapee who had used a milk bottle on the Detective Inspector at the time.

"You take him Jack, get your stick out and have it ready, use it if you have to - he's a nasty type" Jock told his mate.

"I'll take the other two."

With woeful expressions on their faces the three crooks climbed out of the basement. Jack took hold of the 'runner' by the arm as soon as he reached the railings.

"It's alright Guv. I'll walk quietly, no need to hang on," the man said.

"Don't leave go of him Jack, belt him if he starts anything," Jock advised.

"Don't worry Jock, he's going in, even if I have to drag him!" his mate replied as he pulled the luckless lout along - his truncheon swinging from his wrist.

"That's the way I like it," Jock said to his two captives. "Now, do you want to go in quietly or the same way?"

"Guv. We know you, you'll have no trouble from us" they answered.

"Pity, I feel like a bush up, just to get warm." The big copper sighed, the three of them walked peacefully to the nick. As they stepped off the pavement to cross the road, one of them slipped to the ground. Jock watched him slip a jemmy down a drain cover.

"That's alright Mick, we'll get it out in the morning. Those things are only three feet deep."

"I just slipped down Guv," the man muttered.

"No Mick, you slipped up." Jock laughed. "Don't worry, I'll supply you with another jemmy for the charge sheet."

"You rotten sod."

The procession entered the station yard and went up the steps to the charge room. As they climbed the stairs Jock watched the men closely and spotted some other housebreaking implements being dropped over the rails into the basement.

"You keep trying don't you?" he said to his prisoners. "I'll just nip down and get them as soon as you are made comfortable." He placed them in the charge room and recovered the gloves, pencil torchlight and a slender jemmy. He took the articles back to their owners.

"Right, empty your pockets - all of you" he ordered. The Station Officer came out of the office and watched them, making a list of each item and who had owned it. Knives; chains; knuckle dusters; gloves; all piled up on the desk alongside another jemmy which had been generously supplied to replace the one that had been dropped down the drain gully. The three were charged by the Station Officer, who placed them in the cells pending CID completing the paperwork. The Detective Sergeant was informed whilst he was in the middle of a losing hand and he took the chance as an excuse to leave the table. When he was given the facts of the case he said,

"That's good, one for each of us for the book."

When he went into the front office and found that the men had already been charged and the arresting officer's names did not include his, he went berserk. Jock never realised that these men could be so petty over such a small thing. He looked at the Sergeant who was acting like a small child.

"Look Skipper, you can have all three if that's how you feel about it."

"You know they can't alter the book. You should have told me that you had information about the job being done. I would have come with you" he said.

"We didn't get the information from a grass, Skipper. We were just patrolling and came across them."

The Sergeant was adamant - he refused to believe that it was possible to suddenly come across such a situation. He passed the rest of the week without talking to the two Aides and refused to allow them to go out again by themselves, especially when they were on night duty with him. He got his own back in his own childish manner when they were on days just afterwards. The two lads were lumbered, with a capital 'L', by the Sergeant when a man was arrested at Fleetwood. The chap was wanted for crimes committed on their patch and arrangements were made for the villain to be held pending the arrival of an escort. Jock and Jack were designated to go and collect the body.

"You have time to get there and back today." The Sergeant grinned, "It might be a little late when you get back though."

A little late, that was his idea of being funny, because by the time they found the times for the train and where they had to change to reach this remote town placed at the furthest point from them in the country, the morning was half way over. They eventually got to the end of their train journey at tea-time, to find that they had another mile to travel to the Police Station. The time for the return journey was ascertained from the ticket office before setting out to the local constabulary.

"We only have an hour to collect him, get a meal, then get back here for the train" said Jock. "So we'd better get a move on." They managed to find the local nick after a ride on the tramcar and a red-faced copper was sitting at the desk.

"You took your time getting here" he said. "We've been waiting all day for you."

The prisoner was brought in for them to sign for, the old copper was in a hurry to get home for his tea.

"Have you got a canteen here?" Jock asked. "We haven't had a meal all day."

"Canteen?" The old copper looked at them as though they were silly. "No, this is a Police Station."

"Well, is there anywhere we can get some grub?" Jock asked. "We'll have to get a meal before we go back."

"The only place you might get something would be in the town." He pushed the prisoner's property across the desk. "Will you sign for him, I want to get away."

"Have you got a car here to take the prisoner to the Station?" Jock signed and checked the property.

"Only a two-seater sports car that the CID use. You'll have to walk or catch a tram." The helpful man switched the lights off and made for the door.

"Oh come on you" Jock said to the patiently waiting prisoner. "Better put the cuffs on him Jack till we get on the train."

"You don't have to put them on me Guv, I won't make a break" the man said. "I won't cause you any trouble."

Jock was now too long in the tooth to be caught like that.

"Possibly not but regulations must be obeyed." He didn't want to lose a prisoner four hundred miles from home. "We'll take them off once we get on the train."

By the time they got to the station they found that the train was already standing at the platform - it was a rush. A helpful porter noticed the handcuffs and said,

"They never told us that they needed a special compartment. Nothing has been booked for you, but leave it to me, I'll fix it." He rushed off and put a 'Reserved' notice on a compartment.

"I'll telephone ahead and make arrangements for a one to be held for you when you change. I'll tell the guard to look after you for meals."

He was a very helpful man and Jock thanked him for his attention. He was the only person who seemed to have any consideration for them all day.

On the long ride back to the Big City the handcuffs were taken off the prisoner. The three of them had the compartment to themselves, blinds drawn and a pack of cards appeared to help them through the hours - and thanks to the staff of the Great Western Railway, they were kept supplied with liquid refreshments on their journey.

Back at the 'Smoke', the handcuffs were replaced and the prisoner delivered to the Police Station. The Station Sergeant in charge of the night duty told them that a message had been left for them to prepare the prisoner for Court the next day. So, by the time antecedents were completed and fingerprints taken, Jock and Jack headed for home at three o'clock, time for a couple of hours kip before early day shift. Thanks Sergeant.

These trips out 'into the sticks' were not unusual. They were a break from routine, as if time wasn't of any great importance. Normally, a long one like the one just done by Jock and Jack would be a two-day job, and on those details they would have the evening free and accommodation provided and all expenses paid. Jock was never so lucky, he never landed such a plum, the only other escort he was elected to do was to Lincoln. He only got that because the prisoner was known to be violent and known by Jock and there was a need for identification. The man was being held in a hospital under guard. He had been examined and found to be healthy, not suffering physically nor mentally, but he refused to talk or move. Things were therefore uncertain as regards transport - should he be moved by car or persuaded to co-operate and travel by train. It was eventually decided to despatch a car from the pool to collect the body. Jock and his mate were picked up by a chauffeur driven limousine and driven direct to the hospital. The prisoner was reclining naked on a bed, covered with a sheet. The local copper indicated him and said.

"We've not had a single word from him. He appears not to hear us."

A doctor was present with them in the ward and agreed with the policeman that there was nothing wrong with the man.

"It took your mob long enough to send somebody along, we've been messed about all day with this chap," the copper complained. Jock ignored him but asked the doctor if it would be alright to move the unwanted patient and, having been given permission to get the fellow out of the hospital, Jock was content.

The doctor shook the man by the shoulder and said.

"There's someone here to see you and to take you home." The body in the bed did not move, till he heard the next voice.

"Right, laddy, on your feet and get dressed, there's a car waiting outside, so move your arse." The villain recognised the Scottish accent at once and reacted for the first time. He looked up to verify his ears, saw the face he feared and said

"I might have guessed they would send you but I'm not moving from here. I'm a patient" and he turned his face to the wall again.

"Either you get up and get dressed, or you go the way you are, bollock naked," smiled Jack

"You can't do that, I'm sick." The man gasped as he swung round in the bed.

"You'll be a damn sight sicker when I drag you along that corridor. Get his clothes Jack." As he spoke, Jock grabbed the bedclothes and whipped them off the bed. He took hold of the nearest ankle and heaved the body off the mattress. There was a bump as the fat buttocks struck the floor.

"Now, you can either walk to the car or I drag you feet first - and don't dare me, I couldn't care less, you've had your chances."

The prisoner knew Jock and decided to walk as quickly as he could past the smiling people but when he did reach the vehicle, he reused to get in. A very short struggle was needed to accomplish this movement and the man lay across the floor of the back seating space. He refused to get on the seat and still refused to put his clothes on.

"Fair enough bonny lad, but it's a long way home, as you want to travel there far be it from me to stop you.They drove all the way back to the Big City with him lying on the floor, the two CID bods used him for a footrest, at least he couldn't jump out of the car and frighten any old ladies. They left behind a crowd of giggling nurses who had witnessed the removal of this awkward customer, and a very worried, perplexed and curious copper, who was left standing wondering about the hard attitude taken by these men from the Smoke.

Once they had reached their own nick, the prisoner decided to get dressed in the Charge Room; he knew he was nicked and would be going inside, so it was a waste of time carrying on with the bluff.

"Well, I knew they couldn't charge me up there - it was worth a try wasn't it?"

The following day all available CID were required for an observation due to the fact that a robbery had taken place - a lot of cash and gems had been stolen. The wanted man had turned up at a seaside resort and had been arrested doing another job. He had escaped after attacking a Police Inspector. It was expected that he would make his way back to the Smoke, where he would be safer than in the rural town. All available men were posted onto railway and bus stations and from the first arrivals of the transport each passenger who alighted was scrutinised - every copper hoping he would be the lucky one to nick the villain. However, the tour of duty lasted all day and the men were thankful when the last bus tram and train had arrived - it had been a waste of time. The man was arrested the next day as he left an underground station at the opposite side of the City. Fancy being picked up by a Detective Inspector as he came off the first train on a Sunday morning, it was good information received that led to his downfall because nobody believed the Detective Inspector was 'just passing' at the time and recognised the man.

The rest of the staff prepared for a normal day's work whilst the man was questioned. Just before knocking off time a report came in of four suspects seen climbing a fence. Everyone went along, uniformed and plain clothes, the whole area was sealed off within minutes - the block of buildings where the men had been seen was completely surrounded. No way could they get out, each garden was searched, outbuildings examined and buildings checked for signs of entry - all without success. The Station Sergeant in charge was still not satisfied so he requested that a member of the newly formed dog handler's section attend the scene. It was dark and cold but everyone had their orders - to remain at their posts until the dog had searched the area.

Jock and his mate were standing in a doorway with the Sergeant when the dog handler arrived.

"Evening Serg, where do you want me?" he said, holding on tight to a vicious looking Alsatian.

"Four suspects are alleged to have been seen climbing this fence," and he indicated the wooden structure beside the house.

"We have searched all the grounds but have not found them. They couldn't get out without being seen. Do you think your dog could find them?

"How do we get in with the dog Skipper?" the handler asked, as it seemed the fence was too high for the dog to jump.

"I'll give a knock at this house, the owner might let us through," the Sergeant said and promptly began to beat a tattoo on the front door, which brought a rapid response. A window was flung open and a surly looking individual yelled out at the group.

"What the hell do you think you're doing, kicking my door like that?" The Skipper explained the situation but it didn't seem to smooth the man's temper.

"There's no bugger in my house and I'm not letting anyone in," and he slammed the window down.

"We shall see about that, helpful sod," grunted the Station Sergeant. He was just going to bang on the door again when it was flung open by the man, who was breathless and appeared very distressed.

"They were in the back room, they have just climbed out of the window."

"Let's go" said Jock - and without speaking to the owner both he and Jack pushed their way into the house - they raced up the stairs and soon found the open window. It led out onto a flat roof of an outbuilding - they climbed through and stood on the roof, looking out over the wilderness of trees and bushes. The ground couldn't be seen in the blackness, the Sergeant soon joined them without the dog handler.

"Pretty hopeless but at least we know the sods are there. I'll keep the observation on all night if I have to."

Jock was straining his eyes, looking down into the darkness, his ears trying to pick up any slight sound.

"There," he snapped and jumped straight off the roof down into the garden. He dived into some shrubbery without pause and grabbed a man who was just trying to climb into the next garden. "Right, you're nicked, where's your mates?"

The man squealed with pain.

"There're only two of us Guv."

"Shout to him to come out then, he won't get away because the whole area is covered and we have the dogs here ready to set loose. If he doesn't come out they will tear him to pieces." Jock had no idea what the dogs would be like chasing anyone - lucky enough neither did the villains. His prisoner shouted out

"Better come out Ginger, they've got some dogs and are letting them loose."

Gingerhead and the Station Sergeant also heard the voices down below. He knew that Jock had jumped down into the garden but couldn't see him. When he heard the voices he also jumped down and his fall was broken by the second suspect. Ginger had just stood up and he took the weight of a fifteen stone copper - it kind of took the wind out of his sails. The Skipper was also at 'sixes and sevens', he didn't know who he had landed on, he said later that he believed he had landed on Jock. However, as he was getting to his feet, he heard a crashing of timber and grinding of splintering bushes. Jock also heard the noise as it was very close to where he stood - he saw the Sergeant standing up - only to be knocked back to the ground again by a figure that came literally flying over the adjoining fence. The two human beings crashed to the ground in a mad struggle and Jock wondered what the hell was going on. He noticed the fight suddenly come to an end and one figure stood up.

"Is that you Serg?" he asked, although still hanging onto his prisoner, he was ready to have another go.

"Yes, it's me Jock. Are you alright?"

"Yes Serg. I've got one here, he tells me there were only two of them."

"That's a lie because I landed on one and another one jumped over the fence on top of me."

"Jack," Jock called up to the rooftop where Jack still waited. "Shine your torch down here, will you."

The dim light from Jack's torch soon lit up the field of battle. Ginger was unmistakable, he was out for the count after being hit with the Sergeant's feet. Another body lay near him and both Jock and the Sergeant recognised him at once as being one of the young probationers.

CHAPTER SEVEN

BURGLARS

The copper had heard the noise of Jock having a fight, then he heard the Sergeant jumping down and, not wanting to be left out of the action, he decided to make his first arrest - rather unlucky for him though, the chap he tried to arrest was his Senior Officer who in turn thought he was a suspect! The lad got a right bollocking from the Sergeant for leaving his designated post.

At the nick, the Station Sergeant drew Jock aside and said,

"About that prisoner Jock, would it be alright if I had him?"

"Well, you landed on him so it's only right you have him Skipper" Jock answered, "He's yours."

"Oh, I was meaning the other one. I was thinking of the dog handler, we got him out of bed to help us and I know you get plenty of arrests. Would you mind if we let him have the credit, it's the first time he has used the dog?"

"Fair enough Serg, I'm on a day off tomorrow in any case and I'd rather not go to Court." Jock was inwardly pleased but his pleasure didn't last long because the Detective Sergeant handling the case stated that they couldn't take it to Court without Jock's evidence. Consequently, he had to go to Court to prove the case. The dog handler was not disheartened about his night's work - for as soon as the men were charged, he telephoned his Inspector and Jock heard part of the conversation before walking out in disgust.

"Yes Sir, it was nearly four hours later before they called me out and by the time I got there, I found that dozens of coppers had been tramping all over the place but my dog soon found the scent. He traced the villains and pointed down into the garden where the men were hiding." He got a Commendation from the Commissioner for his work because these were early days and a load of bull had to be pushed from one senior officer to the next, so as to ensure that their cushy jobs were not taken away.

BURGLARS

Jock and his mate dropped on an unusual incident shortly afterwards as they were patrolling the main road on the way back to the nick. It was 1 am when Jock saw the movement in the darkness.

"Hang on Jack, am I seeing things." Jock pointed up a long garden towards a house. "There's a man and woman there and it looks as though they are trying to break in."

"You can't be sure that they are trying to screw the gaff, they might be the owners locked out." Jack was dubious.

"You go up the side street Jack, I'll go up the drive," Jock told him and he waited till his mate started to walk along the side street before going towards the couple - he was fairly close to them before the female looked round and saw him.

"Copper" - the word shot out and both people decided to do a disappearing act - talk about fear lending wings, those two really hoofed it on the approach of the law. They separated and Jack shouted.

"I'll take this one," and he ran after the scampering female.

"Trust you," muttered Jock as he went after the other burglar. After a few minutes chase he arrested the man and took him back to the pavement to await the arrival of Jack with the other prisoner. Several minutes passed and still no sign.

"Come on, we'll see them at the Nick" he ordered the cowed man.

"You'll be lucky Guv, I don't think your mate is fast enough." The man actually smiled as though he had a secret. They waited at the Police Station for nearly half an hour before Jack made a noisy entrance, struggling with the flashy female.

"Get in there you sod!" he yelled, and pushed her down onto a chair. "You bastard, do that again and I'll really thump you."

"What's the matter Jack?" Jock was really curious, this was the copper that liked all females.

He soon discovered the reason, Jack had chased the woman thinking she would be an easy catch but when she started running she had kicked her shoes off. Jack had passed the high-heeled shoes as he raced after her. The long run was bad enough as far as he was concerned but he never expected a resistance when he caught her. When he grabbed hold of the woman's arm, she let him have a strong right arm and a hard fight began. It was only then that Jack realised that he was fighting a man dressed as a woman. It turned out that the prisoner was a deserter from the Royal Navy who had borrowed another set of clothing from a friend's mother - he was really a 'queer' in all senses. When he was stripped and searched the Station Sergeant grinned.

"You arrested him so I'll give you the pleasure of searching him," he said to Jack.

The ladies clothing was slowly removed by the prisoner, he did a striptease for Jack as the dress, stockings, suspenders, bra and French Knickers were taken off. The man was obviously enjoying his search.

"Are you a bloody queer aren't you?" asked Jack.

The owner of the clothing was contacted and asked to collect the gear - she was also asked to bring the man's uniform with her. When she arrived at the Station with the required clothing, she passed some information onto the Station Officer, which didn't seem to surprise him too much.

"Gary has been 'tomming' around he town quite a lot recently. I didn't like the company he has been with and I think he's caught a dose. The way he has palled up with Nobbie since he came home on leave makes me wonder if he hasn't passed it onto him."

'Nobbie' of course being the sailor, who admitted that he had enjoyed the pleasures of life with his best friend. Medical evidence later proved that the amorous attentions had resulted in him contracting an infectious disease. Sex seemed to be an accepted thing amongst the criminal fraternity and their female followers. The local villains were all known to Jock - he knew where they lived and who their associates were. Also, he had acquired the knowledge of the villains' different methods of obtaining cash and goods which belonged to other people. From the small-time thief who would pick up anything lying around which didn't belong to him - and this included shoplifting, to the breakers. The majority of them would resort to violence without any provocation. The good villains, if there was such a thing, offered no violence when arrested.

Patrols centred around the shops at the weekends, watching shops, cycles, cars, people (in case of purse snatching). Watching and listening, eyes open for any suspicious character, passing or carrying or removal of goods. Ears open for any chance remark about crimes committed or being planned.

Jack and Jock moved into one of the amusement arcades which was packed as usual by members of the criminal fraternity. It had often been suggested that these places were dens of iniquity and should be closed down - granted, they were thieves kitchens. At least one knew where to go to look for some particular person should he be wanted. It was also in these places that jobs were planned and discussed, talk was loose and goods exchanged hands - there were always willing and eager buyers for a bargain.

As they mingled with the throng, they heard an argument going on amongst a group of local yobs. A red-haired female was the centre of the heated discussion and as Jock and his mate drew nearer.

"Here Guv, settle this will you?" said the girl.

"Are they real or not Guv?" one of the men pointed to the enormous boobs which the girl carried, with obvious pride.

"Look you sod, I've already told you, they are real - I don't wear falsies. Here, does that satisfy you" and she opened the front of her dress and lifted both of her enormous breasts out.

"There, they are real, aren't they Guv?" She turned to the man and said "I suppose you want to have a feel - just to make sure." She covered the top part of her body before the man took advantage of her offer. She was typical of the tarts who were friends of these men and they were the cause of more trouble than enough. The females often were the instigators of fights and crimes, often they would also join in a fight. If they went out with a thief on a job, it was good cover to either kiss and cuddle, or even engage in actual sexual intercourse if necessary to put any inquisitive person's mind at rest.

A jewellers shop had been broken into and several rings and watches stolen. All eyes had been centred on the heaving flesh of the redhead as she struggled to fasten the buttons of her dress to hide her female charms. Jock had his eyes elsewhere and had noticed a movement amongst the throng which aroused his suspicions.

"Watch the door Jack, stop anyone going out."

Jack didn't question the order, he knew that Jock had seen something and he reacted at once. He pushed his way to the exit and stood there, ready to stop anyone. Jock made his way towards a group of men in the arcade; he had seen something being passed but had been unable to identify the object. He was now going to question and, if necessary, search the men. However, they saw him coming and split up; they pushed their way through the crowds and avoided Jock and as they approached the door they all ran. Jack was taken by surprise by the crowd who bore down on him, he grabbed one of them but realised he couldn't hold the man and also stop the others. So, when Jock came out of the arcade close behind the mob, he realised he had a chase on his hands. He ran after the man who he had seen in the centre of the group - Jack started to walk his prisoner down to the Station and he watched Jock haring along the road, going like an Olympic champion.

Jock's legs couldn't go any faster as he put all he could into his run and, slowly, he was gaining ground. Suddenly, he realised that the market had closed - there were very few shoppers walking around, the Council workers were out cleaning the rubbish away and washing the roads. Jock was wearing crepe soles and as soon as he went onto the wet surface, he lost his grip on the surface. Down the slope he went, gathering speed like an ice skater, legs frantically waving as he strove to keep his balance. He went so fast down that slope that he passed the villain. The man stopped and gaped at the sight and when Jock eventually reached a dry part of the road and thankfully halted without going on his backside, the man was doubled up on the pavement laughing his head off. He knew he was nicked, with Jock in front of him and Jack behind him.

"Guv, that's the best laugh I've had for years." He gave in gracefully and said "I thought I was fast, but you left me standing."

Jock didn't know whether the man was taking the Mickey or if he had believed Jock had actually slid down the road on purpose.

"Right, let's have a look at what you're carrying."

The man said "There's no need to search me Guv, these are what you're looking for aren't they?" The giggling man produced a handful of gems from his pocket. "I didn't think you'd seen us."

Jack's prisoner was also in possession of some of the stolen articles. They both admitted receiving and named the persons responsible. The statement of 'Honour amongst thieves' resulted in the arrest of two other men.

BREAK-INS

Occasionally, there was an outbreak of crime committed by the same villains who were feeling lucky. The mode of operation pointed towards the same gang or person. Lock-up shops began to receive the attention of unwelcome customers during the hours of darkness and they didn't use the front doors. The Detective Inspector decided, in all his wisdom, that all days off and leave would be cancelled until the persons responsible were caught. This meant that nearly all duties were half nights or night shift, for the observations which had to be kept. Naturally the ones detailed to keep these nocturnal observations were the 'Aides to CID' So, once again, Jock and his mate were out in the cold with a roving commission and orders from the boss to 'Catch the Bastards' or else!

One of the favourite ways into these premises was through the roofs, which allowed the thieves to work in peace as the patrolling coppers wouldn't find any broken windows or doors. Night after night the streets were watched and rooftops patrolled. It was generally easy to gain access to the roofs of the buildings as they were all attached in blocks; dozens of shops could be checked without coming back down to street level. One night Jock left Jack watching a special section of the area whilst he went to stretch his legs and examine another street close by. As he walked along in the shadows, he suddenly saw a flash of movement beside a name board over a shop on the opposite side of the street. Out of the corner of his eye, he knew that he had seen a face. The man was watching him but, not turning his head, Jock carried on walking at the same pace until he went around the corner. Once round the corner and out of sight of the villain, he ran like hell to where Jack was standing huddled up against the cold.

"Come on Jack, I think we have them," he said, "they're on a roof top in Station Road." As the pair of them trotted along, they met a uniformed man who tagged along to render assistance. Jock indicated the point where he had seen the man on the roof and it was decided that he would approach the premises from the front. Jack and the wooden top would cover the back in case the culprits made a run for it.

"I'll climb up the front of the shops and turf them out." Jock volunteered to face the unknown intruders.

He walked down the street alongside the shops and once he had passed the premises where he had seen the man's face, he began the hazardous climb up the front of a neighbouring shop. As he pulled himself over the edge onto the roof he saw two men emerging from a skylight; as he stood up, they spotted him and ran. They raced along the rooftops towards the spot where Jack was waiting and on the way they came to an office built over one of the shops. The only way past it was to ease along the covers of a sunblind. The crooks got past the hazard safely and Jock had no option but to follow. The fitting bent and creaked under his weight and he cursed the two men under his breath; he expected the wood to give way at any time and cast him down to the road below. His luck was in and he rounded the structure to gain a firm footing once more on the roof and he continued the chase. At the end of the line of shops the men climbed down into a back garden - they had spotted the two coppers waiting for them in the street. They had just reached the ground when Jock arrived at the roof above them, he took in the situation at once. The coppers couldn't get to them due to a high fence; the villains could disappear in a maze of gardens with numerous exits, unless they were stopped at once.

"Sod them, there's no way," he knew what he had to do and, without hesitation, he took a flying leap off the roof - aiming for the two men - hoping they would break his fall. He was lucky but one of the villains was not, he took the full weight and gave Jock a soft landing. There was a good scrap with the other man as he strove to get away and he was soon joined by his mate who was beginning to recover. However, Jack gained access to the garden through a nearby house and came to Jock's assistance.

The men were charged with shop breaking. They admitted all the other offences put to them by the DI but the next morning at Court, they both complained to the Magistrate that they had been brutally assaulted by Jock.

"Did you strike these men, Officer?" the great man asked. Jock looked at the two pathetic brutes standing in the dock; how could he deny it when one looked at the mess he had made of their faces.

"Yes Sir," he admitted.

"Why?" asked the learned Magistrate, although he already knew the answer but wanted a reply for the record.

"It was in the middle of the night Sir, I was by myself and there were two of them. They didn't want to be caught so they ran, I caught them but they didn't want to be arrested and I was compelled to protect myself."

"I see Officer, you did a good job." Not indicating whether he meant arresting the men, or giving them a good hiding.

"Any more questions or complaints?" he asked looking at the prisoners.

"No sir" came the glum reply. Consequently, a future train robber and a future Police murderer began another prison sentence.

STRANGERS

"Let's go for breakfast Jock." Jack could eat like a horse and was always hungry. On the way down to the all-night café they noticed a good crowd of the local yobs had gathered around a coffee stall which was situated close to the café.

"Quite a lot around for this time of night" Jock said, as he indicated the mob. Both coppers automatically registered the names of the local thugs who were gathered together around the stall. Inside the café, they found a dozen people enjoying the warm atmosphere and Bill, the owner, actually sitting down, looked very tired.

"I've been very busy, I could do with a break to catch up on some work in the back" he said. "I'll fix your grub for you before I clean up."

The coppers took their meal to the back of the café, sitting facing the door; in this position they had a clear view of anyone entering the shop. A few more people came in, obviously revellers on their way home after a night on the town - some of them carrying an excess of liquor. Then a couple of men came in and after ordering coffee, they sat at a table close to the door.

"A couple of strangers Jack," Jock remarked. His mate nodded because his mouth was crammed full with his second bacon sandwich.

"Hy unda hmmdy ar oo" he spluttered in a seemingly foreign language.

Jock who had come to understand the feeble guttural speech said,

"I don't know, I'll ask them" and made his way down the café towards the strangers. He sat on the edge of the seat facing the men, who eyed him suspiciously.

"Hello mates, I'm a copper, who are you? Where are you from? And, as my mate asks, what have you been up to?"

The strangers sat in silence looking at Jock with their mouths open, until he said

"Look here, when your mouth is open, use it. Either to eat, drink or talk. At the present moment I want you to talk. Who are you and where are you from?"

"How do we know you're a copper?" asked one of the customers with a broad Irish accent. Jock showed him the warrant card and said,

"I'd better tell you that my mate is like you, he doesn't speak English, he's mad when his temper is roused and the quickest way to get him annoyed is to refuse to answer questions." Jock had caught a glimpse of Jack's reflection in the shop window as he came along the café, stuffing his mouth as he approached.

"U dy ne U oo?" - the sounds emitted from his mouth as he glared at the two men. He was annoyed at having his meal disturbed. The newcomers blanched visibly.

"How did you know we were strangers? This is the first time we've been here and have just got off the tram."

"Where are you from?"

"We've just come from Liverpool and are looking for somewhere to sleep."

It was impossible to explain to these men that the Big City is divided into Divisions and Sub-Divisions, and that the place was like hundreds of very small towns, each with several separate beats, in consequence, all the local villains were known to the local Constabulary. A stranger stood out like a sore thumb.

"Y Ieery uggers" Jack expounded.

"What did he say?" said one of the men as he wiped breadcrumbs off his face.

"He said that you are a couple of lying buggers and that you are going down to the nick for further questions." Jock translated the garble. They allowed the men to finish their coffee before taking them to the Police Station.

"Nigh Bill," they said as they went out into the cold night air with their prisoners.

"Nigh Guv" came the response.

"Guvnor, give us a chance, we haven't done anything on your manor," one of the mean pleaded with his big Scotch copper.

"We'll see about that in a few minutes, the nick is just along the road. If you're clean, you have nothing to worry about," Jock answered. As they walked along the silent street, they noticed the crowd had gone from the coffee stall.

"Queer, all of them going so soon. I wonder if anything has happened." Jock was curious so he stopped, with their unwelcome guests, and asked the proprietor the question which was uppermost in their minds.

"What's happened to the mob that was here a short while ago?"

"There was a fight Guv."

"Coppers?"

"No," the man replied, "a couple of Irishmen got done up."

"Where are they now?" Jock asked.

"They went home after the gang left, one of them wasn't too good. They put him down and put the boot in quite a lot - his mate took him away."

"Right, thanks." Jock and his mate continued on their way.

Once in the charge room the men dejectedly sat down on the form.

"It's no use Paddy, they've nicked us. You told me we would be alright down here," one of them complained to his mate.

"How the hell was I to know that they would be waiting for us, somebody must have grassed on us?" his mate answered.

"What have you brought them in for?" The Station Sergeant was annoyed because his game of cards had been disturbed.

"We're just going to take them upstairs for questioning Skipper. We thought we'd better let you know they were on Station premises." The Sergeant was relieved.

"Right, keep them up there till six o'clock and give them to Early Turn," he gratefully returned to his game of solo.

The Irishmen were taken upstairs to the CID office and separated. Statements were then obtained from them both regarding their various nefarious activities. Once the proof was down on paper, Jock and Jack obtained all their antecedents, fingerprinted them and took them down for the Charge to be read out. Once again the Desk Sergeant was disturbed, but he was in a better frame of mind knowing it would only be a couple of seconds work - in fact he had been winning which had made him happier.

The case was ready for Court, thanks to a few short cuts and the men were bedded down for the night. A message was sent to the Police at Liverpool CID to inform them that they had the two men in custody. They were wanted at Liverpool for robbery but were charged with other offences and were to appear at the local Court at 10am that day. This meant, of course, only a couple of hours sleep for the two Aides before they had to attend to give evidence.

MURDER

After the hearing, the Irishmen had been disposed of to the custody of the prison service, and Jock and jack returned to the office to complete the books and to sign off duty till their shift started at 10pm. They wouldn't have much time with their families before returning to work, however when they showed their faces at the Station they found things in a turmoil.

"Just the blokes we want," said the Sergeant on duty in the office

"Sorry Serg, we're on nights, we've had no sleep and have been at Court all morning and we'll have to go home to get some shut eye before coming back on duty."

"That will have to wait, sorry. We're short of men due to last night's do." Jock looked round the crowded office and asked how they could be short of staff, especially with the number of men present.

"There are a lot of enquiries to be done, everyone else is busy with the murder."

"What murder was that Skip?" asked Jock.

The Sergeant went into detail about the two chaps who had digs together, they'd been involved in a fight the night before and one of them was very badly beaten up. His mate had helped him home and put him to bed. He found him dead in bed that day. All the CID were engaged in enquiries, trying to find out who had fractured the man's skull.

"Two Irishmen you said Skip? There were two Micks at the coffee stall last night who were done up by the mob." Jock told him.

"Did you see them?" The Sergeant was suddenly alert. "You'd better come with me."

"Not now Brian, I'm busy." He went into the Detective Inspector's office. The Sergeant was not to be put off because he knew why the boss was getting his knickers in a twist.

"It's about last night Guv. Jock and his mate were on duty last night." The Inspector looked over the piles of paper that were gathering on his desk in front of him and glared at the two Aides as the Skipper closed the door.

"What the hell have these sods been up to then?"

"Tell the Guv what you told me," the Sergeant requested, and the story of the mob at the coffee stall and the subsequent happenings was related. The Inspector was interested and grunted.

"Where would we be without you idle sods. If you two buggers hadn't been sliding off for a cuppa, you wouldn't have seen them. I keep telling you that work is on the streets, not in the cafes."

They didn't enlighten him that they had nicked two blokes in the café but waited as he pondered over his new information; one could almost see the gold plated machinery ticking over in his head.

"Did you recognise any of the mob at the stall? How many were there?"

Between them, Jock and Jack related over a dozen names of local yobs.

"Are you sure?" the boss asked. When he was satisfied that the coppers knew the villains he said, "Right, bring them in now."

"Guv, we're on night duty, we've been at Court all morning and we are on night shift again tonight. We haven't had anything to eat."

"Always thinking of your bloody bellies. This is more important than feeding your faces, I want them bastards brought in, at once," the Detective Inspector bellowed.

So, it was straight out onto the streets to look for fourteen thugs. Jack moaned.

"Why the bloody hell do we have to do it all by ourselves, with all them idle sods sitting on their arses in the office?" He was really in a bad way, missing his grub. "It'll take us hours to find these sods, I'll die of starvation."

To sustain his stamina for a couple of hours, they called into a local café and ordered a fry-up. The girl passed Jack's plate over to him as she laid the other in front of Jack.

"Bloody hell" gasped Jock, and frantically dropped the plate down in front of him. "The silly bitch, she's kept the plate hot, it must have been against a flame for some time." Even as Jock was looking at his painful hand he could see it getting very red and a blister began to appear. By the time he finished his meal, he was sucking the offending digit and roundly cursing the stupid woman. After reluctantly paying for his torture, he left the café, still sucking the burn to ease the pain.

"Where do we go first?" Jack asked, although he already knew the answer.

"The usual place, the amusement arcade, it's bound to be the best" Jock muttered. So the pair of them started on their long search towards the villains' favourite retreat.

God was on their side, as they stopped at the doorway and looked in at all the familiar faces.

"You hang on here, I'll go and weed them out," Jock ordered before commencing a slow search of the place. As he reached various yobs and recognised them as having been at the coffee stall the previous night, he said to them.

"You're nicked. You don't want to be done for resisting arrest and assault on police do you?" Naturally the amazed thugs knew that a stretch inside would be the result of such charges, so they didn't argue. "Right, just go to the door and wait for me there." The message was brief but the villains knew that something was on so they all obeyed. By the time Jock had finished his search of the stinking place and had returned to the doorway, he found a dozen thugs waiting patiently with Jack.

"Right lads, you lead the way down to the nick," Jock ordered.

"What's on Guv, why are we nicked?" was the general question on all the lips of the crowd.

"You have some questions to answer," they were told. They had no idea what was waiting for them, nor why this big Scotch sod had nicked them, but due to the fact that he had arrested so many of them at the same time meant that something serious was in the air. Consequently, they didn't argue with him, although it didn't stop them moaning and complaining as the procession wound it's way down to the Police Station. A lot of those present had seen him deal with Pete some time back; they knew he could be a nasty chap to meet in a fight and wasn't worried about the odds. Consequently, Jock had no trouble marching the crowd into the nick. As they walked behind the mob of villains Jack grinned at Jock.

"When we get this lot settled down I think I'll treat myself to some dinner."

"We won't be that lucky, gutsy," grinned Jock, "I bet the DI will think of something else."

"Straight upstairs lads. You know the way." Jack pushed into the lead, even though the whole crowd were regular visitors to the CID office, he wanted to warn the boss about the new influx of people due to join the crowd already in the office. The prisoners were all herded into one corner to await the attention of the Guv - who was soon on the scene.

"Is this the lot?" he asked, looking daggers at the motley mob.

"Two more to come Guv" Jock answered.

The DI delegated all the staff to get written statements from the newcomers and turned on Jack and Jack who were just slipping out of the door.

"Where the hell do you two think you're going? There's a lot of work to be done here" he said.

"Yes Guvnor, but we still have to find the other two."

"Oh alright, but don't be long, I've got some more work for you." The boss reluctantly let them go.

The door closed behind them and they gratefully headed for home, for a meal and a few hours sleep; they had been on duty for over eighteen hours.

"The DI is doing his nut about you two. He's been waiting all day to see you." He finished his drink, "I think he'll be very annoyed if you don't call in and see him for a chat."

"You mean we're nicked, one said, Honest, Guv, we ain't done nuffin."

"Honest? You don't know what it means, and as regards not doing anything, you mean you haven't been caught?" Jock grinned and ordered another round of drinks. "It's your turn, isn't it?" he asked the other villain.

Drinks finished, they all headed back to the Station where the DI was still slaving away at paperwork.

"Here are the last of them Guv" Jock told him.

"Right, get statements from them both about last night" he grunted as he glared at the prisoners. "I want a word with you before you start." He told Jock that the dead man's watch and wallet were missing, apparently removed during, or after, the fight. None of the other men had admitted to this offence, so pressure had to be placed upon these two so as to identify the guilty party.

"See if you can crack them Jock. We want the bastard that took the gear."

The statements were obtained with regard to the fight, the men didn't argue, 'fair enough' was their attitude, 'we've been nicked, but why so much trouble over a little punch-up?' They were curious. Both denied emphatically any knowledge about the watch and wallet, everyone had a go at them, but they stuck to the story, just like the others had done.

They were bailed out till the next day and as Jock showed them off the premises they asked what all the fuss was about.

"Murder," they gasped, "You're joking?"

"No, you and your mates worked him over, his gear was nicked and he died as a result of his injuries. That's murder."

"But we didn't nick his gear," the men pleaded, they were really worried.

"If you find out who it was, and it wasn't one of your mob, then you might be lucky and get away with it," Jock told them.

"We'll find out who the bastard was Guv and we'll let you know. We're not going to carry the can for anybody."

"We'll be here at ten o'clock, so you'd better get your skates on, your time is short," Jock advised.

They completed their diaries and, paperwork done, they decided to go along to the café for a cuppa.

"I'll have a bacon sandwich as well Bill." That stomach just couldn't be filled.

After refreshments, they walked round the town, checking the rear of the shops and arcades. As they passed one arcade a man came out and followed them. He walked past and they recognised him as one of the thugs they had brought in that morning; he turned into an alleyway just ahead. As they reached the corner, a whispered

"Guv!" came to their ears. They stopped and stood with their backs to the alley, glancing along the street casually as the man gave them the information they had been waiting for.

"Does that get us off the hook Guv?" the hidden figure asked. "The lads want to know."

"You'll still have to be at the nick in the morning, but we'll check this out," Jock told him.

The next morning at 9 am the two coppers arrived on the doorstep of a local second-hand shop in the town centre. The owner was questioned regarding recent purchases and he produced a book with all the details of transactions.

"A watch, you said?" he asked as they scanned the document. "Yes, I remember a lad bringing one in. Here it is" and he pointed to an entry in the book. "And here is the watch" he said as he took a watch from the showcase. The person who had sold the watch had produced identity at the time of sale, the name and address was the same as had been given to them the previous night.

"He didn't sell a wallet as well?" asked Jock.

"No, but I'd recognise him again," the shop-keeper said.

Jock thanked him and handed over a receipt for the watch and then they headed for the address which had been given to them. A pasty-faced youth came to the door in response to their repeated knocking. He was a loud mouthed and scruffy individual and he objected strongly about being disturbed before dinner-time.

"What do you want?" he demanded.

"We want you mate, you're under arrest."

"What do you mean, under arrest?"

"Get your bloody clothes on, you're nicked." It seemed to be the only language these blokes understood.

"What for?"

"This, and don't worry about the time, you'll have plenty of that where you're going." Jock dangled the watch in front of the chap's nose.

"I don't know what it's all about." The man was going to be awkward.

Down to the nick they all went and straight up into the CID's office. They pushed the reluctant thief into the Detective Inspector's office where he was looking at the list of latest crimes; he hadn't been on the premises very long and was annoyed at being disturbed so early.

"What is this all about?" his surly request was to be expected.

Jock laid the watch on the desk in front of him in answer to his question, the timepiece seemed to magnetise him for a few minutes. "Where did you get it from and who is this?"

"He sold the watch to a secondhand shop in the market Guv. He's the one that nicked it, and also the wallet" Jock stated. It made the day for the DI - murder solved and property concerned recovered - all inside one day.

"I have no idea what this is all about" the prisoner said.

"We shall soon find out. Sit down there" the DI instructed as he turned to the two Aides. "Send the Sergeants in and get back to work, you won't find criminals whilst you're sitting on your arses in the office, they're out on the streets."

No word of thanks or a 'Well done lads', just the usual curt order. They went, leaving the villain alone with the four senior Detectives; he was well and truly questioned and, much later, admitted taking the dead man's property. Although he denied being involved in the fight, he insisted that he was only having a cup of tea at the coffee stall when the fight started. It couldn't be proved that he had struck any blows, so the DI settled for the charge of robbery, which the man admitted. Naturally the Guv signed the sheet as arresting officer and claimed the arrest, all down to his intelligence and capability. When the man appeared in Court it was indicated to the Magistrate that the prisoner had decided to join the army, he was just awaiting confirmation. The case was adjourned for one week.

"Either you sign on for 14 years in the Army, or I'll send you to prison for 14 years. The choice is yours," was the advice given to the prisoner.

He joined the Army!

PROPERTY

Property is a word that can send shivers through the hardest and most seasoned copper. The stuff causes more trouble than enough, whether it be found, stolen, prisoner's property, or stuff relevant to a charge. The Station Officer ensures that the goods handed into a station are entered into the correct book and it is then allotted its correct place of rest. The property cell was for items large or not of great value; the Station safe was for valuable goods. The cell used to become full of cycles and it could be a nightmare going into the place to find some specific object. Prisoner's property was checked and re-checked and carefully placed in an envelope with the name written on, and then placed in the cabinet. Any property handed to a copper in the street had to be recorded at once in his pocket book (only things of importance went into those books), the goods would be given to the Sergeant at the Station, who would check it and sign the pocket book. Officers have been cautioned, fined and even sacked because of 'property'.

During his spell as 'Aide to CID', Jock was detailed, with all of the others, to assist the uniform branch during an election. A uniformed PC had to be in attendance at every school or hall which had been used for the election. The hours were long, at least a twelve hour day, from the time they opened until the booths closed. Sometimes a PC was designated to travel with the boxes, depending upon whether or not they already had an escort when the transport arrived at their station. The Presiding Officer might decide to take his own car with the box in it. In this case the copper would have to travel with him, the Presiding Officer would not be in the least worried about how the copper was to get home. Jock had arranged with the Inspector to go straight home after the booth closed, providing he wasn't needed for escort. As it happened he was in luck and had a meal and a few hours kip before getting up early for an observation job.

The days used to drag on the Poll, there were the same stereotype collection of volunteers, teachers and civil servants who somehow managed to arrange to be selected for these 'extra cash jobs'. They worked in pairs, as everyone knows, whether this is to provide company for the staff, or just to provide more jobs for the teachers, Jock never found out. There never seemed to be any friendliness amongst the volunteers, they always sat like complete strangers, very rarely talking to one another. Nearly all the women took their knitting so they were paid to knit their own jumpers; activities were only interrupted by the usual lifesaving liquid - tea. Often these people would take their own brew, some of them even took thermos flasks so as not to share with the others. *Once* Jock managed to get a cup in all his service.

The worried clients would creep into the room, they would become completely lost at the various boards covered with numbers. Sometimes streets were included on the boards but generally only the voter's number. Naturally the old, poor-sighted, or the idiots never knew their numbers and approached one of the tables where two grim faced women sat looking like Spanish Inquisitors waiting to pounce.

"Address?" the question would be barked. When given, a look of disgust would appear on the face of the clerk, "Wrong table."

When eventually the poor creature reached the correct position and gave their address, the clerk would glance through the Voters List and note the number alongside, she would repeat the number out loud for the benefit of her companion who would write it on the stub of a ticket. The other piece of the ticket was then handed to the voter, who would then retire to a cubicle to record his vote in secret. The slip would then be inserted in the box under the eagle eye of the presiding officer. Jock noted that the slip had a number which corresponded with the stub retained by the clerk, just like a raffle ticket. Who said that the British voting system was secret? If anyone really wanted to check the way a person had voted, it would be difficult, but not impossible.

The number of people attending the chambers of horrors varied during the day. A rush at first as some workers called in on their way to their labours, then quiet till lunch-time. The afternoons brought a steady trickle of shoppers and retired residents, but the evenings brought the crowds. It was during one hectic crowded session that a woman handed a broken old pair of specs to Jock. Fastened with tape across the nosepiece and one lens cracked, but he still obtained the name and address of the finder and inserted the particulars in his pocket book, then put them in his tunic pocket. Nine o'clock, voting over and the box collected, he headed for home.

A week later he was called in front of the boss, and as he stood on the old familiar carpet he wondered what on earth he had done wrong this time. A serious expression was on the face of his boss as he looked at the PC standing in front of him. Reading from a sheet of paper in front of him, he asked,

"Where were you on duty during the last election?"

Jock wondered what had happened to be questioned like this. He didn't answer his senior officer, who asked a further question.

"Was any property handed to you?"

The day's events flashed before Jock's eyes and he suddenly remembered the old spectacles, what had he done with them? Damn it, he had put them in his tunic pocket after he had made the entry in his pocket book. In answer to the SD Inspector's next expected question, he told him what had happened in detail. The property was placed in his pocket and he had not worn the uniform since that date. He had been up early the following day and had forgotten all about the old glasses.

The old man ordered a Sergeant to call at Jock's house to verify the facts. He returned shortly afterwards with the specs and informed the boss that they had been found where Jock had stated. The Inspector then examined the pocket book and noted the entry.

"You're a lucky man you know. There are two things that saved you. Firstly, the value and type of the property, and the fact that you had a good excuse, being in uniform for only one day. Secondly, you had entered the article in your book. Take warning from this incident, property is very dangerous and could cost you your job, or worse. The old woman who had lost the specs was in her corner shop and, naturally, her one and only pair of glasses was the subject of discussion. The couple who had found them and had handed them to you entered the premises and heard them talking. The lady was informed the glasses had been handed to the police and, naturally, when she called here there was no record in the book. So, don't forget in future, it doesn't matter what the goods are, or the value, hand them in as soon as possible. Now you can go and return these to the owner.

Jock was never so glad as when he handed the specs over to the grateful old woman.

"Thanks dearie, but you shouldn't have bothered, they were only old ones, I very rarely use them," she said sweetly as Jock went to hunt for villains - they were safer to handle than property.

CAR THIEVES

He met up with his mate at the nick, and the first remark was to be expected,

"We might as well go and have our grub before we start." So they headed for their usual café and Jack could also enjoy his favourite pastime, watching the women go by as he ate. Jock often wondered if he was ever going to stop filling his face, it didn't seem to make any difference how much he ate; he never got any fatter.

"Come on, let's go" Jock said. Jack reluctantly followed his partner back onto the streets, it was dark and most of the workers had already gone home and the shops were closed. It was the quiet period before the night-life started and people began to head for the pubs, clubs and theatres. As they strolled along, Jock suddenly pulled Jack into a doorway.

"Hang on," he said as he indicated a group of youths gathered around a couple of cars which were parked on a bomb-site.

"Look at them."

The four youths were all attempting to gain entry to the cars.

"There are two cars, so that is two separate attempts. Shall we nick them?" said Jack

"No, let's hang on for a bit, it's obvious that they are after something, if they don't get in they will try something else."

After several minutes the gang gave up their attempts and moved away. They followed them, only stopping for a few seconds beside the cars to note the index numbers and the damage to the doors caused by the would-be thieves. Another car received their attention, but as it was on the main road the men left it unopened, after the cursory examination they moved on to look for better prospects. Eventually the crowd crossed the road which led to another Police area, they walked past a Police Telephone Box and entered a dark side street. It could be seen that vehicles were parked on both sides of this street.

"We're off our toby now Jack, I'll ring the nick. With all these cars here they're bound to have another go and will probably strike lucky. I think we may as well get the van down in any case." They made the necessary call to the Office and shortly afterwards the van arrived, the spare driver had come along also to render assistance if it had been needed.

"Can you go round the block to the bottom of the street, there are four yobs down there having a go at the cars?" Jock requested.

The van driver obliged and moved off with his mate. The four villains had no idea that the law was closing in on them. The plain clothes men split up, one on each side of the street and, moving slowly, keeping close to the hedges, until the suspects could be seen. They were working their way along the lines of vehicles trying each one. Eventually they were in luck, or so they thought, they had found a car unlocked. Quickly the youths crowded into the vehicle and waited for the driver to pull the wires loose from under the ignition switch, he crossed them over and was successful in his attempts for the engine fired. Just as it did so a couple of coppers appeared beside the car, one on each side.

"You're nicked, bonny lads" and as he recognised the men, "Again." And a couple of future car dealers and two eventual train robbers were once again arrested by Jock. Before they could even start to make excuses, the Police Van pulled alongside. The prisoners were placed in the Maria with Jock and his mate as escorts. The spare driver drove the other car back to the office. The four yobs protested their innocence very emphatically to the Station Sergeant, but it was like water off a duck's back, he knew them all. The following morning at Court they maintained the plea of innocence.

"It's a fix. We were just on our way down to the coffee stall beside the river." They also denied being the owners of all the car keys found on them, saying 'They had been planted by the law'. As if that would have been done.

GANG FIGHT

The following night the two of them stood beside a pub at the main junction of the town.

"Quite a bit of activity tonight" Jock remarked, as they leaned against the wall looking at the busy pavements. He was referring to the unusual number of villains who were gathering at the junction.

"The sods are up to something Jock," his mate agreed.

They mingled with the throngs and were soon chatting to one of the groups.

"What's cooking tonight then, going to a ball?" Jock asked one of the locals. The yobs told him quite readily that the gang were waiting for another neighbouring mob to arrive, then together they were all going to another area close by, where there was a dance being held. This was on a district used by another two different gangs. It was going to be a case of 'Tit for Tat' due to the fact that some of their mob had been put in hospital recently by their opposition. Not that they needed any excuse for this gang warfare. The intended army were all armed with their usual weapons, cutthroat razors; flick knives; stilettos; jack-knives; hammers; knuckle dusters; choppers, Commando style knives (with the knuckle duster attached); coshes of all shapes; lead pipe; pick-axe handles; chains - ranging from dog leads and toilet chains to the heavier industrial type and several had open razor blades sewn into the peaks of their flat caps.

As Jock was chatting with his informant, a crowd began to gather round them. A couple had already been on the bottle to build up their courage for the coming fight. One of these saw Jock and said

"He's a bloody rozzer. What the hell are you talking to Old Bill for?" he snarled. There's only one way to talk to this type of person and that's not to be polite. They only know one language and that's theirs, to show any sign of worry or fear would spell disaster. So the inquisitive drunk was told in no uncertain terms to get lost, as the conversation had nothing to do with him. Naturally, he got annoyed.

"Don't get stroppy with me Fuzz, or I'll fill you in. I'll mark you." Indicating that a knife or razor would be used. The beer was already talking.

"Listen, Pratt, you couldn't do it, so belt up."

"There's a lot of us here copper, we could do you up no trouble at all. We'll eat you alive." The alcoholic voice crackled.

"Oh, piss off, you load of shit." Jock ground out. "If you want to have a go, you're welcome to try." He glanced at his mate, at least he looked in the direction where Jack had been standing, only to find that the other copper had gone. He eased his stick up into his sleeve, realising he was alone.

"Right, laddy, come on." He spoke to the beer soaked bloke. "Try me."

One of the local mob took hold of the stranger's arm and spoke to him.

"If you start anything with him he'll slaughter you. He's the one that took Big Pete and his mob on by himself," he whispered fiercely to the man. "Get out while you can, he'll crock you for life, if he doesn't kill you."

The advice soaked into the antagonist's brain, even he had heard about Jock's run-in with the leader of the local mob and as common sense sifted into his blurry brain.

"Well, we have a good fight lined up for tonight and I don't want to miss it," he said and drifted away to blend in with the others.

Jock looked around as the crowd dispersed, they surrounded a bus which was just drawing in, yelling and shouting at the rest of the Army who were on board. Soon they joined them and were on their way to the intended battle ground. Jock saw his mate standing beside a 'phone box.

"Where the hell did you get to?" he asked.

"I thought there was going to be trouble, so I was going to 'phone for help if they started. You were stirring it up with that block and I knew that I wouldn't be any good if the whole crowd started," was his mate's feeble excuse.

"Oh, never mind, let's get this info across straight away." Jock went into the box and passed the information onto the local police station. The news was passed onto all surrounding stations about the forthcoming battle. All cars and available men were directed to the scene.

Jock and his mate were out of luck, by the time they reached the nick all the cars had gone and they couldn't get a lift. The results of the fight were discussed for a long time after the affray and everyone had seemed to enjoy themselves. Jock's mate had also enjoyed himself due to all the villains being at the fight, there was no danger of crime. So he got stuck in and had a good meal!

CHAPTER EIGHT

THE PIG MAN

THE PIG MAN

Out of the blue the information came,

"The Guvnor wants to see you," the man in the communication room told him. When he entered the Detective Inspector's Office.

"Yes?" said the man, looking up at him enquiringly

"You wanted to see me, Guv?"

"Not me lad," he answered, "Who told you that?"

"Communication Room." Jock replied, "I'd better go and check and see if they have made a mistake." When he questioned the copper about the message, it was soon realised how the mistake had been made. 'Guv' to a CID man meant the Detective Inspector, but to the uniform it meant the Divisional Inspector, so he headed up the stairs to see the old man.

"Hello Mr MacGregor, I have some news for you. From today you will be posted to your local station where you live. This will save you travelling time and there will be quite a few of you starting for the same reasons. The nick is very short and the transfers will bring it up to strength. All arrangements have been made, so just contact them to find what shift you are on. I'm sorry to see you go, but I know things have been a bit strained at times. I'm sure you'll settle down at your new nick, at least until you get into Special Branch. That's if you still intend to apply."

"Oh yes Guv, I still intend to apply."

"If you have any gear at the nick you can get the van to take it across." The old man stood up and shook hands with him before he left.

So Jock was posted, out of the blue, to the station where he lived. He was now one of the coppers who had the honour of working under Dirty Dick. He didn't intend to stay in his present quarters because of the conditions. Doors and windows didn't fit properly and they let in cold blasts of wind; most of the bedrooms were over the stables and extremely cold, with condensation running down the walls; the living room had a concrete floor, and a faulty damp course allowed water to soak up the walls. On one occasion, when returning from night shift, he found the place full of fumes, the pet budgie lay dead in its cage. Luckily enough, Puggle had closed the living room door so the fumes from the fall of soot had not affected the family. Jock was constantly complaining, asking for another house or for repairs to be carried out, but to no avail.

His first day at his new Station was faced with apprehension. It seemed a long time since he had been on beat duty and it was like starting as a new boy, regardless of his numerous arrests for crime and paperwork regarding traffic offences. As he stood in the line of fresh new faces awaiting the Sergeant to show his face, he glanced around the relief but he didn't know any of them.

He wondered what the supervision would be like and if there were any like the Inspectors and Sergeants at his old nick, the type who seemed to take great delight in chasing young coppers. His question was soon to be answered as the door banged open, nearly six o'clock, so the Skipper was late.

"See me after parade, you're late." said the Sergeant glaring at the other new copper who came in just behind him.

Jock stood at the end of the line, next to the Sergeant, he was taken by surprise at the skipper's attitude for this chap was the one that his wife had nicknamed 'Dirty Dick'. Considering the way he carried on in relation to his job, it didn't seem possible that he should chase the coppers for trivial things. The man must have been in a terrible hurry to take the parade because he had forgotten to bring all the required books with him. Apart from having to go back upstairs to collect the rough book and the list of stolen cars, he also had to go back to inform the Inspector that the men were ready for inspection.

Apparently the Inspector had got fed up waiting for this and was having a cuppa in the front office. The Skipper was delegated to inspect the men; naturally he was fed up with rushing around and barked at the coppers.

"Right, show your appointments."

Dutifully, all the men produced their truncheons, pocket-books and whistles, holding them up in front so the Sergeant could see them as he carried out his inspection. He went round the line, finding fault with each one. Jock was last, on his extreme right, the Sergeant glowered at him.

"Where's your whistle?" his voice was almost a snarl.

Jock had already made up his mind that he didn't like this man and was being awkward on purpose, he looked the Skipper in the eye, it was now or never - it was obvious that his whistle chain led into his top pocket.

"It's in my pocket Sergeant" he answered.

"Well!" the voice grated as the owner waited for the whistle to be shown to him.

"Well!" Jock echoed - he was going to be just as nasty as this chap.

"I asked you where your whistle is," the Sergeant repeated, really getting annoyed now. Jock turned his head slowly and began to examine the supervising officer, from his brown shoes and civvy trousers right up to the multi-coloured shirt which could just be seen over the police raincoat.

"I told you that it's in my pocket" and fastened his eyes on the man's shirt. The Sergeant had the grace to blush when he realized that Jock had noticed the fact that he was wearing civilian clothes under his police raincoat.

"Right, return your appointments," he ordered, and the implements were duly replaced, the missing whistle was not mentioned again as the Skipper laid down the law about working their beats properly, before marching them out. As the men were all strangers they had to check their beat books and maps as soon as they reached the streets. They would have to refer to them constantly as they patrolled their beats.

Jock was one of these, as he sat in a police box having a smoke, he checked the necessary books with care because he wanted to learn his ground as soon as he could. After a few minutes, as he was preparing to leave, he saw the figure of the tall Sergeant coming along on his bike. The man went past the box and approached it from the rear, where there were no windows. Jock went outside and quietly closed the door but continued looking at his books. Without looking up, he noticed the shoe caps appearing into his view.

"All correct, Sergeant" he said. The Sergeant showed his face as he was greeted.

"Are you lost then?" he asked, pointing to the beat book and the map.

"Lost? Not me Sergeant, in fact I'm just feeling my way" Jock responded sarcastically. The bugger was just falling into the trap.

"Feeling your way, are you blind?" the smart-Alec was certainly leaving himself wide open.

"Blind? Not me Sergeant, in fact I'm anything but that, you should know that" came the truthful reply.

"What do you mean, why should I know?" the perplexed Sergeant asked.

"This morning for instance, Skipper" Jock stated "You were wearing civvies under your police coat."

"So what. What I wear or what I do has nothing to do with you," the man blustered due to the fact that a police constable should get onto him about his dress, this made him mad. Jock continued,

"Then you come on parade late and began to have a go at the youngster who followed you in," continued Jock. "You were just taking advantage of your rank," Jock went on unaffected by the Sergeant's rage.

"Look lad," the jib got under the skin, "I've told you to mind your own business or else you'll be in trouble."

Jock decided to drive the knife in deeper.

"I wonder who would be in trouble Sergeant, if the commander got to know about a certain man, who goes to a certain place and takes his uniform off and changes into old clothes. This chap then gets a wheelbarrow and goes round the town collecting swill and then he mucks some pigs out before putting his uniform back on to patrol the streets."

"Eh!" the man blanched. "Where do you live?" he asked. "I don't know what you have in your mind, what are you cooking up?" The Sergeant was in a flat spin when he found out where Jock lived, he was looking for a way out of this. "Quite simply, Sergeant, I told you that I was feeling my way. I want to know exactly how I stand with supervision. If I want a cuppa or a smoke without being chased I would be quite happy. Mind you, I can work my eight hours on the streets, but the chap that chases me around had better be doing his own job according to the book. I know damn well that you take the piss, and I could have them stripes off your arm like greased lightening," Jock spoke bluntly to the chap before him.

"Are you trying to threaten me?" asked the worried man.

"Why should I threaten you? You asked me what I had on my mind and I have told you. After all if I had wanted to be nasty, I would have reported the matter a long time ago."

The Sergeant was obviously cowed, he had no guts, pleading with this new copper not to cause any trouble for him.

"After all Jock, we're all in the job for the same reason."

"What reason is that Skipper?" Jock knew that he had the man on the run.

"For a living of course, there's no reason why we shouldn't get on well together." He was crawling now. "Any time you feel like a cup of tea or a smoke, it will be alright. You won't say anything about my little part-time job, will you?"

"Right, Sergeant. I enjoyed our little chat" and Jock started to walk away. The Skipper called after him.

"By the way Jock, if you fancy a drink now, you'll find the bus canteen is OK."

"Thanks," said Jock waving acknowledgement and continued his walk round the streets to get to know his beat.

SETTLED IN

During the following weeks it became quite apparent that Dirty Dick was the odd one out with regard to Supervision. The new promotion scheme had been making its headway and the Sub-Division Inspector was now a Superintendent. He was a canny enough chap who never bothered anyone, a wealthy man in his own right, he owned his own property in the country. He didn't have to rely on the Police salary for a living. He had, however, a weakness for the hard stuff at times, but never in uniform. This wasn't all that often, but he worked according to the letter of the law.

It soon became obvious that there were no social facilities at the station, this was due to the fact that they had been short staffed and nobody had bothered. There were no children's parties, outings, whist drives or the old football pontoons. Jock questioned several Sergeants and the Inspectors about this face, he chased around and tried to get some interest going but nobody was interested. One of the older men at the nick said. "The last kids' party we had was a flop. Everyone just stood around the walls, it was hopeless, the place was freezing cold."

Eventually Jock pestered the Superintendent and suggested that something should be done. The old man had the answer and told Jock to take over the problem himself as all the other coppers refused.

"Organise a dance Mr MacGregor," he said. "And let me know when you have done that. I like a dance, and so does the wife."

So, Jock was nominated as Secretary of the Social Club; he was also Secretary of the Children's Party. Not only was he levered into these two positions but he was also granted the jobs as Chairman and Treasurer of both groups. That was no joke, so he decided to use these positions for his own benefit. The dance hall was booked, band arranged, cloakroom tickets bought and arrangements for attendants. Dance tickets bought and sold, prizes obtained for the dance, drinks and other entertainment were all fixed up. The boss allowed him to wear plain clothes in order to carry on with all the duties. Local businessmen were contacted and raffle tickets sold.

Every day the old man would ask him how things were going, the fever took hold of the other men. They didn't mind going to a dance, as long as someone else did the work. It was a swinging success according to everyone but Jock didn't have time to enjoy it himself as he had to supervise everything. The results proved that Jock was a born organiser.

And soon everyone was asking him for the date of the next dance. Outings to various places were also arranged. Jock got the bookings fixed up and also the coaches. Meals were arranged on the road and bills paid by him. He arranged for various local publicans to go with them to the races, they of course provided the drinks en route. Visits to different breweries never came too often for coppers of all ranks, naturally this was also one of Jock's jobs.

The children's parties, now that was a different kettle of fish. Apparently, the parents of children who wanted to go to the party also wanted to go with them. Jock laid down the rules, those who could go; get the grub; presents for everyone; games and visiting personalities to provide entertainment for the children. All the presents were obtained by him, by scrounging round the big stores; he collected all the broken toys and also the yearly allowance from their charity funds. Nothing was paid for by the men at the nick. He got a lot of cash from the football and cricket sweeps and pontoons he ran, which paid for meals etc.

He also arranged a whist drive for the parents whilst the party was on; he visited warehouses to obtain food and any other article required. Consequently, due to all of his requests to transport all of this material he was compelled to ask for the use of the police van. Eventually, the Superintendent called him into the office.

"Mr MacGregor, you've been pestering me constantly for the use of the Police Van ever since you came here."

"I'm sorry, Sir. It wasn't for my own use; it was for the Station."

"I know that you've done a lot of good since you came and that the work you have put in was for other peoples' benefit," the old man continued, "So, to avoid you having to keep asking me for the van, I have decided to send you on a driving course. In that way, you can bloody drive yourself, without coming to me, OK?"

A new chapter in Jock's life commenced. The stress and strain of a Standard Driving Course and how to drive a car seemed simple; until one attends such a course, one never knows just how much there is to learn. If anyone can pass a preliminary course, they say that they can drive. If they pass any other course then they are experts, the best in the world. After introduction to the course, the classroom work commenced for a few days, with general instruction regarding vehicle construction, reaction to steering, braking and acceleration. Students had to learn the car from top to bottom, from bonnet to boot. Naturally, the Highway Code was deeply involved and had to be learned word-perfect from back to front and this was necessary for the final exam, which was also in writing. At the end of the course several tests were set up in various cars, they had to find the faults and repair them.

Before setting off on the public roads the Instructor had to satisfy himself that his three pupils were safe enough to be allowed out. So each car had to be driven on the private track first. It was on this private roadway that Jock and his two mates were tested with regard to their capabilities. As the other two men had previously driven police cars and only needed an official test, they were alright. Jock was the one they were worried about, the Instructor wasn't interested in them, he concentrated on Jock.

"You only have a motorcycle driver's licence, I understand?" After a quick drive along the rod and a few turns, he ordered Jock to return to the office. He soon returned with the Inspector, who took his seat in the front.

"Right, Henderson. The instructor states that you lot are fit enough to put the public at risk." The PC nominated took his place in the driver's seat as directed.

"OK, let's see if the instructor is right. Of you go."

Five minutes later the drivers changed over when the Inspector said.

"Right, Clarke, your turn." Before each driver commenced driving, the Inspector examined his driving licence to ensure it was alright. Eventually, it was Jock's turn and as he took his place beside the Inspector he handed the driving licence across, as ordered. The licence was taken from Jock and examined.,

"You crafty bugger," the Inspector turned round and said as Jock was making himself comfortable in the driver's seat and adjusted the mirror.

"Why, what's wrong Inspector?" he asked in an innocent voice.

"You know bloody well what's wrong," was the reply, as the offending paper was thrust in front of him, and a thick, pudding like finger stabbed at the address. Obviously he was inferring that if any copper examined the licence, he also would notice that the holder lived in a Police Station and must be a copper.

"I'm sorry, Guv, I can't help where I live."

"Never mind, just get cracking, and don't forget we don't want to finish up with a long thin car. You're not driving a motorcycle now." The Inspector settled himself well down into his seat; it was obvious that he wasn't taking any chances. He was soon put at ease as the driver went through all the preliminaries of checking instruments and mirrors. After making sure that everything was in order, he started to drive, this included a brake test at the first opportunity. All the time he drove Jock gave a commentary, explaining what he was doing and why. The Inspector turned in his seat and looked at the man sitting beside him with a quizzical look on his face. After fifteen minutes he said,

"Right, back to the office."

The instructor was patiently waiting for the return of his car and when the vehicle drew up he approached it, in time to hear the Inspector in the process of pulling the other two drivers to little bits with their faults. As he started to get of the car Jock asked,

"What about me Sir?"

"You," he got back into the car, "You must think we are a lot of bananas down here, coming along here with that story, I only have a motorcycle licence - I haven't driven a car before."

"Sorry, Sir," Jock interrupted him, "I never said that I hadn't driven a car before. I made a clear statement that I only had a licence to drive a motorcycle. I didn't get a green ticket when I left the Army."

The Inspector said, "I knew as soon as you sat behind that wheel that it wasn't the first time you had done it; I bet you've driven more than some of our 'First Class' drivers. Why didn't you take a test on cars?"

"I haven't got a car and I couldn't afford one."

"This commentary business as well, these blokes never said a word and they have driven Police vehicles." He glared at the other two men.

Jock told him he had been on the cars as observer and had listened to the driver talking to himself. He told the Inspector who the driver was.

"Know him well," the man grunted. He then informed the Instructor that he could put the public at risk with the three of the novices.

Over the next six weeks, the course which followed was hard work but Jock was pleased to pass, like all the others who had got through. He was only allowed to drive Police cars without a wireless fitted. Other courses were to follow later, going from the lowly Class Five into Class Four, when he was capable of driving the van; later still the Advanced Course which allowed them the Class One. The previous courses were stiff but did not compare with the final one. Loads of tests and paperwork; long distance driving, fast driving, chasing bandit cars, answering calls and skid tests. Every make of car was driven during these courses, including buses. The final test had two examiners in the car, one at the back and one alongside him so they could see exactly how he handled the car and could also feel the slides. A fast drive was followed by an emergency stop and finished off with a chase. The driver of the bandit car was an Instructor, who would try all tricks to throw the Police Car off. The driver on test, however, had to stick to the rules of the Highway Code and the Training

Manual. He had to drive with safety and still he hadn't to lose the bandit nor break the law; if he did any of these, he would fail.

Jock reached the top grade which allowed him to drive any car, make or type, buses, wireless cars, vans, non-wireless cars, 'Q' cars and squad cars. The 'Q' cars were used by officers in plain clothes under cover, like the squad cars. In fact, anything on wheels he could drive.

Only a uniformed Policeman holding he rank of PC was allowed to drive a car with a wireless fitted, consequently when a squad car was out with the CID the driver had to be a uniformed man in plain clothes. He then drew the plain clothes allowance but was not required nor wanted for the investigation of crime jobs, that was left for the other members of he crew, except on Divisional 'Q' cars, when one car was fully manned by uniformed men in plain clothes. The other vehicle was operated by the CID with a uniformed man at the wheel.

There was strong competition between these two crews, as each tried to outdo the other with the number of arrests. It was a hard grind to reach the position of driver of one of these cars and the drivers had to be fully fit to handle the situations they had to face.

Back at the Station, a Policeman had to wait to be posted onto driving duties, in the meanwhile he carried on with normal coppering. Jock also had his normal Social Secretary's job to do, apart from walking the streets. There were a few drivers at each station who were authorised to drive the wireless vehicles apart from the drivers who were only classified for driving vans or spare cars. This system was operated to allow the wireless car drivers to have a break from the strain, and even occasionally they were allowed to walk the streets, just for a rest.

Jock carried on with the organising of outings, parties, dances and whist drives and used the vehicles whenever he needed them, with never a hint of suggestion from anyone to assist him. In fact, after one party when the children were collected by their parents, each one was loaded down with fruit, toys, paper hats, presents, paper hats etc., each one hanging onto their balloons and one copper turned round to Jock and said,

"I bet your kids did alright out of this."

Despite the snide remarks and the fact that Jock's children hadn't got as much as some of the other children, Jock had done that on purpose to prevent any complaining or allegations.

The Force was changing for the best, a lot of new blood was being introduced, as young chaps joined and the old-timers retired. The old gang were on their way out, taking a lot of bad habits with them. With so many young coppers in the job, the shortage of cash still prevailed, after all a copper only got four pay rises during his service and had to wait nearly twenty years before reaching top pay. Jock, as Social Secretary, was approached on several occasions by other members of the Force who asked if he could fix them up with part-time jobs. As some of the new members were married with children, they wanted a bit extra cash just to feed their families. Jock, with all his contacts in the local industries, was to say having constantly that he would 'see what he could do'.

One thing led to another, he had to keep a list of all the interested men and Jock's list of potential employers also grew and eventually he started making arrangements for some of the coppers to begin their spare time jobs. He soon had them all working for a few hours a week. As the project increased he had every man, Sergeants and Inspectors included, on his lists.

The only one missing was the Superintendent, who did not need any extra cash because his police pay was only pocket money as far as he was concerned.

Jobs with removal firms had traditionally been held by firemen who had plenty of spare time but they didn't like the coppers intruding upon their 'perks'. Eventually the two forces joined and both worked in unison; pay was standard for all the work i.e. two shillings and sixpence an hour. The other jobs that Jock managed to get for the chaps included escort jobs; protection; breweries; loading and unloading ships; lorries; driving; labouring; shops; breakers yards; welding and burning. In fact anything that needed an extra man.

Jock kept a comprehensive list and any chap could come along and ask for anything, from four hours to a twelve hour day if he was on his day off. So, if a copper came along and said,

"I'm day off tomorrow, can you fix me up all day?" the available job would be delegated to him.

Jock kept a full list of the station duties, so he knew what shift each man was on. A man posted on the early turn started work at 6am and he would do his police duties until 2pm, go home and get changed and report back two hours later to the part-time job where he would work until 8pm. The men who were on the afternoon shift and started work at 2pm were delegated to moving furniture etc. at 8am and worked until midday. The night duty coppers filled in the four hours between midday and 4pm. All for ten shillings a week. What a life, when educated intelligent men were compelled to slave away as low paid navvies in order to earn sufficient money to feed their families. At least it was money earned honestly and with their own sweat.

THE CIRCUS

Jock was constantly getting posted as 'Acting Sergeant' when he wasn't on the wireless car; sometimes he even got the job when he was driving the car around. One day he was detailing the men to their various duties and had been informed that the circus was coming to town and he had to ensure that it got through OK.

"Right lads, I have a nice little job for four of you," he told them. "If you keep your noses clean you may even get a free seat at the big show." He detailed the men whose beats took in the area where the lines of vehicles and animals would pass. It would be their job to supervise the movements of the large creatures and also to direct the traffic; they would also be on hand when the circus got settled in. For them it meant strict watch on the crowded streets, for Jock it meant he had to walk back and forwards along the line of animals and keep in touch with the coppers as well. (There were no personal radios in those days!!).

Once on the site where the owners caravans were lined up and the telephones connected, the smaller animals were already settled in, plus the big cats. Everything was in readiness for the large animals. As Jock wandered around the site he was halted by a conversation between two circus hands and he listened for a short while then made his way to the owner's caravan.

"Have you been having any trouble with fires recently?" he asked. The owner of the circus looked surprised,

"Yes we have. Why do you ask?"

"Have you offered a reward?"

"Naturally, we have had so much trouble that I offered a reward of £500 if anyone was caught trying to set fire to the animal tents." He looked at Jock hopefully, "Have you caught somebody?"

"No, but I think you'll be having company very shortly because I overheard a conversation which interested me a few minutes ago. May I wait?" Jock asked. The boss was curious, and agreed that the copper should await the mysterious expected guest.

"Certainly, have a drink" and Jock was offered a chair and a bottle was produced.

"Or shouldn't I ask when you're on duty?" he grinned.

"I would be able to down a drink of tea after sniffing at the elephants backsides."

He was just enjoying the hot brew when a commotion was heard outside the van, there was a loud banging which gave the impression that the owner was needed urgently. Two circus hands came in, pushing a man in front of them.

"We've got him Sir" one of them said excitedly. "This is the man, we caught him starting a fire. He was in the animal tent." The owner looked flabbergasted towards Jock.

"How did you know?" Jock ignored the question.

"Ask them what exactly happened and what the man did to start the fire."

The owner of the property started to cross-examine the two hands and eventually obtained their description of the affair.

"Totally incorrect, I saw them and heard them talking," said Jock after they had given their version. "They knew that this man was drunk, he was smoking a cigarette and one of them knocked the fag out of his hand and it landed on straw but not in the tent and it didn't catch alight. If there had been a fire it would have been their fault, not his. If I'm not mistaken, they would be after the reward you offered." He indicated that he knew the prisoner as being a local drunk.

"If you care to give me the dates of your fires, I'll check up on him, and more than likely you'll find that he was in prison."

"He couldn't have heard us talking because my mate doesn't speak English," said one of the circus hands. Jock was engaged with his telephone call but he turned round to the man and said,

"I don't know whether he speaks English or not but both of you speak German."

"They are both German" explained the owner, "How did you know." Jock told him that he could understand the language.

"Hold on a second," he halted the conversation until he obtained the particulars over the telephone, "It is as I thought, he spends most of his time in prison; he was inside on three of the dates you gave me," as he pointed to the drunk.

"We'll take him away and charge him, he won't give you any more trouble. Hang on a second." He opened the caravan door and shouted to one of the coppers who had walked along with the cavalcade of animals. "Taffy, here," when the youngster came across he asked him to remove the drunk and charge him. "Drunk and disorderly, the usual."

As the drunk was escorted away, the owner turned to his employees.

"You two, get out, I'll see you later." When they had gone, he turned to Jock and once again suggested that he have a drink, more stronger than tea; once again the offer was refused.

"Well look, I have to give you something, after all you have saved me a lot of cash. I know what" he said as he rummaged in a drawer. "Take these" and he held out several tickets for the show. "Just alter them to admit the number in each party, it's the least I can do."

"Well, if you insist, I'll pass them onto the chaps who helped with the animals."

"Right, now if you'll excuse me, I have a lot of work to do; I have to find some men to put the big top up tomorrow."

"Don't your men do it?" asked Jock.

"They help, but the brute force comes from the local volunteers" the owner explained, "I usually give them a couple of quid each."

"How many do you need?" Jock was interested. "I can fix it for you."

"I'll want about fifty, where could you get them from. Christ, if you can get them it will save me a lot of running around." He indicated the time that the men would be required.

"I'll give everyone two pounds that turns up." Jock left a very happy circus man behind him as he headed towards the nick. For a few days afterwards the call of "Hey Rube" could be heard around the station, and often reached the ears of a puzzled 'Super'.

FUNDS

It was quite apparent that the Social Club couldn't operate only on voluntary contributions, nor could they rely upon Charitable help. Consequently, Jock had to run various methods of raising cash, such as football pontoons, numbers games, raffles and sweepstakes. The lists of members were placed, as in all Police Stations, on the canteen notice board, showing the members, winners, total amount of stake and the weekly or monthly winners. A deduction was made towards the children's party. However, fate is always ready strike, all good things come to an end and even the kids were to suffer when the new Gaming and Lotteries Act came into force.

The Superintendent waylaid one of the Inspectors and designated him to find Jock. The Social Secretary had to see him in his office. Bill, the Inspector, was a pleasant chap a little older than Jock.

"I think you're going to have some trouble with this new Act," he commented.

He was right, for when Jock entered the office he noticed that the Guvnor had a copy of the new Act on his desk in front of him.

"Come in Mr MacGregor, I'm afraid that I have some bad news for you. Have you read this new Act?"

Jock admitted that he had seriously condensed the pages.

"I don't think it will concern us much," he said.

"It will, because all of these things you have going at the Station will have to come to an end. They are unlawful according to the Act and I will not have the law broken at this Station while I am in charge."

So began hours of arguing and debates between the Superintendent and the rest of the staff. Naturally all the men wanted the system to carry on as before, but the boss would not be moved. As far as he was concerned the matter was closed and he ordered that all the lists be removed from the notice board. The men were downhearted to say the least, moral was low and naturally discipline began to get sloppy. Jock could be a bad tempered awkward devil when he was roused. It took a lot to disturb him but was a stubborn cuss; the Superintendent found that out when Jock informed him that he wanted to appeal against his decision.

"That's up to you Mr MacGregor but you're wasting your time." So the appeal went forward, from one rank to the next; each Senior Officer backed the Superintendent's decision until Jock requested that it go to the very top, much to everyone's surprise. Eventually the call came for Jock to attend the office to discuss matters with the boss.

"Well Mr MacGregor, I suppose you'll be happy now. You've been given permission to operate your football systems and the raffles etc. Here is the memo, apparently you were right, but there are five points which you have to observe. I will want to check your books every week also." Jock read the memo and smiled.

"Don't worry Sir, I shall abide by the regulations and will have the Club's books etc. available for you at any time."

The Inspector, who had discussed the problem with him previously, looked at the memo.

"That's no good Jock, it says that all money taken shall be paid out as winnings. None must be retained." He was surprised that Jock had accepted the findings. "Neither the Social Club nor the Children's Party will benefit if all the cash is paid out."

"Right Bill, all the winnings will be given to the winners, but I will be holding my other hand out for a donation towards the Kids' Party. I don't have to keep any books for the kids, as I am the only one on the Committee. The residue, after the party has been paid for, will be given as a donation to the Social Club; it will be shown in the books and not even the books can question a donation." Jock explained how he intended to operate. "I'll be working according to the rules as far as the Guv is concerned."

"Crafty sod" said the Inspector, "But what if they don't want to make a donation. They might not have children."

"Before they are accepted into the sweepstake, they will be told that I will be expecting the usual donation," Jock answered. "In the event we do get an awkward one who refuses to pay, I'll just cross his name off the list and he will then be barred from the raffles, draws and sweepstakes; he will also find that there are no spare time jobs for him, and neither will there be any trips to the races or breweries."

"That's blackmail!" Bill explained.

"Call it what you like, they will all know the rules beforehand; everyone will be happy, the Super will have his books, the men will have their usual winnings and the donations will help pay for the kids' party and then of course there will be the dances and outings."

CRASH

"Will you book the car out Jock?" The Station Sergeant was patrolling officer for the day and as he couldn't drive the spare car, he had to use Jock's services to drive him round the town. "We have to pick the Chief Inspector up," he explained.

That was the trouble with being the spare driver, being a general dogsbody at everyone's call, although sometimes he was never needed, there were also times when the driver couldn't get a meal. This was one of those days!

"Where to?" he asked the Skipper as they drove out of the yard.

"I'll show you" he was told, for after all Jock was still pretty new to the area. After driving for a while, Jock recognised the pace as he drove along.

"Aren't we off our patch?" he asked. The Sergeant told him it wasn't far to go.

"Stop outside the Railway Station" he ordered, "Just here." The Sergeant indicated a space at the side of the road and Jock gently parked the car between two other stationary vehicles and switched off the engine.

"Whereabouts are we?" Jock enquired as he looked around street. The Station Sergeant didn't answer the question directly but a few seconds later he

"Here he is coming now."

Before he finished speaking Jock realised that the boss was not the only one approaching the police car. He started to sound his horn but the frantic blast did not deter the driver of a heavy lorry who was in the process of reversing his very large vehicle; he obviously intended to park it in the same space that was already occupied by the Police car. Slowly but surely the lorry drew nearer and Jock wound his window down and started to shout but his voice blended with the crowds of people who were all trying to attract the driver's attention. As the back end crumpled the wing, the Sergeant jumped out, having regard for his own safety. The Chief Inspector also saw his lift to work doing a disappearing act under the big lorry and he ran to warn the man who was still blissfully unaware of what was happening. The boss stopped him and they both came round to the back of his lorry, the look on the poor man's face when he saw a little Hillman Minx stuck right under his tail end; the back of the vehicle was actually touching Jock's windscreen.

"Good God!" he yelped and nearly burst into tears, he had visions of going to prison for life.

"Never mind," said the Chief Inspector, "Is your vehicle OK?" Whether it was or not, the driver didn't look, he just said that it would be.

"Right son," the boss said. "If you're alright just push off and forget about it, we'll not be doing anything." The amazed driver couldn't get back into his cab quick enough and soon he was just one of the many drivers who were guiding their vehicles through the busy streets; he hadn't even been asked for his driving licence. Coppers were queer buggers, hit somebody else and they would have reported everything, but smash one of their cars and nothing happens.

The Chief Inspector turned his attention towards Jock and asked him if the car could be driven. He watched Jock as he pulled the crumpled wing away from the wheel; after a while he considered that he had moved the torn metal enough to allow the wheel to be turned.

"I think we can manage now," he said.

"Good, drive us back to the nick, I will take it from the corner. If anyone else wants the car for the rest of the day, just tell them that it's booked out to me," the boss told him.

Jock walked the short distance from the corner to the nick with the Station Sergeant. He didn't see the car again until the following day, when the car looked like new, no signs of any damage. Whoever had repaired it must have been working overtime. The Station Sergeant approached him later during his tour of duty.

"I want ten bob off you" he demanded.

"Ten bob! what for?"

The Skipper explained that it was for a tip for the mechanic who had repaired the damage to the police car, it had been decided that they should pay ten shillings each.

"You'll be able to get blood out of a stone a lot easier Sergeant. I wasn't the cause of the damage, you ordered me to go there. We were off our patch to pick the Guvnor up, so I don't see why I should pay out of my small wage." The Chief Inspector could easily have afforded to pay the lot without any hardship, which he did.

It was just as well that the car had been repaired for shortly afterwards Jock was informed that the Superintendent wanted the car booked out. After he had entered the details in the book, Jock sat in the car awaiting his passenger and after a long wait he decided to go and look for the boss. He found him, sitting in the front office having a cup of tea.

"Your car is ready Sir." Jock informed him.

"Oh don't get on to me Mr MacGregor, I'm coming." He finished the few drops of tea remaining in his cup and turned to the duty Inspector.

"Always getting on at me this man." He slapped Jock on the back, "But he's one of the best. Well come on, I haven't got all day, I'm waiting for you Mr MacGregor."

Jock drove the boss home, obviously he had been visiting again and had one over the eight. This was only one of the many journeys he had made with the Superintendent; he had got to know his wife and daughter quite well, especially after he had to climb several flights of stairs sometimes, with the body of his boss slung across his shoulders. It was only on Jock's insistence that he got rid of his Landrover and acquired a secondhand Rolls Royce.

"A Landrover is not very comfortable for your family to ride in Guv. Why don't you give them a treat and get a decent car. You could afford something more in keeping with your position, something like a Rolls Royce." So the old man took his advice; he called him over one day to look out of the window.

"Mr MacGregor, what do you think of it?"

"You know Guv, I keep asking you to come and examine my house, one of these days we'll be blown out by the draughts." Jock said as he drove him home.

"Yes, I know, I keep forgetting." The boss thought for a while and asked Jock what shift he was on the following day.

"Late turn, beat duty."

"Have you got a television?" the boss asked. When he had ascertained that there was a television at the MacGregor household, he said "Right, I'll see you at two o'clock."

"I'll be at work."

"Tell the Inspector you have an appointment with me. Make it half past two, that will give you time to get down from the nick."

So Jock had just got in the house the following day when his boss knocked at the door.

"Hello Jock, Mrs MacGregor," he greeted them before making himself comfortable in one of the armchairs.

"Switch the Telly on Jock." Jock was flabbergasted.

"Hey, you've come to examine the house not to watch T.V."

"I know, but I have one of my horses running this afternoon and I want to see how he goes," the boss looked pitifully at Jock.

"House first, then the Telly."

"You're a hard man Jock," the old man complained, and he reluctantly levered himself out of the comfort of the armchair and proceeded to carry out his inspection. He finished off lying full length in front of the fireplace, with his head inside the grate looking up at the chimney.

"The silly sods," pardon me Mrs MacGregor, "but they've put it in wrong." He pushed himself back on to his feet. "I'll get in touch with the Surveyors Department straight away." He then adopted the reclining position once more, "Now can I have the Telly on?"

Jock obliged him and they sat together drinking tea and watching the racing until Jock reminded him that he was supposed to be on the beat.

"OK I can take a hint, and I won't forget about your house." He took leave of Puggle and walked along with Jock up to the Station. He was as good as his word, for it was not very long afterwards that Jock was granted a brand new maisonette; the only trouble was the distance he had to travel to work.

CHAPTER NINE

KNIFE FIGHT

KNIFE FIGHT

Jock's first night duty at his new Station and he was on beat duty. All five coppers were on parade when the breathless communications officer came running in.

"There's a knife fight at the dance hall." The whole relief ran upstairs to the yard to await the van driver who had to book the van out. A traffic Patrol Car was just going out and the driver stopped when he heard Jock shouting for him.

"What's wrong?" he asked.

As soon as the cause of alarm was pointed out to him he agreed to take two of the coppers in his car, so Jock and Jim got in with the driver and his operator. There were four of them, enough to sort any problem out and it didn't take long before the car pulled up at the dance hall. As they were getting out of the car a man in evening dress indicated a youth leaving the building.

"That's one of them." The driver grabbed hold of the person who had been nominated as one of the contestants in the dance hall.

"If you have a knife on you, I'll use it on you."

Jock never saw the outcome of that little incident because they were called away to another fight which had broken out in a nearby passageway. The brawl soon broke up when the blue uniform arrived on the scene; the crowd separated into two groups, both left the passage by different doors, one on each side of the passage. Jock followed the crowd that went through the door on the right whilst Jimmy and the wireless operator followed the ones who had gone through the other door.

It was the first time that Jock had ever been in this building, he didn't have the faintest idea where the door led to, until he suddenly found himself on the dance floor. The place was crowded, the tables and chairs placed around the sides of the hall were all occupied by between four to eight people. The Master of Ceremonies came across to him and said.

"Where are the rest of your mates?"

"I don't see any reason why there should be any more policemen here, it all seems quiet" he answered.

"It is just now 'cause you're here, but I want all that crowd put out" he said as he indicated the section of people he meant.

"They are the gang that have been using knives." Jock looked at the crowd and realised that he could have handled the situation much better if there had been some support but he couldn't walk away from the problem now and he told the Master of Ceremonies that it was his responsibility to tell the persons to leave.

"Just tell them over your loudspeaker that you want them out, I'll do the rest."

"OK it's your life," the man said, and he made the announcement which was received with hoots and catcalls from the gang. Silence then fell over the occupants of the dance hall as Jock made his way to the first table; two men and two women sat and looked at him as he approached. One of the chaps had his feet up on the table and was chewing gum, he had an insolent expression on his face as Jock looked him in the eye.

"Right laddie, you heard what the gentleman said, he wants you out."

The man smirked and looked towards his mate for support, he didn't stop chewing nor remove his feet, but said with typical cockney slang,

"I paid me free and six, I ain't going out."

"Never mind looking at your mates for help son, I'm talking to you and you alone, nobody else, so are you going out quietly or do you want to go the hard way?" Jock eased his sleeve back to disclose his truncheon, "I can drag or carry you out if you want."

When he had finished speaking he reached over and took hold of the heavy table, picked it up and placed it to one side, the sudden removal of the support from the man's feet nearly knocked him off his chair and by the time he had turned round the group were all standing up.

"Alright Guv, we don't want any trouble with you, we're going," said the other male member of the small group, holding both his hands up in front of him, palm forwards as if to fend of any trouble. Jock promptly ignored them as he moved onto the next table which had eight persons sitting at it.

"Right, your turn, follow them" he ordered, and without any arguments the party collected their personal articles up and followed the people from the previous table towards the exit.

Jock moved slowly along the line of tables, never once did he have to raise his voice; on some occasions he just indicated with his hand that the troublemakers should follow the example of their friends. Other people decided that discretion was better than valour and left without being ordered. Slowly and gently the whole bunch were being ushered out of the premises without any trouble, then suddenly a shout arose from the centre of the crowd.

The wretched Maser of Ceremonies had been stupid enough to get mixed up with them and one of the former dancers had decided to sort him out. Jock pushed his way through to the man's assistance and dragged his adversary away from his victim, who appeared to be unhurt. Everything would have been alright even then but for a burly, half drunken labourer who shouted out to the rest of the crowd.

"Come on, let's do them, there are only two of the bastards." The fight started, with Jock right in the middle. He strained his head over the mob looking for the other copper who had been mentioned, for no doubt that is what the chap had meant. Then he saw Jimmy, his mate, he was standing near the door with his back to the wall, swinging one of the tables from side to side as the attackers tried to reach him. As he observed this happening, he didn't have time to appreciate the fact, he was too busy looking after his own defences. First man he wanted was the one who caused the row, second was the one who shouted. He lost the first fellow because of the crush of the crowd and he was left with the man's collar and tie wrapped around his fingers. His right arm went around the neck of the man with the loud mouth and he tightened the grip until his stick was underneath the man's Adam's apple. This way he could lift the man onto his toes or lower him down if required, he was protected from the front. Someone jumped on his back and he reached over, grabbed a handful of hair and pulled tight, he was protected from the back.

Jock knew that he was in a dodgy position due to the report that knives had been used. He would rather have had his back against a wall but as he was surrounded by the crowd, he realised that it was impossible. That is why he provided cover for his body as quickly as he could. His hands were engaged but his feet were free, anyone that was near enough was in danger of feeling their weight. A flash of steel on his right made him swing the bodies around him, the swirling motion knocked the nearest people over as the person on his back swung outwards, suspended only by the great handful of hair in Jock's hand. A chair came flying at him, down goes his head and up come his two protectors to take the blow. Any legs he could see received a tremendous blow from his boots, groins and kneecaps proved to be the best deterrent and bodies began to collect around him. He wasn't gentle, he meant to hurt them for he knew that his life depended on the blows he delivered.

Unexpectedly, after he had began to wonder how long they would keep coming, he heard a shout.

"Look out, the law is here." 'What the hell did they think I was?' Jock wondered as the crowd began to make a dash for the exits. Still holding on tight to the two bodies, he saw one of the swing doors open. There, framed in the opening, stood the Inspector with the Section Sergeant beside him. The other three night duty coppers standing behind them. From the floor it was impossible to see exactly how many coppers had arrived, but it looked quite a lot.

"Been having a ball Jock?" said the Sergeant coming over. "Here, I'll take this one" and he reached over and removed the man from Jock's grip.

"Leave go of his hair." He dropped the unconscious man on top of the others lying moaning and groaning on the floor around him. "

Fourteen, not a bad night's work." He looked at the man still being held by Jock. "I think you can drop him as well." Jock then released his other prisoner and dropped the senseless troublemaker on the pile of bloodstained bodies.

"Are you alright Jock?" came the voice of his mate. "When I saw you stuck out there right in the middle of them, I thought you'd had it."

"You seemed to be having a swinging time when I saw you last," replied Jock, grinning.

"Well, either you were an expert dancer Mr MacGregor and wore all your partners out, or you were a lousy dancer and they all tripped over your big feet." Another voice broke in, it was the Inspector.

"Are you alright Jock?" he asked, looking at the big bloodstained copper.

"Fine Guv, just getting warmed up when you lot cut in and took all my partners away, they were fighting to have a dance with me," Jock laughed.

Fighting was still going on at the exits as police arrived from all the surrounding stations, the Inspector ignored the row and detailed the Sergeant to arrange for vans to take the injured to hospital and cars to ensure the prisoners were taken to their nick.

"All these will be down to you, of course, Mr MacGregor, it will keep you busy for the rest of the night." This was a simple way of saying, 'Take it easy'.

Apart from the dance, it turned out to be a quiet night, with thirty five arrests, fourteen knives collected, twenty three needing hospital treatment but none serious enough to be kept in.

ATTEMPTED MURDER

Early days, cruising round in the wireless car just waiting for something to happen. Taffy was his wireless operator and they were anticipating calls for break-ins found by cleaners, or trouble when unwanted guests were being put out of their digs. At 7 o'clock, the call came.

"999 - Call for Police" and the address followed.

"Another Irishman getting kicked out because he came in drunk I expect," Jock grunted when he realised the address was a private house.

They were only a couple of hundred yards from the location, consequently they pulled up outside the house in a matter of seconds where a small gathering of people were standing at the entrance of the house.

"Hang on Taffy, I'll deal with it." Jock left his mate on the wireless and approached the house.

"Righto, where is it?" he asked, meaning the room from which he expected to find a half tight and awkward Lodger.

"Last room on the right, downstairs. I'll show you," a girl in her teens said.

They walked down the passage together and she indicated a door.

"In there."

Jock went in expecting trouble, he got it, but not the type that was in his mind's eye. A body lay draped across the bed, a young girl, massive head wounds which covered everything with blood. Quickly he checked to ensure that the girl was still alive and noted the injuries.

"Christ" he muttered quietly. "You're in a right old state lassie." He looked towards the doorway, the other girl stood silently watching him.

"Go out to the car and tell the policeman I want an ambulance urgently. Then tell him to get in here, quickly now." He knew that every second counted if was going to save the girl. His assistance came straight back and informed him that the message had been passed on.

"Good lass, now you need not stay, but tell me what happened, who done it?"

The girl started to sob.

"My mother, the axe is on top of the wardrobe, here she is now." She added the last information when a woman came into the room. Jock noticed that the lady in question did not seem to be distressed or in any way affected by the gruesome sight. He carried on with his job, ripping the sheets into strips for bandages, but it was impossible to find a clean piece as the sheets were all red. He had straightened the girl out so he could work, the number of wounds to the skull was terrible, he suspected a couple of possible fractures and made rolls to lay around them. Whilst doing this he spoke to the lady.

"Do you know anything about this?"

The woman just nodded, so Jock decided that before anything else was said he had better caution her. The words didn't seem to penetrate for she just stood watching. Taffy pushed his way past her and entered the room.

"Christ, Jock, what's happened?"

"Taffy, get on the wireless and ask for the duty officer to attend, also the Detective Inspector. Attempted murder. This lady has been cautioned, the weapon is on top of that wardrobe. Now move it Taffy." As Taffy left the room the woman spoke.

"Is she going to be alright? I didn't mean to hurt her, I borrowed the axe yesterday, I'll give them it back." Jock realised that the poor lady was not responsible for her actions and he asked the girl what had happened. Once he had received the full story from her, he asked the youngster to take her mother out and 'give her a drink of tea or something'. The husband was in no condition to speak to him as he worked, so Jock spared his feelings and left him alone in his misery. They had been a happy family and had just returned from their holidays, the girl should have been going back to school for her first day since the holiday, now she was on the brink of death.

Taffy returned with the information that the Inspector had already left the nick for the location.

"Anything I can do, Jock?" He was a bit white about the face as he looked at the bloodstained body.

"Nothing else we can do Taff, but wait for the ambulance." He had just finished speaking when the Inspector entered the room.

"How's things Jock?" was his first question.

"At least forty separate wounds to the head, Sir. Weapon was the axe on the wardrobe there. Caused by the mother. I have cautioned her, she is in the kitchen I believe having a drink of tea. The ambulance has been called and also the Detective Inspector."

"Will you go with her in the ambulance Jock, I'll arrange for your car to be taken back to the nick," the Inspector asked.

"Right Guv, but there is one thing I have to do. They will have to operate, so I want to see the husband and obtain his permission, it will be required." He went with the Inspector to where the husband stood in shock and, naturally, the man gave his permission straight away.

The ambulance arrived and the man quickly put he girl on the stretcher and took her out to the waiting vehicle.

"Guv, I'll go with them in my car, you take Taffy back because there isn't another authorised wireless car driver on duty," Jock informed the duty Inspector.

"Right Jock, I'll see you later."

Jock accompanied the unfortunate girl till she was placed in the care of the doctors at the casualty department. The doctor began to take off the dressings that Jock had put on, the ambulance man had not touched them for the short journey. As he removed the makeshift dressings the doctor looked at the bloodstained copper.

"Who put these on?"

"I'm sorry, I did. That was the only stuff I could use at the time; she had a lot of curlers in which seemed to have taken most of the blows. I took them out to prevent any undue pressure and so they wouldn't open the wounds up again."

"That's alright officer, I'm not complaining, you did the best thing, including your ring bandages" the doctor said. "We'll have to take her to the theatre so we'll have to get permission to operate."

"I'm afraid the injuries were caused by the mother, but I did ask the father and he gave his consent. I thought it would save time."

"Good lad, right Sister, let's have her in" the doctor ordered.

"Can you hang on a second." Jock was left talking to the Staff Nurse when a female came in. She was the beautiful woman police lady from his old station and she was in plain clothes. She spoke to Jock in a very superior tone of voice.

"You have to report to the Detective Inspector, he is downstairs. I'm in charge here now."

The Staff Nurse scowled at her, she didn't like this official attitude the girl was adopting.

"You're not in charge here, I am. Now if you must wait, you can wait outside. I don't want you in my department." The female copper was compelled to leave and sat outside, her face was made with rage when Jock left. He hunted around downstairs for the Detective Inspector, and eventually found him taking a statement from the doctor in charge of casualty.

"What do you want Jock?" he asked.

"How's the girl?"

"They are just taking her in for operation. Your WPC told me you wanted to see me and that she was in charge up there" Jock answered.

"I don't want you, I think you've done enough."

"He saved that girl's life if I'm correct," interrupted the doctor. "He did everything that was right and I have to congratulate him. As regards your lady being in charge of the young lady, she'll find a lot of trouble from the Ward Sister if she hears her say that."

"Have you had your breakfast Jock? If not, you'd better go and get it and collect that bloody female from up there, take her back to the nick with you. Take my car."

"Thanks Guv but I have my own outside. So long doctor, Guv. I'll see you later." Jock went to find the W.PC and gave her the good news. He took the irate bitch back to the Station, where he had a good wash down to get rid of all the bloodstains.

"Alright Taffy, you lazy sod, where's my tea. Cushy job you have, sitting on your fat backside all day."

They had just finished breakfast when the next call came through, it was a '999' call for Police regarding an alleged robbery. It was stated that the assailant had been armed. Three minutes after getting the call Jock got out of the car, just a split second after Taffy. The cashier at a local fairground stated that a man had held him up and that he had threatened him with a flick knife. They obtained the description of the wanted man and began their search of the area, he was spotted a few minutes later and after Jock had chased him for a few hundred yards, he was arrested. Jock hauled him back to the police car and searched him for the flock knife. They found the missing cash but could only find a single bladed clasp knife on him; no signs of any flick knife. The owner of the cash insisted that it had been a flick knife he produced, the blade just shot out he insisted in his statement. Jock tried like blazes to make the blade shoot out, without success, until he realised that by having the knife blade partly open he could make the blade come out quickly.

The problem was to keep the blade open a little bit when he produced it in Court as evidence. The solution was to hold it in his small change pocket, the point stuck into the material, so when he pulled it out the blade was already on its way out. When the Magistrate asked to see the knife he jumped visibly when the blade shot out.

"I don't seem to be able to get this to work officer," he said examining it closely.

"No Sir, it takes a lot of practice, which makes me believe that the prisoner had used it quite often" Jock answered.

The baffled Magistrate was satisfied with that explanation and found the man guilty. When he was taken down to the cells, the prisoner said to Jock,

"Guv, can you show me how to do that, I've been trying for months to get it to work for me." He didn't see Jock's torn pocket.

ACCIDENT

Jock was posted on night duty and was spare driver, not much for him to do, so he asked the Section Sergeant if there was any chance of taking four hours time off due to the fact that he was due to be at Court at 10am. He would be able to get a few hours sleep.

"OK Jock. If everything is quiet, you can have it" the skipper agreed.

Just before two o'clock, when he was preparing to go home, a request came in for the van. A Policeman had arrested two prostitutes and needed transport to take them to the station. The Duty Inspector who had just started at the nick was on the scene assisting him.

"What the hell does he want me for. They could bring them back in the Inspector's car, couldn't they?" Jock complained.

"Sorry Jock" the Sergeant answered, "but it was the Inspector that ordered the van to be sent. Anyway, it won't take more than a few minutes."

Naturally Jock couldn't refuse, so he booked the van out and made his way to the Police Box where the prisoners were being held. The Inspector's car was parked outside the box and he stood talking to the PC who had mucked up Jock's time off. The two females were sitting inside the box awaiting their carriage. It was an extremely wide road, enough room for six lines of traffic; the road was very quiet and so Jock passed the box and completed a 'U' turn and stopped behind the duty officer's vehicle. The only other car to be seen on the was nearby a mile away, heading towards them, so Jock's turn did not cause any anxiety to anyone.

Jock got out of the van and opened the rear door of his transport to allow the passengers to enter; they were ushered inside by a very worried Inspector. He hung onto the girl's arm in case she ran away, ordering the PC to do likewise. Once in the van the door was locked behind them. After he had closed the door, Jock moved back towards his driving seat, and automatically he glanced to the right and saw that the car travelling towards him was still a long way off. The young copper jumped in the front with him, coming from the pavement side and pulled the door shut behind him.

"OK Jock, sorry to drag you out but his nibs was with me. It was his suggestion that we should nick the girls."

Jock reached down and switched the engine on but before he did so, the sliding door of the van was slid open again.

"I'll see you at the station," said the Inspector, leaning in. What a stupid thing to say, thought Jock, naturally he would see them at the nick. Even if he wasn't going to accept responsibility for the arrest of the two prostitutes, he would have to take the charge. Best thing to say in such circumstances is 'Right Sir' and then it happened.

An almighty crash sent the van forwards, even though the brakes were on. The Inspector was slung from the doorway and landed on the pavement. Jock quickly looked in his mirrors but could see nothing behind him; he got out of the van and walked round to the back and saw the mess. The car had been travelling along the road had run smash into the step. Jock looked for some reason for this to happen but could see none. Here, on a road which was seventy five feet wide with no other traffic on it except him and this other car; the driver of the private car had chosen to run straight into the back of a stationary Police vehicle.

"What the hell do you think you're doing?" he asked the man who was sitting petrified behind his wheel. The man was dumbstruck and tried to gather his thoughts, seeking some logical reason for trying to commit 'Hari Cari'.

"Er, I thought you were going to move, my foot slipped on the brake, I mean the clutch. I didn't see you, you were in a shadow." He paused for breath as he thought of another excuse.

He was not the only man who was panic-stricken for the Inspector had also started.

"These prisoners will have to be taken to the Station, I will get the Traffic Sergeant out to report the accident." He telephoned from the Police Box and requested another van be sent to collect the prisoners. A neighbouring station answered the call for assistance and a van was sent to the scene, the driver knew Jock and as the prisoners were being transferred to his vehicle he said.

"I see you have worry guts here," indicating the Inspector, "he was a Sergeant at our place and were we glad to get shot of him." He looked at the damaged car which was wrapped around the back of the van and said,

"I bet that sod had something to do with that, he's a jinx."

"Don't you try and move this vehicle till the Traffic Sergeant arrives," instructed the Inspector.

"No way Sir," replied Jock looking at the tangled metal. The other driver laughed.

"Be seeing you Jock, Cheers" and drove away leaving the Inspector pacing up and down as he awaited the reporting officer. Jock took the opportunity to sit in the van to have a quiet smoke.

The Traffic Patrol Sergeant posted on night duty, he had the job of reporting any accident involving a police vehicle. He didn't take long to arrive on the spot and began the investigations. He examined the position of the two cars, noted the absence of skid marks, then turned to the people involved. First he spoke to Jock and as he was talking, the Inspector butted in to give all the relevant details.

"Do you mind Inspector? I will talk to witnesses later," said the Sergeant. The hapless driver of the other car was then questioned.

"Right," the Sergeant said, "Let's get them apart."

As it had happened, the front bumper of the car had gone under the step of the van. The heavy step had smashed all the front of the car but no damage had been caused to the van. The Sergeant headed for his car.

"So long Jock, Goodnight Sir."

"Hey, just a minute Sergeant," the Inspector stopped him.

"How am I going to get the van back to the Station?" The Sergeant looked at him as though he was silly.

"You have the driver here, what more do you want?"

"But aren't you going to suspend him?" The Inspector was under the impression that every driver had to be suspended from driving when he was involved in an accident. In actual fact, it was only those cars where there was doubt about the cause.

The Traffic Sergeant was amazed with the Inspector's remark.

"Suspend him, Sir. Why should I do that? He only came here on your orders and he parked where you wanted him. You could have taken the prisoners in your car and the other vehicle wouldn't have hit his stationary van. No Sir, I am not suspending him," he muttered as he walked away. "If anyone should be suspended, it should be you." Lucky enough, the chastised Inspector didn't hear him.

It was no consolation to Jock for he didn't get his four hours time off, it was four thirty by the time he got to bed and was up again at nine o'clock to go to Court.

TIME GENTLEMEN, PLEASE!

Things began to change for the better in the job, from everyone's point of view. Someone, somewhere, had decided to alter the Policeman's lot - which was not a happy one. Several different systems for working the shifts were placed before the coppers so that they could discuss them and eventually pick the one they wanted. A vote was taken and a three week system was commenced. This meant that night duty only lasted three weeks and was preceded by an early day shift, and this suited the young coppers who wanted a bit more night-life. The refreshment period was increased by a full fifteen minutes, that meant a copper was allowed three quarters of an hour to enjoy his meal. Although the six day week wasn't altered, a scheme was operated so that they could have two days off together.

Time off was incurred when a copper worked any overtime. A Sergeant or over would place the time worked onto his card and he could then take time off if there were enough coppers on duty. The Force fell over backwards for the athletic type of person; they were allowed four hours each week if they entered in any team or sporting event. Whenever they asked for time off, they were granted it, regardless of how many coppers were on duty. They always seemed to be asking to get away early but always had plenty of time left on their cards.

It worked against the other coppers because sometimes they would be detailed to take time off when there were plenty of chaps on the shift. This annoyed some coppers who were saving their precious hours for some special occasion. Also, this affected the new system of payment. It had been decided to grant payment for any time on the cards and a lot of hard up coppers relished this idea, to get paid for overtime seemed the answer to their problems, but to be told by a Sergeant, 'You have time on your card, take four hours off', broke a lot of hearts.

DRY HUMOUR

The Superintendent caught Jock in the canteen.
"Have you got much to do today Mr MacGregor?"
"I was just going to wash the cars Guv."
"Well, I was wondering, seeing that it's Sunday if you could find time to wash my car. Can you fit it in?" the boss asked.
"I don't know Guv, I have the spare car to do, then the wireless car, the van and the CID car. There is mine and Cyril's to do, and the Inspector and Sergeant have asked us to do theirs" Jock told him.
"You rotten bugger. Do you mean that the Inspector and Sergeant come before me?"
"Well a dollar a time isn't to be sneezed at in these hard times Guv," said Jock, grinning.
"So, I suppose you want me to pay you as well?"
"We do a first class job Guv and we might even slip it in early for you" Jock answered. "That's if you want us to."
"Alright, you bloody robbing Scotsman, let me know when you are ready." The Guvnor agreed to the terms.
The various cars had been cleaned and dried off before Jock went in search of the Superintendent. He found him in the front office signing the books.
"Got the keys Guv?" he asked.

"What keys?"

"For the Roller, we're ready to start" Jock told him.

"It's alright Jock, I'll bring it in for you." He slammed the Occurrence Book shut and jumped up.

"You must have rushed the others, I hope you make a better job with mine."

"Now Guv, I told you we do a first class job, in fact I was wondering if we could put up a car wash sign to get more customers." The Superintendent looked hard at him.

"You know Mr MacGregor, I never know when you're taking the piss out of me." They left the office together and went to collect the huge Rolls Royce.

"Just here Sir, that will do fine." Cyril called as the vehicle purred into the yard.

"Be careful with it now." The Guv was worried about his new possession. Jock said, "Don't worry, Guv. The wife will be proud to ride in this by the time we're finished."

The Superintendent obviously didn't trust them for he hovered around all the time they worked on the car.

"You know Guv, we should get danger money as well," Jock spoke from the top of the step-ladders. "It's like scrubbing a back yard standing on top of a pole."

The ancient showpiece was shining like a new pin. The boss went round the car with an eagle eye and when he finished his examination, he looked up and saw the two drivers standing to attention, shirt sleeve order with braces, and caps on the backs of their heads; brushes were held on the slope over the right shoulders.

"Bloody silly sods" he muttered. "You should have the brushes on your left shoulders." He climbed quickly into the car to drive away while the car was still in one piece and as he did so the two coppers marched to the front of the vehicle.

"Change arms," a voice bellowed out. The brushes were transferred smartly to the correct shoulder.

"Slow march!" came the next order and in true military manner the pair commenced to move slowly along in front of the car, serious expressions upon their faces.

"Shift your bleedin' arses!" the Superintendent bellowed from the window of the car, his order was assisted with a prolonged blast upon his horn. The noise he was making soon attracted the attention of the office workers and windows were flung open as the curious onlookers gazed at the unusual sight.

Eventually the boss capitulated.

"All right, you win, I'll pay you later." Having received the promise, the two drivers marched smartly to the side and presented arms, in this case brushes, as the above drove past.

"Mad sods, and get those bloody brushes cleaned before next parade, they are filthy," he snarled.

A little humour, droll perhaps, but the job was too serious to do well on sordid matters. A copper tended to make light of all problems and difficulties, sorrows and tragedies. Death and suffering were constant companions with the copper on the beat. Suicide and natural deaths or foul play all had the same end result, a PC had to deal and relatives had to be informed. A mother or a wife must be told of the loss of their loved one; there was no easy way to do this. Jock generally obtained the assistance of a close neighbour prior to calling at the house. Normally the serious look on his face was enough to give the news, they knew then. The friend stayed behind to give solace and comfort; sometimes the death was just another cruel blow to some family (the cold icy hand of death could twist the guts of even a hardened copper and if he let it dwell too much on his mind, he would drive himself insane).

Bodies had to be taken to hospital to be certified by a doctor as being dead (if none had attended the incident). The unlucky participants in the game of life and death would then be taken to the mortuary where they were stripped by the copper, who had to search the clothing and list all of the articles. The list was checked and signed by the mortuary attendant. The body would then be labelled on the big toe, pending an autopsy. During the many visits that Jock made to various morgues, he couldn't help but notice how very similar all the attendants were in looks; they all looked like walking corpses. Ambulance men and firemen used to adopt the same attitude towards these serious cases, they had to otherwise they would break down, and sometimes they did.

CHAPTER TEN

DROWNING

DROWNING

A nice quiet walk around the beat was just the thing to rest from the strain of driving on '999' calls. Jock ambled up the road towards the Police Box, he would have a smoke and make his ring. He passed an old lady sitting on a low wall.

"Hello luv, are you alright?" he asked her.

"Just a little out of breath duck" she answered. Jock left her and carried on the few yards to the box and as he made his ring he said to the operator,

"Can you send an ambulance up here, there's an old lady here and I don't like the look of her."

"That's nothing lad, I don't like the look of my old lady and there are a hell of a lot more people that I don't like the look of, but I can't get an ambulance out to take them away." Jock hung the phone back up and returned to the old lady, she was still sitting on the low wall.

"Look love, I don't think you are too well, I've sent for an ambulance." He put his arm around her as he knelt on the ground beside her and he then realised that he was talking to himself, she was dead, another one for the records.

It didn't take long to complete the report and Jock was out on the streets again. Everything was quiet, but not for long. A voice rang out!

"Officer, Officer, a boy has just fallen in the river," a young female gasped out the information. Jock didn't wait to get her name, seconds counted, he raced towards the river. It was in spate after very heavy falls of rain, it was a raging torrent and much higher than normal. He saw a group of people standing beside the river bank where the incident had happened. A distressed man was soon identified as the father.

"What happened?" Jock asked. He looked at the fast swirling water and knew that if anyone had gone in there the body would be swept away by the current; the water was too rough to discern any particular object.

"My son has fallen in, he was playing on them planks when he slipped into the water."

"When did this happen?" Jock enquired, wondering how the father happened to be on the scene.

"I don't know, he was with his mates" and the man pointed to a couple of youngsters close by.

"When he fell in, they came and told me, and I came straight along."

After questioning the lads and verifying the man's address, Jock realised that it was over half an hour since the boy had gone into the water.

"Look Sir, your wife will be worrying so why not go and keep her company. I'll get some other men out and we'll search the river banks." The distraught father realised that he couldn't do any good just standing there and agreed to go home. Jock sent one of the lads to the Police Station to inform them of the incident, whilst he commenced to walk along the river bank. H knew in his mind that it was a waste of time but by some act of God, the lad might have been able to struggle ashore further down.

With the river in flood as it was, the search was called off till the water had subsided. Four days later, when he was posted on the van driver's job, a call came in regarding the sighting of a body in the river; another job for the van driver, naturally.

"I'm on my way Skipper" Jock said. "Can you call the doctor out, it'll save me taking it to the hospital."

Down at the riverside, he met the informant who indicated where he had seen the body. Although the floods had gone down quite a bit, there was still a very strong current running; the body was entangled in some branches overhanging the surface; Jock slipped into the current and forced his way through the thick sticky stinking mud which covered the bank sides and the river bed. With a struggle he managed to disentangle the body and clutching it tightly, he made his way back to dry land. When he arrived another copper helped him to drag the corpse away from the water; the doctor had also arrived and he examined the body.

"Do you know, if I hadn't seen you pulling it out from the water I would have sworn that death was due to a heart attack." Anyone could tell that the lad was dead for the flesh was already rotting and falling away. In any case, I would swear that he was dead before he hit the water. The body was placed in the van and taken to the mortuary. Jock returned to the station to be swilled down by one of the other drivers to get rid of the mud, slime and remnants of rotten flesh from his uniform before he went home to find a change of clothing.

SUICIDE

Not all deaths are caused by accidents and not all of them are messy. For a short while afterwards Jock called into the front office where the Station Sergeant was working hard for a change.

"Want a cuppa, Skipper? I'm making one for the lads." The Sergeant, naturally, welcomed a drink but before Jock could leave the office a couple came in; Jock, standing beside the counter asked quite casually.

"Can I help you?" He didn't realise how much he was going to help in the next few minutes. The couple started to complain bitterly about the father of the lady; apparently he lived with them and they were objecting to his dirty habits and constant drunkenness. They finished their dialogue by indicating that they had been locked out. The patrolling officer had entered the room during this time and had listened with one ear to their ratings.

"Well, it's your house, if you haven't got a key you can break in," Jock informed them.

"We've just had the door made burglar proof and we think he's probably done himself in." It had taken them a long time to reach the most important fact.

"Quick Jock, see if you can find something to open the door," the patrolling officer ordered. "I'll see you round there."

It didn't take Jock long to find a case opener in the canteen, and he ran towards the flat which was only a few hundred yards away. As he entered the door of the building he saw the Patrol Car coming along; he ran up the stairs and was followed by the duty officer. By the time the Station Sergeant reached the top of the stairs Jock had forced this so-called burglar proof door and together they went through the house. Jock checked the rooms on the right hand side and the Sergeant checked those on the left.

"I've got him Skipper," Jock said. The man was in the kitchen, lying with his head on a pillow in the gas oven. He dragged him out into the passage. The skipper turned the gas off and opened the window while Jock started his labours, trying to revive the man with artificial respiration.

"The sod, he's drank half a bottle of rum." The owner had recovered from the shock of seeing his door broken open and was now looking for other faults. "I bet I'll have a terrible gas bill next time." Jock carried on working. The Sergeant telephoned for a doctor and for an ambulance and he also telephoned the Station to order his sandwiches. Jock still worked on. Eventually, after much gas and queer noises had issued from the apparently lifeless man, the ambulance man arrived - panting after his climb to the top of the stairs - he spoke to Jock.

"Shove over, I'll give you a break." Just as well because Jock's arms felt as though they were ready to fall off. They changed over and he moved into the nearest room out of the way, the occupant of the flat was standing at the door watching them fighting for the old man's life.

"I could do with a drink" he said.

"So could I" Jock replied.

"We're in the wrong room, the drink is in the lounge," the man said. "Unless you make do with this" he said as he lifted the bottle of rum up.

"It's all he left."

"That'll do" Jock said and had just lifted the bottle to his lips when a deep voice sounded in his ear.

"Hello, what do you think you're doing?" Jock looked round at the Patrolling Officer. "Me, I'm going to have some refreshments after all the work I've just done, I'm ready for it."

"All right, but don't drink it all, leave some for me, after all I've done all the work telephoning," the Skipper said.

After wetting his tonsils, Jock went back to see if he could assist the ambulance chap but found the Doctor had just arrived. An injection was quickly given and a few seconds later the Doctor pronounced the man dead.

"You must have been just a few seconds too late," he said.

If only the couple had acted with more sense he could have lived, but, Jock wondered, did they want him to. As soon as the verdict was given the man and woman stated that they would not stay in the house that night. They left, leaving the coppers to lay the dead man on his dirty bed and leave him for the Coroner's Officer to deal with the following day. There was obviously no affection there, nor was there in the family that Jock was called to next.

It was just another '999' call for the Police. Jock pulled his car in to the side of the road beside the man and woman. It was a very select area with large detached houses.

"Did you call for the Police?" Jock's wireless operator asked them.

"Yes, it's our son, he's locked us out and we think he's committed suicide." They pointed to the elegant house beside them, "We can't get in."

"Right, we'll soon find out." Jock got out of the car and started to run towards the house. The woman came running after him.

"Stop, Officer, Stop."

"Why, what's wrong?" Jock enquired.

"I don't want you to cause any damage getting into the house."

"Have you got a key then?" Jock asked because if he didn't have a key then he would have to break in to the place.

"Yes, we have the keys, but he has locked it from the inside and the keys won't work," the woman said.

"Well, in that case, we will have to break a window or something so as we can get inside." Jock was perplexed at the woman's attitude.

"Look madam, you tell me that you believe your son has possibly attempted to take his life and yet you refuse permission for us to break in."

"That's right, we don't want our property damaged" she insisted. Jock walked away from her and examined the doors and windows, then went over to his mate.

"Wilfy, try and keep these two busy while I have a go at the back."

"Can I have your key please?" Jock asked the woman, who told him again that it was no good, although she gave him the required article. He passed it onto his colleague.

"Just mess around with it for a while, try to give them the impression that it might work."

He then left the small group and slid around to the rear of the house. He soon found a window that only had a catch on it, he joggled it a few times to loosen the catch and then with a few quick bumps with his hand in the right place, released the catch. He pulled a dustbin across and climbed into the kitchen. So as not to alarm the owners, he closed the window behind him and replaced the latch. He then had a quick run round the house and found a teenage lad lying in one of the bedrooms; he was wide awake and just ignored Jock when he entered the room.

"Are you OK son?" Jock asked him, but he got no reply. Not wanting to waste time on the lad who was obviously going to be awkward, Jock returned downstairs and opened the front door.

"How did you get in?" The man and woman were more interested in the house than their Son; Jock considered they could have first asked about him, but they didn't seem worried. He left the couple still complaining about his entry, wanting to know if he had caused any damage breaking in. The pair of them started a search, looking for some damage. Meanwhile, Jock was looking for anything the lad might have taken. He found several bottles and boxes in the kitchen and asked the woman if she could drag herself away from her search for a few minutes.

"Can you tell me what was in these boxes and bottles?"

"They are all empty, but they had quite a lot of tablets in them, do you think he's taken them all?" The lady could only give general suggestions for the containers.

"Lady, your guess is as good as mine, only he can tell us." He called on Wilfy to call an ambulance and then returned to the bedroom and spoke to the lad once more.

"How are you feeling?" He still got no reply and after making several attempts to find out what he had taken, Jock gave up and went downstairs again.

"Wilfy, can you collect all the bottles and boxes here and put them in a plastic bag? If the lady or gent can tell you what each one was called, or what they were for, just write it down so we can tell the doctor." The couple in question were still checking the house to see if anything was missing. Jock returned to the son and sat on his bed.

"You don't mind do you?"

He purposely ignored the teenager, took out his pipe and baccy and slowly began to fill his pipe. The lad's face was a study as he watched Jock lighting his pipe.

"You don't mind if I smoke while I wait?" He struck another match to kindle the tobacco and then puffed away for a few seconds to get it going. Once he was satisfied that it was burning, he pushed himself back on the bed and rested his back against the wall. The lad lay quiet for a while, perplexed that nobody was making a fuss about him.

"I'm not going to hospital" he suddenly burst out. Jock turned his head and glanced at him.

"If you don't want to go then nobody can force you," he said and then returned to enjoy the pipe which was burning well.

"You are like my parents, you don't care," the lad said sullenly.

"Listen to me sonny, I spent over five minutes talking to you, without getting an answer. I was asking you about the tablets that you have taken and you didn't bother to look at me let alone answer. If that is the way you treated your parents, then I don't blame them for not being interested." As he was getting no reaction from the lad, he was compelled to adopt this attitude with him.

"Alright then, I'll tell you. I took the lot, everything that was in the house. I'm not sorry and I'm not going to hospital," at last he had told what he had swallowed.

"Fair enough bonny lad, if you want to kick the bucket, it's up to you" and he took another few puffs of his pipe, seemingly ignoring the dying man. After a while, he glanced at his watch and asked the lad why he had done it.

"It's my parents, you should ask them," was the outburst from the young chap. "Tell me, why do you keep looking at your watch?"

"Well, I have other things to do but it will be a waste of time for me to leave now. I'll just be called back when you kick the bucket so I might as well hang on - I was just seeing how long you have to go."

"You're cold blooded," said the lad going a bit whiter than his already wan complexion allowed him to.

"Could be, but not on this occasion, I'm just doing my job," Jock told him as he re-lit his pipe.

"Where are my parents?"

"Downstairs, probably still trying to find out how I got into the house." Jock smiled, he had at last got the lad to talk and that was a beginning, although he was giving the impression that he couldn't care less and was waiting for the lad to die; he was actually waiting for the ambulance to arrive.

He eventually got the story out of the youngster. The reason was simply a family matter, they were Jewish, in fact a very rich family whose name was known in every house in Britain and the lad had started courting. The trouble was the girl was a Gentile and the family strongly disapproved and refused permission for the two to get married.

"They always get their own way" he complained.

"Is she here?"

"Who, your girlfriend?" Jock enquired. "Why, should she be?"

"I thought she would have come" wailed the lad.

"Look son, you've proved that you don't love her by taking those tablets - she will be left alone - and your parents will have got their own way again. With you dead, there will be no wedding and they will be happy." Jock again looked at his watch and thought the ambulance was taking a hell of a long time to get there.

"I suppose you're right but it's too late now isn't it?" said the lad who was getting weaker.

"No, we might be able to have it pumped out if we hurry" Jock said as they heard the ambulance, "Come on."

Together the pair left the room, Jock supported the lad as they passed his parents

"Sod you both," said the lad. The ambulance chaps took him on a stretcher and placed him in the vehicle.

"Are you coming?" one of them asked Jock.

"Just a minute Constable, I want to know how you got into my house?" the owner had been searching all the time his son had been lying dying.

"I'll see you down there," Jock called after the driver and then he turned to the man who was holding him by the arm.

"I have only one thing to say to you sir."

"What's that?" asked the householder.

"Piss off," and Jock shrugged the hand away and walked to his car, leaving the millionaire standing with his mouth open.

A quick drive to the hospital where they assisted two nurses to hold the lad down whilst a doctor struggled to insert the tube down into his stomach.

He lived, and married the girl of his choice.

RECEIVING END

Early days - how Jock hated this shift, crawling out of bed in the middle of the night. However, it turned out to be a fairly quiet day, apart from the usual burglar alarms set off by a sleepy cleaner or dozy office personnel and a few accidents, all of a minor nature. Ernie, who was posted on late turn arrived at quarter to the hour, this allowed Jock to get away before two o'clock. He slipped his leather coat on over his uniform and adjusted the leather helmet before starting his steady drive home. He wasn't in any hurry (he got enough of rushing around when he was on duty). He knew Puggle wouldn't have his dinner ready till he arrived home; this was a normal thing due to the number of times he was late because of his work.

He drove along in the line of steady moving traffic, the roads were packed, no way could anyone overtake or drive fast because of the amount of traffic on the road. Keeping a safe distance behind the car in front, he suddenly saw a lorry turning from the outside lane of vehicles which was coming towards him. He knew what the man was trying to do, fed up with waiting to turn, he believed he had seen a gap in the traffic and accelerated to enter a side street which was on Jock's left hand side. The man hadn't seen Jock's motorcycle as he cut across the line of traffic. Jock slammed his brakes on and swung the bike round to the rear of the lorry. He missed it by a hairs breadth, only to be faced with another van, the driver of the second van intended to enter the same side street - he was using the lorry as a cover as he cut the corner. Although Jock swung his cycle to the left in an attempt to miss this fresh danger, he was out of luck due to the speed; the other chap was using his right foot too much. The crash was inevitable. Jock's bike struck the wing of the van, the sidecar carried on along the road following the route he had been going. If the driver of the van had maintained his correct position on the road and had travelled right up to the junction, Jock would have been safe. As it happened, he was thrown over the handlebars. He put his arm up to protect his face as he saw the corner of the windscreen was in line with his head. He came to a sudden halt and dropped down on the ruins which had once been his pride and joy. He put his left hand out to fend off the impact of the metal; he sat there on the wreck of his motorcycle and watched his sidecar moving along on it's own, looking up at the driver of the van who was looking down at him from his window.

"You stupid bloody bastard," said the van driver. A car slowed to a halt beside him, it was the vehicle which had been following him, the driver got out and grabbed the van driver by the neck.

"Why the bloody hell don't you learn to drive, you nearly killed us." Apparently, he had been caught unawares also by the lorry and the van. He turned and assisted Jock to his feet.

"I am a bus driver, if you want a witness, I'll give my name to the police, you didn't have a chance."

A woman who had been standing at the corner also came to Jock's aid.

"I think it's disgusting, people driving like that. I'll be a witness for you; my husband is a policeman."

A motor cyclist who had been riding behind the van also had a go at the worried driver of the van.

"You'll have to go to hospital mate," he said to Jock. and while the other two witnesses tried to stem the blood flowing from a great gash in Jock's head, he stated that he would get the police and an ambulance.

As Jock stood there amongst the ruins of his motorcycle, he said to his helpers.

"If you're willing to go as witnesses, can I have your names and addresses?"

"Don't worry about them, we'll give them to the first copper we see; look, there's an ambulance coming now," the man said.

Jock could see the white vehicle coming along and knew that it wasn't an emergency ambulance. It was moving slowly with the line of traffic travelling in the opposite lanes.

"That one's no good," he told the man. The ambulance was then stopped by the motorcyclist who started to have an argument with its driver. The two people who were tending to Jock's injuries helped him across towards the vehicle.

"I'm sorry mate, but I'm not an emergency accident ambulance, this is a maternity ambulance," the driver was tell them. "I don't know this area."

"Look mate, you'll have to take him, otherwise he'll die, look at the state he's in." The motorcyclist was insistent, even if he didn't consider the feelings of the new patient. Eventually the man relented as Jock's helpers had already opened the back door of the ambulance and pushed him in.

"I don't know any of the hospitals around here," he moaned.

"There's one just up the next main road" the woman said.

As the driver started to head towards the place indicted, Jock spoke through the dividing partition.

"It's no good going there mate, that's a fever hospital." However, the driver just wanted to get rid of his unwanted cargo and soon pulled in to the front of the isolated building, ignoring Jock's constant warnings. A Sister came out of the front door and had an animated argument with the driver.

"I'm sorry, we are infectious diseases, we don't have any facilities to deal with accidents," she told him.

"Well, where can I take him?" the driver asked.

The poor lady couldn't tell him, so Jock called from the back of the vehicle.

"You have a choice of two, they are both about the same distance away, I'll show you the way."

The driver had the option of staying there, or accepting Jock's offer; no doubt he never recant to his mates that a patient had to direct him to the hospital. As he pointed out the way, Jock grinned to himself as he thought about his helpers, they would never pass any First Aid exams. Don't move the patient he had been told, yet they had dragged him to his feet and assisted him across the road to the waiting ambulance.

Once he had reached his destination, the driver jumped out and ran for assistance, he wanted this nut case off his hands before he died. Later, as Jock waited for x-rays, the door of his room opened and in walked his mate, the one who had taken over the wireless car. He had come to interview the rider of the motorcycle. It was quite some time later when he asked for names and addresses that he found out who he was speaking to.

"Christ, Jock, I didn't know. I'll let your wife know straight away."

After he had gone, Jock struggled up to look in a mirror to find out why the copper hadn't recognised him; his face was a proper mess, the whole of the side of his head was swollen to twice it's normal size; his hair had been cut away from a gash twelve inches in length. All of his face was blackened with the bruising; he couldn't recognise himself. The nurses arrived and took him for his final examination and Jock found out later that he had a fractured skull, two broken arms and a broken leg. Ah well, it could have been worse.

Puggle had a hard time during the following weeks, with having to take the latest member of the family to hospital every day. Now she had Jock at home, complete with plasters, he couldn't do much for himself. It would have been much kinder for her if they had kept him in hospital; instead, he was picked up every morning and taken to hospital for treatment.

On one occasion the plaster was removed from one of his arms.

"Hmmm" the doctor said thoughtfully. It was an unintelligible remark to Jock but obviously meant something to the medical profession. He gently placed the arm on the top of the bench.

"Look at this" he said to Jock. "That should be straight," he had laid both his hands on the top of the arm, "Like that," and as he uttered the last two words, he lifted both feet off the floor. His full weight came down on the arm and it snapped. "That's better" he said as he looked at the limb once more. "It's as straight as I can get it."

"Thanks a lot." Jock was taken by surprise. The plaster was then replaced on the freshly broken arm.

After two minor operations on his head, he was sent to a convalescent home for a couple of weeks; after his rest, he returned home to find that the solicitors had been busy sorting his claim out. He had to go to Harley Street on four separate occasions to be examined by different specialists and eventually the case was settled out of court, to Jock's advantage. Although he knew that the Specialists and the solicitors would be claiming a lot more cash than he got, Jock was happy with his share. He could afford to buy a car, the motorcycle being written off; he also had enough to put down as deposit for their own house.

All the time he had been off work he had never seen any member of the police force. He had never received any of the presents normally given weekly to men who had been in hospital or injured. When he went back to work, he found that the social side of the Station had ground to a halt; there were no outings, dances, parties or spare jobs. As none of the coppers at the Station had bothered while Jock had been out of action, he decided to let things remain as they were. So, the job of Social Secretary became open for any volunteer.

HELPING HAND

Although he tended to blend in with the background, the boss had decided to have him working as spare driver until he built up his strength. As these duties were mainly cleaning the cars and playing billiards with the van driver, Jock soon got fed up, so he took every opportunity to go out with the van driver.

"Jock, are you coming?" his mate yelled. "We have a box of oranges to take up to the kids home."

It was a recognised thing for any perishable goods to be distributed or disposed of by the duty officer. In this instance, a case of oranges had fallen off the back of a lorry going to market, naturally they would go rotten in time, so it had been decided to give them to the Children's home. All the time, Jock had been working at that Station, this routine had been carried out.

It didn't take long before they stopped outside the cookhouse and unloaded the goods. "Do me a favour Officer," the person in charge said, "Don't' bring any more here."

"Why, what's wrong with them?" asked the astounded driver.

"Nothing wrong, they look lovely, the trouble is we get far too many" the woman told him. "Come here and I'll show you." She showed the two coppers a huge mountain of rotten fruit at the back of the cookhouse buildings. "We have to throw them all out, and we have no place to put them. It's a terrible job trying to make arrangements for someone to take them away. The trouble is you know, people say 'Oh those poor kids' and everything is just palmed off on us. These poor kids get more than my own kids do, so please, no more."

Her message was passed on to the other neighbouring Stations.

SPARE DRIVER

"You can do my car now Jock, I won't be needing it for some time," the patrolling officer told him.

"Righto guv" Jock answered as he went out into the yard and took off his tunic, pushed his hat into its usual position on the back of his head and then lit his faithful old pipe before starting to wash the car. All the washing finished, the van driver was helping him to polish the vehicle when suddenly a scream of tyres attracted their attention, and the wireless car came tearing into the yard.

"Silly sod," said Cyril. "He could have met you going out."

The area car jerked to a halt and four coppers jumped out, dragging another man with them, it was obvious that the prisoner did not intend to go with them because he was struggling violently. It was an uneven contest, slowly but surely the body was dragged, punching and struggling to the charge room.

When the party reached the four steps that led up to the charge room door, the man grabbed hold of the handrails, straddled his legs and braced his feet against the bottom step.

The coppers tried all possible ways to make him release his grip and shift his feet but failed dismally.

"I'll give them a hand," said Jock after he and the van driver had watched the struggle for some time. He strolled across to the group, transferred his tin of polish from his right hand to his left one and then as he reached the rear end of the prisoner, his right index finger travelled sharply upwards between the man's legs.

"Oooh," the startled man released his grip on the rails and jumped up the steps in one quick movement. As Jock returned to finish the polishing he saw a man coming from the corner of the yard, he didn't know who he was but there was another couple of men still standing beside some equipment.

"From now on officer, you're a film star. I nearly pissed myself laughing when I saw that little bit of assistance you gave. It's the best laugh I've had for years."

The rest of his team joined him, they were also chuckling about the way the prisoner had jumped up the steps.

"I think, we shall keep that bit in it, shows that a little bit of persuasion can be more effective than force." The men introduced themselves as a team making a film, officially, for teaching recruits all about crime, arrests, and charge procedures.

"The prisoner who you helped up the stairs was one of our Sergeants," they told Jock. "No doubt he will like to know who was such a close friend, but we won't tell him, he can wait until he sees the picture."

PLEASURE

A stroll in the evening is a marvellous way to relax and to take things easy. Sometimes nightshift can be like that, with everything quiet and no villains around, no crimes being committed, and no local yobs around to disturb the peace and tranquillity. On a Summer night this would have been marvellous, but on a cold winters night, it was miserable. A howling wind blew and bit into every bit of exposed flesh, cutting like a knife. This was one of the times Jock was taking a spell from driving, to settle the nerves a bit and to allow some other driver to get his pulse rate going to danger level. Jock was trying to keep warm, muffled up with all types of clothing to keep out the icy wind, but his attempts were futile, he was still frozen stiff as he headed towards the river bank.

Head down against the wind, he thought he had heard a moaning sound. He stopped and listened and it came again; the sound seemed to come from the courtyard of a block of flats, it was pitch black and he couldn't see anything. He started to walk in the direction of the noise and when he estimated he was close to the place, he switched his torch on.

The scene that lay before him caused him considerable astonishment. A female stood before him, naked, her dress rolled up to the neck, she was held in the clutches of a Yankee sailor who was similarly dressed, not including the dress of course; he was minus his trousers and his shirt was wide open. He was suitably attired for the occasion to say the least. The undulating movements did not falter, even when Jock was close enough to see their goose pimples.

"What the hell do you think you're doing?" A silly question to ask as it was quite obvious what they were doing.

"I'm just saying goodnight," the American answered, panting a little, one must admit.

"How old are you?" Jock asked the girl, who couldn't roll her dress down because of the close proximity of her boyfriend.

"Twenty" she answered. Jock didn't think she looked it but asked her where she lived.

"In the flats here" she said. Standing in the middle of the yard with this chap and saying 'Goodnight' in such a fashion, if anyone had been returning home late they would have seen her in all her glory.

"I think you're being a bit silly then, why don't you go and find a place more private in case someone does see you, they may complain." Jock insisted they move away. They disengaged their clutches and headed across the yard. Jock continued his patrol and just around the corner standing in a shop doorway he saw a man who was huddled up against the cold, shivering.

"What are you doing here?" Jock asked him, and checked the property at the same time.

"I'm waiting for my mate, he's saying goodnight to his girl." The man looked frozen stiff.

"Are you cold?" Jock asked him.

"You betcha," the yank answered.

"Well the cold didn't seem to be worrying your mate, Goodnight." Jock left the unfortunate sailor and carried on at his regular three miles per hour stroll. The end of the shift couldn't come soon enough for him, he would finish work at six o'clock and be back again at one forty-five to take the wireless car out again.

FISH

Not everyone is a lover of fish. Jock didn't like it at the best of times, he wouldn't thank anyone for offering the stuff and consequently his day was due to be ruined when the next '999' call came for the Police.

Apparently, a man had gone berserk with an axe and a knife. He had smashed windows of neighbours' houses with bricks and had even thrown a pushbike through one of them, his own home was damaged and his parents had run out in terror.

"See what it's all about Jock."

Sixty seconds later they pulled up in front of the group of prefabs where a small crowd had gathered, and the father of the man introduced himself. The man was out on licence from a mental home, he'd had a relapse.

"He's going for everyone, he'll kill somebody."

"Where is he now?" asked Jock.

"In the house," answered the father as he turned to console the lady of the family.

"Right, Bill, will you go round that side and I'll go this way, first one that finds him keeps him happy. The other one gets the duly Authorised Officer out, good luck." The two coppers made their separate ways around the house. Of course it would be my luck, Jock thought as he saw the nut sitting in the kitchen; he was sitting at the table eating boiled fish. The smell of that was worse than the sight of the large dangerous carving knife he was eating the fish with. A hand-axe lay on the table beside the plate.

"Hello, any chance of a cup of tea?" Jock asked as he entered the room. The man didn't raise his head he just squinted at him out of the corner of his eye and tightened the grip on the knife till his knuckles showed white. He suddenly pointed to the pot, with the knife

"Some there."

"Ta" said Jock as he collected a cup and began to fill it from the pot; as he did so he saw his mate going past the door.

"We don't want everyone joining our party do we?"

"No."

"Right, we'll sit and have a cup of tea together shall we," and Jock signalled to his mate. "We should be nice and quiet in the kitchen, shouldn't we." His mate took the hint that he had to get the Duly Authorised Officer out as quickly as possible and that Jock would keep the man company whilst he was eating.

As soon as he saw that Bill was on his way to the wireless car, Jock sat at the kitchen table facing the man, who was apparently enjoying his boiled fish. He eyed the axe and estimated his chances of grabbing it before the man struck out with it. The chap seemed to read his mind, for even as he was transferring some fish to his mouth with the carving knife, he reached over and drew the handle towards him. He looked up into Jock's eyes.

"Tea alright?"

"Yeh, sure, it's lovely. Thank you." Smiled Jock

"That's alright then," his dining companion said. "Try some fish?" The thought of eating that repulsive foodstuff turned Jock's stomach.

"No thanks."

Like a flash, the knife came up and the point was embedded in Jock's neck; the slightest move sideways would result in a cut and if he tried to move backwards it was a certainty that the man would follow with the implement, and it might go further in. Jock considered the safest way was to amuse the chap.

"I said have some fish." The voice was sinister and it was an order not a request.

"I thought you were enjoying it so much, I didn't want to leave you short by eating some of your meal." Jock tried to pacify the man, "But if you insist."

Without a word, his companion indicated the pile of plates on the table, Jock took one and put it on the table in front of him; the knife was removed from his neck and was used to transfer some fish from the other plate onto his.

"That's enough for me, thanks," Jock eventually said. "There won't be any left for you." He was terrified that the nutter was going to pile all the horrible stuff onto his plate.

"That's alright, there's plenty more in the pan." The remark was like a death sentence for Jock as he commenced to eat the food. The man watched him start before he returned to his own meal. Jock ate as slowly as he possibly could, trying to hold a conversation with his companion. Time drew on slowly but surely and his plate was replenished, under duress; his guardian had offered him some more when his plate had become empty and when Jock had politely declined, the knife struck once again. As the blood trickled down his neck he realised that he must carry on this pretence, cursing the late arrival of the Mental Health chap.

The conversation covered every subject he could think of. The man was willing to talk, as long as Jock ate his fish. 'OK, anything to humour him' he thought. The man was definitely getting a bit edgy and restless. He suddenly jumped to his feet when a very small man entered the kitchen.

"Hello Arnold! Have you been a naughty boy again?" he asked. The big chap looked down towards his boots.

"Sorry Sir," he said. The small newcomer took him by the arm.

"Look what you've done to this poor man." and he pointed to the two wounds on Jock's neck which were still allowing the blood to trickle out onto his collar. "Now say you're sorry to him."

The bleary eyes focused on Jock.

"Sorry Sir," he muttered.

"I think you'll have to come with us for a short holiday, don't you think?" the newcomer said.

"Yes Sir," and the mentally deranged person placed a flat cap squarely upon his head and headed for the door, where Jock's mate was standing. He suddenly stopped and snatched the axe and the knife from the table, then slowly he turned to Jock and handed them across.

"Will you wash my knife and fork please?"

Jock took the offered implements gratefully; he had believed at first that the man was going to use the weapons.

"Thank God for that, I thought you were going to make me eat some more fish," said Jock taking them from the chap.

The nutter laughed all the way to the mental hospital.

ACCIDENTS

Jock pulled the car into the station yard, he was going to get cleaned up while his mate caught up with the list of stolen cars. He sponged the blood off his collar and put a couple of sticking plasters over the cuts before joining his colleague. A call had just been sent out for them to attend an accident. Three minutes later they pulled up at the road junction at the edge of their ground. One vehicle had been travelling towards the town centre at a high speed. It had been travelling too fast to negotiate the roundabout and had struck a lamp standard. As the driver was trying to leave the hazard, the car had stopped suddenly, when it knocked the lamp post down on top of a police box. The police box was demolished completely.

"Good job the beat man wasn't having a quiet smoke in there" said Bill as they approached the incident. The Section Sergeant had scrounged a ride with them as they had left the Station Yard. He got out of the car with the other two coppers and went to examine the car. They could see that there were five people still sitting in the vehicle. The first glance showed that the car didn't seem too badly damaged, apart from the front end. The bumper was smashed off, the radiator caved in and the bonnet was buckled.

Jock opened the driver's door without any difficulty, he didn't have to ask the driver if he was alright because he was sitting comfortably in his seat, both hands on the wheel; his head was tilted backwards over the seat, his eyes were wide open looking unseeingly at the interior of the roof. His passenger sitting beside him was being examined by the Skipper. The pair of them glanced up and looked at one another.

"Dead" said the Sergeant, "and not a mark on them."

Jock nodded slowly

"And we have another three in the back Skipper." The blunt statement was brief but not as short as the time it had taken to wipe out five human beings; all had broken necks due to whiplash. The unfortunate group were removed to the mortuary after death had been certified. Jock measured up the scene of the accident and waited for the breakdown vehicle to arrive and remove the car. They sat in the car as Jock wrote out his 'Yellow Peril' (as the report books were called - they were used when any person had been injured or killed). They stayed on the air, available for any call for assistance as he wrote. The rain began to fall, gently at first, then slowly increased until it was a downpour; it pounded on the roof of the car, the sound nearly obliterating the wireless. Jock dropped his report book, pushed his pencil behind his ear and switched the engine on, he was already in first gear and moving by the time the message came across.

"Accident, not known if any injured. It is believed that one of the vehicles contains handicapped children."

The car was already speeding towards the notified scene of the collision, he drove with great regard for the adverse road conditions, the fact that someone was in need of urgent assistance was also considered. The rain was really tossing down and visibility reduced as Jock drove along the outside lane of a major road.

"Slow down Jock, for Christ's sake," the Sergeant squealed from the back seat.

"If it was your kid, bleeding to death Skipper, could you say that?" Jock snapped at the man. "We didn't ask you to come with us for a joy ride, remember, this is never a pleasure trip."

"I can't see where we are going, we'll crash" he yelped.

"It doesn't matter a tuppenny hoot whether you can see or not Serg, I'm the one who is driving" Jock answered, "If you don't like it, just close your eyes."

Luckily, most traffic had pulled into the side of the road because of the bad visibility and the amount of water on the road. The wipers could just about serve their purpose and when the car eventually stopped at the scene of the accident.

"Bloody hell, Serg, I think this is one for you to deal with," said Jock. He got no reply from the back of the car because the Skipper was curled up in a corner, his eyes tight shut. Jock and his wireless operator got out from the warm dry vehicle into the deluge.

"You take that one Bill, I'll do the other." They each had a single decker bus to deal with, the occupants, apart from the driver and one adult attendant, were all mentally and physically handicapped children. The youngsters had been on their way home and by a multi-million to one chance both buses had collided. The kids were in a state of panic as there was nobody there to pacify them. Both drivers and the adult attendants were injured. Due to the condition of the passengers, it was just impossible to find out who had been hurt. A fleet of ambulances was called to remove the patients to hospital. The Council had to be contacted, to try and find out the names and addresses of the kids, arrangements had to be made to convey the children to their homes and to remove the two buses.

After all measurements had been obtained for the reports, Jock attended the hospital to ascertain the extent of the injuries in order to complete the reports. There would be a good pile of 'Yellow Perils' to list everyone involved, so he decided to start writing in the car as he waited for Bill to empty his bladder. He said later that it wouldn't have made any difference if he had wet his trousers due to the fact they were so wet with the rain. He glanced in the back as he entered the car.

"Asleep?" he asked.

"No, at least I don't think so" Jock answered.

They drove to the police station to complete all the paperwork, the Skipper just disappeared and never scrounged a ride in a wireless car again. Luckily, this accident happened in an area where there was no dispute with different ambulance authorities, as it sometimes happened in such a large congested area; some streets were actual boundary lines for different stations. Jock and other drivers had experienced difficulty in obtaining an ambulance when the accident was on a boundary. Even though the call had gone through normal channels, the drivers had refused to go, they referred the call to the other ambulance station, which in turn refused to go. On more than one occasion, Jock had been compelled to put injured persons in his car and take them to hospital himself. It should not have been necessary, as arrangements had been made for the first station called to attend the scene and deal with it. If it was later ascertained that the incident was not on their ground, then the expenses would be met by the correct authority. These arguments, however, were in full swing at the time the buses collided and that is why Jock was pleased that it happened where it had. He couldn't see how they could have taken so many people to hospital if there had been any dispute.

THE BELL

Driving the wireless car constantly for eight hours a day, minus refreshment time, proves to be a tremendous strain on the man behind the wheel. Calls for his services are quite regular; no sooner is one completed than another request comes along. Then another high speed drive along crowded streets, when the driver has to consider all aspects of safety, stopping distances, space between vehicles which may allow a possible overtake, what other drivers are doing or could be going to do, and also, to some lesser aspect, watching the movements and anticipated movements of pedestrians. A five minute drive was capable of producing a very heavy sweat, even though the driver himself felt calm and relaxed and capable of handling the car; it was the sub-conscious that caused the strain. Jock had a habit of sticking his pipe in his mouth when on a call and it was surprising the number of stems that he bit through due to the sudden tightening of jaws.

Nerves could not be ignored when a copper was posted on wireless car, for when two men were posted together for three weeks, it was essential that they must be compatible. They had to be able to get on well with one another because anything could happen, they had to be able to trust each other and be able to converse. Some coppers considered that the area car was a cushy job and they crawled to the Sergeant responsible for the duty roster. In his early days as a driver, Jock was lumbered with a newcomer to the station, the man was full of his importance and forever talking about his experiences on wireless cars. He was told that he had never ever been on a chase until he had been on a one with MacGregor. As it transpired the man was a very nervous person and this came to light on his first day working as the wireless operator for Jock.

"That chap doesn't like the look of coppers, does he?" The remark came out of the blue, it was half past eight in the morning and the wireless man was dozing in his seat.

"Who, which one?" he said as he tried to rouse himself and focus on the question which he had only faintly heard. Jock was already turning the car round to head the way they had just come.

"That man, on the motor bike. He was coming along behind us when he overtook that car, he saw us and suddenly turned round and headed the other way."

As he was explaining this, he had accelerated quickly and was gaining on the motorcycle. The rider looked over his shoulder and spotted the car so he started to put a move on. The crossroads were ignored by the man on the motorcycle as he sped along.

"I think we'd better have a chat with him" Jock said as he dropped the car into a lower gear to enable him to boost his speed; then with his foot down on the pedal he began to close the distance between them. Jock was compelled to drive according to safety regulations, whereas the motorcyclist just didn't bother. Jock positioned the car for each junction so that he could either slide it round fast or brake if required. It was a fast drive considering that the area was built up, most of the roads were straight with other roads cutting straight across them, there were several 'T' junctions. Jock was obliged to use his horn practically all the time. He had found that intermittent blasts were better than using the bell; the bells were not much use in a fast chase really because the sound didn't travel ahead of the car, it was lost in the exhaust and echoed amongst the buildings. This fact seemed unknown to the wireless operator for he pushed his finger on the button and kept it there and as the car lurched and braked he slid around on his seat.

"Sit back in your seat and rest your head against the headrest" Jock warned his operator. The order was ignored, simply because the chap couldn't press the button if he sat back and he wanted it pressed. He was on a chase and all police cars sounded the bell when they were after criminals, were his obvious thoughts. Jock was too busy concentrating on his quarry to worry too much about the man sliding round beside him.

"Christ, he's going straight past the school." Jock swore because all the kids were on their way to school; the motorcycle roared past the school without any incident. Jock slowed down, just in case; the youngsters had heard the horn and the bell, plus the sound of the screaming engine and they all stood on the pavements cheering and waving. Several minutes later they had to face the same problems at another school but before they got there Jock lost his operator. Well nearly lost him, the man had slid off the seat and was jammed on the floor beneath his wireless, his finger was stuck in the hole which held the bell push and he couldn't get it out.

As they hurtled past the second school, Jock moved his car to the offside of the road; he intended taking the corner fast because the roads ahead turned back on themselves and he knew that he would be able to cut the motorcycle off. The motorcyclist was riding close to the nearside of the road and was not in a position for a fast turn at that point. However, he must have suddenly realised that he would be trapped if he went straight ahead, for he swung his handlebars round and tried to take the corner.

"Silly sod, he'll never do it" Jock muttered as he noted the man's actions. He was right, because the front wheel hit the kerb and mounted the pavement, the chap leaned the bike over as much as he dared in his attempt to avoid hitting the wall. He was lucky in this aspect, but his chain had jumped off when he had hit the kerb. The machine was useless, and he came to a halt with a grin on his face and a police car alongside him.

No casualties, except for an elderly lady who had been standing at the gate of the end house, she had seen the cycle heading for her and she fainted. Jock left the car and took hold of the rider by the arm.

"You're nicked bonny lad. We'll get all the details sorted out afterwards.

He took the man with him as he walked up the corner to see how the lady was, she was standing up when he reached the gate.

"Are you alright madam?" he asked.

"Yeh, ta officer. I would just like to get my hands on that bleeder for just ten seconds. He nearly gave me a heart attack." The good lady did not realise that the culprit was the man standing beside her.

"My own sentiments entirely. I couldn't hit him myself, but I bet you would really give him something to think about; I'm sorry that I wouldn't be allowed to let you hit him though," Jock answered.

"They should bring back the birch for sods like him."

"Steady, lady, do you know that this man is the one you're talking about. You might hurt his feelings. Now, I have to see whether any of those children were hurt as he drove through them." Jock was holding the offender by both arms.

"You wouldn't hit him when I wasn't looking, would you?"

The unlucky man gave sudden yelp and lurched against Jock. Justice had been served Jock realised, as he turned back to the lady.

"I knew you're too much of a lady to hit anyone and this poor man's nose is bleeding, he must have hurt it when he fell of his bike." The woman didn't answer, she just grinned.

Jock walked the man back to the car, the bell was still ringing as the wireless operator tried to disengage his finger.

"Some chase, wasn't it?" the prisoner said.

"Whose bike is it? Did you nick it? Jock asked.

"No, it's mine," came the reply.

"Never mind, we shall soon check it out when we get to the nick," Jock told him as he placed the man in the back of the car and then leaned across and used the wireless as the operator was not in a position to do so. He requested that the van be sent out to collect the motorcycle and then requested a friendly neighbour to keep an eye on it until the police arrived.

"What the hell is that bell ringing?" the Station Sergeant asked as Jock took the motorcyclist into the charge room. Jock grinned.

"Come and have a look Skipper."

The Sergeant went out with him and approached the car which was standing apparently empty but had the bell going all the time. When he looked inside, he saw the disgruntled wireless operator jammed in the bottom of the car beneath the wireless, with his right index finger stuck in the hole.

"Can't you do something about that?" he asked Jock.

"Yes Skip, cut his bloody finger off." Between them they twisted and pulled at the luckless copper and eventually released the offending finger.

After the offences had been sorted out and the man charged, the bald-headed wireless operator turned to Jock and said.

"We did alright there didn't we?"

"If that's what you like but let us get this straight. Regarding that bell, the controls of this car are the responsibility of the driver, your job is the wireless and you will only ring the bell when I ask for it. Understand?" grunted Jock.

Jock wasn't too happy about his new companion and after the next call he made his mind up to get rid of him.

"We will go," he told the operator when the call came over the warless, "Tell them we'll deal." The request was for assistance by a Police Officer being assaulted by a crowd of men. Calls like these had to be answered as quickly as possible because a copper could be killed in minutes when the boots went in.

Jock drove like the wind and assessed the movement of the traffic ahead. He noted all gaps in the line of cars which could be used for overtaking; every possible build up of traffic was considered and acted upon. Crossroads come up, two cars in front of him and two more travelling in the opposite direction. Jock quickly considered the situation and took up his correct position to pass.

Suddenly, the bell rang. The wireless operator had come to life, he just couldn't resist the temptation of that button.

"Stupid sod," Jock exploded. The vehicles in front of him had stopped at the sound of the bell, the road was blocked, were the cars coming towards him also stationary? A blur of possibilities flashed through his head; the other drivers would be wondering where the car was that had sounded the bell. Acting in that half second, he dropped into a lower gear and moved to the right hand side, flashing his lights and sounding the horn. It was the only way past the hazard, without causing an accident. His split second reactions had left the other cars standing at the junction and he swung back to his correct side and resumed normal driving.

"You stupid bugger. I told you not to touch that bell, you nearly caused a pile up there."

It had been touch and go but luck had been on their side and they continued on their way to the fight. This had been one of those occasions when the bell had been dangerous. It happened more than once, such as when a dear lady driver cautiously approached the traffic lights at a 'T' junction. The lights were in her favour and she gently turned the car to the right. A long line of traffic stood at the junction waiting to cross, but just as she was in the middle of her turn, a bell sounded. The woman turned her head, looking this way and that as she tried to see who could be ringing the bell. She was so intent on her search that she forgot that the steering was still on; the result was inevitable, she hit one car after the other - the poor drivers saw her coming but couldn't take any avoiding action as they stood in the line at the lights.

She blamed the bell and the result was that every car with a bell attached that had been working in that district was suspect. Al the drivers had to be traced and statements obtained from them, to find out if any of them had sounded the bell at that particular time. Every ambulance, fire engine and police car was checked, with negative result. It was eventually proved that the sinister noise had been a fire alarm on a building which had gone off accidentally due to change of water pressure.

CHAPTER ELEVEN

FAMILY TROUBLE
(DISTURBANCE)

FAMILY TROUBLE

Jock only had one more call that evening with the Bell maniac, a request for Police assistance. Jock knew the location well, he had been to that particular house on numerous other occasions, it was a husband and wife job. As he approached the premises he saw a crowd had gathered outside the house - this was most unusual. When he stopped the car he saw the lady of the house standing in the middle of the crowd, she was wearing a nightdress covered in blood.

"Hang on here, I'll deal with this," he said. As he approached the woman he noticed that she had been battered around the face, the blood appeared to be coming from her nose. He examined the injuries, ignoring the yelling crowd who were mostly drunks.

"Did he do that?" he asked. "He hasn't hit you like that before." Jock suspected that she had a broken nose.

"Yes, he came in and started all over again, he's inside with the kids."

"Well you'll have to go to hospital, I think your nose is broken. Is there anyone that can look after the youngsters?"

"My sister lives down the street, she'll see to them." Jock obtained the address from her and spoke to his mate, he asked him to call an ambulance and then to go and collect the sister. He placed the injured woman in the police car to wait for the ambulance to arrive and then he went into the house. The husband was sitting in an easy chair, he looked up when Jock entered.

"Oh, it's you again."

"Yes mate, today is the thirteenth and it's your unlucky day, this is the thirteenth time I have been here and you are nicked," Jock said. "Let's go."

"What about the kids?"

"You should have thought about them before; we are getting your sister-in-law to look after them."

"What if I refuse to go?" He was going to be awkward.

"That will be fine by me bonny lad. Let's put it like this, your wife is going to hospital as a patient, you can join her also as a patient. Nothing would give me greater pleasure. Now get outside."

Jock's ultimatum and his tone of voice convinced the wife beater that it was easier to hit women. The ambulance hadn't arrived when they went outside; the wireless operator arrived with a breathless woman who was to look after the children.

The two women clung to each other for a short while and the tears flowed; Jock separated them and told the sister to see to the youngsters.

"They are asleep at the present but I think they will keep her in for the night. He'll be kept at the Police Station for a while, so it will be left to you to stay the night with the kids, OK?"

The ambulance still hadn't arrived so Jock decided to take the injured woman with them to the Nick. "Tell them to make arrangements for the ambulance to pick her up at the nick."

The lady was eventually taken away for medical treatment; it was disclosed that she did have a broken nose so the husband was charged with causing grievous bodily harm. This was one of the few cases that Jock allowed his name to go on the charge sheet as he would be called to give evidence about the previous troubles. Normally he would let anyone have the privilege of having the arrests put on their names, this was handy for a copper trying to get promotion or into the CID. He never had any trouble getting 'rid' of a body, even the permanent members of the CID had asked for their names to be included on a charge sheet.

MIND YOUR BACK

Jock managed to make certain that the bell maniac was not employed on he wireless cars again, he also asked that he be consulted before a copper was posted with him. He settled for two youngsters who took it in turns to work with him. They were both a lot younger than he was, but they were both willing to have a go if required. At the same time, they were capable and obeyed his instructions without question. This arrangement did not suit a lot of the older coppers who were used to having a cushy posting as one of their perks.

One of these lads had a rather high pitched voice, effeminate one would say. This was his only problem and Jock tried to get him to talk in a deeper tone. The reason for this was that often they were called to disturbances where dockers and stevedores were involved and if his mate had spoken, it could cause an embarrassing situation, especially with that type of person. It was on one such occasion that he proved his worth; they were on night duty and driving along the main road. Jock spotted a bottle party going on outside a public house, a crowd of dockers were having a good old punch-up and bottles were being used as weapons.

"Hang on here Mick, stay on the wireless, I'll see to this." It was his first night duty with the man so he didn't want him hurt. He recognised the type involved in the fracas and knew they didn't worry about putting the boot in, or hitting a copper. If Mick had got mixed up with them and opened his mouth, they would have had no hesitation about taking his trousers off.

He ran across the road and got stuck into the mob, not caring how hard he hit them, grabbing two of the big men he banged their heads together, left another hugging himself between the legs, gave a fourth one a backhander (and as his stick was up his sleeve) the man went down poleaxed. He reached out for another contestant and suddenly saw a man staggering backwards, then another shot past him so close that he brushed against Jock. Quickly he glanced behind to see where these chaps were coming from. A crash of glass came as the last min hit the ground and Jock saw Mick standing there behind him, with his stick in his hand.

"Sorry Jock, but I saw them coming up behind you, I just couldn't resist it, after all they would have got you." Jock grinned, the dockers might take the Mickey out of his mate's voice but they couldn't take the Mickey out of his stick that was something they appreciated.

"Come on, let's get this lot into the car."

They loaded the six unconscious men into the car and took them up the rod to the police station.

"Hang onto these Skipper. There are still a lot more down there." They then returned to the scene of the fight. The main road was deserted outside the pub but when the car turned down the adjacent side street, they saw that the fight was still in full swing. Another police car was at the scene, Jock recognised the men who made up the crew, they were from another Station; the driver and his operator were in the middle of the fight.

"Come on Mick." Jock invited the youngster to get stuck in and together the pair of them went to assist the other coppers, four extra hands and four extra feet soon made short work of the punch up. Ten battered bodies were flung into the backs of the police cars.

"Where the hell have you been Jock? It certainly took you long enough to get here," the driver of the other car complained.

"They have been shouting their heads off for you on the wireless and when they couldn't raise you they sent us along."

"We were already out of the car dealing with it, we've already taken half a dozen down to the nick" Jock told him.

"You could have answered the wireless, we would have still come to give you a hand" the man complained.

Mick saw that Jock wasn't going to blame him for not doing as he was told so he spoke up.

"It was my fault because Jock told me to stay in the car but I got out to give him a hand, I forgot to book off the air."

"That's alright, don't do it again though, we always like to know what is happening around us," said the other copper who knew how blood pressure could be affected when action was imminent.

When they got back into the car and prepared to take the other prisoners to the station, Jock told Mick to give the Control Room a shout.

"Give them our location and let them know how many prisoners we have, tell them we will be at the local nick re charges."

The drunks had a right good time in the charge room, they would have willingly killed one another, it was only the presence of the coppers which prevented this happening. When they had all sobered up they were charged and bailed out and walked arm in arm towards their homes, the best of pals.

Jock and his mate had to deal with an accident as they waited for the drunks to sober up. It was just a simple message which came over the air.

"Accident. Call for Police" but when they arrived at the scene, which was on a dual carriageway, they realised that this was going to be a night of grief for at least two families.

A heavy lorry had broken down on a straight stretch of the road, a couple of teenagers had been doing a 'Ton-Up' on a motorcycle, they had ran into the rear of the lorry and had actually moved it slightly. The lad's head was opened up like a slice from an orange, whilst the girl didn't seem to be hurt apart from a compound fracture of the wrist. It was only when Jock was undressing her at the mortuary that he found she had a broken neck. A message was sent for the parents to be informed and Jock retired to the canteen to write his reports and to have his breakfast.

HOSPITAL MESSAGE

Mick learnt another lesson when he went into the Communications Room to make his list of stolen cars up to date. He had agreed to do a hospital message although these were normally done by men on the beat, or the 'Noddy' riders.

"It shouldn't take long," he said apologetically, showing the message to Jock.

"I can't understand why they send these things out at night time. The real point is that the family have only to go and collect the clothes of the dead person to be notified officially, they could at least allow them to have a good sleep. I don't suppose anyone would go back to bed after getting this news in the middle of the night."

It was an unfailing fault of the night duty staff at the hospitals, as soon as a person died they passed the information to the local Police Station, asking them to inform relatives - to contact them after nine. So it was not a very pleasant mission they were on but one they were used to doing.

"Sixty one, isn't Mick?" Jock asked as he checked the numbers of the houses. "Mick, are you asleep?" Jock asked. "Is it sixty one we want?" His colleague had actually been engaged in checking his stolen car sheet with a list of cars found, which was just coming over the air. He looked up and agreed that was the correct address. He shone his torch on the front door of a house as they moved slowly

"Passed it" he said. Jock reversed the car and stopped outside the house; he got out of his vehicle and gave a few hearty bangs on the woodwork. It was loud enough to waken anyone inside, but on this occasion he got no good results. Several more loud crashes on the door did not waken the tenants and, after several minutes, he had only succeeded in getting everybody else in the street out of bed, but not the ones he wanted. One or two of the neighbours actually ventured into the street to find out what was the matter.

"You won't get any answer there Guv," one of the men said when he could make himself heard above the sound of Jock's feet kicking away at the door.

"Why not?"

"There are only two people live there and they are both deaf and dumb," the man grinned.

"Hell, just our luck." Jock was disgruntled and Mick asked him what he intended to do about the message.

"We could leave it for early turn to do but they would have to catch them as they were leaving the house, otherwise they would be in the same predicament as we are now. We could stick the message through the letterbox, but I don't think they would like that. I think we'll have a go and try and waken them." It was a challenge to him and he didn't like leaving a job undone. He asked the friendly neighbour if he had a ladder.

"I haven't got one, but I know where I can borrow one." So, still in his pyjamas, he went along the street to a friend's house to borrow the required article. Jock surveyed the windows upstairs to see if any of them were open but he was out of luck because they were all apparently locked. When the man returned with the ladder he asked him if he knew which room the tenants slept in and when this was pointed out they lifted the ladder up to the sill.

Everyone stood and looked at each other, the neighbours automatically considered that this was a job for the coppers to do and Jock had been hoping for a volunteer but Mick wasn't having any of it, he was engrossed with his writing. So Jock had to climb up the rickety step ladder and try to open the window, he pushed and pulled at the old sash, wishing that it was a more modern type which could be opened quite easily. The damned thing was hard to move but he slackened it enough to get the blade of his jack-knife in between the sashes and slide the catch aside. His problems were only starting because when he tried to slide the bottom sash upwards, it absolutely refused to move. Regardless of how much force he applied, it remained as though it was nailed shut. He turned his attention to the upper half of the window; he started it moving by forcing his knife blade in the space between the window sash and the frame.

Next he got his finger tips in the space and heaved downwards, he put all his weight on the woodwork then, with a lot of shaking and banging, he managed to get the thing down about eighteen inches. It did not make the slightest difference as he tried every trick of the trade, he just couldn't get it down any further. As it was, he was balanced on the very top rung of the ladder and it wasn't a very robust piece of timber. He shone his torch into the room and saw the couple sleeping peacefully, undisturbed by the fact that someone was trying very hard and noisily to break into their bedroom.

The moment came when he had to make a move, the space allowed was such a height that he couldn't step over and even if he stood on the window ledge he would have no handholds. He tried everything that was logical to squeeze through the gap, without success, and it became obvious that the only way in was to go through head first.

Once he managed to get his shoulders through the narrow gap he surveyed the interior of the room; he looked for some hand-hold inside to assist him in. So, wriggling and twisting, he managed to get the upper half of his torso across the window, till eventually he was standing on tiptoe on the window ledge. He knew that he only had to move forward a few more inches before he began to swing like a see-saw on the top of the window. It had to be done as it was the only way in, the pressure of the sash across his pelvic area was nearly crippling him as he heaved himself across the wood. All of a sudden, he plummeted towards the floor, holding his arms above his head to break the fall when he hit the floor.

He suddenly came to a halt, his feet had caught on the top of the window sash leaving him dangling upside down. 'Christ, I'd never make a cat burglar' he thought as he surveyed the room from his bat-like position. Pressing his hands against the floor and pushing upwards, he managed to free one foot and this foot was forced against the wall as he again did his press-ups. A heave, and the offending restriction was released. The sudden freedom sent his body hurtling to the floor; he rolled on his shoulders and finished up at the other side of the room, right alongside the bed. Dragging himself up on to his feet he used the bed as a means of leverage. On his knees he looked straight into the sleeping man's face. Peace and bliss was written all over it, obviously he did not suffer the aches and pains which attacked Jock's body, his shins hurt like hell due to his quick slide over the top of the woodwork and, in the process, he had lost most of his skin.

Jock withdrew his torch from his pocket and looked at the sleeping couple and, shaking the man's shoulder, he waited until the bleary eyes were open before shining the light upon himself. This was so the chap could see that it was a copper who was sharing his bedroom with him and his wife.

He quickly realised that something was wrong; Jock placed the torch on a chair beside the bed to enable them to see one another. His knowledge of sign language was virtually nil, however he did succeed in his quest as a light of understanding sprang into the man's eyes. He reached across his sleeping wife and switched the bedside light on and then shook her awake. The lady woke as quickly as he had done and she flashed a quick glance at Jock to acknowledge the fact that she knew he was there and then she concentrated on her husband. It was a miracle how these people can talk so quick to one another, the hands moved so fast that it was not possible for an inexperienced individual to see and register the movements.

The wife knew at once why Jock was there and she got out of bed. 'Cor, I wish these youngsters would wear something decent when they go to bed' Jock thought as the young lady swung the bedclothes down to reveal that they were both starkers. There was nothing ladylike about the way she got out of bed either, her knees came up to her chin as she rolled backwards and then the whole of her body came up, her legs swinging outwards over the edge of the bed. Crossing to the other side of the bedroom to get her clothes, she commenced to dress, ignoring Jock but occasionally glancing at her husband as he spoke with his hands.

Jock suggested that he take them to hospital in his car but the man declined, indicating that they had their own vehicle. Jock looked for his escape, a glance at the window, but no way was he going to attempt to squeeze through that small gap again. He walked over past the girl and closed the offending aperture and as the couple completed their dressing, he went through the door and painfully made his way down the stairs to the car where Mick was waiting.

"Message delivered Mick, and my bloody legs are killing me."

JUVENILE

'Oh for a quiet night but that just wasn't possible' Jock cursed as he rubbed his tortured legs but he was soon disturbed with his first aid.
"Sound of breaking glass."
The call over the air was directed to them for action; before the address came across, the engine had been started and the car had burst into life, when they received the location, Jock said:
"Hell, that's just over the bridge."
A jeweller's shop window had just been broken and the thieves were helping themselves to the contents. The problem was that between them and the police car was a one-way street. Jock decided to take a chance and swung the car round; to go by the legitimate route would mean a several minute delay and as it was night time and there was very little traffic on the road, he made up his mind. A quick race through the forbidden territory without seeing another car. As they crossed the rise and the lights came down, they saw two men running from the burgled shop. One ran down a side street beside the shop and the other went down the road.

Jock stopped the car.
"After that one Mick," and the youngster was away like a deer down the street. Jock swung the car into the side street and his lights soon picked out the other chap, as soon as the criminal saw the lights coming towards him he tried to give the impression that he was just a drunk staggering home. He leaned over a garden wall and made retching sounds, well all drunks do, don't they?
"Right lad, you're nicked," said Jock getting out of the car. The man tried his hardest for several seconds but he was a lousy actor, especially when Jock shone his torch over the wall to display a beautiful pile of jewellery and watches which the man had tried to dispose of as he had leaned over the wall. He hadn't been successful in his attempts to get rid of the property for when Jock searched him, he still had a couple of rings and two watches in his pockets. He sat the man in the car and they waited for a couple of minutes until Mick arrived with the other prisoner.

"Searched him?" Jock enquired.

"Not yet."

"OK let's see what he's got in his pockets." They emptied the man's pockets and found that he had not been able to get rid of his share of the spoils. So the villains were whipped off to the nick with all the proceeds, within five minutes of having committed the crime. Charge sheets were signed so that all the details could be filled in later by the Station Sergeant, then they were back on the streets again, ready for action.

GRUB UP

"Will you bring the cakes in Jock" the chap in the Communications Room asked as they headed for the car. "Dennis is on a job." Dennis was one of the men who normally collected the nightly goodies from the cake shop. He was one of the men who had taken the place of the pedal cyclists, they had been issued with Velocette Motorcycles which were lightweight machines and run very quietly. The nickname for these bikes was 'Noddy' and the men detailed to ride them were, naturally, called 'Noddy Riders'. The bikes could cruise quietly around the streets to check property and all the messages which had to be done were the responsibility of these men. One of the jobs of the night duty riders was to call at the local cake shop and collect the cakes and pies. The delivery man who brought the fresh supplies had to dispose of the old stock and as the previous days supply were just thrown out for pig food, it had become a standard practice for the night duty relief to take some to the Station. The bags of food were placed in the canteen for anyone to help themselves.

As they patrolled the streets they sighted the delivery van as he stopped at one of the big shops and they pulled the car in behind the vehicle. The driver looked towards them and waved, holding his hand up with five fingers spread out, indicating he would see to their needs in a few minutes. When he had finished stacking the trays of fresh food onto the counters at the rear of the shop, he piled all the old stuff onto a tray.

"Help yourself," he said pointing to the pile of sausage rolls, pies and cakes. They took the bags of food to the Station and placed them in the canteen, ready for the chaps who had to take an early meal. It seemed a harmless practice to collect the scraps which would just be fed to the pigs, but nothing ever runs smoothly, something always seems to go wrong. On this occasion it was a brand new Inspector, still feeling the weight of the pips on his shoulder; it was not normal for the Supervision to check the canteen on night duty but this chap was new and probably worried about his new job. He was checking to ensure that none of the coppers were in the canteen who shouldn't be there. He barged into the room and glowered at the motley collection of bodies, who were either playing cards, feed, or sleeping in chairs.

The Supervising Officer checked his list with the men, to satisfy himself that everyone had booked in. The spare driver, whose job it was to make the tea, looked up and asked.

"Want a cup of tea, Guv?" The Inspector agreed to have a cup of tea because he would be out patrolling whilst the coppers were having their breakfasts. As the driver poured the hot tea out he said

"Cake sir, or a sausage roll?" indicating the spread of food on the counter.

"Is it someone's birthday?" he asked.

"Not that I know of Guv" the driver answered.

"Well, what's this lot for, where did they come from?" the new man asked.

"They are spares Guv," the tea boy explained and he was compelled to tell the Inspector exactly where the food came from.

"This is going to stop. I will not allow it."

"Guv, these are spares, they were just going to be thrown to the pigs."

"Not the pigs at this station, I assure you." The new boss was as good as his word for he contacted the owners of the food shops and the system came to an end. The drivers had to leave a credit slip for each shop, accounting for each item of food which he removed from the premises. It just wasn't possible to get even a crumb from that date.

NO STOMACH

The following day, after the inspector had decided to stop the cake fiddle, they were on late turn having just completed the quick change over by finishing work at six am and back again at 2pm. Jock was posted van driver, having a break from fast driving. He had helped the spare driver to clean all the cars, the Superintendent had been taken home and all the other little jobs the drivers had to do were completed. Jock decided, therefore, to have an early break; he was going to have a fry-up and wanted to get his done before the chaps came in from beat duty. An oven was supplied in the canteen for those who didn't want to, or couldn't afford to, buy food from the counter. He could get his meal finished with and have a game of cards with the area car men when they came in, after all it's not possible to have a game of solo when the table is covered with greasy plates.

He had fried some sausage and egg, beans and a fried slice of bread made a good meal and he enjoyed his grub. He had just started to tuck into his meal when the door of the canteen opened and the new Inspector came in.

"Oh, are you having your tea?"

A bloody silly question because it must have been obvious to the simplest of people that Jock was indeed eating, in fact he had just stuffed his mouth full of sausage when the question was asked. Jock looked at the man with an enquiring look on his face, the man looked ill and definitely worried. He emptied his mouth and swilled it out with a drink of tea before speaking.

"What's wrong Guv?"

"Are you van driver?" Another silly question, he knew damn well that Jock was van driver because he was always checking the postings. Jock wasn't going to argue though, he just answered.

"Yes" and continued to eat his meal due to the fact that the man was taking so long to get to the point.

"I was wondering if you would like to come with me." The Inspector faltered as he spoke.

"What's on then Guv?" Jock asked as he swallowed a portion of fried bread. The Inspector looked at the greasy mess spread before Jock and looked as if he was going to be sick right over it.

"There's been an accident and I have been asked to attend."

"The wireless car will deal with that Guv, there shouldn't be any need for you to go" Jock told him, through a mouthful of beans.

"It's an accident on the railway, the car is there and they have asked for me." The man's face seemed paler than ever.

"I have cleaned your car Sir, it's full and ready for you in the yard." The Inspector blushed so quickly that Jock could see the line of red move over the paleness.

"I know, but I would like to you to come with me Mr MacGregor. I haven't had to deal with anything like this before and the Station Sergeant suggested that I should discuss the matter with you. I am told the body is in a bit of a state."

"Right Guv. You'll need the van in any case." Jock stood up, collected his plate and put it in the oven and drank his tea in one gulp.

"Righto Guv, let's go." He ran out of the canteen and slid down the handrail to the yard below. The engine of the van was running by the time the Inspector reached it. A few minutes later they were drawing to a halt beside the wireless car. The driver of the car met them.

"Hi Jock, bit of a mess, hit by an express."

Jock looked at the Inspector with his lovely clean uniform, hat dead straight, pips gleaming and even carrying his leather gloves; he certainly looked the part of a supervising officer but wasn't going to be any use here. He reminded him of Lt. Jones the first time he met him on the bomb site.

"Give me a hand Jim," Jock opened the back of the van and opened the lockers under the seats and they pulled the stretcher out and collected the large rubber sheet.

"Any idea who it is?" asked Jock.

"Not yet," Albert answered "But we think he was one of the gang working on the line."

"Sir," Jock aroused the Inspector who seemed to be in a trance. "Sir, we'll have to know who the man is and also find out if there were any witnesses. We'll also have to get the train examined when it reaches its destination. We'll require a statement from the driver and guard of the train, we'll also want a statement from the signalman of this stretch. Do you think you could make a start while we collect the body?"

"What?" the Inspector shook himself when he realised Jock had spoken to him. "What did you say?"

Jock shrugged, 'What's the use' he thought but out loud he said nothing.

"Nothing Sir, I was just wondering if you would give us a hand, it'll take four of us to carry the stretcher."

The crew of the wireless car took up positions at the front end of the stretcher and Jock held the handle at the back alongside the Inspector. The rubber sheet was laid across and allowed to hang down towards the ground.

"Any idea where he was when the train hit him Albert?" Jock asked as they trudged alongside the track.

"Down beside the signal box, I believe."

They struggled along over the loose stones towards the point indicated by the driver,

"Round about here I think Jock."

The small group began a slow search along the railway line, every piece of ground in between the lines and at the side was closely examined as they looked for parts of what was once a human being. As they worked they kept looking along the tracks, they didn't want to end up like this chap, spread over half a mile.

"I don't want to finish up like this," Albert said, as he held up part of an arm, glancing along the lines once more as he placed the limb on the stretcher alongside the slowly gathering pile. The wireless operator retrieved part of the leg attached to a piece of groin and threw it on with the rest of the bloody flesh. The Inspector's face was drawn and white but he never spoke as Jock picked up part of a head, identified by the ear and some hair.

Slowly, the pile of flesh, broken bones, tissue, fingers and intestines began to mount and the stretcher got heavier.

"It doesn't seem possible for anyone to weigh as much as this" Albert said. "Are you sure there is only one man." After they had covered over a half a mile along the track Jock said,

"I don't think it's worth while going any further, do you Guv?" said Jock

As the Inspector didn't reply the men began to cover the gruesome remains with the rubber sheet, drawing up the hanging side and fastening them together. The long plod back to the railway station began, with a ball of flesh measuring about three feet across balanced on the stretcher. It was difficult climbing up the stairs because the ball had a tendency to roll off, it was only held in position by Jock pushing it back on and holding the back of the stretcher up as high as possible to keep it level.

"Are you alright Sir?" The Inspector was taking this new aspect of Police work very badly.

"Er, yes Jock, I'll be alright," he answered.

"Look Guv, you sit in the van if you wish and we'll get finished here." They had found one brown shoe with a foot in it and a key ring with three keys but apart from that they had no means of identifying the body.

The three coppers left the Inspector sitting in the front of the van and went their own ways to try and discover who the dead person was. Jock contacted the Station Master and made arrangements for the train to be examined and for the Police to get statements from the crew of the train. He then went down to the signal box and obtained a statement from the man on duty. They all met on the platform and discussed the details of information. One of the porters had seen a workman walking along the side of the track. He believed he was one of the workmen who had been working on repairs to the track. Various other witnesses had also given descriptions and statements of how the man had been walking alongside the line, although he had been about four feet from the rails he had been sucked into the side. The body had been rolled along all the carriages and chopped up by the wheels. Enquiries had been made and the man's name obtained, the wireless operator had checked all the cars standing outside the Railway Station to see if the keys which had been found on the track fitted any of the vehicles. He had eventually opened one of the doors and had checked the Registration Number over the wireless and in this way he obtained the name and address of the owner, the name matched the one already obtained.

"Right Albert, I'll whip him down to the morgue, see you at the nick." The Inspector was sitting in the wireless car when Jock returned to the van and he got out when he saw Jock.

"I wasn't going to sit in there with him" he muttered.

"Leave the door open Guv, it'll let the smell out" Jock told the Inspector as he started the engine.

"Where are we going to now?"

"First, the hospital and next to the morgue, that is if he's dead." Jock grinned at his boss.

The bloody carnage stank.

"We'll have to send a message to inform his wife won't we?" The Inspector held his face close the open door to catch the breeze.

"Not in this case Guv, we'll do it ourselves under the circumstances because it's on our patch," Jock replied.

It didn't take long to get to the hospital and Jock pulled up outside the casualty wing.

"Hang on Guv, I won't be long." Jock got out of the van and opened the back door. Climbing inside he unfastened the rubber sheet so that the doctor could examine the remains and as soon as the knots were undone the pile of flesh slopped out all over the big sheet. A gasp and choking sound came to Jock's ears and he looked up just in time to see the Inspector running for a hedgerow, vomiting profusely as he did so. Jock left him and went inside the building, a nurse met him and let it be known that she was in charge.

"Can I help you?"

"Yes Sister, I need a doctor to certify death, the body is in the van outside" Jock informed her.

"I'm sorry but you'll have to bring him in here for the doctor to examine him" she answered very starchily.

"Normally I would agree with you nurse but not on this occasion" Jock told her.

"I insist that the person be brought inside before the doctor can see him" she answered.

"Nurse, normally I get on well with hospital staff, this is the first time that anyone has got me annoyed. I want to see a doctor now, is that clear." Jock realised that this was one of the old crusty type who thought she was Florence Nightingale.

The problem was solved when he saw a man in a white coat coming along the corridor, he left the nurse who tried to prevent him and went to the man.

"Are you a doctor?" he asked.

"Yes, can I help you?" the man said.

"That's what the nurse here said but I'm afraid she didn't mean it. Yes you can Doctor, we have a body in the van outside and I need it certified dead. Nurse here insisted that I bring it inside."

"No trouble officer" the doctor said as he gave the Sister a dirty look and headed for the door with Jock. He went towards the front door of the van and Jock stopped him.

"I think most of his head is at the bottom end Doc." The man obliged and headed for the rear door.

The Sister pushed against Jock and made to get in the front door, Jock tried to stop her.

"I shouldn't go in there lass, the chap is dead." She pushed him away.

"I have to be with the doctor, anyway I have probably seen more dead persons that you have" she replied smugly.

"OK if that's the way you want it" and Jock let her climb onto the steps and stood behind her holding his arms out. She gave one gasp and after one look at the pile of fetid, mutilated meat, she fainted, falling backwards into Jock's waiting arms. He carried her back to the hospital, passing the young doctor who was standing weakly at the back of the van. As Jock walked past, he began to retch and vomited his inside up. Jock laid the nurse on a trolley and called another nurse to see to her.

"She's had a bit of a shock" he explained and just then the doctor came in.

"Sorry about that doc, but it had to be done" Jock said.

"Yes I know Officer, I only wish it hadn't been me that had to be the unlucky one. I wouldn't have your job for a million pounds" he said before making his way to the washroom.

"Sorry lass, but I did try to stop you" Jock said to the Sister who was just coming back to reality.

"It's my own fault, I thought I had seen everything, I never want to see anything like that again. I'm used to them being whole and in one piece."

Jock returned to the van ready to remove the carnage to the morgue, the Inspector was sitting on a wall waiting for him, he still hadn't got over the grim sight.

"Come on Guv, it won't be long now."

At the mortuary the attendant looked at Jock.

"You're joking aren't you. How the hell am I supposed to put that lot on a stretcher?"

"Put it in a drawer."

"How can I tie a label on his toe, I can't find his bloody feet," the man moaned.

"I don't think you'll have another like this so there is no chance of getting mixed up with the customers is there?" Jock said.

They carried the sheet into the morgue between them and laid it on top of a drawer and untied the knots again. The body flowed out and spilled into the drawer and Jock pulled the sheet away and folded it up. A few alterations of the pile of bones were required to make the pile level enough to slide back into the freezer.

"I'll wash my hands Guv and then we'll be off," remarked Jock to the Inspector.

"Right," replied the Inspector dully

As Jock returned to the building to rinse the blood off his hands he gave the particulars of the deceased to the attendant and bade him goodbye.

The Inspector climbed back into the seat beside him and they drove towards the given address.

"What can I say to her Mr MacGregor?" he asked.

"Don't worry about it Guv" said Jock.

The van pulled up outside the Council house where the man's wife was waiting for him.

"Come on Guv" Jock said to his boss, "It'll be easier for you than it will be for her." A middle aged lady opened the door.

"Do you know the lady next door?"

"Yes ducks, she's a friend of mine" the woman answered.

"Her husband works on the railway, is that right?"

The lady acknowledged the fact and confirmed the name that Jock had in his possession. She also agreed that her neighbours had a car and confirmed the number. Jock knew that they had the right man and told her that there had been an accident and a man had been killed.

"We believe it was your friend's husband. We will have to tell her so she may appreciate some comfort after we leave. Could you come with us?"

"Certainly Sir," the lady was only too pleased to go with them. When Jock knocked on the door the Inspector was twisting his hands together, he was in a terrible state. The lady of the house opened the door and Jock knew straight away that she didn't have to be told.

"I saw the police van and I knew that something was wrong, it's Ted isn't it?"

"I'm sorry lass, yes it is," Jock said. The look on the three faces had already convinced the widow.

"Can I go and see him?" Jock could hear the rumbling sound in the Inspector's throat.

"No ducks, I wouldn't."

"Why not? I would like to see him," she insisted.

"It wouldn't bring him back ducks and it wouldn't do you any good, just leave it for the present" Jock advised her.

She had appeared to have taken the news fairly calmly but Jock guessed that the information hadn't really been absorbed, it would hit her later.

The Inspector was quiet until they arrived at the nick when he said,

"Thanks Jock, I wouldn't have managed myself." as Jock was parking the van.

"Part of the job Guv."

"Yes, but I spoilt your tea."

"Spoilt my tea? No way Guv, it will soon warm up in the pan."

"You don't mean to say that you can face that fried meal after seeing that lot?" the Inspector asked.

"Guv" Jock said earnestly. "Life goes on. If we stop to think of all the death, suffering and gruesome sights, we would be driven mad. You'll have to learn to forget it."

"I couldn't face anything to eat" the Inspector said as Jock booked the van back in. He ran up the stairs to the canteen where three coppers were sitting waiting for him to have a game of solo.

"Make a four Jock?"

"Yes, wait till I put my tea on to warm up," and Jock poured himself a cup of tea as he waited for the food to warm up.

BANK ALARM

The next day saw Jock sitting outside in the sun, all the cars had been cleaned and polished, except the patrolling officer's car and he was out on the ground. It was a beautiful day and he puffed away at his pipe, still in his shirt sleeves and his cap pushed to the back of his head, it seemed as nobody wanted the van driver today. He was content to sit there and wait for the gaffer to bring his car in to be cleaned, he had already washed it and it only required a good polishing.

They had a strange Inspector today, he was on loan from a neighbouring Station due to the fact that the chap that had been out with Jock on the railway job had gone sick. Eventually, the car swung into the yard and stopped beside Jock.

"You won't be going out again for a while will you Guv?" The Inspector knew Jock because he had covered his ground on the 'Q' car.

"Will you be long with it?"

"No Guv, it's only due for a polish now. I've already washed it." Jock picked up his rags and tin of polish as he spoke, "I'll start straight away."

"OK it's all yours" and the Inspector went into the front office leaving Jock to get on with his labours.

Very soon the whole of the vehicle was covered with white polish. Jock stood his tin of liquid on the front bumper with one of his rags and commenced wiping the surplus powder off the metal. He stopped for a few seconds to fill and light his pipe, he wasn't in any hurry because the spare driver had taken the van out for some property as he needed a bit of practice. All the wireless cars were out and the CID had the spare car out. So, the only vehicle left on the premises was this duty officer's car and that was a lovely streaky white colour. He puffed at the pipe, making sure that it was well alight and then re-commenced his attack on the bodywork.

Suddenly the alarm bell started to ring, it was immediately above his head so it was impossible for him to ignore the sound. However, he did ignore it as he knew he didn't have a car to use to answer any call. There was only this one and it already had a driver. He rubbed the polish off the windscreen ready for the Inspector. The Superintendent came running from his office.

"That's the alarm bell ringing," as if Jock didn't know.

"Where's the driver?"

"There's only the duty officer's car Sir and he's in the front office" said Jock as he carried on with his work.

"Why doesn't someone do something, where is everyone?" The boss was worried, the panic bell was ringing, a bank hold-up was in process and nobody was worried. He ran into the front office seeing as Jock ignored him and shortly afterwards he came tearing out again, chasing the Inspector, the Section Sergeant and the Detective Inspector in front of him, apparently these were the only coppers in the office who didn't seem to have any work to do.

"Come on, get a move on!" he fluttered round them like a terrier trying to coax them into the car. Jock opened the driver's door for the Inspector to get in but the crafty old so and so got into the passenger seat at the front. The other two made themselves comfortable in the back seat.

"Will you drive Jock?" the patrolling officer asked.

"It's your car Sir, it's booked out to you" Jock explained.

"I know, but I'm not used to fast driving and you are. Anyway, I don't know this toby very well" was the excuse.

Jock didn't argue any more, he just made himself comfortable behind the wheel

"Whereabouts?" he said as he switched the engine on.

"Midland Bank" he was told and once he had the engine running he selected bottom gear and raced the vehicle towards the tight turn at the entrance, leaving behind a grateful and relieved Superintendent. A quick swing on the wheel, a pull on the handbrake and then he accelerated to the road. No traffic on his side but a solid queue on the opposite side of the road going the same way that he intended had come to a standstill. He slid the car out into the main road, headlights on and sounding the horn, this car did not have a bell fitted. He drove alongside the other cars on the wrong side of the road towards the traffic lights. It was a crossroad he was approaching but the turning to the left was a one-way street, he didn't have to worry about that, he could see the traffic coming towards him which was also stationary, the only danger was the stuff coming from his right - and that is where his eyes were. He automatically checked the time. He did this because he knew that there was a five second delay before the lights turned to green for the danger traffic to move. It was tight and as he passed the right hand side of the bollard and slid the car round in front of the stationary traffic he saw the lights change out of the corner of his eye. One danger hazard passed safely, ahead of him he knew there was a busy main road, traffic would be travelling in both directions and there would also be a lot of illegal parking on both sides of the street - it was Saturday and the town was crowded with shoppers. Numerous buses used this stretch of the road so he had to cope with the bus stops which could cause hold-ups.

Engine racing and building up speed the car whistled through the crowded thoroughfare, swerving and swaying. He eased on the speed and touched on the brake, lights still flashing and horn still sounding and he was through the worst part, giving the locals a thrill. Ahead of him he saw a bus travelling in his direction; it was approaching a double bend, islands were situated in the centre of the road and if he got caught behind the bus he would be held up until it had completed that stretch of the road.

He estimated his distance and speed and compared it with the speed and position of the bus and then he decided quickly to cut the corner on the wrong side of the bend and raced past the island and the bus. Back onto his own side, he picked up speed again and soon he was stopping outside the bank, which still had the bell ringing.

A few pedestrians glanced at the copper walking across the pavement, dressed in shirt sleeves and braces over his shirt, hat on the back of his head and smoking a pipe. As he entered the bank he was met by the manager.

"Sorry officer, it was a false alarm."

As Jock headed back to the car he saw that the rest of the coppers were just extracting themselves from the vehicle.

"It's alright, just a false alarm" he told them. The Sergeant indicated the interior of the car.

"See that brown patch, that's mine."

"That's the first time I've ever been on a '999' call and I bloody well hope it's the last," said the Detective Inspector

"Christ, lad, you chaps deserve the extra pay you get for driving like that. When you have been driving all day at those speeds it must take it out of you, mentally as well as physically," said the Patrolling Officer.

"Extra pay? You must be joking Guv. We don't get any extra for being a first class driver, mind you if you could arrange an increase it would be appreciated." Jock grinned as he headed for his seat in the car.

"Let's have a nice quiet drive back Jock, about sixty miles an hour will do" the Sergeant suggested as he settled down in the back of the car.

"How fast were we going Jock?" the Detective Inspector asked.

"Couldn't say Guv, I was too busy watching the road. I only travel as fast as I can do with safety." Jock switched the engine on and gave it a few revs. before he said, "Bugger it." He got out of the car again and walked to the front where he retrieved his tin of polish and the duster, they had been standing there all the time.

As he returned to his seat and placed the cleaning articles down between the seats the Inspector looked at them with astonishment.

"Do you mean that they have stood there all the time were driving. I would have thought they would have been blown off." The skipper was leaning forward on the edge of his seat. "I would love to be on a real chase with you Jock, they have told me that it is something that I'd never forget."

"Would you Serg? well you never know your luck," Jock smiled, the man was talking like a rooky. He drove the car quietly back to the nick to wipe the rest of the polish off.

"I'll just leave the mileage down to you Inspector, it will save booking the car in and out."

He'd almost finished his chores when the other driver arrived back with the van.

"Come on you lazy sod, you should have finished that hours ago. I'll give you a game of snooker."

"As soon as I have dusted off. If you weren't so bloody lazy you would give me hand but then I don't suppose you want to get your lovely hands dirty," Jock answered.

Anyone listening to these two calling each other names, and the slanging arguments between them, wouldn't think that they were actually the best of pals!

FIRE

They were in the middle of a 'quiet' game of snooker when the alarm bell went again; they ran into the front office to find out the reason.

"Pluck up as many of the chaps as you can Jock, take them to the High Street to help out, there's a bloody inferno going."

The van driver was designated to collect some traffic signs and place them at strategic points so as to close the main road off and divert the traffic. Whilst these orders were being given, they could hear the fire bells clamouring incessantly one after the other as the engines raced to the centre of the town. Two huge departmental stores were well alight. By the time Jock had collected five coppers from the different beats and took them to the incident, he saw that the five-storied building was well underway. The heat was so strong that the shop windows on the opposite side of the wide street were exploding, goods displayed in the windows were actually beginning to burn just from the heat.

The whole of the town centre had come to a standstill, it was engulfed in flames and smoke - the traffic consisted of fire engines. Occasionally a loud roar or an explosion heralded the fall of a wall or a whole floor, the flames shot up hundreds of feet into the air. All evening and well into the night the fire brigade slaved, trying to prevent the inferno spreading along the line of buildings. They were still coughing their way into the heat when Jock went home at ten o'clock.

The following day showed the fire out, being constantly dampened down by a few firemen. It proved a miracle how quickly the site was cleared once everything was over. A veritable small army of men swarmed over the place, removing the rubble. Very soon new concrete foundations were erected and mountains of timber surrounded the area; a huge basement gave the first signs of the size of the intended project as pillars of concrete and tons of cement were soon visible. From the ruins a new building was emerging, one could see it grow day by day and in a very short space of time the modern structure was nearly completed. Jock sat in the wireless car watching the relay of lorries shifting the remnants of building material from the site, he noticed that the procession of vehicles seemed to be loaded up with anything that was lying around, including timber. The wood appeared to him to be of fairly good condition so he was curious; he stopped the foreman and asked him where the lorries were transporting the rubbish to.

"We just take it out into the country and burn it. We have to keep the site as clear as possible. Why do you want to know?" the man answered.

"I was going to build a shed in my back garden and I was looking for some old timber," Jock told him.

"What size shed did you intend to make?" the foreman asked.

"Just a small one, about eight by six."

"Where do you live?" the man asked. "I'll drop some in for you."

Jock remembered the last time he had wanted some firewood and the lorry load of boxes had been dumped into the front garden.

"No it doesn't matter, I wouldn't want to put you to any trouble."

The man wouldn't be put off.

"No trouble, you'll be doing me a favour. The lorry would be able to do two trips in the same time as it would have taken him to go out to dump it. I have to clear the site."

As Jock didn't live very far from the new building the man knew it would be easier to drop the stuff there than to pay for a man and a lorry to do an hour's drive. He was insistent, so Jock gave him the address. Before he went in for refreshments he decided to call at home and warn Puggle about the wood coming.

"I asked him for a few bits of wood for a shed and told him just to drop it in the path. I'll take it through when I come in from work."

However, he got a shock when he did finish work, because the front garden was covered by a tremendous pile of timber of all shapes and sizes. Thick plywood in whole sheets, even windows and doors were included. The biggest timbers had been placed on the bottom to lay the other stuff across, this was to protect the flowers and the remainder was neatly laid on the top to a height of about five feet.

'Hell, it's like a timber yard' he said to himself before going inside. Puggle nearly laughed her head off when she saw his expression.

"They didn't even knock. The first time I knew about it was when I looked out for the bairns coming home from school. I nearly died laughing."

He contacted the foreman the following day who said

"Did you get the wood alright? Was it suitable?"

"Well it's more than I expected, how much do I owe you for it?" Jock asked.

"Oh forget it, it would have cost us more to transport it. You saved the company some money, they should be paying you," the man replied.

"It seems an awful lot of wood though, are you that it'll be OK?" Jock didn't want any trouble.

"Of course it will, can you use it? That's the main thing" the man said as he laughed.

"If you have any left I'll get one of the lads to collect it."

"I'll use it alright, if there's any left my neighbours will be glad of it." Jock expected to be busy for several days taking the timber into the back garden, due to the fact that they lived in a terrace and the only way into the back garden, and he didn't relish the idea.

"It's a 'Bob a Job' week you know," said Puggle coming to the rescue. Both of the lads were in the scouts so the following day he saw the entire pack of scouts on the doorstep, waiting for instructions. Jock told them where he required the different types of wood etc. to go. Inside an hour they swarmed round like worker bees and had moved all the wood into the back garden, and no damage to the house in the process. The lads were all paid, cards signed, and away they went looking for some more work.

A beautiful shed was the final result, not only for him but also for several of his neighbours as well. One chap took the remnants, sawed them into small lengths, then chopped them up into firewood, which he sold.

A GOOD JOB

The man who made the firewood was a queer one; canny to talk to; he was a Scotsman. He had five children and owned an old Ford Popular motorcar. How he managed to squeeze his whole family into that car was nothing else but a miracle. Jock used to see him all over the town cleaning windows; doing gardens; mending fences; repairing cars; there seemed no end to the work he would do to make some money. Jock was talking to his next door neighbour as he was putting the finishing touches to the shed.

"You managed to get rid of all the scraps then Jock?" The man was curious, wondering where all the small pieces had gone. Jock told him about the fellow along the street.

"That amazes me," he said," I wonder what he really does for a living?"

"He used to work for a bank but he packed it in to start work at the car factory, he gets more money there."

"Does he still work there then?" asked Jock.

"Yes, he's one of my gang actually. I'm foreman there and he does permanent night work, and do you know, he'll ask me for four hours extra work every night. Mind you when I go round he's finished the work and is sleeping on a pile of old sacks, he sleeps there till knocking off time."

"How can he get four hours extra work and do his normal eight hours and still find time to sleep?" Jock couldn't understand that.

"Well, it's an agreement with the Union, they have decided exactly how much work a man should do in his eight hours. He just gets that extra to do, the work is laid out on the floor for them and whenever they complete their allotted amount then they are finished. Normally the chaps just sit and play cards for over half the night and some of them, like him, go to sleep."

"It sounds like a worker's paradise." Jock was flabbergasted.

"Well they earn very good money but it mustn't be enough for our friend along the street when he has to do odd jobs all day long," the foreman said.

Once a year the little Scotsman would squeeze all his family into the tiny car, they used to travel up to Scotland to his home town, just to visit the family and have a holiday on the cheap.

FIRST HOLIDAY

Jock's first holiday was taken with the whole family making themselves comfortable in a houseboat. An advert appeared in the Police Review, stating that a retired copper had two such boats for hire near the sea. Jock arranged with a friend who had the similarly sized family to spend a couple of weeks on the boats.

At the time they both owned a motorcycle with a sidecar and the kids were crammed into the sidecars and the wives sat on the pillion, the trusty old bikes were on their way, taking both families on their first holiday. All the luggage was piled up on the carriers. Naturally, the weather decided to try and stop them because it started to rain, gently at first and slowly increasing. Jock's motorcycle gear wasn't good enough to prevent the downpour entering. Puggle got into the sidecar with the baby on her knee, at least they were dry, but Jock got wetter and wetter by the second. The rain lashed down and the wind cut through his clothing, even though he crouched behind the windscreen.

Suddenly there was an explosion, loud enough for Jock to hear it over the sound of the wind, he felt the back end going and guessed the horrible truth. A puncture on the rear end, in this weather, damn, damn, damn.

They pulled into the side of the road to examine the damage and found a gash about three inches long in the wall of the tyre. They could mend the tube alright but even with a gaiter placed inside the tyre, it wouldn't take the pressure needed for the back wheel, there was only one thing for it. The tyres had to be changed, the one from the side car had to be used for the back wheel but the trouble was the amount of work needed. The weight had to be removed from the pannier, the wheel had to be taken right off and then the sidecar tyre had to be removed completely, leaving the motorcycle balanced on one wheel and the stand. The rear tyre was patched and put on the sidecar and the good rubber was then placed on the back wheel, then and the chain and all the little bits replaced. Then off they went, everyone dry except the riders who couldn't get any wetter. The heavens opened before they eventually found the two houseboats and got some temporary relief. For the whole fortnight the wind howled and the rain came down.

After ten days the other copper had decided that he had to call it a day, he had been rained off and packed his bags and went home. Jock managed to buy a secondhand tyre for two shillings and sixpence from a local garage. It was very nearly new but the chap at the garage had no further use for it. The holiday was damp, windy, and uncomfortable but it was all they could afford at that time. It was a change and they hoped that the next one would be better.

They had to wait for another five years before they could afford to have another holiday; this time they hired a caravan at Lulworth Cove, two weeks basking in the sun, it was a real Indian summer. These were the only holidays that Jock could afford in all the time he was in the Police Force. Why worry, they had each other and the children, but it would have been nice not to have any financial worries so that they could give the kids some decent holidays.

WAGES

"Can you call at the brewery Jock?" asked the patrolling officer. "They are collecting the pay today and want an escort."

There had been a spate of robberies in the area recently and a lot of people were getting worried. Normally this company contacted a different taxi firm each week, the route taken to the bank was varied each time and they returned a different way, anything for safety. Although this method was good, the owner of the brewery was still worried and had asked the

Police for escort. The extra protection was Jock's car, which had to follow the taxi with the cash.

At two forty-five he stopped at the office of the beer manufacturer and later was discussing the needs of the manager. Everything went smoothly, the cash was picked up and returned to the office, and they escorted the cash into the building to complete their job.

"Drink?" asked the man, laying the money bags down. "You don't mind if I carry on with my work while you drink do you?" He produced two glasses and four bottles of beer.

Quite innocently, Jock agreed that it wouldn't make any difference to them and the cold beer was poured into the glasses and they began to enjoy the afternoon drink, thinking that the chap had some paperwork to do. The man started to carry on with his duties, much to the displeasure of the two coppers who were just about to enjoy a nice quiet drink. The man was testing samples of new beer, a mouthful from each sample, then a gargle around the interior of the mouth, and then the liquid was spat out into a nearby sink.

"Would it be alright if I saved this one for later on?" Jock asked after several such tests, which sounded like a pig eating swill.

"Not at all" the workman said, "There's plenty more there if you want it."

They thanked the man, he was very generous, but they had been put off this particular brand of beverage - and Jock never volunteered for the escort duty again. In fact he only entered these premises once more whilst he was working at that station. The occasion arose when he was on the car during night duty, an alarm had gone off and they were sent to deal with it. The night-watchman was contacted and he showed them the new alarm system; there were invisible rays all over the place, plus pressure pads. Whenever any of the rays were broken or a pad stood on, a light came on the large board in his room. A red light indicated that an alarm had been set off in one of the warehouses, but as they stood looking at the board, another light came on.

"That's queer" the watchman said. "That's the back fence." Another red light flickered, then another.

"Someone is moving through the factory" the employee stated. He traced the line of movement and told Jock which way to go so as to capture the intruder. Following his directions, the crew from the wireless car moved quietly through the warehouses and spotted a shadowy figure creeping along in the dark. They stopped the man and found he was a copper, he had heard the alarm going off and had climbed over the back wall hoping to catch some thieves, he didn't know about the new system. It transpired that the original alarm was due to a case falling down and breaking the ray for a split second. So everyone went back to work and left the watchman to go back to sleep.

CAR CHASE

It had been a fairly quiet night, they hadn't even obtained any drink from the brewery, not that Jock would have appreciated one during the night. They were sitting in the car at the Station, just after they had finished their breakfasts.

"I think I'll go and catch up with the stolen cars," said the wireless operator as he dragged himself out of the car. Just then another car drew up alongside, it was the area car from their sub-station. Albert, the driver, came across and had a few words with Jock before he too went into the front office, leaving his wireless operator in the car talking to Jock. They each sat in their own cars, smoking and chatting through the open windows and, as always, one ear was reserved for the wireless.

"Hang on Tom, I think that one is coming our way. Nip out and get the others," said Jock suddenly.

Shortly afterwards, Albert and the wireless operators returned and Jock explained what he had heard over the wireless. A County Force was having trouble with a bandit car, a burglary had taken place but the thieves were disturbed and were being chased by the Police. Several roadblocks had been set up but each time the vehicle had rammed them; coppers had been injured and a police car was now in pursuit. The man was wanting assistance but the County Force couldn't help. The chase was heading towards the Big City and the police car would soon be out of wireless contact. It was requested by the Information Room that some other wireless car should try and make contact so as to keep the vehicles in wireless contact. Jock considered that the route the bandit's car was taking would bring them towards them - towards a 'Y' junction.

"You take the top road Albert and we'll cover the bottom one." The two area cars sped out of the yard and each moved towards the road they were going to cover. The streets were deserted, market traffic hadn't started to move yet and it was too early for the morning shifts to be out. Jock built up his speed as he made towards the junction where he anticipated the bandit would be. Travelling at about seventy miles an hour, he saw the first car coming round a bend in the road, closely followed by another.

"There they are" he said to his operator and explained that he would have to inform the other police cars of the sighting. "Slide down in your seat a bit and keep the handset in your hand."

He swung the car across the road, switched his lights on full and drove alongside the kerb on the wrong side of the road, straight towards the speeding bandit. At first it looked as though the other car wasn't going to move, the cars drew nearer and nearer, then at the last second the driver of the other vehicle slowed down and swung his vehicle away from Jock. As soon as the bandit's car cut across the road, Jock switched his lights down, he didn't want to blind the copper driving the police car, who also swung across the road after the thieves. Once the two cars had passed him, Jock braked, swung his car into a skid and turned it to face the way he had just come, even as he was skidding round he was changing gear, down into bottom, ready for some quick acceleration.

"Right, now let's see what he can do. Have you ever been on a chase before young un?" he asked his operator. The lad acknowledged the fact that he hadn't. "Right, as I told you before, slide down in your seat and rest your head against the back of the seat. If we stop suddenly you won't get whiplash or a broken neck. Knees up against the dash and keep the handset in your hand. Now get through to Control Room and ask for car to car, tell them that we are following the bandit car, and require the car-to-car communication to keep other cars up to date. Just repeat everything I tell you and you'll be alright. We always inform them of our speed, direction, junctions approaching and the ones we pass. This allows the other cars to assess exactly where they can go, or whether they are too far away to do anything. OK?"

"What about me?" a plaintiff voice came from the back of the car and Jock took a quick glance at the owner of the voice.

"How the hell did you get here?"

It was the section sergeant who had mentioned that he would love to be on a real chase with Jock.

"When they came running out of the office, I came with them" he said.

"Well, you're here now but I could have done without you. Your extra weight makes a bit of difference in the speed of the car. However, you'll have to do the same as the operator, rest your head against the back of the seat, that'll save you getting a broken neck, and wedge your knees against the back of the seat to stop you being thrown forward if we hit anything hard."

The wireless operator had already taken up his position and had got the air open so that every car in the Big City would know exactly what was going on. A large junction loomed up ahead just as Jock was building up his speed. It was a staggered junction and to avoid having to slow down and steer through it, he moved over to the right hand side of the road where he had good vision straight along and then shot past the crossroads at ninety miles an hour. The information was spoken by him and repeated by the operator. Slowly they began to close the gap between the other police car and the bandit was in sight. Junction after junction was passed, crossroads and intersections were safely negotiated. The lad on the wireless did as he was told; he kept cool; calm and collected. Jock glanced at him 'Not a bad lad on the wireless, considering the way things are going' he thought. Sometimes wireless chaps got all excited when they were in a chase and started shouting and often began to swear over the air. The results were terrible, words were indistinct and the screeching made one cover the ears.

Each message was related, word for word, as Jock had dictated over the air; speed, distance to next junction, and their position in relation to the other cars. A good straight stretch of road ahead but it was obvious that the County car couldn't catch up with the bandit

"I'm going to signal the other car to let me past," Jock said, as the other two cars were running along the centre of the road. A flash on the lights, which was quickly acknowledged by the County man, he eased his car into the side and Jock slammed his foot further down and swished past the other car. The convoy of cars screamed past the Police Station at over one hundred miles an hour and the office staff all stood on the front steps to witness the spectacle.

"He's going straight down, good," Jock muttered, more to himself than anyone else.

"What's the speed?"

"Hundred and twelve," came a plaintiff voice, barely audible. It had been the first time the wireless operator had looked at the speedo.

"Christ, what did you want to know the speed for?"

"The last time I had the Skipper in the car he said he wanted to go on a chase with me, he kept asking me how fast I had been going, it was only to satisfy his curiosity." He looked in his mirror to see if the Sergeant was sitting up as he couldn't see him.

"Are you alright Skipper?" he asked.

A grunt came from the back, apparently the Sergeant was still there.

"We're going to put him off the road at the first chance but first, we'll give him the chance to stop. As soon as we get alongside, signal him to stop but don't try to open your window because we'll be blown out with the blast." Every time Jock tried to move alongside the bandit car the driver swerved towards him in an attempt to push the police car off the road.

"He's trying to force us off the road. We are going to stop him." The wireless operator repeated the message.

Jock waited until the time was right and then using full power he slid the police car close up to the other vehicle. The driver looked when he saw that the copper car was close that he couldn't swing his wheel at all, there was no way that he could force the police vehicle off the road. Jock took a quick glance.

"There are two of them in the car," he said. He moved his car further forward, checking the right moment; he waited until his back wheel was level with the front wheel of the bandit car and then acted.

Wheel to wheel, a quick flick of his steering wheel to the left and then back again at once to the right was enough to swing the back of his car over a few inches. That few inches was just enough to hit the wheel of the other car. It knocked the steering wheel from the driver's hands; he lost control and was unable to steer the vehicle which was spinning round and round.

Jock had anticipated his car going into a skid after the contact and had automatically countered by adjusting his steering. The Police Car slid sideways along the road, with Jock constantly watching for oncoming traffic whilst at the same time observing the actions of the bandit car as the driver struggled with the steering wheel.

"I think he's going to hit that side turning," he said suddenly. He allowed his car to move round slightly so that he was travelling backwards in a straight line; he gently applied his brakes to slow down but when he noticed that the thieves vehicle was going to hit a low wall, he applied his brakes and stopped his car. He selected a low gear and was moving towards the crash before the car had come to a halt.

The Police Car stopped alongside the crashed vehicle and the Sergeant jumped out, accompanied by the wireless operator. They grabbed the passenger as he tumbled out of the wreck, the driver got away and ran down the side street. Jock swerved his car round the stationary vehicle and followed him. The crook ran into a garden, hoping he had not been seen, but was very much surprised when he felt a hand on his collar as he crouched under a hedge.

"You're nicked, bonny lad" Jock said.

He put the man into his car and returned to the scene of the incident. As he arrived, the County Police Car screeched to a halt, closely followed by six other wireless cars who had been monitoring the chase. They had been trying to get into position to stop the bandit if he turned off in their direction. The other prisoner was also laid to rest with his mate and Jock went to meet the Traffic Sergeant who had arrived just then.

"I heard it over the wireless, Jock so I tagged along. I knew I would be needed. Any damage to your car?" They went to examine the Police Car to ensure that there was no damage done. "I heard you say that he was trying to put you off the road, he came off worse didn't he?" The skipper grinned, he was becoming used to Jock's brushes with the villains who would not stop for a copper; they always seemed to come off worse. As they were talking, a stranger came along and spoke to Jock. It was the driver of the County Car.

"Were you the driver of that Police Car?"

The Traffic Sergeant stopped writing on his pad and looked up at the man.

"Why, did he do something wrong?" he asked.

"No Sergeant," the chap appeared to be embarrassed at the question, "He didn't do anything wrong as far as I was concerned. We chased that bloke all the way from his last crash into your area, I couldn't get anywhere near him, then this officer came along like a bat out of hell. He passed me as if I was standing still. They tried to put him off the road a few times but I haven't seen driving like it in all my service, he was great."

"Good, you are a witness then," the Skipper said. "Regards his driving, he is a Class One driver, there are no better."

"We're going to the Nick with the prisoners, so if you'll just follow me I'll show you where it is," Jock turned to the County copper.

The other patrol cars had dispersed, each returning to their own respective stations, the County Car and the Traffic Sergeant went with Jock to the nearest Police Station. The Station Sergeant greeted them as they entered.

"Well done Jock, we were listening on the wireless, another couple of bodies for you."

"No Skipper, give these to the County blokes," Jock replied. The copper from the Constabulary couldn't believe his ears.

"I can't do that, you stopped them and arrested them, they have done warehouse breaking, jumped a few road blocks and injured a lot of coppers."

"So, the crimes were committed on your ground, the coppers who were injured were from your Force, the accidents at the road blocks were on your ground, they were your cars that were damaged. These two chaps will have to go to your Court, so why shouldn't you charge them? I don't want to spend a full day visiting your Court and I don't need the arrests. I don't think the Serg or the wireless operator would want them either."

His observations were confirmed by his two passengers, neither relished a long journey and loss of sleep just because of two villains. The discussion was broken by the Station Sergeant.

"Telephone for you Jock, it's Control Room."

That call was the first of many to follow in a very short space of time. The Officer in Charge of Control Room had called to congratulate the crew on the arrests and the correct use of the wireless. The Officer in Charge of the County Force also telephoned and thanked them. The commendations came in thick and fast and even collected from the Chief Constable of the County and the Commissioner of Police, Station Superintendent and Divisional Commanders also sent their messages to the crew of the car.

"That is another brown patch on the back seat Jock," the Sergeant said later. "I must have filled my trousers a dozen times. Tell me though, we were travelling at seventy miles an hour in one direction and they were driving at about seventy miles an hour going the opposite way. We were both on the same side of the road, what would have happened if he had not slowed down and swerved to miss us?"

"Hit him, Skipper," Jock said tersely.

"Shit, how did you know he would swerve?" the man persisted.

"He'd been chased a long time, he was under strain, he had jumped several road blocks, he had hit some coppers, he had a load of stolen gear on board and he didn't want to stop to get nicked. Therefore, he was bound to try and avoid a crash which would result in him being caught. At least that's what I thought," was the reply.

"Well, what about the time you hit him, he went into a skid? You could have finished off doing the same as him," the Sergeant remarked. "After all, we were doing about one hundred and twenty when we hit him."

"He hit me, Skip, don't you remember and after all, we didn't crash, did we?"

"Well, I always said that I wanted to go on a real chase with you, now I have and believe me, I kept shitting my pants."

"Are you sure Skip? I thought you always smelt like that." Jock laughed. He tried to get rid of the Sergeant but the man clung like a leech, whenever he was on the same relief as Jock he would occupy the back seat of the wireless car. On this occasion, they drove sedately back to the nearest nick to enjoy a cup of tea. The Sergeant disappeared into the front office to give his version of the marvellous ride he had just enjoyed.

RIDE HIM COWBOY

They didn't get time to enjoy their cuppa before another call came across the ether for them to deal with.

"Cattle straying. Round them up and pen them down for the night." Wasn't a normal request which was given to a Police Car. As it so happened, these particular creatures were cows and they were only about half a mile away from the Station, the animals were just grazing on the main road, at least they would have given that appearance if there had been any grass available. A dozen hefty cows trotting along the main road in the middle of the night would give anyone a heart attack, or some drunk could think he had a dose of White Elephants.

"It's a bloody good job we didn't meet them when we were on the chase Jock" his mate exclaimed. "

Yeh, I think we should head them up to the common, it will only take ten minutes, it's off our ground but there is nowhere else nearby that will accommodate them."

As the car moved up towards them, the leaders began to break into a trot, quickly followed by the rest of the herd.

"We don't want to scare them, they could turn off down any of the side streets and then we'll be in trouble." Jock considered the problems they would face if the cattle did get into the small side streets. "Look, I'll shoot off down the street and get to the next junction before them and stop them going down it. Once they get passed, I'll try and get to the next street before they do."

So it was arranged, the wireless operator began his first lessons as a cowhand, moving slowly along behind cows, uttering a quiet 'Gerralong you sod' every now and again. In the meanwhile, Jock was engaged driving like blazes. He had to drive the full length of two streets and be in position waiting for the animals, which only had a short distance to travel in comparison. Eventually, they approached the vicinity of the common where they hoped to dump the creatures but there was an extra large complicated junction to be negotiated before the grass was reached so Jock had to call up for another car to assist.

The calls came thick and fast, other wireless operators were quick on the mark as they considered the situation. The ribald remarks included the usual, 'Get along little doggy, Ride him Cowboy' and 'There's rustlers in them thar hills'. With the assistance of the other two coppers from the other car they managed to get the cattle bedded down for the night and they all returned to their respective patrols.

LAYABOUT

Early days came along, another one of these killer shifts, getting out of bed in the middle of the night and cycling to work still half asleep. All his service Jock thought that he would never get used to those hours. He was posted van driver so he would try and get forty winks in the drivers' room, he didn't feel up to scratch owing to a nagging pain he had endured for some days. He spoke to the spare driver about it, the man just laughed.

"After a day off?" he asked, querying whether Jock was going on the sick.

"I didn't want to but this pain is worse than ever. I think I'll see the quack about it and confirm if my suspicions are correct."

"What do you think it is then?" his mate asked. "Too much beer?"

"I'm going sick Serg." he announced as he went into the front office at nine o'clock, leaving the other driver laughing her head off.

"Righto Jock, having a day off?" the Skipper replied. Nobody seemed to take Jock serious.

"No, I've got appendicitis."

"Righto, if you say so. I'll see you tomorrow," said the Station Sergeant.

Jock mounted his old trusty steed and rode slowly home. As he was going past the local paper shop he heard a cheery call.

"Morning, changed your transport?" It was his own doctor.

"Morning Doc, I was just coming to see you," he replied as he dismounted and asked the medical man, "Why does everyone laugh when I tell them that I have appendicitis?"

"Is that what you have? Well then you'd better come in so that I can have a look," the Doctor replied with a smile on his face.

The surgery was close by and very shortly afterwards Jock was instructed to go home and prepare for the ambulance which the Doctor was ordering for him. Puggle looked surprised when he entered the house.

"Have you taken time off?" but when Jock informed her that he was going to hospital for appendicitis, she laughed. It was only when he packed his pyjamas and the ambulance arrived at the door that she believed him.

"It's just a touch of wind." The Casualty Doctor was dubious about Jock's diagnosis.

When Jock suggested that he should go home, the man told him he would have to be admitted so that the Doctor could examine him.

"I thought you were a doctor," Jock said in some surprise. "The specialist will be coming on his rounds shortly, he's the one who will decide."

Jock was allocated a bed and he had just made himself comfortable when the great man and his retinue arrived. The procession made its way slowly round the ward till they stopped at Jock's bed.

"Ah, this is the man who thinks he has appendicitis. Let's have a look then," he said as he pushed his finger in at the spot indicated by the patient. Having been reassured that the pressure did not have any effect, he whipped it away quickly.

"That hurt?" he asked as Jock nearly hit the ceiling. "We'll have to operate at once." Jock gratified him by telling him that he had eaten no breakfast, so there was no danger of his breakfast being shared between the staff later on.

"Can I 'phone the wife?" he asked the Sister who was tagging along behind the crowd.

"Yes, but don't be long," he was told.

Jock grabbed his dressing gown and crept past the group of doctors to make his call.

"Have you told them at work yet?" Puggle asked.

"Not yet, I'll have to get some more change. Bye." Jock hung up and headed back to his ward where the surgeon and the trainees were still waiting but there was panic stations at his bedside. Two porters stood with a nurse, they were looking for the patient who had to be operated on urgently.

"Come on, they're waiting for you in the theatre," the nurse informed him. Jock was pushed onto the stretcher and was sitting up putting the gown on ready for surgery as they pushed him past the doctors.

"I'll see you in a minute," said the specialist, looking round.

A mad rush along the corridors followed, with Jock trying to pull the large white stockings on and at the same time fit the hat on his head. He was eventually trundled into a room where everyone was dressed in green.

"We haven't had time to give him a prelim," the nurse said as she handed the file across.

"We've been waiting for you," the man said as he glanced at the papers. "I'll just give you a small injection, you'll only feel a little prick and when you wake up, it will all be over."

The required injection was soon given but Jock did not pass quietly into slumberland as was anticipated, he was engaged in lively conversation with the doctor and the nurse for some time. Eventually, the door leading to the next room opened, which was as Jock could see, the operating theatre, and another man in green stuck his head out saying

"What's wrong, we're waiting."

The doctor who had injected Jock was frankly amazed at his resistance to the attempts to put him to sleep.

"I don't know, he just will not go off." The nurse told Jock that he should have been asleep and in the operating room.

"You shouldn't fight it, your eyes should be closed now."

That was the last thing that Jock heard, he was operated on within an hour of seeing his own doctor and started his week's rest in hospital. The following day when the specialist came on his rounds, he stopped beside the bed.

"Feeling better? You should be after getting rid of that thing. You were a lucky chap, we just caught it in time." He turned to the Sister and informed her that Jock could get up and sit in the Day Room.

As the procession moved onto the next bed, Jock was ordered to get up and get dressed, and make his way to the Day Room. His mind was in a daze, time had gone but as far as he knew it was only a few hours since he had been admitted, and now he had to get up straight after an operation. The nurse pulled the curtains around his bed so that he could get rid of the open backed gown and climb into his pyjamas. He clung tightly onto the dressings with both hands as though his whole inside would fall out. Sliding his feet over the side of the bed he rolled over and landed on his feet in a crouched position; he had to straighten up and slowly, still maintaining pressure upon the vital spot, he eased his body upright. At last he stood straight and felt pleased with his performance, until he realised that his locker was on the other side of the bed and that was where his clothes were!

A long, slow, painful movement began as he moved one foot a few inches and then the other. Slowly but surely he shuffled his way to the locker for his pyjamas. Another problem faced him wen he reached his goal; he had to bend down and open the door. This was absolutely impossible, he thought, but when the garments were gathered together and placed on the bed, he breathed a sigh of relief, but then the shock of the next move struck him. How could he bend down and pull the trousers on and then fasten them with one hand? The pains grabbed at his torn muscles as he struggled to dress but he won, then after succeeding to lever his dressing gown on he relaxed because now all he had to do was complete the last hurdle and head for the Day Room.

One inch at a time with each foot, both hands in his dressing gown pockets, pressing hard on the stomach muscles, he eased his way along the ward. The distance never seemed to get any shorter, the pain never eased, but then at last he faced the door. He was considering which hand to remove from his torn muscles when the nurse came along.

"Come along, it's dinner time, you'll have to hurry back to your bed."

Bloody hell, it had taken him over two hours to put his pyjamas on and walk a few yards. Now, the return trip started, the dinner trolley passed him before he was half way; he felt like asking for a lift as they were travelling faster than he was. The meal was waiting for him when he arrived at the bed, it was cold. His remaining strength was needed to consume the meal, before he stretched out on top of the bed for the afternoon nap. The following week soon passed and he was discharged. He lugged his suitcase along to the bus stop, changed buses three times, and then had a full mile to walk home. That was the decider because he knew he wasn't fit, he was glad to get out of bed but he knew he couldn't face the copper's life for some time. This was confirmed by his doctor the next day.

"It will be at least three months before you are back at work, in the meantime you are to get as much walking done as possible."

The following weeks produced miles of perambulations; just going for the morning paper meant a three mile walk, right round the outside of the local park. Several times the doctor saw him stepping out and stopped his car to take him home.

"I told you to get some walking in to strengthen your stomach muscles, but I didn't expect you to walk nearly as fast as I drive."

After a couple of months Jock felt that he should be back at work and he began to pester the medical advisor, asking to be returned to duty; after several requests the doctor gave in.

"Only if it's on light duties. I don't want you to start driving or getting involved in any fights because you can still burst the inside stitches."

Jock agreed to look after the weakened part of his anatomy as much as he could, stating that if he went on driving duties he would be spending the first month as spare driver, or on van duties. And so ended his long holiday and he went off to organise his return to work.

CHAPTER TWELVE

BACK TO WORK

BACK TO WORK

His first tour of duty was, as he anticipated, working as the spare driver so whenever anyone wanted transport, he was the dogsbody. Nothing very energetic about that job, he just rested his guts and then was back on the wireless car once more; his mates were glad to have him behind the wheel again. The first call came after a few minutes.

"Accident." Experience had taught him that when a call came in regarding an accident, it wasn't just a slight bump. Drivers tended to exchange names and addresses only if the cars were damaged, if it was a serious incident and anyone was injured, then they shouted for the coppers.

Arrival at the scene proved this to be case. However, they saw an ambulance parked on the offside of the road, just past the traffic lights. The front of the vehicle was actually on the pavement. Under the ambulance they saw a motorcycle and, tangled up with the wreckage, was the rider of the machine. The driver of the ambulance was sitting in his seat, whilst his mate stood beside the crashed vehicle.

"How the hell did this happen?" Jock asked the driver's mate.

"God knows Guv. We were going on a call, I saw the lights coming up and saw that they were on red, he made no attempt to stop. I shouted at him to watch the lights but he didn't even touch the brakes; the lad came from the right and we hit him in the middle of the junction."

As the man was giving his statement Jock had laid flat on the ground so that he could examine the mess underneath and try to work out how to get the injured man out. He was considering whether he could get him free without calling the Fire Brigade out. He looked up at the ambulance man.

"Did you say you were going on a call when this happened? Have you informed your Control about this?" The man admitted that he had not done so, someone else had called for the Police.

"I got straight out to see if I could help this chap," was his excuse.

"OK, don't worry, we'll see to it." Jock shouted for his mate and when Mike came across he asked him to call another ambulance for the motor cyclist, and also to get an ambulance to deal with the incident that the damaged vehicle was going to. He indicated that the Supervisor of the Ambulance Service should be informed so that he could attend because one of his own cars was involved. As his requests were being relayed Jock slid, face down, underneath the ambulance to examine the injured party; he wasn't conscious but had a steady pulse and there was quite a lot of blood around which seemed to be coming from the rider's leg.

"Have you got a jack in your kit?" he asked the uniformed attendant. Jock went to his own car and brought his own jack and slid back under the ambulance, the other jack was produced by the ambulance man.

"Will you check that your handbrake is on please?" Jock asked, as he took the second jack. Once he had been assured that the heavy vehicle would not run away when he lifted it up, he placed one of the jacks under the front axle and adjusted it, before he started to pump it up. The ambulance man crawled in beside him.

"You'll get your uniform dirty under here mate," said Jock. As the man was insisting upon helping, he told him to take his own jack to the other side of the motorcycle and start pumping it up. As the ambulance began to lift, Jock slithered under the axle and attempted to move the machine but it was resting on the rider and jamming against the exhaust. He pushed his way out and asked Mike to find a rope.

"The two rope will do Mike."

He checked that the ambulance man had pumped his jack up as far as he could and then went back under the van; he ensured that there was enough clearance to haul the cycle out once it had been lifted off the injured man. The rope was passed underneath and he fastened it to the front wheel.

"Will I pull now Jock?" asked Mike.

"Hell no, you'll pull his bloody leg off, it's just hanging on now," Jock shouted back. He asked the ambulance chap if he had any levers in his tool kit and was informed that there were two tyre levers which could do. Jock thought of them and said, "We'll need something else to act as a lever." He pondered for a while and then crawled out from under the wreck and, going straight to his own car he picked up the large black first-aid box and took it back to the motorcycle.

Mike looked at him in astonishment, wondering why he was taking the box underneath.

"You aren't going to put splints on him under there are you?"

"Silly sod, I can hardly move under the chassis," Jock laughed as he eased the large box as close as possible to the motorcycle to use it as a levering point. The bars were put under the bike and pushed down over the box, on the other side the ambulance man was watching closely. Slowly, the frame was lifted; Jock was lying on his stomach and, pressing hard with his arms he slowly lifted the bike. There was a terrific strain on his arms when he had forced the bike up as far as it would go and gritting his teeth, he asked the ambulance man if the cycle was clear of the injured man. Once he had been assured that it would be safe enough to move the machine he shouted to Mike

"Pull, Mike." The reactions were automatic and the battered remains of the motorcycle was hauled out from underneath. As it was withdrawn, Jock saw the shattered remains of the cyclist's leg and he guessed that the pelvis was injured as well. The man couldn't be dragged out without splinters on.

"I think we'll have to treat him for a broken spine as well as his legs, what do you think?" Jock was speaking to the ambulance man, who occupied the space under the vehicle with him.

"I think you know what you're doing without my help," the man answered. "I'll get some splints out of the back."

"No need, we have some here," Jock said as he opened his first-aid box and took out the bundles of interlocking splints. Between them, two experienced men worked together, placing the splints in place and then fastening them.

"At least you won't feel anything" Jock said to the still unconscious motorcyclist.

Eventually, the injured man was ready to be moved. Jock shouted out to his mate to push the stretcher underneath. He didn't have to shout really, because Mike was on his hands and knees at the front of the vehicle, watching the first-aid work, and the stretcher was ready to slide under. There was no room to lift the man on, even if they could, so as they were restricted with the space they started to ease the man onto the stretcher, feet first. Mike slowly pushed the stretcher forwards and, at the same time, Jock and the ambulance man eased him up onto the canvas until the motorcyclist was clear of the ground.

"Right Mike, ease him out, slowl,y" said Jock as he watched carefully to make sure the body did not catch on the underside of the ambulance. "Right, let's get out of here and get some work done," said Jock once it was clear.

He collected his gear and returned them to his car.

"First time I've used a first-aid box when it was closed" he said to Mike.

The driver was still sitting in his seat as they began to take the required measurements for the accident report. The injured man's name was in his wallet, so all that remained was for another vehicle to arrive and remove the casualty to hospital. The driver seemed to have recovered enough to be questioned by the time his supervisor arrived in another ambulance; at the same moment, another ambulance came on the scene, much to be expected as they were from the same station. A third one passed them on the way to the incident which had been earmarked for the first one; four ambulances being used at the same time because of one accident. Arrangements were made for the removal of the cycle. Witnesses were obtained and the ambulance service made its own arrangements for the removal of their own vehicle. That was another call completed.

"We can write it up after breakfast Mike, "better let them know we're available for action again. We can drop the name and address of the motorcyclist into the nick so his relatives can be informed."

BABYSITTING AGAIN

When they were at the station getting washed, Jock was requested to see the Inspector before he went out again.

"Ah, yes, Jock" the Inspector replied to his demand. "I want you to take the Sergeant out with you."

"That's nothing unusual Guv, they're always jumping in the back" Jock answered. "They're always trying to scrounge a ride these days."

"I know Jock, but this one is different - he's a bit new. He's just been made up and I want you to keep your eye on him and help him out. See that he doesn't get into trouble."

"Righto Guv, I'll see to it" Jock replied. So, another babysitting job started.

Before long they heard an urgent request for any vehicle on call to attend an accident. Apparently the car that covered that area was busy and the vehicle on the adjacent beat who would normally do the call was engaged. It was some distance from their station and as no other car responded to the request.

"We'll do it Mike," said Jock.

As they approached the location of the accident they were faced with a traffic jam, the roads were really blocked with cars. Jock drove along the offside of the traffic so he could get to the cause of the holdup; he stopped the car at the junction just before the scene of the accident.

"Mike, turn all the traffic up that side street so as to bypass this part, you can turn these others back as well," he said as he indicated the few cars that had gone past the junction. "When you've got them moving, see if you can get some pedestrian who is feeling like doing some work and he can take over the control of the traffic, and this will let you came along to give me a hand."

Jock drove along the pavement, forced the gawking pedestrians out of the way, and once the past the pile of cars he pulled back onto the road and said to the Sergeant.

"Will you get all those cars to turn round and go along that next street. That will take them along to the next junction where Mike is. Start with the ones nearest the accident and swing them round, the rest will follow. Then, if you can get someone else to direct traffic, come back and see me. I'll have a look at this lot."

It only took him a few seconds to round round the jumble of crashed cars to get some idea of the injuries and the number of people involved. He wasted no time to check each individual case, all he wanted to know was how many were hurt and, if possible, the extent of the injuries. As soon as he had gleaned this information he raced back to his car and called an urgent request for at least seven ambulances because there were fourteen injured people that he had counted and some of them looked serious.

He informed control that the road was completely blocked and that traffic diversions were in operation, he also asked for breakdown vehicles to be sent to clear the wrecks. This road was the main road from the city and the traffic was very heavy. As he spoke on the wireless he saw that the skipper had managed to get the traffic moving so he called to a member of the public who was standing gaping at the accident.

"Can you nip along there and ask that sergeant to come back here, you can take over directing the traffic if you want to." The man, newly promoted to point duty, ran off to deliver his message. Jock was in the first car attending to one of the more serious cases when the Sergeant came along.

"Right Sergeant, nip along there and get Mike, tell him to get a move on and get back here. Chop, chop, now Serg." The young skipper did as he was requested and returned shortly afterwards with Mike.

"Work together Mike, check each car, find all the serious cases and treat them. Don't worry about cuts and broken limbs or crush cases yet. Deal with haemorrhage, heart cases, or anyone in danger of fire from leaking fuel." Although Mike was a little younger than the Sergeant, he'd had more experience with road accidents whilst he had been with Jock.

"What about the position of the vehicles, how the accident was caused, and the drivers' statements?" the Sergeant asked.

Jock didn't stop working on his patient during the whole of the conversation and he didn't stop even now.

"Sergeant, I've told you what to do, now get on with it." The tone of his voice made even Mike jump, he'd never heard Jock speak to anyone like that before. The skipper realised that there wasn't time to argue or pull rank as he was new to this sort of thing.

Jock ignored the man and concentrated on his hospital case, once he was satisfied with the injured person's condition, he called a woman over from the pavement. The elderly lady came across at his request.

"Listen ducks, just stay with him, talk to him and just try to give him a bit of comfort. There's nothing else you have to do."

Leaving them together, he moved on to the rest of the occupants of the car. One had gone straight through the windscreen of the car, his face was a multitude of cuts, 'slashed to pieces' as some may term it, and he was unconscious. There was a very deep cut across the forehead which was bleeding steadily. Jock soon placed a pad over it and pulled it tight and then eased the man out of the broken glass and laid him alongside the other one.

"There you are ducks, you have two now, this one will not give you any trouble either."

The other two passengers of the car had broken limbs but were wide awake, groaning and complaining with pain. He saw that they had minor cuts but nothing serious and he couldn't waste precious bandages on them.

"Just sit where you are, don't try to move for a few minutes and you'll be alright. I'll be back to see to you in a few minutes." He left them complaining and moved on to the next car which was a taxi, the driver was unconscious, face and leg injuries, and quite possibly the chest had been injured. He was breathing OK and there were no signs of blood coming from the mouth or ears. Jock couldn't see any other signs of excessive bleeding. He decided that he could wait for the ambulances to arrive and turned his attention to the two female passengers trapped in the back seat. They were shaken up and suffered from cuts and bruises, and again he considered that bandages could be used to better causes and told them to remain in the cab until the ambulances arrived.

His next stop was a horse and cart, the driver had been thrown off and had landed on his head by the look of him. The Sergeant and Mike must have gone straight past him as he lay amongst the pile of scrap metal which he had been carrying. A quick examination proved that he had broken his right arm, it was a Smith's fracture, the wrist had shattered and the bone protruded from the joint. Blood was coming from one of his ears and this was what had given Jock the idea that he had a fractured skull. Jock eased him out and laid him on his side in the 'prone' position, because of the bleeding, a pad was then placed round his exposed bone in an attempt to keep it as clean as possible. He then applied a short splint to prevent the hand from flapping around and causing more damage.

His next problem was the horse near to where he was standing, it was trapped in the shafts and kicking violently to free itself from the restriction. He took his pocket-knife out and cut the traces which held it then, grabbing hold of the bridle, he tugged and assisted the animal to struggle free of the wreckage. It scrambled to its feet and stood there, terrified and shivering, 'poor old bugger' Jock muttered as he examined the creature. He was pleased to find no sign of any injury so he led it to the pavement and fastened it to a lamp-post; here it would find plenty of people who would talk to it and find something for it to eat. He then turned his attention to the fourth vehicle which looked in a proper mess, both sides were crumpled and very little glass was left in the windows. Five passengers were trapped inside and the doors would have to be forced to get them out. He put his head inside and asked a totally senseless question, just for the sake of talking to them and getting some reaction.

"Are you alright in here?" the stink of booze met his nostrils,

The question provoked an immediate response, the language was blue as the company and they all answered in unison.

"Bloody comic are you? What the hell do you think we're all doing in here, playing with one another?"

"We are all cut to pieces," the driver told him.

It was obvious that they had all been cut, what would they expect, with all that glass flying around.

"Right Guv, we'll get you out as soon as we can," said Jock having made sure that none of the injuries was serious.

As they only had minor injuries, he left them and moved on to the next car where Mike and the skipper were trying to extract a female from the wreckage.

"Broken back I think Jock," said Mike glancing up.

"Better safe than sorry Mike, how about the other one?" indicating the other woman in the car.

"Don't know yet but she has been talking to us," said Mike as he carried on with the job he was doing.

Jock went round to the passengers side and asked the girl how she was feeling and if she had tried to move. He was guessing that she would be trapped as well as her friend.

"Can you move at all?" he asked.

"I really don't know, I haven't tried, my legs hurt a bit," she answered.

"As soon as we've finished with your friend, we'll get you out and have a look at them," Jock promised her. She smiled bravely as she turned her head to watch Mike and the Sergeant who were in the process of getting her friend out of the car.

Jock began to examine the metal which was wrapped around the front of the passenger. It was going to be a harder job getting her out than her mate; the whole body of the vehicle had been pushed back and the bulkhead was resting against her legs, jamming them against the seat. The door was crumpled and refused to open.

Jock reached across her and removed the keys from the dashboard and went to the boot, hoping to find something that would assist him to get her free. He was in luck, a couple of iron bars and two tyre levers were amongst the tools stored there. He started work on the door and soon made short shift of it, very soon he had it ripped off.

As he worked he thought to himself about the girls legs, 'bound to be some bones broken, I'll have to get some splints for them'. He left the girl to get some first-aid gear from his own vehicle as the first ambulance arrived. Jock stopped him.

"Up on the pavement and push that bloody nosey bunch out of the way. There are two at the other side waiting for you."

The driver didn't question his orders and just mounted the pavement and drove straight through the gaping throngs, they scattered and cleared out of the way. He stopped beside the police car and Jock indicated where the injured people were.

"Thanks a lot Missus," he said to the woman who had sat with the first casualty.

"They'll be alright now." He collected his first-aid box from the car and headed back towards the trapped woman. Another ambulance came along and Jock shouted for the driver to drive along the pavement to where the other injured were.

"The driver of the horse and cart and the taxi driver are waiting for you," he said.

Mike and the skipper had finished their jobs when he reached them.

"Serg, we've got four away to hospital but when the rest of the ambulances arrive they'll need to know where the bodies are. Will you see to this, see that all the injured are removed, take the most serious ones first." He pointed out where the people were and indicated the car with the drunks in it.

"There are five of them in there, they are trapped but only have minor injuries. Could you see if you can get the doors open for them?" He turned to Mike and asked him if he would tend to the man in the last vehicle.

"I don't think he's hurt much, if he isn't then just leave him and give me a hand."

Jock pulled the driver's seat out of the car so that he could get inside beside the trapped lady, he then noticed that the passenger seat had been set forward for a small person so it would move back a wee bit.

"We'll try to move your seat back a bit so as to ease the pressure on your legs" he told her but the seat refused to slide backwards so he got the tyre levers on the go. He heaved and strained and pulled but the release catch didn't work. More pressure was applied under the slide, a slight movement but still the bolts held.

"Cor Miss, you'll have to do a bit of slimming. You must weigh a ton!" he said to the girl and laughed. "I just can't shift you."

He knew that the slightest movement would be hell for the girl if the bones were broken and started to grate together. "I'll lift you this time" and he put the iron bars under the seat frame. He lay on the ground outside the car and put both his feet against the bar; he forced his legs straight, sweat ran down his face and then suddenly there was a sharp crack, the resistance had gone. He was just getting up when Mike returned.

"He'll be OK Jock, what can I do?" said Mike as he looked at the girl.

"A couple of splints and straps. Once we get the seat loose we can put the splints on between the legs and fasten them together before we try to move her," Jock explained. "Make the splints at a fixed angle so that the knees won't bend." He went round to the other side of the car and got inside; he now had to force the other two bolts but he couldn't lay down to do it this time. He pushed the iron bar under the seat frame and, bent double, exerted all his power trying to lift the dead weight. The strain was terrible, more so when one looked at the awkward position he was standing in. He stretched his muscles to the limit but the reward was sweet when the bolts eventually snapped.

"Oh my legs," the girl suddenly screamed, as the pressure was taken off them and the blood started to pump its way around once more.

"Right Mike" and Jock knelt down beside the girl who had settled down slightly after the initial shock of pain. "We'll be fiddling around for a bit so don't get embarrassed."

"I don't see why I should be embarrassed, you've had your hand up my skirt already" she said and she actually laughed.

This statement was true because when Jock and Mike had fitted the splints on they had to be placed between the legs and the straps had to be passed from one side to the other and pulled tight. This had resulted in her legs being fastened tightly together and her skirt was nearly round her neck.

"Right lassie. I am now going to try and move your seat backwards, we'll then turn it and get your legs out of the door first." Jock made it sound easy but it didn't work that way at all.

He climbed over into the back seat and even though he pulled the seat back as far as it would go, he couldn't shift the legs because they were well and truly jammed under the dashboard. There was no way to shift them, even though the whole of the dash was removed.

" Try and pull the seat to the other side of the car," a good idea of Mike's but that didn't work because of the handbrake and gear lever.

"I think we'll have to take the roof off, or you can live here," Jock told the girl. He asked her if her legs were hurting.

"No" she answered. "It's not too bad sitting here." Anyone would believe that she was really enjoying it, being the centre of attention. The skipper came back and told Jock that all the injured had been removed.

"Everyone except these two" he said, indicating the girl and the man in the last car.

"OK Serg. get him out of his car and stick him in an ambulance. We shouldn't be long here. The trouble is this young lass is enjoying this, every time I get in the car she gives me a cuddle."

"I could think of better places for doing that" the girl said, laughing. The Sergeant glowered and turned away to the other man, muttering about people not taking things serious, the buggers treat it like a joke!

"Right Mike," Jock returned to the job in hand, gear lever pushed forward he knelt on the back seat but he couldn't get his arms right round the seat frame. He tried twisting the seat without any luck. He shuffled round to the front again and said.

"Let's try on top."

"I'm not in any position to argue, seeing that you have me well and truly tied down," the girl giggled.

Jock moved his feet until he had one on each side of the girl's seat; he bent over and tried to get his hands right under the seat but with no success. He shifted his hands from the framework and pushed them under the girl's buttocks and as he lifted he told her to put her arms around his neck.

"Pull tight, it'll make it easier" he muttered as he took her full weight. She obeyed his request but couldn't resist a crack.

"Eee I like this," she said as she nibbled at his ear.

"Behave yourself, somebody might be watching." He eased her body up as far as he could and slowly lifted the legs out of the twisted metal. Her body was pressed tightly against him.

"The feet are free Jock" said Mike and slowly Jock started to gyrate, turning the legs towards the door.

"Can I take her weight now, Jock?" asked Mike. Jock just grunted, it just wasn't possible for him to get rid of his burden due to the way he was crouched and the hold he had on her. He saw the Sergeant appear behind the other copper.

"Can I help?" he asked.

"I wish you could" grunted Jock, "But I'm afraid that she doesn't want to let go."

"Not likely, I'm enjoying this." The girl laughed as Mike reached inside to take here weight.

"Hey, your hands are cold." Mike had touched her bare bottom with his cold hands. Together they managed to get her out of the car and laid her on the stretcher which was waiting for her.

"There you are lassie, that will make you look more decent again. We'll see you later," said Jock pulling a blanket over her.

He turned to the other coppers.

"Mike, will you begin at this end and start getting all the details for the accident report." He asked the Sergeant if he knew how to use the wireless and when he was informed that he could he said,

"Refer to the time of the message, it's on the pad, give them the exact location of the incident, how many vehicles are involved and the number of injured, and then ask for breakdowns again for someone to collect the horse."

"Horse?" the Skipper was surprised. "Which horse?"

Jock indicated that the animal hadn't been injured and pointed to where it was tethered. As soon as he left, Jock began to get the same details as Mike only he started at the opposite end of the crash (they would meet in the middle), and then the job of getting the road clear began. He had many willing helpers from the watching crowds (they had their uses sometimes). The cars were virtually lifted off the road and bumped and bounced into the sides, where they would remain until the breakdown wagons took them away. These were soon in attendance for Control had warned them as soon as the first messages came in. Two 'heavies' took two cars away and promised to be back shortly for the others and the cart was pushed into the gutter, and the pile of scrap was put back on it.

Mike went down to the junction where he had started the traffic diversion. Two well-meaning dockers were waving their arms around frantically, really enjoying their brief attachment to the police. Mike thanked them and released them from the job and then let the vehicles proceed along the normal route. Jock had done the same at the other junction, before climbing behind the steering wheel of his own car.

The engine was ticking over when his mate returned.

"Nearly fourteen minutes Jock, you must be getting old."

"Surely it took more than that?" The Sergeant wouldn't believe that it was possible to do so much work in such a short space of time.

"Time flies when you're busy Serg., especially when there re plenty of helpers," Mike answered, and just like an old copper he relaxed back in his seat as the car moved off.

"Are we off to hospital now Jock, to get all the rest of the particulars?" Jock agreed that was the general idea and suggested that he let Information Room know where they were going, just in case they were required.

The job they had to do next was like sorting out a gigantic jigsaw puzzle, with bodies and vehicles. Trying to ascertain who was driving which car and who were the passengers; names and addresses had to be obtained from all concerned, plus the extent of their injuries, and particulars of driving licences and insurances also had to be noted.

"What happened?" "How did it happen?"

Endless repetition of the same question to different people. A man who appeared to have two noses attached to a gory mass of flesh instead of a face spoke to Jock in a barely audible voice.

"Jock, will you tell them that I'm OK I don't want them worried." Jock just couldn't recognise the man nor his voice but answered,

"Of course I will, but you'll be getting discharged soon, do you want me to hang on and give you a lift home?"

The man's own mother wouldn't even recognise him but he wouldn't let him know that, he might even be an old mate of his, he knew that from personal experience.

"Who do you want me to tell?" he asked. "Just my old man at the 'Fourteen Tits' was the reply. The penny dropped, Jock knew the slang nickname for the dockside pub and he also knew the owner and his son. The son was getting married the following week and had invited Jock to the wedding. He didn't change his expression as he answered,

"Yeh, I know that, but do you want Cilla told?"

"She was with me in the car, if you see her just let her know that I'm feeling OK."

He was more worried about the other people than himself. Jock chatted with him for a few more seconds until the medical team took over and he moved on to finish his enquiries. He gave the driver's particulars plus the description of the vehicles to the Hospital office so they could claim expenses and then he returned to his car.

"I have a call to make on the way back, but you can book back on the air Mike."

He stopped at the pub as he was going past and told his acquaintance that his son had been involved in an accident and that he would probably be kept in Hospital for the night. He didn't enlarge on the injuries nor the rest of the carnage he had just witnessed. No deaths, but a bloodbath for all that. He headed for the station to clean up.

NEATLY SLICED

Before they reached the sanctuary of their own Nick, another call came over concerning an accident.

"We're not far from there, tell them we'll deal with it" Jock said. About half a minute later they arrived at the location given; the road was clear and there was no signs of any accident.

"Queer, better check that location Mike." His operator soon verified from Information Room that they were at the place given. A motorcyclist stood beside his motorcycle watching them and Jock drew in alongside the man.

"Have you seen anything of an accident around here? Someone called for the police." The man made no attempt to move from his cycle but said, "That's right, it was me." Jock drew the car into the side of the pavement and they got out.

"What do you mean, it's you?" Mike asked.

"Well, I had trouble with my engine and was just bending over trying to fix it when I was hit by a car that went past."

"Any damage?"

Apparently the force of the blow had been enough to throw the man over onto his motorcycle, the car hadn't stopped. When he had picked himself up and stood the bike back onto its stand he felt the pain in his rear end. He found that he couldn't sit down, so he called the police.

"Let's have a look" Jock said. Reluctantly the man turned round and showed his back end.

"Better call an ambulance Mike," Jock informed his operator. The Sergeant just stood and gawked at the man's mutilated posterior. The trousers had been ripped wide open and nearly all of his buttocks were exposed; the flesh had been cut off cleanly just as though it had been done by a bacon slicer.

"We're getting an ambulance for you, to get that seen to." Jock obtained the man's name and address and gave him a slip to produce his documents at a later date.

"Where do you want the bike taken to?" he asked. The rider asked if relations could be informed about the accident and he said that they would look after the bike, which was not damaged. The ambulance soon arrived to take the man to Hospital and for some reason, when they put him on the stretcher, he insisted on lying face down. They continued the journey to the Nick where a message was sent to the relatives about the man's predicament and they were asked to collect the bike.

"We'll have to report it as a hit and run" said the Sergeant. Jock looked at him in surprise.

"Talk sense Serg. the amount of traffic on that road, it's dark, and some silly sod sticks his arse out. What do you expect? Anyone could hit it and would the driver know? I'd say the best we can do is to stick it in 'Yellow Peril' and mark it down as an error on the part of the driver, that is if he had even seen the cyclist."

Mike asked whether they should book back on the air again but Jock declined the offer.

"By the time we get cleaned up and get all the reports done it'll be knocking off time."

BUTTONS

There was pandemonium at the station the following day when they booked on duty. Apparently, a local shopkeeper had called in to complain about the fact that he had found a button from a Police Uniform. Nothing unusual about that but he had picked it up in his shop and he swore that it had not been there when he'd locked up the previous night. Consequently, with this allegation suggesting that some copper had been in his shop during the night the CID had been busy. Every uniform which had been left at the station was checked and they had also been to every copper's house and checked all the jackets and topcoats of the men who had been on duty during the time when the shop had been closed. Both late turn and night shifts had been checked by the plain clothes men. It appeared that due to the fact that the wireless car had been engaged all the time and they had the Sergeant with them, Jock and his colleagues were not bothered and they were eliminated from the enquiries.

Every copper was suspect and questioned, it was amazing how many buttons had been found missing and Jock knew just how easy it was to lose them. Climbing into and under crashed cars, climbing walls after suspects, or even a simple fight could result in threads being snapped and eventually the button would fall off. The shopkeeper didn't report any property missing, he was only interested in the mystery of the button. Still, it left a nasty taste in the mouth whatever the circumstances - the results were that the 'Rubber heel squad' appeared on the ground. These senior officers worked in plain clothes from other Divisions and investigated the activities at any given Station where an allegation had been made which couldn't be proved. They would check every PC from the time he left the nick to how he worked his beats, times were also noted and if anyone did anything wrong he would be in for it. All late turns and night shifts had to be worked according to the book and anyone nipping in for a cuppa and not working according to the book was in for trouble. Those who disappeared into the gents toilets or railway stations for a game of cards would be in serious trouble, and like the chaps who used the all-night cafes, they could expect marching orders.

SAFE BLOWERS

This team had been working their patch for two weeks. Jock was on night duty again and things were quiet, apart from the usual disturbances plus the inevitable road accidents. Occasionally, the peace was broken by a burglar alarm going off. Once the bells started ringing there was little chance of catching anyone because any person with any common sense would run. However, more sophisticated silent alarms were being brought into use and these gave the law time to reach the place before the bell started. They would then catch the villains on the job, or just as they left the place. It was to one of these that Jock's car got called that night.

A factory broken into, suspects on the premises. It was on his patch and within the recognised time that the car slid slowly and quietly to a halt. As he approached the factory Jock noted that no alarms were sounding, he had already switched his lights off so as not to warn the villains during their nocturnal pastime. No sirens or bells, no blazing lights, engines screaming or tyres complaining when the brakes were slammed on. This type of thing was only for the public to digest on TV or films.

"Have you been here before Jock?" the Sergeant asked.

"No, first time," Jock answered. "Don't slam your door." Jock got out and left his door open.

The car had been stopped some distance from the building and they continued on foot. They moved quietly, not using their torches as they began to check for any sign of forced entry. As they walked along, the tranquillity of the silence was broken by the clamour of the alarm bells; after a few seconds the shock wore off and they became accustomed to the sound.

The noise had also disturbed the two men inside; it must have been a much bigger shock for them, having just broken in and working in the darkness. The reality of the fact that the coppers could turn up at any moment soon became evident to them because they dropped everything and ran. What a pity, they ran straight into Jock.

"That's far enough lads, you're nicked" he told them.

They were regular thieves and offered no violence or resistance when they realised that the law had them. As the Sergeant and the operator came up, Jock asked them to take the villains to the car while he checked the inside of the premises and as he went into the front door, one of the villains called after him.

"Watch how you go Guv."

Jock couldn't understand the significance of the advice until he reached an open door at the end of the passage. A strong smell made his nostrils twitch; he recognised that aroma - it was explosive. No sooner had his brain recorded the fact when he was hit by a blast of air, accompanied by fumes; it wasn't strong enough to harm him and he saw by the light of his torch that he safe door was hanging by one hinge. The blighters had just set the charge when the bells had gone, poor buggers, all that cash there and they hadn't even seen it - so near yet so far. They would still be charged for attempting to steal it.

Mike had called for the key-holder and the CID. The Duty Inspector arrived with the plain clothes men and informed the car crew that they could take the prisoners to the Police Station and he would look after things there. At the nick the men were put in the cells to await the return of the 'brains', the charge sheet could be signed at breakfast time, so they resumed patrol.

STINKERS

It wasn't long before their services were required again - a request for them to contact a nearby station, personally, and as soon as possible.

"I wonder what's wrong?" Mike asked.

"Probably one short for the card school," Jock answered. They had often called in at the same station during night duty and had a game of solo as they had their refreshments.

It wasn't for the card school though that they were needed. The Superintendent had demanded that a roadblock be set up and the CID plus the Inspector would be out stopping and questioning all drivers. Vehicles had to be inspected and the men checked. The CID, of course, would be the brains in case a possible crime was suspected. The wireless car was requested to be available in case any car tried to jump the roadblock, in which case the wireless car would have to chase and stop them. The local wireless car was engaged on another job and that is why they had called for Jock to stand by.

It was a dreary job, just sitting at an angle to the road so they could drive off in either direction and at the same time watch all the vehicles being stopped. After countless stops, which proved negative, they saw a sudden increase in activity around an estate car.

"Hello, what's going on there?" The Sergeant was awake.

The Inspector and all the CID were gathered around the car in question - there were also a couple of uniformed men. The crowd thinned out for a while as other cars were stopped, the driver could be seen.

"Hell, it's a woman" Mike exclaimed. "

No wonder they were all interested" Jock replied. "A bit of crumpet to chat up, and probably looking at her legs."

The crowd re-gathered around the car once more and suddenly there was a commotion - the door of the car was opened and a melee of coppers moved backwards and forwards as the driver fought them. The crew of the wireless car wondered what the hell was going on. The mob moved away from the stationary vehicle and they caught several glimpses of bare legs, right up to the bottom!

"Bloody hell, they're nicking her" Jock said.

"Can't be, probably all just having a feel," Mike answered as he gazed in awe at the silk clad legs which were being waved frantically in the air. The owner of the legs had long flowing blond hair. The cavalcade slowly made its way across the road towards the CID car and, with a struggle, the body was pushed inside and a crowd of coppers squeezed in also before the car was driven away.

The Inspector came across to the wireless car.

"Jock" he said. "That car has to be taken into the nick and you're the only one who is qualified to drive it, can you take it in and I'll bring you back to your own car?"

Jock, of course, couldn't refuse so he left his two mates sitting in the comfort of the warm police car and walked over to the vehicle indicated. The inside of the car was packed out with clothing and private goods, all except the driver's seat. Getting in he switched the engine on but as he did so, he opened the window wide. Christ, Inspector, what have you got here, he thought. The smell was terrible, so revolting and nauseating that Jock put his head out of the window to drive the car, going as fast as he could. He was glad when he at last reached the police station and got out.

As he turned to the grinning Inspector who was waiting he said, "You rotten bugger, you knew that was a mobile sewer and that nobody else would drive it, so you picked on me."

"I knew it stank Jock but you were the only one who was allowed to bring it in. I didn't realise it was as bad as that," he answered. "Come on, I'll take you back to your car and I'll buy you a cuppa when you come in for breakfast. You'll be coming in for a game, won't you? I'll have to charge this bloke first."

"Bloke! That was a woman wasn't it? We saw the skirt and the legs and the long blond hair," Jock was surprised.

The Inspector laughed. "You should have seen the face, it was like the back of a bus, with a moustache and a long beard. I don't know whether to get a WPC or a PC to search it. Anyway, I'll let you know when you come in."

"Righto Ralph, I'll see you." Jock got on well with this Inspector and he liked him. He wasn't like some of the sods who got too big for their boots and had no sense of man management. The Inspector dropped him off beside his own car so that he could carry on with his duties.

When the roadblock was called off they made their way to the station for breakfast.

"Jock," a voice called out his name. "Our car is still engaged, can you do another call for us?" The duty Sergeant came out of the office with a piece of paper. "It shouldn't take you long."

The crew looked at one another, shall we or shan't we, attitude. Mike accepted the message from the supervising officer.

"Neighbour states she hasn't seen her friend for a long time, she thinks something is wrong," he read.

"Bugger waits till the middle of the night to 'phone up" Jock exclaimed. "Righto, let's go."

It didn't take them long before the car stopped at the terraced house, which were let off in flats of single rooms. They had no trouble finding the 'friendly neighbour' - she was waiting beside the front door - oh what faith she must have had in our Police.

"What's the problem?" the Sergeant asked her.

The lady explained that she had not seen the tenant upstairs for nearly two weeks. The skipper suggested that the person may be away working, or on holiday, but the woman insisted that was not the case.

"Why did you wait till now to call us?" he asked.

"It's all them maggots which keep falling down from the ceiling." Jock's head jerked up at once when he heard that.

"OK we'll have a look."

As they approached the upstairs room he could smell it.

"Have you been up here before madam?" he asked the woman. She admitted that she hadn't so Jock told her to stay in her room because he guessed what was waiting for them in the locked room. As they forced the door open the full force of the smell hit them and a rat scurried from the bed where a half eaten body lay; the whole mass was heaving as though still alive but the mass was only the maggots. Holes lay where the eyes should have been and the flesh of the stomach had gone as well as nearly all of the innards. The man had been dead a long time and the rats and maggots had taken over. The stink was terrible so they closed the door to leave him in peace once they had obtained all the details they needed for their report.

"What now Jock?" the Sergeant asked.

"Well, it's a Coroner's officer's job, and also the local Council to fumigate the place. The local nick will do all that." He hesitated a while before adding, "I think I'll get my own back on the Inspector for sticking me in that car. I think you'd better call the Inspector and require him to attend, Mike."

As it was the job of the nick to deal with any sudden death, it was right that the Supervision attend; also the CID Information Room came back and told them that they were on the way, so Jock and his mates left them to it. He saw them later in the canteen and the Inspector grinned.

"We were a right of couple of stinkers tonight Jock, you got your own back."

SUSPECT

After refreshment, they cruised along the quiet streets just checking for broken windows or anything that looked suspicious. There was always a chance of seeing an unguarded light as a job was being done. Quite often they caught people in doorways as they tried to force the doors; this type usually worked in the early part of the night and had a female accomplice. The presence of the female was obvious, if caught in the doorway, they would just be having a quick cuddle and anything else that went with it. However, to find a man hiding in a dark doorway in the middle of the night meant one thing, there was villainy afoot. So, as the car moved slowly and quietly along the silent street, Mike and the Sergeant shone their torches into the darkness.

"Hold it Jock." Mike had spotted something.

As he applied the brakes Jock looked into the darkness of a shop and in the shade he could just make out the figure of a man; they got out to question the person and to examine the property. The man refused to give an account of himself and also refused to allow the coppers to search him.

The Sergeant drew Jock aside.

"What do you think?" he asked. There was no signs of any attempt to break in to the premises and the man didn't look like a villain but Jock had a feeling in his bones about this man and he advised the Sergeant to carry out his duty according to the book.

"You have the right to search him under Section 66 but as he will not allow you to do so, I would suggest you take him in and let the Inspector sort it out at the nick."

The man adopted a very truculent attitude and refused to co-operate so the Sergeant informed him that as far as he was concerned he was a suspected person, loitering with intent, and he was going to take him to the Police Station for further enquiries. The man objected but the skipper refused to be put off and bundled him into the waiting car, he resisted at first till Jock told him he would be done for resisting arrest if he wasn't careful.

So, the very irate man was driven to the local nick with Jock hiding his smiles. In the Charge Room, the Sergeant gave the details to the Inspector, as per the book. The Inspector listened but was watching Jock with a very quizzical look on his face as the skipper went through his routine. Once the Sergeant had finished talking, he spoke to the man.

"You heard what the Sergeant said, have you anything to say in answer to the charge?"

The man was livid, this was a blow to his pride, but there was no way out for him but to tell the truth. He was a Superintendent from the 'Rubber Heel' squad.

"Why didn't you tell the officers at the time, it would have saved a lot of unnecessary time and embarrassment? You realise of course that I will have to record these facts in the Occurrence Book?" The Inspector told the crew to get back on patrol. What happened to the Senior Officer who had been nicked, nobody every found out, but he wasn't seen again and the rest of the team were taken off the observation in that area. When the cars changed crews the Inspector stopped Jock.

"You rotten sod, you knew he was a rubber heel didn't you?"

"I didn't arrest him Guv" he said.

"I know, but you could have warned the Sergeant."

"Guv, that chap was out looking for trouble on our patch so he was out of luck. He now knows that we do our job properly and according to the book, he now knows there are no favourites."

"You're a crafty bugger Jock."

"Whatever you say Guv, now if you don't mind, I'm off to bed."

POISON

A good five hours sleep and Jock was up, shopping and odd jobs done, and ready for the next night shift. Now that there was every chance that the rubber heel was scared off, there was a good chance that things would get back to normal. Coppers would be taking the usual liberties, such as the crafty cuppa or having a kip. One man in particular had missed the time he spent in the canteen because every night at midnight, breakfast time and at four o'clock, he could be found stretched out sitting on one chair and feet up on another. A cup of tea rested on the table beside him as his head went back, his mouth fell wide open, as he snored. Whenever the door banged, he automatically reached for his cup and took a swig, just in case it was a Sergeant or Inspector - he was more or less regarded as a piece of the furniture, until one night when one of his mates decided to lace his tea for him. He had slept for about half an hour and the tea was, as usual, cold beside him. A special cup was mixed for him with salt, pepper, mustard and vinegar all stirred in together and whilst the contents were still circulating his mate, who had mixed the horrible brew, opened the canteen door and slammed it shut. The sound of the door was like an alarm clock to the sleeping man, his feet came off the chair, he reached out and, before his eyes were open, he took hold of the cup and poured the contents down the gaping orifice which he called a mouth. Quicker than it had gone down it came out. He spat the poisonous liquid across the canteen and jerked upright at the same time. The stuff looked and smelt terrible so God knew what it tasted like. He glared round the laughing coppers and then spotted the culprit standing beside the door ready for a quick getaway.

"You bastard" he yelled as he made a bound for the man, chairs and tables flying in all directions. His mate was quicker than he was though, he was outside and sliding down the handrail towards his waiting Noddy, its engine was running and he jumped on and was driving out of the yard before his enraged pal had reached the bottom of the steps.

Still spitting the vile fluid out of his mouth, he grabbed hold of the nearest cycle and started to pedal furiously after the other copper. Once more his luck was out, the cycle had been left there on purpose, the nut at the crown head had been slackened because when he tried to steer he went over in a heap. He was sitting on the ground beside the bike when the duty officer came in. The Inspector stopped his car alongside the forlorn looking man.

"All correct Sir." came the usual greeting.

"If you're all that tired why don't you get yourself into the canteen where you generally sit?"

The copper was left speechless.

CRUMPET

A new woman Police Officer arrived at the nick; she was a beautiful blond and she knew it. She declined any conversation or advances from the ordinary copper but fell over backwards to rub shoulders with Supervision; she never went into the canteen at meal times, not like the other old battle axe who never left the place. No, this one sat at the window of the women's room, combing her hair or doing her knitting, she only went out on the streets with the patrolling officer in his car.

One night when she was the only WPC on the Division she was required to attend another Station to look after a female prisoner. She trotted daintily across the yard just as Jock was going out.

"Hold on, I'm coming with you" she ordered. It was the first time she had spoken to Jock. As she spoke the grasped the door handle and opened it and as she made herself comfortable.

"Hang on a bit Miss, this is a wireless car, if you want transport you'd better see the Inspector," said Jock.

"I've already spoken to him and he told me to get a driver to take me over" she answered.

"I'm sorry Miss," said Jock, "but not in this car, you'll have to get the spare driver or the van driver to take you." He refused to accept her as a passenger. "We're on wireless duty and not allowed to leave our own ground, if we got a call with you in the car you could find it may take you hours to get where you want to go."

"I'm in a hurry and I'm not getting out of the car, you have to take me." She replied very tartly, it was more an order than anything else.

"If you're not out of this car in thirty seconds, I'll drag you out personally, now get out." Jock had taken as much as he was going to from her. The tone of his voice was brusque, nobody had spoken to her like that before and she didn't like it.

"I'll report you to the Inspector" she said as she got out and slammed the door behind her.

"Why didn't you take her Jock," Mike asked.

"I wouldn't want the Sergeant to get his hand away while I'm driving" was the reply. The car drifted out of the yard.

"Jock, you know damn well that I wouldn't do a thing like that," came the shocked voice from the darkness at the back of the car.

"You lying sod, you were just itching to get your hands on her, just like everyone else at the nick. I didn't want you to be enjoying yourself while I had all the work to do."

"Get out of it, you Scots get, I wouldn't do anything in the back of a Police Car." The Sergeant was really put out with the suggestion.

"Don't kid yourself Skipper, I've seen it happen before" said Jock as the memories flooded back.

PROTECTION RACKET

"The old bugger's at it again, I bet," said Jock as they raced along the High Street.

"You know this place then?" asked the Sergeant.

They were answering a call for assistance to a club owned by a foreign gentleman and his family.

"Yes, I know it, we've been here quite a few times. He runs the club with his wife and his son and daughter also help him. There are a few chaps in the kitchen but they're no use whatsoever when it comes to trouble."

"Do they get a lot of bother there then?" asked the Skipper. Jock smiled.

"When anything does start, he'll have a go by himself, and his wife is just as keen to help."

"When was the last time?" the Sergeant asked.

"Last time we were on nights, we had a call. A crowd of seamen pushed their way in and demanded a meal and some drinks. He told them it was a private club and he couldn't serve them. They started to get nasty and began to wreck the place, so he just picked a glass up and chopped the first bloke in the face. One of the other seamen tried to prevent this by putting his hands in front of the man's face; the result was he got his hands cut to pieces. I had to take the two of them to hospital to get stitched up. He was lucky because the ship was sailing the following morning and no charges were pressed. The rest of them ran like hell when the blood started to fly."

The car was screaming along the main road at that moment towards the club and Jock suddenly said

"There he is, the little sod's at it again." An angry looking man was running along the main road behind a couple of terror stricken thugs and a woman was chasing behind them.

Jock stopped the car in front of the men being chased and grabbed them.

"Hang on mate, we want to talk to you."

The men were really frightened.

"Keep that mad sod away from us, he'll kill us," they pleaded to the coppers. The club owner arrived just then, brandishing a large carving knife and his wife had a huge piece of timber with a large nail sticking through the end.

"Hang on Silvo, what's the trouble this time?" Jock asked the panting man.

The proprietor explained rapidly in broken English that the two men had entered the club; they were involved in the protection racket and were demanding money as a weekly payment. When they were refused, they had started to cause some considerable damage to the place; tables and chairs were thrown about; heaters which had been standing on the tables had started small fires. The owner had grabbed a large knife which was nearby and he had attacked the two thugs. His first blow had partly removed an ear from one of the men and the other chap received a large slash along his arm. They rapidly took to their heels.

"Now look, Silvo," Jock said, "I've told you before about this, it's our job to sort out any trouble, not yours. Whatever your problems, you should send for the Police."

"I know Mr MacGregor, it only takes you a few minutes to get here but in that time they could wreck my place. This is my own, my living, and also that of my family and I'll protect them," the little man said.

"I know your problems but just go easy with the clubs and knives." Said Jock although his sympathies were with the man.

"But, Mr MacGregor, they are always bigger than me and there are always at least two of them. These are the only things I have to protect my business with."

"If you cause injury to any of them, I can't protect you from the law. If they want to lay charges against you they can. You can't attack and injure people, and you could lose your licence, one of these days, you'll be out of luck."

The two prisoners willingly admitted their reasons for being at the club, especially when Jock suggested that if they weren't taken into custody they would have to be released. They didn't want to face the irate owner and his wife again, so they were carted off to the nick after hospital treatment.

This business of protection needed stamping out, it was run by vicious thugs, but the owners needed protection from them because they took their lives into their own hands if they retaliated. This is what happened to Jock's friend, the boxer, he was sure of that, but his death went down as suicide.

CHAPTER THIRTEEN

CHANGING TIMES

CHANGING TIMES

Back to the nick for grub and a game of cards, they booked in and ran up the steps to get started. They were met with a deathly hush, the canteen was empty.

"They must be out on a job," Mike said.

"No way," Jock answered. "There are no cups lying around and no breakfasts left." The usual thing when a call comes in during the meal break was for all the coppers to drop everything and run.

"I'll get the van driver to make a four up" said the Skippr as he headed for the drivers' room. He was met with a wall of smoke because the room was crowded. All the night shift men were watching a blue movie but the Skipper had seen them all so he returned to the canteen.

"I think we'll have to just make do with three, the others are otherwise engaged."

Things were certainly changing in the job, even new cars were brought into use, more powerful and more comfortable vehicles. Gone were the days of driving in unheated cars with the wireless operator scraping the ice off the inside of the windscreen so the driver could see when they were on a call. Uniform was also changing, with regular issues of different styles each year; thick ones for winter and thin for summer use, shirts with collars and ties came into force; new shorter-type overcoats and new raincoats. The ceremonial tunics were not replaced, they were only to be used for town jobs. The boot allowance stopped and footwear was issued, shoes for drivers and boots for the copper on the beat. The loss of the ten shillings a week was felt by everyone and when the chances came to earn a bit of overtime for cash, everyone jumped at it. The main job was for attending football matches and even when Jock was driver on the van he managed to get there. He drove the chaps across, back to the nick and then took an hour off duty; he then raced back to the football ground to complete four hours extra work for payment. It was worth it financially.

UNDERCOVER CARS

One of the problems of being a first class driver was the demand for his services. Apart from driving the wireless cars, he could be used for 'Q' cars, undercover cars, crime, squad, or flying squad vehicles.

The driver on all of these cars was a uniform man, except he wore plain clothes. He was treated as a driver and not involved in any of the crime work, nobody else but a Class One driver was allowed to drive these cars and again, the plain clothes gave an extra ten bob a week. On the Division, two "Q" cars operated, one of them was a 'CID' car and was used this time to get round their informants and to clear some of the backlog of work they had. The other car was all uniform men, they came from different stations so knew the whole division quite well. This car always worked as a team and there was a great deal of competition between the two cars. The "Q" cars were changed every week and a different car was used so that the local thieves didn't get to know the car. They were all high powered vehicles such as Rovers, Humber Super Snips, or Jaguars.

They were allowed to get dirty and often disguised with roof racks and boxes tied on the top. The men never dressed in their best suits, they just wore overalls, old clothes, or anything that made them look less like coppers.

On one such posting, Jock heard an usual call. Things had been fairly quiet that night when the wireless came into life - requesting all cars to stand by. Then a call addressed for the action of one individual car came across the air. The call was repeated with the reminder that it was only for the car which covered that area. The crew was informed that a naked woman was seen walking along the main road. The time was three o'clock in the morning.

"Shall we have a run along Jock?" asked the sleepy Sergeant in the back.

"Well it's on our ground, Skipper. If you want to go, fair enough," Jock said. There was nothing else to do.

"A young woman be buggered. She must be ninety if she's a day," the Sergeant spluttered angrily.

Going by the number of Police Cars cruising past, it appeared that none of them had received full instructions from Information Room. The lady, of course, was mentally deranged and was collected by the local wireless car and dealt with.

The next day a young Aide to CID asked them if they were going past Divisional HQ "I have to be there for an interview."

The lad was hoping to be made up and the Skipper asked Jock if they should take him.

Jock agreed that the chap should save his bus fare and they would drop him off. "How are your figures?" he said, referring to the number of arrests that the man had

as this was one thing that was essential.

"Not too good this month," the budding CID man said.

He was in luck, for just before he was dropped off at his destination Jock suddenly stopped the car.

"If you're short there's a couple of likely ones just gone into Woollies." He described the men to the Aide, who entered the building. Jock stood on the pavement where he could see all the doors and as he waited he could check everyone who came out of the shop. He didn't have to wait long before the two suspects came out and he stopped them.

"Excuse me, I'm a Police Officer, I want to ask you a few questions."

"Piss off, you big cant," was the reply - short and sweet! The answer was to be expected, be polite with this type and they think you are soft.

As they turned to go they suddenly found that the other two members of the wireless car were standing behind them and the Aide approached them coming from the shop.

"Would you like to repeat what you've just said?" asked Jock.

Naturally the two men didn't want to know for they were like all their type and yellow when outnumbered. The voice changed into a wheedle.

"Look Guv, we ain't done nuffin."

"I'm not too sure about that, we're taking you in for questioning. You're nicked, get in the car."

The men were placed in the back seat, the Skipper asked if he was sure and the Aide asked what they were being arrested for.

"They're yours, they've been up to something. You're the CID man so you'll be able to come up with something. They'll tell you all about it." Jock answered as he climbed in behind the wheel.

The Aide questioned the men as he sat in the back of the car with them but he hadn't managed to get any answers which satisfied him. At the Nick they were placed in the Charge Room and he turned to Jock.

"I don't want to know anything about them. You arrested them, so leave me out of it." He was afraid of being involved with something that may ruin his chances with the CID Board. Before Jock could pass any comment, the Station Sergeant came in.

"What have you got this time Jock?" he asked.

The big driver of the 'Q' car was just beginning to explain the situation when the PC from the Communications Room ran into the room and gasped.

"Armed robbery Serg, three men with guns."

Jock took a quick look at the message as he passed it over to the Serg. who noted the details.

"We'll go Skip, keep your eye on these till we get back. See what they've been up to." Next second he was out of the door, following his two mates. If he'd looked over his shoulder he would have seen the grey haired Station Sergeant, gazing sadly after him, shaking his head as he jumped into the high-powered vehicle. Before the car had reached the scene, the occupants heard the instructions, any car going to assist at the robbery was to approach with care, this meant that they hadn't to start ringing any bells to warn the thieves.

The undercover car slid slowly to a halt some distance from the house in question and the crew walked around the property. They examined the doors and windows before returning to their own car and waited for the others to arrive. It wasn't long before two other wireless cars drove quietly into the street and stopped beside them. The four uniformed coppers got out and greeted them, asking instructions. It was arranged that they should go in the back way. Jock and the other two plain clothes men would enter by the front door.

"Alright with you Skip?," Jock asked, knowing full well what the answer would be.

Naturally the little plump sergeant did not want to be left out of any action and said, "Count me in Jock, I'm willing." The wireless operator merely nodded his head, knowing he was outnumbered, and slowly walked towards the house behind the other two. 'Why the hell did I have to be posted on the car with these two mad sods?' he wondered sadly, knowing full well that if he walked into this house he may not walk out again if the guns started blasting. A quick check of the watches showed the time was nearly up. The seconds had crawled past as they had stood outside the door.

"Right Serg. here we go. Good luck." Jock knew that they were going to need all the luck in the world as their chances were very slim, but after all they did get paid for doing the job.

As Jock threw himself at the door the two retaining screws which held the lock snapped from the impact of his fifteen and a half stones. Before it had hit the inside wall he was racing along the narrow passageway. His eyes were glued on the door at the end and just before he reached it he launched himself forward, shoulders hunched. The flimsy wood shattered under the impact and he was inside, his momentum carried him into the room and before he rolled across the floor he had noted the occupants of the place.

Two men stood inside the place, one near the window holding a rifle in his left hand, the barrel of which was pointing towards the window. He seemed obviously on edge and concentrating upon the noise coming from the rear of the building which was caused by the other coppers trying to break in. The second man stood nearer to the middle of the room, facing the same way. He was holding a shotgun in his right hand and the barrel pointed towards the floor. It was towards this person that Jock made his attack.

He rolled across the floor in a ball and as his feet hit the carpet, he launched himself at the man in a flying tackle. As he went forward his hand reached out to grasp the barrel of the gun. As he cannoned into the man, he managed to get hold of the metal and clung to it like grim death. With Jock's weight and speed, the man fell over backwards and hit his head on the fireplace with a crash. His grip on the shotgun relaxed at once as he was rendered unconscious.

Jock's sudden entry into the room had taken them both by surprise. The man with the shotgun didn't know what had hit him and his mate was in the very process of turning round when he was met with a violent blow to his face. As Jock had taken possession of the shotgun, he had swung it like a bat towards the man with the rifle, straightening upwards as he did so. As the butt of the shotgun hit the man and shattered his nose, he screamed in anguish and clasped both hands to his face. The rifle dropped unheeded onto the floor. Jock climbed to his feet and pushed the two barrels of the gun into the man's ear.

"Where is your mate?" he asked.

The villain knew what a shotgun could do and he was suffering more pain than he could stand. Tears ran down his face, running channels through the blood. The miserable sod just indicated a cupboard under the stairs where the other man had run to when he had heard the other coppers trying to break into the back of the building. Leaving the injured criminal lying on the floor he walked over to the cupboard door.

"Right laddy, I have your friend's shotgun here and I'm going to count to three, then I'll fire both barrels into your little cupboard. One, Two .." but before he reached the last number the door slowly opened.

"Slide your gun out first and then come out yourself on your stomach, hands first" was the next order. A revolver was eased out of the opening. Jock pushed it aside with his foot before he bent down to pick it up.

"Right, you get out" he said. The man's hands came out and he then slithered along the floor until he was clear of the cupboard. The wretched figure glared up at his big captor. Jock belted him with the butt of his shotgun and he joined his friend in the land of nod.

"I hate these buggers who have to use guns to prove just how big they are," he grunted. He turned round to the injured man.

"You, pull your mate across there beside the other one, then lay down between them."

For a few agonising moments the man took his hands away from his nose so he could obey the order. As soon as he had moved the body towards the fireplace, he lay alongside the two senseless men and returned his hands to his face. Satisfied that his orders had been carried out, Jock took his battered old pipe out of his pocket and lit it.

"I think I could do with a smoke now" he said, speaking to the Sergeant who stood speechless beside the door.

"Bugger me Jock. If I hadn't seen that with my own eyes, I wouldn't have believed it," he said. "In fact, I did see it happen and I still don't believe it, we've only been in here a couple of minutes." The gang came thudding in from the back and quickly took the situation in.

"Ah, you got them Skip," said the driver of one of the cars, indicating the three bodies.

"Not me lad, Mr MacGregor got them all," said the Sergeant, and he then went into detail about the scrum he had just witnessed, which caused some laughter from the uniformed men. A faint voice came from the passage door, which made them all look round - it was the wireless operator.

"Is everything alright Sergeant?" he asked. "Do you want an ambulance?" Jock indicated that the first aid men would not like the rubbish being put in their vehicles.

"No, we'll take them straight to the nick." It was arranged that each car would take one of the criminals down to the Station for safety reasons.

"What have you got this time Mr MacGregor?" asked the old grizzled Sergeant. In answer Jock placed the three weapons on the desk in front of him.

"Another three Skip. Use of firearms, breaking and entry and resisting arrest."

"Right Jock, by the way the CID have sorted your other friends out. They have admitted twenty-four other jobs. The charge sheets are ready for you to sign."

"Can I have one?" said a voice interrupting them.

It was the Aide to the CID, who was hoping to get one of the prisoners as it would help him with the Board if he told them that he had just arrested an armed villain.

"You get bugger all lad, on your bike," the Sergeant told him. "Jock brought these in and you didn't want to know anything about the others till they coughed up."

The prospective candidate left the room, looking very downhearted.

"Why the hell did you put me down as arresting officer?" asked Jock. "You could have given them to the Skipper here, he needs them to get his promotion."

"You'll do, Jock, by Christ you'll do. If you get any more bodies in they'll do away with the CID." The senior member of his car laughed.

Jock left them and went into the front office to sign the Charge Sheets and while he was there he scrounged a cup of tea from the Communications Room, before returning to the Charge Room.

"By the way Jock," the Station Sergeant asked. "Can you tell us who had what regarding the guns? None of these others seem to know what happened."

Jock indicated which gun had been used by the different criminals and told the Station Sergeant that the bodies had to be shared between the cars. "One for each car Skipper."

"But you apparently nicked them all by yourself," the old man said.

"OK Skip, but give one to each car and give the Sergeant the one for our car, after all everyone was there" Jock insisted.

"As you wish." The Station Sergeant wasn't surprised at all.

The charge sheets were signed and all the cars resumed patrol after the prisoners had been placed in the cells to await the attention of the CID whose job it was to prepare them for Court.

"Come on Jock, let's go and have a cup of tea somewhere," the Sergeant suggested.

He didn't realise that his driver had already been scrounging the old standby, but to keep them happy Jock took them to his own Nick to fill their bladders.

Well that was another job done with, no Commendations this time and no medals, although the Sergeant insisted that Jock should get a gong as big as a frying pan, at least they hadn't been put on the carpet.

"Where shall we go this time?" the Skipper asked as the car pulled out onto the road.

"How about the riverside?" suggested the Wireless Operator.

"I suppose it's as good as anything around here," Jock answered as he headed the car for the dockside area. There were a few factories and warehouses in that area and there were some dingy places which could invite a few criminals. As they crawled along the filthy streets they intercepted a call to the local car requesting a plain clothes man attend to render assistance.

"We'll do it," Jock said, and the Wireless Operator informed the Information Room that they were close by and would deal with the call.

They parked the vehicle some distance from the address, which was a foundry, and walked the rest of the way. They spoke to the manager in the office who was rather surprised when three plain clothes men responded to his request within minutes of his 'phone call. The man was obviously distressed due to the fact that he had found a warehouse door had been forced because the building contained valuable metal ingots. The lock had been forced during working hours and there were security men on the gates, so no metal had been taken from the site. He knew that it must have been someone in his employ who had committed the offence. It would not be possible to say how much had been removed without doing a complete stocktaking check.

He took the coppers to the store and showed them the ingots. Due to the large number of men employed on the site, it would be difficult to make any enquiries, however as it was obvious that the goods had not been removed from the premises, it appeared that the thieves had hidden their booty and would try to take it out when they left the factory.

"Bugger me, it's heavy," said Jock checking the weight of the blocks. The manager explained that there was a quarter of a hundredweight in each one of the ingots. Jock discussed the situation with his mates.

"If they try to carry them out they are bound to be spotted. I think we should do a stakeout on the gate Skip, at least until the men go home. What do you think?" He gave the final option to the Sergeant.

"Well they couldn't carry them out, they would have to use transport and if they had a bike they could only take one at a time, even then the tyres would be flat. If they had a car then they would try to take the whole lot out in one go." The Sergeant had to say something.

Jock asked the manager if any of the men used cars and left them on the premises during working hours. He was told that only about eight men used the premises for parking their cars, everyone else used the faithful old pedal cycle.

So it was decided that the exit from the factory would be covered as the men left. The Sergeant and the Wireless Operator stood on each side of the gate. Jock stayed in his car watching all the vehicles coming out. When the whistle went the men simply poured out of the gate. The Skipper and his mate watched them looking for the telltale signs of a heavy load. They didn't have to wait long before Jock spotted an old Ford Popular car coming out. His suspicions were aroused and he called to the Sergeant.

"There he is," and drove after the car. He soon stopped the vehicle a short distance from the gate.

"Good evening Sir. I'm a Police Officer."

"Yes Guv, what's wrong?" asked the driver tried to bluff his way out.

"There's been a load of gear stolen from the factory and I wonder if you would be kind enough to open your boot for inspection. We are checking all the cars, just in case."

"What for? I haven't done anything wrong. I've just finished work and have to get home, the wife will have the tea ready."

"I'm sorry Sir but it won't take a second," Jock insisted.

"Not bleedin' likely. I work in the foundry and have just finished work."

The Sergeant arrived on the scene at that moment and the irate man looked at him.

"If you're in charge, I'll report you to your Inspector. I tell you I'm in a hurry and haven't done anything wrong."

The Skipper looked flabbergasted at the outburst but Jock had reached the end of trying to persuade the man, he grabbed the door handle and flung the door open.

"Out!" he snapped. "I've asked you, now I'm ordering you. Open that boot."

As the man was reluctant Jock reached inside and took hold of him by his collar and assisted him out of his seat. When the boot lid was unlocked and lifted the driver gasped.

"Good God, how did that get there. I didn't know it was in there." The boot was filled with ingots of precious metal, laid nice and tidy one on top of the other.

"I don't know who could have put them there, I didn't know about them, honest."

"You're nicked mate," Jock told the man, "and your mate" indicating the passenger of the Ford.

"Someone has grassed on us haven't they?" the passenger asked.

They sent the Wireless Operator to get the manager before he went home. Upon his arrival at the scene Jock asked him to identify the ingots.

"Is this lot yours?" The manager examined each one.

"Yes, our stamp is on each one. Twenty ingots, worth about £5,000 each."

"Will you press charges?" Jock asked.

The manager agreed to allow the law to take its course and he would go as witness. Jock made arrangements for the local van to call at the scene to tow the car in and remove the ingots to the Station. The two men pleaded guilty to breaking into the store and taking the goods.

"How did you know it was us Guv?" Jock laughed, he wasn't going to tell them that the car was nearly running on its rear wheels only due to the weight it carried; the front tyres were hardly touching the ground.

"It doesn't matter who squealed, the result is just the same isn't it?" Jock knew from experience that to drive a Ford Pop with a load in it made the steering very difficult. They waited on the scene until the van arrived, just in case the metal ingots were stolen again.

"Busy today, Mr MacGregor?" The old Station Sergeant was joking because he knew that this team were always working hard.

"What have you got this time?"

"Just a couple of naughty lads who have been stealing from their boss."

"Where's the gear?" referring to the items alleged to have been stolen.

"We left them in their car. The wireless operator is helping the van driver to bring them in." Jock informed the Sergeant what the property consisted of.

"Another nice one for the book Jock, they might even admit to doing some more jobs," the boss remarked.

They did not admit to any other stealing, not even to the CID so once the property was checked and put in the cell for safe keeping, the charge sheets were signed and the car was back on the road again, with its ever keen crew looking for some more work.

MOTORBIKE MUGS

The next day started off very quiet. They cruised around the building sites, shopping precincts, dockyards and factories without any call coming over the air for them. Their eyes were forever seeking and their brains working as every unusual happening came before them. The logic possibilities worked out automatically.

"I don't like the look of them," said Jock as he pointed to a couple of youths walking along on the opposite side of the street.

"Who are you talking about?" asked the operator. Jock once again indicated the men in question and pointed out the fact that a man had just parked his motorcycle a short distance ahead of them and the owner of the bike had disappeared into a shop.

"I bet they'll have that bike," he said. "I think they'll come this way." Consequently he pulled in at the side of the road, opposite a side turning. "If they do come this way, I'll turn them down that side street."

"I think they're just looking at it," the operator said. He had hardly got the words out of his mouth before the two men jumped onto the motorcycle. The rider kicked it into life and accelerated straight along the street towards the waiting Police Car but Jock had already made his plans. The car swung across the road just as the motorcycle reached the junction with the side street and the rider had no option but to swerve the bike into the turning so as to avoid hitting the obstruction which had suddenly appeared in front of him.

Jock picked up speed quickly until he was just behind the stolen vehicle. He maintained that position until he wanted the rider to turn into another side street and he then accelerated and slid the police car at an angle in front of the bike, and once again the man was compelled to turn. Eventually Jock had manoeuvred the stolen cycle into the road where he wanted them to be and rode alongside of them.

Whenever they increased their speed so did Jock and when they braked so did Jock. The thieves began to panic because they couldn't get rid of this strange car which had dogged them since they had got on the bike. Their panic increased more when they suddenly saw a parked lorry in the narrow street; it was close to a wire fence which ran around the nearby building site so it was impossible to pass on the nearside. It was also not possible to pass on the offside because the car was being driven very close to them. All ways were tried by the rider to lose the car but he couldn't, there was only one way and that was to stop. Rather a pity because they were travelling too fast to stop and at the last second, the rider flung the bike onto its side, the vehicle scraped along the road surface before halting. The rider and his mate had both managed to get off without any serious injury and as soon as they hit the ground they started running.

The Sergeant and the Wireless Operator got out and chased the pillion rider whilst Jock followed the rider along the street. The poor sod was puffing and panting, looking with fear in his eyes at this queer cuss who was intent on running him down. He raced alongside the high wire fence, looking for an opening through which he could escape. The police car moved slowly beside him, getting closer all the while until the man didn't have enough room to swing his arms in the space between the police car and the fence. Suddenly he saw what he thought was an escape, the fence seemed to come to an end and he quickly ran into the opening. Jock gently eased the car to a halt and completely blocked the entrance. He had been round this area before and knew that this was just a small cul-de-sac. The man was trapped, there was no way out for him and the wire mesh fence was too high for him to climb.

Jock got out of the car and leaned against the bonnet. He took out his faithful old pipe and began to light it. He watched the man as he frantically tore and scrambled at the wire but he was like a rat in a cage, he was trapped. After a while Jock said gently to the villain.

"You might as well give up lad, you'll never make it. I'll tell you what, after I've had my smoke I'll come and get you, you could get a good hiding but if you come across here and get in the car I'll forget all about the belting. Fair enough?"

The desperate man was dejected, more so as he saw his mate being led along the street by the other two coppers. He shrugged his shoulders and made his way meekly to the car, opened the door and climbed inside. The Wireless Operator was most surprised when he saw the man give himself up as Jock just sat on the bonnet of the car, smoking.

"Right Serg, we'll go and try to find the owner of the bike shall we?"

They went back to the scene of the crime and waited for the owner to return. In the meanwhile, a message had been sent requesting that the van be informed of the need to collect the cycle. The owner arrived and was greatly distressed to find his machine had been nicked. Jock introduced himself and faced a barrage of abuse from the rider who wanted to know what the coppers were paid for. He couldn't even leave a motorcycle for a few minutes. He was speechless, but not apologetic, when he was informed that the cycle had been recovered and the thieves apprehended. He accompanied the coppers and the prisoners to the nick, where he made his statement.

Charge Sheets were signed and the car was once again on patrol, leaving the paperwork to be done by the various sections concerned. That was the beauty of the system, the copper on the street brought the bodies in, the Station Sergeant charged them, the assistant station officer placed the prisoners in the cells and looked after them appropriately, i.e. washed and fed them. The CID took statements and prepared the case for court and the typist put everything down on paper for them. They even had a Coroner's Officer whose job it was to deal with all sudden deaths after the coppers had done the original work.

CANDID CAMERA

Formalities completed and the car was once more driving gently round the streets, looking for anything suspicious.

"What do you think of that one Skip?" said Jock as he indicated a car parked in a side street behind some shops.

"What's wrong with it?" asked the puzzled operator. "It seems to be parked in a funny place, it's out of the way for the shops and they must have passed a lot of parking places to get here. It can't belong to the shop owners because they have their own places to leave their cars."

"You're right Jock," the skipper acknowledged. "You have to keep your eyes open lad to spot these things. It isn't Jock's job you know," he added, addressing his remarks to the young wireless operator.

"I think we'll park up for a smoke Skip and see what happens." Jock was already parking his car where he could watch the mysterious vehicle and he manoeuvred his car into such a position that he could see the vehicle without being too obvious and also be in a position to drive out quickly. His hunch proved to be correct again.

"This is it Skip" he suddenly said and the engine which had been ticking over quietly burst into life and the car hurtled forward and slowed to a halt in front of the parked vehicle. Three masked men were in the process of getting into the car, having reached it at a run. The police car screamed to a halt.

"One each," said Jock. He chased a man who was carrying a blue money bag. The chase began with the portly Sergeant running like hell after one of the men and the young Wireless Operator chasing the other. Jock's quarry led him a dance and finished in the main road through the crowds of shoppers they ran and suddenly the man threw the money bag at Jock. Jock ignored the bag and carried on with the case and eventually the man was brought down at the rear of a public house. The battle was short and sweet, the hunter and the hunted fought silently until at last, with his arm held in a lock, the villain was propelled back along the main road towards the car; the man was bent double trying to ease the pain.

As they approached the point where the bag had been disposed of Jock noticed that the people were acting in a curious manner, just as if they were on 'Candid Camera'. The money bag lay fully exposed on the sidewalk and everyone was walking past and looked at the bulging bag. It was like a rock in a river, the tide moved past on each side. All eyes were turned as they looked at this unusual object, they could guess what it was, but nobody made any attempt to pick it up.

"Right lad, you dropped it and you're nearer than me so you pick it up," said Jock when he and his prisoner reached the object. The man obeyed and carried it back to the car.

The Sergeant arrived, slightly out of breath but hanging on tightly to one of the other prisoners, who was placed in the back with his mate. They waited several minutes for the third member of the crew to return, he was very deflated when he did get back and he was more than subdued and nearly in tears when Jock and the Skipper started to take the Mickey out of him. They piled the insults on really heavy.

"Too much of the other last night, that's your trouble. I bet you didn't get any sleep last night."

It didn't make any difference really that the youngest member of the crew had let his prisoner get away. They had the other two, who soon coughed up the information needed to pick him up. They squealed on him and couldn't tell them enough about other jobs they had been involved in. The third member of the gang soon added his voice to the choir and told about jobs they had done, he also included other men involved with their various shop and house break-ins.

"Let's have a look at the gear they have gone to the trouble of getting" the big Station Sergeant said. Jock picked the blue bag up, undid the string and pushed his hand inside to grasp the contents.

"Sod that," he muttered and withdrew his hand like greased lightning.

"What's the matter Jock?" the Sergeant asked.

"You just stick you mitt in that bag and you'll soon find out," Jock said.

The Skipper grinned, he thought that Jock was just having him on. He too inserted his hand in the bag to get the money out.

"Christ!" he yelled and threw the bag away from him. Money scattered in all directions but, mixed up with the notes, were several snakes. It was the feel of these creatures that had caused their hands to be withdrawn quickly from the bag.

"Bloody silly sods, putting them in with the money," cursed the Skipper. The snakes slithered all over the Charge Room floor but were quickly disposed of. It transpired that the villains had broken into a large pet shop and the owner had put the snakes inside to protect his cash.

"I only put them in there to frighten anyone who tried to take the money out," he said.

"Frighten? They put the shits up me," the Sergeant exclaimed.

"Oh they're harmless, people buy them for pets," the owner replied.

"They're harmless now" said the Sergeant as he looked at the pile of dead snakes.

"That's the best place for them."

The days on 'Q' cars were usually very busy, with numerous arrests and incidents. This meant that the mornings were taken up with the Court cases, whilst the afternoons and evenings were for police work.

TRIPLE MURDER

They got a shock when the news reached them. Their friends, who often played cards with them, had been shot and killed. Murdered, in cold blood. God knows that every copper who leaves his family each day to go to work may not return. This was one of those days. Three coppers down, catch the one who did it were the orders of the day, for more women were widows and more children had lost their fathers. All because of one person's hate of authority. Apparently a prisoner in the CID office had suddenly pulled a gun out and run out of the office. A uniformed man who bumped into the chap in the passage had a gun pushed into his stomach, the trigger was pulled but the gun didn't go off. A very lucky man. The man ran out of the station, chased by the Station Sergeant, through some gardens and the back door of a house. The owner of the house ordered the fellow from his property and booted him out into the street. Another lucky man. The Station Sergeant chased him along the street and was overtaken by a copper on his 'Noddy' motorcycle, who was also intent on catching the man. Further along the road came a police car, the Inspector who was driving saw the man being chased and, standing beside the car, he asked the man what was going on. Gun pushed into his stomach, trigger pulled, and he was shot in cold blood. The Inspector was dead. Unlucky man.

The motorcyclist caught up on him, the gun was aimed and the trigger pulled. Another unlucky man.

The Skipper closed the gap and closed fast on him. The killer stopped, aimed and fired. The Sergeant dropped down dead. Another unlucky man. The sadistic murderer ran off and escaped. All cars were ordered to be filled up at the start of every shift and guns had to be drawn. This man was dangerous. Every call had to be treated as genuine and attended with the utmost urgency.

There were several sightings, reported sightings and false alarms until one more call came over the air.

"Any car, any car!" came the anxious request.

Jock had just filled up with petrol and they were on their way to the station to collect their arms when the call came.

"To hell with the gun, tell them that we'll deal with it," Jock exclaimed as no other car was available. He accelerated swiftly and the huge fast car sped along towards the 'phone box where the suspect was supposed to be. Another car came on the air, informing the Information Room that they were also available but didn't know where the telephone box was. They required assistance in getting there, the Skip and the Operator didn't know where the location was either, so Jock had to drive at breakneck speeds, avoiding all the other cars and jay walkers, and at the same time direct the other car. His instructions were so clear that as they arrived at a road junction, the other car screamed to a halt in front of him.

The 'phone box was just around the corner and Jock realised that they would have just as far to run from where they were stopped so he switched off the engine and got out, followed by the other two men.

The sound of tyres complaining about the harsh braking alerted a man in the 'phone box. He looked out towards the sound and saw a police car stopping and three coppers in uniform getting out. He dropped the handset and took a gun out of his pocket. As the three wireless car men began to make their way towards the box, he levelled the gun and began to fire at them. As soon as they saw the gun they all dived to the side where they were hidden by the box. Whilst all this had been going on, Jock was running like a mad man, coming from the side, his crepe soled shoes made no sound on the pavement as he closed the gap. The three coppers crouched in safety and watched him running towards his death, not realising that the sound of their tyres had given him a few extra seconds to get closer to the man.

The gunman seemed in a daze, wondering where the coppers had gone. He hated uniforms. He glanced to the right and saw Jock, closely followed by the Sergeant. Whatever passed through his mind will never be known, he may have thought that Jock was being chased by the tubby little man, however, he made his mind up and turned to face the new enemy. He raised the weapon and began to aim it at Jock. Jock's heart was pounding and he was gasping for air, his legs were just a blur as he raced along. He was almost on the man when the chap had realised that these fellows were also coppers and as he pulled the trigger Jock ran into him without slackening of his speed.

There was the sound of an explosion as the pair of them, locked together, fell to the ground. Jock held on tight to the gunman, considering his plight. He didn't feel any pain but had the strong smell of explosive in his nostrils. The gun had been aimed at him and it had gone off but what had happened? He pinned the killer to the ground with his weight as he sucked fresh air deep into his lungs, then the deathly silence was broken by the Sergeant as he panted up to the scene.

"You rotten bastard, you've killed Jock." He had been slightly to the side of Jock and some distance behind him and had seen the gun being raised. He had heard the explosion and saw Jock falling. He was most surprised when Jock his raised his head.

"I think I'm alright Skip," he said and eased himself off the prostrate man.

The killer still held his gun tightly in his right hand but he didn't move for the shot which had been intended for the copper had been deflected and he had shot himself. The bullet came out of the back shoulder blade. He lived for a full week after that and he got no sympathy from the coppers. Before very long the whole place was covered by police cars and senior officers, CID and mixed with the newspaper men who had been listening in on the police wave length.

"Come on Skip, let's go and get a cuppa," Jock muttered to the Skipper. "There's enough of them here to deal with it now." They quietly left the scene to have a well earned cuppa, but as soon as they entered the office, they were ordered to report to the Chief Superintendent. They were on the carpet again and got a right old rollicking for not obeying orders. The orders had been clear enough, they had to collect the firearms as soon as they had filled up, they of course, hadn't done that. They were all reprimanded.

So much for a copper's job, but then, they were getting used to that now.

CHAPTER FOURTEEN

NEW JOB

NEW JOB

The application for Special Branch was at last getting some attention for Jock was detailed to attend for interview. He eventually joined a great line of hopeful applicants standing in a corridor as they waited patiently for their names to be called. At last it was his turn and when his name was called he was ushered into a room where three grim faced men sat behind a desk. They gazed silently at the new applicant as he stood on the small carpet in front of them. Jock was used to being on the carpet so he stood quietly to attention, looking at a point just above their heads. Eventually the questioning began and he was grilled and questioned for some considerable time before he was detailed to attend other rooms for examinations.

From one room to another he went, questions and answers given in the languages he was being tested on, reading, writing and general conversation were all part of the examinations. After he had completed the interrogations he went for lunch and after he had eaten he returned to the corridor and joined the line of men who waited there. He noticed that the number had been reduced considerably since they had started that morning. When it was his turn to go back into the room he found the same three grim faced men sitting in the same positions, they seemed to be engrossed in a file of papers which lay on the desk in front of them - it was Jock's file.

"Seven languages?" It was more of a statement than a question.

"Why did you wait so long before you applied?" the stern faced man in the centre of the group asked.

Jock explained how he had attended evening classes to polish up his grammar and vocabulary and that he wanted to be certain that he would pass any exam he was given, and not trust to luck. Apparently most men applied to join the Branch as soon as they had enough service in. They fired several more questions at him before he was allowed to leave and with never a change of expression.

"Wait outside please," said the man in the middle.

A bored looking detective lounged in the corridor. He had been on duty outside the room all day and probably that was enough to make anyone look fed up.

"What did they tell you to do?" he asked.

"They told me to wait outside" explained Jock. He was then told to go into a nearby office and join the others who were waiting there. He found two other men sitting in the room when he entered and they glanced up at him as he entered and then carried on with their conversation. A short while afterwards another man came in and it became apparent that they all knew one another. It turned out that they had all gone to Cambridge and had been in the same Police class. They were relying on shorthand and one other language to get in the Branch and were more than amused when they found out that Jock did not know Pitman's shorthand.

"But old boy, one never gets anywhere these days without knowing shorthand. They need it in this job you know."

Apparently out of three hundred applicants the list had been reduced to the four of them and Jock was the only one that did not know shorthand. He felt as though he had lost all hope and did not stand a chance. Going by the smug expressions on the faces of his fellow applicants they thought the same way.

"What exactly do you do then, old boy?" the Oxbridge accent came as near as possible to being sympathetic. "They must have some reason for asking you to stay behind. Have you any other language you can speak, apart from Scottish?"

As he had been asked, and being a bit fed up with their attitude, Jock decided to rub it in and he really laid it on for the pleasure of seeing their faces drop. As he told them the extent of his qualifications they looked at one another and looked sick and deflated.

Some time later they were all called back, one at a time, into the office where another round of questions began, before being allowed to go home. A week later Jock received a message which informed him that he had to attend for duty at New Scotland Yard. His dreams had come true at last; he had made it after all the hours of study and the long spells of sitting in a hot classroom with a raincoat over his uniform.

It was with some trepidation and a touch of curiosity that he reported for work at the appointed time and faced his boss. It was the same grim faced man who had sat in the centre of the small group at his interview. He insisted that dress was expected to be perfect at all times due to the fact that one did not know when their presence would be required in a Ministry or Embassy building. He was informed that in future his dress would consist of a dark suit, white shirt, dark tie, black shoes, bowler hat and an umbrella. If the weather was inclement then he would have to wear a dark raincoat or overcoat. Naturally a briefcase would be required for his correspondence. Jock was now one of the 'Bowler hat brigade' as the coppers called them.

"Report to your Inspector in the main office!" were his instructions.

He couldn't miss the main office due to the fact the whole Branch was accommodated on one floor of the building. There were a few men in the room as he entered and introduced himself. An elderly man eased himself out of an armchair with his hand extended and he told Jock that he was destined to be his new boss.

"Welcome to the mob. Hope you live to enjoy it. If you would care to pull a chair up I'll try to put you in the picture of what the job consists of, what you'll have to do and what you can expect whilst you're with us. I'll also try to give you a brief idea of the opposition. It's going to be a long session so if you want to smoke please do so. We'll have a break for coffee later on."

He introduced the rest of the men present before they settled down.

"Your first job every day will be to purchase two newspapers, these ones," and he showed Jock two foreign newspapers. "It will be your job to get them every morning, read them properly, and that means every word. If any article attracts your attention, translate it and type it out and submit all your reports to me. Make sure that every report is correct in all ways and if there are any spelling mistakes or they are not tidy, you will get them back to do again."

"Now, to work. This department consists of five squads; the other four are responsible for the run of the mill stuff. Our squad is like the CID is to the uniform branch, we do all the enquiries, translations, escort and other dirty work. Our job is security and this means working with the Intelligence Departments of this country and others. Intelligence and Espionage are a dirty business so don't forget it. You can't stop and feel sorry for your opponents, it's a case of getting in first, fast and hard. In this line of work if you don't get them, they'll get you, they'll devour you, kill you or make your name like mud. The job involves theft, blackmail, minor crimes and can even include murder."

"You'll find that your opposition has a Department called 'SMERSH', its job is entirely devoted to murder and assassination. One of the men, who was a self confessed assassin or executioner, was called Bogdan Stashnynsky." (Jock later confirmed the existence of this murder squad when he heard of Nikolai Khokhlov, who signed his own death warrant when he defected in 1954. An attempt was made on his life in Frankfurt in 1957 and it was only prompt medical attention that saved his life).

"The KGB also have another squad which is called the 'E and E Squad' and their job is to assist any agent who has been arrested or is about to be arrested. It's for evasion and escape. They assisted such persons as Maclean, Burgess and Blake. Blake was actually helped to escape from Wormwood Scrubs. When Kim Philby was given assistance to get to Russia, he was given a job and a home. Though he was something special for he was one of the top men in Intelligence and had been working for the Soviets for a long time. When he was working in America the CIA began to suspect him so he was transferred back home and eventually was sent to the Middle East and it was from the Middle East that he escaped to Russia.

To do your job properly you'll have to make enquiries at all possible places, such as different registries i.e. The Aliens Registration Office; Criminal records; Bush House; Records of Births; Deaths and Marriages; Libraries; Secretaries of various Political Parties, and even our own Special Branch Registry. We are the only ones who have access to this place. Some foreign visitors will have to be accompanied at all times so this will mean long hours, not much good for a family man I'm afraid. (Jock later found this to be true for he was with them from early morning until late at night and they had put their lights out. He would then have to make his own way home. Puggle would be sitting waiting patiently for his return, anxiously praying he would be alright. The next day, he would be away again early).

You were kicking the backsides of naughty members of the public when you were in uniform but from now on you'll be treading carefully amongst the corns of Diplomats; Nobility; High Ranking Commissioners and their families; High Ranking Police; Civil Servants; Government Officers and Ministers. These will all require special handling, in fact like us, you'll be walking a tightrope or walking on thin ice. Dangers are always present when you deal with certain members of this class. There are people who have little regard for the law and play for higher stakes than the ordinary thief, human life is cheap and expendable to them.

In your attempts to obtain information, it will be essential to make contacts. Residents of other countries are the most obvious and as this part will be left to you, you'll have to make your own groups of informants. Most people wonder about the double life of a spy, how much of what they read in the papers is true? A spy is arrested or another being exchanged, but what is a spy? What does he do? The public neither know nor care, nor do they appreciate how far some countries will go in order to obtain information. Getting information has always been the job of Diplomats who are accredited officers sent to obtain such information about the countries where they are sent to work. The professional Intelligence officer, disguised as a Diplomat, works outside the code of honour and if he's caught he'll be declared a persona non grata."

"The Soviets, and some of their followers, operate on a saturation basis by using official covers. They pack their Embassies with Intelligence Officers, they also use these in their other offices. Because the KGB chairman is both a member of the Council and the Police Bureau, he outranks the Soviet Minister of Foreign Affairs. Consequently he can secure a high proportion of posts for his Intelligence Officers. It is estimated that there are over sixty percent of the staff in a Soviet Mission who are believed to be spies. In the Third World countries this number is greatly increased. On top of that, we'll find western countries will have to use the local labour to work as drivers and gardeners etc, whereas the Russians will not allow any other person except their own people inside their Embassies."

"They also include the International organisations for their spies. The most important, where the spies operate from, is the United Nations with all its different branches. Over twenty Russians have been arrested or expelled for their activities whilst working with UN. With over thirty-six Russian agents working for Russia in the Scientific and Cultural Organisation, it shows how far they will go to collect information. There are moves afoot at the present moment to try and reduce the number of such people who work there. Sergei Nikhaibovitch Kudragatsev was a senior KGB officer who had been publicly exposed in various countries as a spy, yet he was given the job of being the Soviet's permanent representative in UNESCO."

"You'll have to forget the names you had for 'Grasses' because from now they will be known as 'Informants'. Your 'Fingers' and 'Tea Leaves' are not thieves, but suspects and activists, and a 'Dodgy Cuss' is not a suspect but a possible security risk. You'll find that all your old slang words have been replaced, such as the ones I've told you, also you'll have to get to know a lot more.

For instance, an agent in a place is a spy who has access to secret material, and an agent of influence is a one in a high place who is able to shape events for the opposition, for example there was Philby. A 'Bag Job' indicates a break in, this is usually to obtain photographs or to collect material."

"During your duties you'll hear such words as 'Black Information', which indicates this was received from some undercover source, whilst the 'White Information' comes from open sources. 'To Blow' means that a spy's identity has been discovered and a 'Case Officer' is the person who has direct supervision of a spy."

"If you hear of a 'Roll Up', you know that a capture has been made, whilst a 'Sleeper' is not a copper having a kip on night duty but an agent who is being kept for future use. A 'Stable' is not a place where they keep horses, it's a roster of women who are willing to help in sexual enlistment."

"Naturally, as I have said, there are many more such phrases which cover such things as cameras, hidden microphones, illegal and even executions. You, Jock, are being thrown into the deep end for you will have to engage in complicated operations with Polish, Hungarians, Russians and Czechs, all people who have escaped from the Eastern Block. You will have to spend a lot of time with them in their homes or at their places of work. Get to know them as much as possible and get to know as much as you can from them for you'll need every bit of help that they can give. If they are willing to set up their own units to get information for you that will be up to them. Make no record of names or addresses. If you have to visit them at home or a place of business, just make sure you're not followed because if the Russians found out about them, they would have no hesitation about killing them."

"It is estimated that about three quarters of information obtained comes from 'White' Intelligence sources such as books, magazines, directories, year books or papers written by some learned society. Those written by experts are on some particular subject they were working on such as mining, commerce, science, aviation or possibly agriculture." This 'White Intelligence' is the type that supplied Jock with a vast amount of knowledge for his job and assisted greatly with his enquiries.

"Whilst all such paperwork is classed as White there still remains the percentage which is classified as being 'Black'. The 'Black Intelligence' information of course comes from the undercover agents and this indicates espionage. The information obtained by this method may have no meaning at all to the person who acquired it however, overall, the small pieces can fit together like a jigsaw puzzle."

"With this type of activity going on, it is necessary to try and prevent it and also to try and stop it leaving the country. We have to try and apprehend the persons responsible and this is one of your jobs."

"You know Jock, even though recruits come from the regular police to join our job you will find that the officers here are not typical coppers. Before you were accepted into the Branch, you were checked thoroughly, references and personal history were all looked into. You are expected to be bright enough to adapt the dress and manners of whatever circle you are moving in. Unlike the CID you will be trained to look for political background and ideas rather than for the direct evidence of a crime."

"Qualifications normally include shorthand, plus at least one other foreign language but, in your case with your vast knowledge of so many languages, you are far more suited in the work which you will be doing. The greatest skill will be to observe and remain unnoticed, just to blend in with the background and to use your knowledge of languages to listen and make note, mentally, if not in writing."

"A spy is selected by taking into account his education, political training, experience, personal and business qualities. Consequently, an agent can get acquainted with foreigners without his behaviour being questioned. The KGB is able to gather information about politics because their officers are generally posted into the press and culture departments, and officers engaged with the questions of technology are in the trades section."

"An agent's cover need not be fictitious; concealment could be through his normal lifestyle or true occupation which has been built up over a period of years. For example, Klaus Fuchs who was working as an atomic scientist at Harwell Research Station, he was sentenced to fourteen years for spying and he went to Russia after he was released."

"The difference between them and us is great, you know, Jock. For instance, one of our Commanders recently said that a good SB man was judged by the fact that he keeps out of public eye. That doesn't mean that you just have to keep out of the way, because you'll have a stack of work put on you every day from different departments, and they have to be answered. The reason is that our work is secret and we don't welcome outside interests. It's impossible for anyone to learn anything about this organisation because we bridge the gap between the Police and Intelligence Departments. As our work is carried out in the full glare of public scrutiny, we are the favourite target for those who have most to lose from our enquiries. We concentrate on various fields of assassination; terrorism; revolution; sabotage; espionage; counter-espionage; protection; surveillance; infiltration; subversion and Intelligence gathering. So you see Jock, we have a lot of opposition to contend with."

"We haven't just the Russians to contend with you know. There are just as many in this country who are as bad as the Reds. You have to consider that the work is hard and tedious, the hours are long, and danger is your companion all the time. Even though our Department is very small compared to Russia and other countries, they can always find various parties, agencies, Councils, Individuals and Trade Unions, even MPs, who try to get rid of our Branch. For instance, the leader of the opposition recently protested during the ABC case, that's the case of Aubrey, Berry and Campbell, he said that the Police must be denied the licence to use their professional position for the pursuit of private, political, religious and moral beliefs."

"The problem, basically, is that the British public are not interested whereas Communists are always working in their own insidious ways. The whole slimy corruption can start in a factory where Union meetings are called; the average worker doesn't bother to attend, it's just a rush home for dinner and then out to the pub with their mates for a quick pint. The Communists, however, have to go to the meetings and therefore when a vote is taken, the decisions are unanimous. When a Shop Steward is appointed, then he must be one of their men so before long the whole factory is taken over."

"The fanatical, well-trained agent or one of his officers can whip up hate amongst the crust of the employees. When an open vote is demanded, the workmen are like sheep, they see all the bully boys and activists in front of them raise their hands. Slowly but surely, sometimes reluctantly, they all follow suit. A strike or action is therefore demanded by the open vote. The Communists create the strikes, as the recent one caused by the NUM, even the most innocent member of the public know the Communists and the trouble-makers who appear regularly on television, but they don't know the ones who are behind the scenes whose faces and names are never known."

"It will not take many large organisations to be crippled by strikes before you find that the whole of British Industry is affected. You can see how such actions could cause serious problems to the economics and production of this country. Foreign agents would not be required in this country if it were not for Special Branch being there. They strive to prevent the collapse of the Industry and to get rid of the spies who operate. They also seek out the British subjects who have joined their cause. Personally Jock, I would say that if all these people consider that the Russians have it so good, they can pack their bags and go to Russia. It would be cheaper to pay their fare. At least in this country we haven't got torture or concentration camps. No, they know when they're well of."

"The aim of Russia is to take over other countries and enlarge their own borders. There is no person moving in that country who is not being watched and reported on. There is no job nor occupation which is not riddled with the secret police or their helpers. Every ship which sails the seven seas has a KGB man aboard, he is really in command of the vessel and the personnel, even though technically the Skipper is in command of the boat. Likewise, every group of individuals, athletics or musicians have a similar person travelling with them. These people do their job well, as many immigrants know, for when some of them escaped and entered the free world they brought with them the knowledge and experiences which would later be used against their tormentors."

(These were some of the people who Jock had to contact and work with and his knowledge of various languages proved to be a valuable asset when he worked with the little groups in the underworld of politics because they would do anything to help him in his tireless efforts).

The Inspector pushed back his chair.

"I think I've given you the facts that you'll need, naturally there are a lot more things you'll have to learn and it would take far too long. If you have any questions or problems, all you have to do is ask. Now, I'll see about you getting your side arms, you'll have to practice at least once a week, you buy your own ammunition of course. There will be some work waiting for you on your desk, I'll show you where your office is.

So, Jock was at last sitting in his own office. He looked at the small pile of papers on his desk and slowly shuffled through them. The first one only consisted of one line, a request from MI5, they couldn't do the enquiries so his assistance was required. He looked at the other memos and found they were all similar, short and brief, and all from different Branches and Departments. His work was starting at last.

The days passed and turned into weeks, then months. Jock was settled down to his new job and he had managed to make several contacts with the underground fighters. The foreigners who were willing to die in their fight against communism.

His contact with former residents of different communist countries was of great assistance to him; one of his best contacts was a former Russian subject, a man who had held a very high position in his country. He had escaped with his daughter as she felt the same way about Russian politics and methods. She ran a magnificent underground movement in Britain that was comprised completely of her own country folk. They, like their leader, couldn't do enough for the English and consequently Jock took full advantage of their organisation. This was only one group of the many he had managed to get operating.

Although the old man could speak perfect English and was a well educated person, he insisted that all conversation should be held in Russian. This was for Jock's benefit in order to assist him with his accent and knowledge of terminology. Jock appreciated this, although he would have appreciated their assistance in writing his reports.

After completion of his work in the office, Jock pushed his typewriter aside and commenced to study his latest requests which had been awaiting his attention and he made a few notes regarding the names he had to check on at Aliens office. Picking up his pile of completed reports, he had checked them and knew that everything was in order; he thought it marvellous how such a large pile of papers could arise from just one small piece of paper with just one line written on it! Naturally, to get a dossier a few inches thick required a hell of a lot of legwork. One of the first things he had to do was to obtain the basic details of each person he had to check on. This was what he had to do now and that was the reason he was going to ARO.

After he had handed his reports in he headed for the stairs.

"Morning Mr MacGregor, going anywhere special?" said another officer as he walked along the corridor.

"Just stretching my legs as far as Piccadilly Place," Jock replied.

"Going there myself, I'll join you if you don't mind," the officer said.

"Are you busy? I have an Embassy job on this morning and it shouldn't take long, would you care to join me so that I can get the job finished today?"

Jock agreed to go along with his colleague to help him out because he knew that regulations insisted upon anyone entering a foreign Embassy or Legation should have a witness present.

They walked across Whitehall and along Downing Street; over Horse Guards Parade and St. James Park, before crossing The Mall and climbing the steps towards Piccadilly. Jock enjoyed these brief walks, together they stepped out briskly and smartly, bowlers on straight and swinging their umbrellas. This was the best part of the job because things were not as peaceful all the time.

From Aliens' office, after they had acquired the information they needed, they walked along to the nearby Embassy. Before very long they were sitting in an office and enjoying a cup of tea with the Secretary, before the questioning started.

"Cigarette?" the man asked, offering the silver container which held the weed.

Jock's companion took one of the proffered cigarettes but, as usual, Jock declined, saying

"I would much rather smoke my pipe, if you have no objection?"

Pipes seem to be an object of curiosity as far as the Eastern Block is concerned, the British always seem to smoke them, so permission was given. Jock filled and lighted his trusty old bowl and then sat back to enjoy it, as he was watched with curiosity. He shook the match out and looked for an ashtray to place the burnt match into but was faced with a problem because there weren't any in sight. Well, he wasn't going to show the British breed up by throwing his matchstick on the floor of the Consul, so he put it in the box again.

The conversation had begun and Jock realised that he was taking a chance when he put the match back into his box, but nothing had happened. He sat listening to his partner obtain the facts he needed when suddenly there was a terrific roar and the office filled with a cloud of choking foul-smelling sulphuric smoke. The Secretary yelled with alarm, or was it terror, and the door of his office burst open as a crowd of armed security men rushed in waving their weapons.

It was some time after the smoke had dispersed when Jock, who was red in the face, managed to convince them all that it had been an accident. He showed them the box full of burnt out matches just to satisfy them. There was laughter all round as they looked at the still smouldering contents and they were satisfied that they were in no danger of being blown up. Everyone thought it funny, except Jock because he had learnt another lesson, never trust a dead match and better still, never smoke in one of their places again.

Once the interview had been completed they headed back to the office and Jock was in more of a relaxed mood, having overcome his temporary embarrassment and they laughed about the incident. As they entered the building and were passing the Guvnor's office, they saw a detective in the passage looking very sorry for himself.

"What's wrong Cecil?" asked Jock's colleague. The man told them that he had just been on the receiving end of the boss's tongue. Through some quirk of fate, even though he was on holiday, he had come into the office just to leave his holiday address. He was an ex naval officer and dressed ready for his leave. He had a navy blazer on with an immaculate pair of greys and his shoes were shining so much that you could shave in them! However, his luck had run out when he was requested to go into the Guv's office. The big man told him he looked like a tramp and if he wanted to look like a tramp he could quite easily be sent back to uniform.

"When you're in this department, you must always be prepared to be sent anywhere at any time. You will always be dressed correctly," he was ordered.

His reasons and excuses were not accepted.

The copper who had just been told off did not appreciate the joke, he was completely filled with misery and his holidays had been spoilt. Jock and his companion left him in his sorrows as they headed back to their own offices to carry on with the mountain of work that each of them had. As Jock waded through the pile of work he was disturbed by one of his Inspector friends. Jock was nearly finished sorting his papers out for the journey so he stopped to chat with his pal.

"What kind of baccy do you smoke Jock?" he asked as he watched Jock filling his pipe. "You seem to like it and you always seem to be content as you sort your papers out or do your typing."

The truth of it was that he was on the scrounge because he had recently been given a new pipe as a present. Although he gave the impression that he had never smoked a pipe before and wanted hints on the filling and handling of the pipe. He wanted to know the secrets and was not wanting to waste money on the purchase of an ounce of tobacco, only to find that he didn't like it; he much preferred to scrounge a fill from Jock and if he didn't like it he could try some other tobacco.

So it was arranged that he should bring his pipe to work the next day and Jock would show him what to do. He had warned him that it was very strong but the Inspector wouldn't be put off and the next morning they met in the canteen and had a cup of coffee. The pipe came out and was filled, under Jock's eagle eye. The baccy was tamped down and lit The Inspector puffed away to get his pipe ignited as the pair of them headed for the stairs which led to their respective offices. Just before they reached the landing, Jock's companion was puffing strongly at the pipe causing great clouds of smoke to belch out and fill the passage, he then grew bolder and continued his puffing, seemingly taking great pleasure in seeing the vast amount of smoke he was creating. Suddenly he started to run, he left Jock and headed for the nearest toilet.

About ten minutes later as Jock sat at his desk pounding away at his typewriter, the door opened and he glanced up at the man as he entered.

"Are you alright?" he asked.

"No, I'm bloody well not!" the man snarled as he stalked across the room. "Sod the bloody pipe, I'm as sick as a bloody dog and I'll stick to my gaspers in future." He then opened the window and threw his new pipe out onto the Embankment as far as he could.

Jock smiled to himself. 'Teach him not to be so bloody tight' - Jock had omitted to inform him of one important thing and that was not to inhale the tobacco because it had proved to be far too strong for a lot of people.

SECURITY

On big jobs the workload increased tremendously. Weddings, Funerals, Coronations, visits by Foreign Heads of state etc. all made it necessary for more premises to be checked and many more people to be vetted. A big detail came and the entire route of an intended procession had to be checked over. This meant that every house and its occupants had to be put through the registries; also, every office block and its employees had to be cleared and every factory viewed with suspicion where it overlooked the route. This route covered numerous miles so it meant a lot of men had to work long hours and do a lot of legwork.

Once this hectic checking had been completed, six men from the squad were delegated for special security and Jock was one of those men. On the Fifteenth of March, a Yugoslavian sailing ship glided into the Thames and berthed at Westminster Pier. Marshall Tito stepped ashore surrounded by his host of security men. As he landed he was met by a crowd of representatives from the Ministry and a large mob of civil servants.

The contingent of British security men were not really needed for the great man was well and truly protected by his own strong-arm mob who apparently carried a great variety of weapons between them.

The peace was broken when some idiot in the watching crowds set a smoke bomb off. Action was automatic and the escort closed tightly around their leader. One of these men stood close beside Jock and looked at the enormous gun which had been drawn. All the other members of the guard had also drawn their guns. Jock spoke to the man and told him that he had nothing to fear as the incident wasn't serious.

"Invinite molia, nije ozhiljac je."

"Jeste il Yugoslavea?" the worried guard, quickly turning to face him, asked him if he was Yugoslavian.

Jock tried to calm the man and assured him that he was a member of the British Police.

"Ja sam Engles. Ja nadin zamilieju." But the worried man was still not satisfied and asked for Jock's identification papers.

"I mate li legitimaci ju molia."

After the papers had been handed over, the man perused them and Jock guessed that the chap couldn't understand them. He questioned Jock about his knowledge of Serb Croat for it wasn't normal for a Britisher to speak their language. Jock explained that he had served in the Army during the war and had been with the Yugoslavians for a while. As soon as the escort had ascertained these facts, he turned to Marshall Tito and spoke to him.

The eyes flicked across and Jock found himself under scrutiny. He was being closely examined by the visitor who eventually he came across, smiling and with his hand outstretched. He grasped Jock by the hand and shook it warmly.

"I remember you. There were three of you working with explosives at the time, am I not correct?" He was grinning broadly as he swung Jock's hand up and down.

"Your boat was sunk by the Germans wasn't it?"

He seemed to remember every detail of their previous meeting. They talked together surrounded by a solid wall of armed men who stood with their backs towards them. The worried men from the Ministry stood on the outside of the circle watching this very unusual display.

"You are dressed very different now, you were nearly in rags the last time we met," the big man stated.

They talked together for some time before Jock managed to get the message from the worried British contingent that they should get a move on.

"I think my boss wants us to go," he told Tito.

"That is one of my troubles, I can't do what I want to these days," replied the Marshall pulling a face. He said goodbye to Jock and returned to the Home Office men and he was soon whisked away to a safer place.

The next morning Jock found a 'request' on his desk amongst all the other stuff. The 'request' was from his boss asking him to attend his office as soon as possible. Naturally, the great man was worried as were all those from the Foreign Office and the Ministry. They all wanted to know about Jock's acquaintance with the visitor to this country. They also wished to know all about the conversation which took place so openly in public, and most of all they wanted to know how Jock knew the Marshall.

"Explain yourself Mr MacGregor."

It didn't take long for Jock to put his mind at ease. He told his boss everything that had been said and how they had met during the war. A huge sigh of relief greeted the explanation for after all they couldn't have a member of British Special Branch being pally with a head of a Communist state, could they?

SMALL PEOPLE

Not all of the people he met were of the same status as Tito for he came in contact with the underground of politics and consequently, various types of folk were involved and they came from all walks of life. The reason was simple because after the war had ended in Europe, it was found that millions of Soviets, and the citizens from their satellite countries, had been left behind in occupied Germany. These included prisoners of war, forced labour, plus a mixture of Balts, Ukrainians etc. who had just moved along in front of the advancing Russian troops.

An agreement was reached to return these people to their own countries. However, after all the returns had been completed, it was found that some thousands of émigrés remained, not wishing to return. These came from all parts of the continent, including the Ukraine, the Baltic States, Armenia, Czechoslovakia, Byelorussia and many other countries.

This tremendous body of people created a veritable hunting ground for the Communists who were hoping to obtain their services as agents for the KGB. Likewise, the western powers also had this prospect in mind for the émigrés would prove easy to recruit and they also wanted their skills and services. These people hated the Russians and their methods, this was one of the reasons they had avoided going back to their own countries. Sometimes whole groups of volunteers could be obtained from the willing sources but Jock was only interested in those who came to Britain to live. This then was the background of the contacts he made.

CALL

Jock browsed lazily through the books and occasionally he would glance at one then return it to the shelf. He would pick up another and appear to be interested in it for a while before that too was returned to its original position. To anyone watching he would look like just another potential customer. Coming to the botanical section he reached up and glanced at several books, turning the pages and then returning them to the original places.

He casually flicked through the pages of a book about flowers, his movements were no different and his face gave nothing away but this particular book interested him tremendously. It was a volume about Chrysanthemums and it had been placed upside down on the shelf.

Jock was interested in this particular book even though he didn't show it. He casually picked the issue from the rack, his code name was Chrysanth, and the book showed that someone either wanted to pass a message or contact him. As he glanced through the pages he noted that the nineteenth page had been turned down. Eventually he replaced the book back on the shelf, after turning the page back. Browsing through the rest of the collection he removed the nineteenth book off the top shelf and after he had completed his examination, he put the book back where he had taken it from. He had received the message. After a few more minutes, he left the shop and stood in the doorway to fill and light his pipe. He used this short time to examine the street, just to ensure that no other person was on his tail or watching the premises.

This shop was one of the many such places that Jock used to either meet, make contact with, or pass messages onto his informants. Using the book system, no written message need be passed or carried and no conversation was made that could be recorded. However, the information he had just received was serious, someone wanted to meet him but he didn't like this because it was dangerous if the other side knew. He was well trained in street surveillance and ensured that he was not being followed as he made his way through the streets to meet his informant. There were a million and one ways to dodge anyone following and Jock was very careful for a lot of lives could have depended on it.

After a roundabout route he came to a row of dingy houses situated in a small back street. Jock had wondered why his contact had requested him to come, surely it would have been safer to meet somewhere away from the house, but whatever the reason he would soon find out. He checked the street once more before stepping down the stairs to the basement. A muttered request came in response to his knock.

"Chrysanth." His reply caused the door to be opened at once and he was greeted warmly by a burly man with a deep guttural Baltic voice. The man greeted Jock with great affection and, taking his arm, he guided him along the passageway which was lined with cabinets filled with books of all kinds, encyclopaedias of knowledge reached from the front door to the back.

"In here." He was directed into the back room where a pretty young woman stood. "My daughter, you have met, yes?"

Jock admitted that he had not had the pleasure of meeting the young woman before.

"How do you do" she said in a pleasant, well-educated voice. She looked intelligent and had clear blue eyes, which gazed openly and frankly at Jock.

"Now" said his host. "A drink and then to work."

"We have so much to talk about my friend," he said, passing the whisky round. They sat down and began to fill their pipes. Jock was waiting for the woman to leave them but his host seemed to realise this.

"Don't mind her, she's one of us, she hates the commies more than I do. She has her own group and that's what I want to talk to you about" and as he turned to his daughter.

"Tell him."

The story she told was brief and concise about agents operating and suspicions of infiltrations into the MI5 and also of movements in America.

"Yes we have knowledge of these rumours but it is proof we need," Jock told her.

"Proof." This beautiful wench seemed out of place in this place. "If it's proof you want, then you shall have it, come with me." She led the way into the front room and as he entered the darkened interior he tensed as he realized there were other people in there. His hand flew automatically to his shoulder holster but stopped short as he recognised the six men who sat quietly in the dim light. The girl switched the light on and her father ushered him to a vacant chair.

Jock greeted the members of the group as he sat down. Nothing was said by them, they just sat and waited for their leader to open the discussion. As Russian was their mother tongue, the conversation was going to take place in that language, as their leader had previously ordered for Jock's benefit. Naturally, if there was anything he wasn't certain about it would be clarified. Speaking in Russian the men could express themselves without bothering to have it translated.

At the woman's instructions they began to talk, starting with the man she had indicated, to begin. They went into great detail one after the other, occasionally the speaker was interrupted by one of the others who wanted to enlarge upon the speaker's words, on some point he thought was necessary. Jock listened intently to each one, the basic comments didn't disturb him unduly for he had already been informed about the 'Mole', believed to be in British security. What he wanted to know was who was the man that everyone was speaking about? He knew how much importance these good folk had placed in their information but he wanted a name as well as the proof.

The basic information given tied two associations together, they were operating against the British yet they were classed as 'Friendly'. 'Friendly they were to some country from behind the Iron Curtain but not to England. It was disclosed that their leaders, called the 'Secretary', were both sons of High Commissioners. Some of Jock's informants had gained entry to the associations to follow up their enquiries. It was the results of their enquiries which they now disclosed to Jock.

A list of possible agents were high level people, apart from the two sons of Diplomats. There were Italians, one of whom could also claim Diplomatic privilege, then came a couple of Americans. These names did come as a surprise to Jock, especially when he found out where they were employed. One of them worked in the White House whilst the other was a member of the CIA. The final figure was the one who was the most important, this was the one that interested Jock. However, his informants were vague about details, all they could say was that he was a leading figure in the British MI5. They couldn't provide his name, only a code name.

Jock considered the situation, the group had done a bit of good work, and it only needed the final touches to clean a few agents up. After each man had completed his statement and had been questioned by Jock, the woman and the father, the young lady turned to Jock.

"Well, what do you think?"

"Nobody is above suspicion" answered Jock. "We have known for some time that there was a mole in MI5 but we want to know his name, we cannot do anything on guess work."

Jock's host interrupted just then.

"Do you know, we've been working on this for a long time now and it has not been without its dangers, so please don't treat it too lightly. We have lost two good men trying to get the information you require. It seems that our enemy have found a new way to dispose of anyone they suspect."

Prompted by Jock, he continued.

"They have built a new type of gun and it looks just like an ordinary umbrella. It's powered by a compressed gas which is released by a trigger in the handle, it fires a very small pellet from its tip. The pellet only leaves a small break in the skin and the plastic dissolves with body heat. The poison is RICIN, which is short for Trichlotinile, which gives all the signs of a heart attack. Both George Markov and Vladimir Kostov were attacked by this weapon.

"I'm sorry about your colleagues but we want this man. We need proof, evidence in writing, photographs, or copies of the originals, and we want his name. I want to thank you all for the good work you have done, you've done an awful lot. A lot more than some people but I'm very much afraid that I must ask you for that little extra. I want every possible place examined thoroughly and every smallest detail obtained. What we need is solid evidence, you may not be able to obtain it but together with some other evidence gathered by your colleagues, it may make some sense. I must warn you once again that the people we are after must not be disturbed in any way, they must not know or be pre-warned of any intended action. Now, if there are no questions we'll go over the whole lot from the beginning."

The group knew exactly what was needed because Jock had impressed upon them so many times that if they had to break in (do a bag job) then they must not leave evidence, so no questions were asked. All they required now was the directions for the big job awaiting them. So the meeting dragged on, all details were discussed and arrangements made to obtain the required documents.

Jock planned each case with the individuals concerned, he knew that these chaps would risk their lives in order to break the corrupt Communist organisations but he had no fears for them on these present assignments. Each one had his orders, or rather suggestions, and he knew that they would carry them out properly and leave no visiting cards to show they had been.

"If you need any more assistance or any more men, just let me know and I'll arrange for some of the other groups to come in with you." He knew that he could get a small army of men to do the jobs if needed, but it was better to keep a small number, if possible. A crowd of people stand out and attract attention but he had no worries about this small group who had seen their homes ransacked and burnt, families executed by the villains they now fought. They had seen torture and punishment, and imprisonment. Jock had similar groups working for him and they all had the same desire, to get rid of the world of communism. They all assisted him faithfully, without any thought of peril or payment.

'They are a good bunch' he thought as he pulled his bowler firmly down on his head and marched along the grimy street, away from the terraced house that looked so very much like every other one in the street.

A week later, a huge pile of papers lay on the desk in front of him. He read them slowly, concentrating on every word, making sure that he never missed any point. Each one was digested thoroughly before placing it on the completed file in its correct place.

After consuming all the details, he numbered them and laid them in their separate piles. Each one referred to a different person, they had to fall in order with his own completed report which would include them all. The only things missing from that file would be the names of the persons who had helped him obtain the vital information. Five different Governments were involved, so protocol had to be considered. The families of High Commissioners were also tied in with the report. CIA were involved and would have to be contacted about their double agent. He also had a colleague to be arrested. There were also the problems of the member of their armed forces who was 'An Agent of Influence' and worked in the White House. Jock realised that the icing on the cake was the case officer in America. The man who received his orders and information from White House and relayed the information on to Russia, he had to be caught. The problem Jock had was his own MI5. officers who were involved in this drama. Once he submitted the report and handed it in to their office he knew that this information would be transferred to America. The agents would then make themselves scarce before CIA could pounce. He would have to warn them first.

'Hell, I can't take a chance' he decided and muttered to himself, and then collected the papers together.

He headed along the passage to his Inspector's office to discuss the situation. He knew what he had to do but required permission first. It took some time to go through the file with his boss and at the end of the talk the Inspector decided that the Chief Inspector must decide. Together they approached the Chief and once more the problem was thrashed out. It was a very highly complicated case and eventually the boss pushed the files across to Jock.

"It is a problem Jock. You have done all the work up until now and I think I'll leave it to your own judgment. Let us know the results."

That cleared up, but he had not been given any suggestion about what to do. Not that he expected any ideas coming from them. They took the view that a good Detective could sort things out without being told. He had already made his mind up about the jigsaw of the various suspects. He knew that as soon as the information and proof relating to MI5 and the American cousins was disclosed, the cover would be blown, for Head Office would warn them at once.

BROTHERS

'Hell, he thought, I cannot take that chance', and decided to break regulations and contact his friend in CIA first. He picked up the 'phone and dialled the number.

"Dry cleaners," a female voice squealed.

"I want to hire an evening suit," he said.

"Sorry, this is a dry cleaners, Sir," the female voice replied.

"I know, but I understand that you hire out," Jock answered.

"Only for special occasions, Sir," she said.

"This is a very special occasion and I want a first class outfit," was Jock's response.

"First class, Sir? I understand, is it only for the one night?"

"Yes it is," Jock told her. "It's very urgent and I want it for tonight at The Hilton Hotel, for six o'clock."

"I understand Sir, in which case we'll do our best to oblige you and see that your needs are met. The name please?" the lady asked.

Jock gave her the name of the person he wished to contact and then hung up and placed the written report appertaining to the American situation, together with the documents his friends had collected, into his briefcase. These were ready for his meeting later that night with the CIA chief. 'Ah well' he muttered. 'The President may as well pay for my dinner'.

He met his contact dead on the dot of six o'clock. They had worked together on previous cases.

"Good evening Mr MacGregor, short of cash again, you want me to pay for your meal?" A typical joke.

"Of course, why else would I want to talk to you?" said Jock, laughing.

"When you walk along you lean over with the weight of cash in your pocket. I feel sorry for you and just want to straighten you up a little."

The pair of them always got on well together, they always had a joke and a crack whenever they met. As they walked to the table which was ready for them.

"Urgent was the message?" said his colleague

"Very, awkward as well," Jock replied.

"How come?" The yank gave his order and Jock decided to make it easy for the waiter and ordered the same. As the waiter moved away to get the meals, he outlined the situation to his friend.

"You mean the man at the top?" the yank asked in astonishment.

"Exactly, now if I put my reports through the correct channels, we will definitely lose them. At least your side will," Jock told him.

"How come?"

"We have this hot potato at the top of MI5 and I have to take these reports back personally to them. What will happen? The cover has been blown and everyone will know, so what will they do because the agents would be withdrawn before anyone could act."

"Correct, we would do the same" his friend answered.

"You have one in the White House, a case officer, and a double in your own department," Jock informed him.

The man, taken by surprise by this statement, slopped his food down the front of his jacket.

"You're kidding?"

"No"

"Any proof?"

"In here," Jock laid the envelope on the table. The agent stopped eating and read the contents.

"Christ" he expounded. "Can I have these?"

"Sorry, originals," the Special Branch man answered. "I have to keep them I my possession all the while, until I hand them in."

"Hell man!" The boss choked as he read the files.

It was quite obvious that the CIA man wanted the papers, he was worried. Jock came up with the solution, to quieten him down, by telling him that he could run some copies off.

"Good, as you have to keep hold of these, you'd better come with me," he said.

"Right, but what about the grub?" Jock smiled at the man's eagerness.

"To hell with the meal. This is important. Come on, I have a 'phone call to make."

He was a man of action and few words. He made a bee-line and before very long he was through to Washington. He made the required arrangements for the White House agent to be arrested and close observations to be kept on the CIA case officer.

"Yes, I have written evidence in front of me at this very moment" he said.

"When can I have the copies?" he asked Jock after he had hung up.

"Tomorrow," was the brief reply.

"Good, let's go and finish our meal because we have something to celebrate now. Don't forget Mac we owe you a big one. Any time you need anything at all, you know where to find me." The yank was grateful.

"I'll remember, but all I want is a name, the one at the top," he said as he replaced the papers back into his brief case. "I'll report this through the usual channels tomorrow, so eventually you'll be notified via the official channels. That will give our friends time to be warned and for your agents to collect the Case Officer and any contacts he may have in America." Jock thanked his host.

"I'll see you tomorrow morning!!" Jock headed back to his own office to begin his massive pile of reports. They would have to be examined by his Chief Inspector for any grammatical mistakes or typewriting errors before being allowed to go to another department.

The contents were checked to ensure they were in chronological order and as each name was read in the report, it appeared as the next in line on the border, with all the others. Eventually he assembled the piles of paper, tapped them straight and headed along to see his boss. The Chief Inspector looked through the massive amount of reading matter which had been placed before him and eventually he looked at Jock.

"Good work, but it looks as though you're stirring up a hornet's nest with CIA"

Jock then explained what he had done unofficially to keep the CIA happy and upon hearing this his boss was a changed man and he cheered up quite a bit.

"Well you seem to have got round that problem and have sorted all the other ones out, except our own." He examined the paragraph regarding the Italians. "We could do some more work on these and see what you come up with." He made a few notes on his pad. "Naturally we will have to take this further regarding the security, so re-type your report and leave them out of it." He collected the file and handed it to Jock. "Right, now we'll go and see the Commander."

The big man read them without saying a word, finally he spoke to the Chief Inspector.

"Deportation, Diplomatic Privileged and Immunity are all involved. You checked these Inspector."

When he had given the affirmative he turned to Jock and pushed the file across. "Right, carry on Mr MacGregor. Jolly good show."

"Someone put the cat amongst the pigeons. We had all the lines tapped and radios were covered, and they all got caught. See you soon." Jock's friend telephoned him a few days later.

Jock knew by that call that someone in a high position in MI5 had used his information to warn the case officer in America that the law was on to them. They didn't know that action had been taken beforehand and it was a trap. A further message from his mate in America informed him that the arrested suspects had been grilled and questioned, but under no circumstances could they get any information from them about the true identity of the man in London, all they knew him by was his code name.

The following days created havoc with Jock's family life, the youngsters had grown up hardly knowing they had a father. The hours were so long and over the next few weeks they grew longer still as all the spies were rounded up. He was getting home in the early hours of the morning when the kids were in bed asleep, and going out to work before they were up for school.

SPIES

Other long spells followed as more serious cases came to life. It even came to a point when days and nights were spent away from home. Some agents spent their time collecting scientific and technical information, as an Intelligence officer's cover is selected by taking into account his education; political and specialised training; and his personal and business qualities. This is so he can be no different from the others employed doing the same work.

Some spies get a lot of money from their activities, such as Gordon Lonsdale, his true name being Konon Trofimovich Molody, a Soviet Agent. He is reputed to have received £45,000 from a British newspaper for his memoirs, after he had been exchanged for Greville Wynne who was being held by the Russians. Lonsdale was involved with the Portland Spy Ring.

It was in this case that a man called Harry Houghton had come under suspicion because of his high living. Special Branch were informed and investigated. This case was already on their books for a Michael Golencewski, who had defected from the East, had been questioned closely. He provided a wealth of information on how he had been successful with sex traps. Fifteen employees of the American Embassy in Moscow had been compromised, the results were that a fairly high ranking official and four others were sent home and fired. Also ten Marines, the entire guard, was withdrawn and replaced.

He also made reference to one agent who was an employee of the Naval Attaché. This man was Houghton, who had been compromised by the Poles in 1958. Lonsdale took over Houghton as a spy and in his control. Houghton was under surveillance and was living with Ethel Gee in a caravan and he had access to secret documents. With this contact, Lonsdale also became a suspect. Packages were also seen being passed and he was followed and went to a house in Ruislip. It was in this house that Helen and Peter Kroger lived. A large team of men were used to keep them all under observation for 24 hours a day. Arrests were made when Houghton was in possession of secret naval documents. Gee also had similar papers. The Kroger's house was searched and a considerable amount of material used by spies was found hidden away. These included printed sheets of a spy's personal cipher (these consisted of groups of figures that were produced at random on a computer. The computers produced a permutation of groups by the million so each group was used only once and then destroyed. It was therefore impossible to break the code). Microdots and microdot readers; high powered short wave radios; false and forged passports and stacks of cash. Microdots are made first by taking a photograph of the required documents and then the plate is exposed through a microscope onto film, this reduces the photograph down to the size of a dot. Once made, they have to be hidden and it has been found that the 'dot' over a letter 'I' is a suitable place.

Five people were arrested in this ring and the Krogers turned out to be Maurice and Cora Cohen who had been wanted by the CIA for over ten years.

Spies and agents come from all walks of life, for instance Guy Burgess who was once a member of the British SIS and the Foreign Office was recruited as a Soviet Agent when he was still a Cambridge University. Kim Philby was also employed by SIS who were recruiting for agents and he was instructed to pay particular attention to University Graduates. Philby had been 'In Place' for over ten years.

There are of course some agents who volunteer their information. These are called walk-in, such as Percy Allan who was a Sergeant who handled top secret documents he stated he was short of money. David Bingham was a Sub-Lieutenant in the Navy. He was also a walk-in but was compromised from the start. He was spotted going into the Russian Embassy and was fed with false information for the Russians. William Vassall was a KGB spy in the British Admiralty HQ and had been compromised at a sex orgy which had been staged by the KGB.

Generally, the members of MI5 were selected and drawn from the Universities or were ex-officers of the Armed Forces. Here is the difference with the Russians whose spies are drawn from all walks of life and they are always on the lookout for other possible agents, not only for their present use or occupation but also for future requirements. The officers are urged to join clubs and churches to give them a solid background and to increase their circle of acquaintances, whom they might be able to entice or manipulate. No one is safe from them and their evil methods, such as Frank Bossard a Senior Intelligence Officer who interrogated prominent scientists who escaped from the East. He was a coin collector and was always short of cash. He was hooked when he accepted £200, he now worked as a spy. The RAF was also involved when Douglas Britton, an RAF Sergeant who was a Signals Technician was photographed accepting money from a Russian Agent and was then forced to work for them.

State organisations were also used by the Russians who set up businesses and then used them as cover for their agents. These included Saxepont Film; Aeroflot; The Matreco; A.B. Sales and the Anglo-Soviet Shipping Line. The UNO Plant hire was set up in Britain only one year before the British Government expelled 105 agents for spying.

When the small number of British Security Officers are compared with the might of Russia, it shows the integrity of the leftists who are falling over backwards to make things difficult for them and are assisting the Soviets, especially when one considers the size of KGB and the different Directorates and Departments within their organisation.

The First Directorate for instance is concerned with espionage and has fifteen departments and employs over 10,000 men. One of those departments alone has a staff of 50 writers who disseminate false information to the West.

The Second Directorate is solely responsible for Counter Espionage; its officers are experts on locks, photography and Audi surveillance. More than 100,000 agents report through this directorate.

Counter intelligence within the Soviet Forces are dealt with by the Third Directorate.

The 4th, 5th and 6th Directorates were taken into the body and control of the Second Directorate in 1959.

The 7th carries out surveillance by entering offices illegally and recruiting agents amongst foreigners. It employs over 3,000 people in Moscow alone.

Forms of communication by Foreign Governments was kept under observation by the 8th Directorate who was also responsible for breaking codes.

9th Directorate provided security to the Russian Government and also had an Administrative aid in personnel division HQ, which also operates a technical and research laboratory in Pusckino. They had another division that was responsible for border posts and subversive literature.

The Individual Division is Inter State and checks on Soviet citizens, both at home and abroad, including Ambassadors down to Chauffeurs. They also keep surveillance on agents of other sections. Everyone whether a Diplomat, athlete, actor, singer or dancer who travels outside the USSR has agents of the Division with them. This division collects all scraps of information possible in all countries and they maintain a biography of everyone who may be of any use to the Red Cause. They collect information on parents, grandparents, education, career, family and friends, political views, works, relationships, financial circumstances, and any dirt which can possibly be used as blackmail. There are over 300 people constantly working on this index.

"Everyone in Russia is involved in spying. Ministries, Committees, Academics and even Tourist Organisations. We are all spies, we do not have Diplomats as the West knows them, and we are engaged in espionage in every country of the world," stated Colonel Oleg Penkovsky, a defector.

There were lighter moments of course, although very rarely.

"You've had a petty hectic time recently Jock, you need a break. With the Coronation coming along, I've made arrangements for you to take it easy. You'll have this detail, to look after these four chaps during the actual Ceremony, and afterwards until the day is over. After that, I will need you in the Abbey. It won't be a hard job, just to keep an eye on the Jewels etc."

So Jock knew why his vast amount of enquiries slowly began to get smaller, he still had a lot of work to do so as he could finish them. On Coronation Day he collected his four foreigners at their hotel, which meant a 4am start for him. This allowed him time to get up, dress, have breakfast and catch the early tram into town. His visitors were getting up early also, so as to take their reserved seats on The Mall. The streets were crowded, troops and police were already lining the Route of the Royal Procession, but the weather wasn't at all kind. It rained, heavens hard, what a day.

All through the morning they sat glued to their seats, trying to look as if they were enjoying it. Jock was inwardly glad when the procession at last returned and the crowds began to make their way to Buckingham Palace to view the newly crowned monarch on the balcony. He then had to escort his visitors to their hotel for lunch, which he was ready for, and he didn't have much interpreting to do as they only spoke to one another and himself.

After tea they all went to the places which had been reserved for them at Scotland Yard. They were allocated seats at a window overlooking the Embankment and County Hall, ready for the fireworks display. It was a great expenditure of cash for the Authority but everyone seemed to enjoy the sight. Jock looked at the mixture of nobility crammed in, with the country's officials and the high ranking police and services all mixed in with dignitaries and the County Hall officials. As tea and cakes were supplied, along with the drinks, he didn't mind, after all it was better than walking the streets.

After the Coronation he had another cushy job. He was detailed to be in the Abbey because he was to be one of the group guarding the Crown Jewels etc. They stood one on each side of the chair tucked into the side, out of sight. The crowds came in the main entrance in their thousands and slowly made their way down to the Abbey and followed the ropes past the Coronation Chair and the Crown Jewels. Jock stood with his mate just watching. There were three of them really but one went for a cuppa, or to the toilet, then came back to relieve one of the others.

The first and last thing they had to do was to check the whole building thoroughly; one had to do the tour of the catacombs and the passageways with their suits of armour, whilst the other two stood guard. The area around the throne was secure with a rope, red in colour, which was strung across the front to prevent the public crossing to the Coronation chair. Two of the men stood there and the other man protected the rear of the Queen's dressing room, between it and the Air Force Chapel. This was the prohibited area, no person was allowed to pass unless they were in possession of a pass giving them the required permission. These orders had been given to them personally by the head of the police. As Jock wandered around the dark corridors and landings of the Abbey he used to try on the old fashioned helmets which lay discarded with suits of armour. He never ever found a helmet big enough! He came to the decision that going by the size of the suits that all of the big knights of old were all very small men.

The public were only allowed to view the precious items at certain times and special passes were issued which allowed certain extra special groups of high personnel to cross the ropes and obtain a closer look at the famous objects. They had, of course, received the usual directions that nothing whatsoever must be touched, under the penalty of being asked to leave the Abbey at once, together with all the other persons on the pass. Only three of these passes would be allowed to cross the ropes each day. Jock and his colleagues had strict instructions to see that these instructions were obeyed. The passes had to be signed by both the Duke and the Dean of Westminster.

The throngs of the common people slowly made their daily walk up the aisles and past the objects of common heritage. Occasionally, a group of high ranking individuals with their Special Passes were passed through the ropes to get a closer look at the magnificence of splendour. Obviously something had to go wrong with all these rules and naturally it would have to occur when Jock was on duty. One of these extra special parties came along and prepared to cross the rope into the forbidden territory.

"Sorry" said Jock as he examined the pass, "We've already had three such passes through today, the full allocation of permission has already expired, you cannot come through."

The decision was made and it was final. The person in charge of the group made his authority known, an insignificant little policeman wasn't going to stop him.

"This is a very Special Group, you have to let them pass." His order was made in vain, Jock still refused permission.

"We have permission from the Duke to come through" the man stated.

"Sorry" said Jock, "I also have my orders."

The Home Office chap argued and insisted that the party must be let through but still Jock refused. The long line of the public was curious about the display and eased their way almost to a stop.

The Home Office man was beginning to get frustrated and sent one of his subordinates to fetch the Duke. The big bull neck of the Duke soon appeared as he came storming along the aisle.

"Who the hell refuses to let them through? I have given permission and authorisation for the party to go through," the Duke demanded when he reached the scene.

"I have," said Jock as he looked at the big man. He had made his stand and there was no going back. He looked at one of the rulers of the country, the man who had done all the required arranging and organisation for the Coronation. "I'm only obeying orders."

"Right, now you have my direct orders to let these people through," he stated.

"No Sir, sorry, they must have a Special Pass which is signed by you and the Dean. Those were my orders."

"Damn it man, I have signed it." The bull neck got even redder, "Isn't that enough for you."

"Those were your own orders, Sir, it will need to be also signed by the Dean." Jock expected the man to blow up, after all it probably was the first time that any one had declined so blatantly to obey

"Get the Dean," he snapped at last, as he towered above the little commoner who opposed him.

The Dean was duly sent for whilst the extra special group of people waited. When he arrived on the scene, he slid under the ropes and produced his pass at once to Jock smiling. "Hello, what's wrong?" he asked.

The Duke soon went into detail and sorted the thing out. It was decided that they should both sign the pass and that would be that.

"Sorry, no. I have my orders direct from my superior, distinctly and emphatically. Only three passes each day. They have already been past. I could not allow these persons through without his direct order," said Jock in reply but he was just being awkward, the other people thought.

"Well, he's right you know, we did say only three such passes each day," said the Dean after a hurried discussion. So it was eventually decided to send for the Commissioner in order that Jock could accept the Special Pass. He gave it and probably cursed Jock under his breath.

"Are you satisfied now?" asked the Duke.

"Sir, if you are happy and satisfied that everyone is carrying out your orders in the same manner, then I am content." He tried to keep a straight face as he spoke to the man.

The Dean smiled in his own benevolent way as he slid under the ropes and gave Jock a wink as he left. The Duke conversed for a while with the Special Party, no doubt passing on his apologies for their delay by such a thick-headed copper. He left them with his aide and as he passed Jock he muttered to him.

"Good job, well done. It's a pity everyone didn't do the same." What would he have done if Jock had let them in? Jock found out the next day when he was called in to the Commander's office. He was required to give a full report of the occurrence and a report was then asked for. The report was already written and Jock handed it over and, once read, the Guv said:

"Good, I suppose you know that the Sergeant has been returned to work? One copy for me, one for his nibs, and one for the Home Office." The reports were separated and Jock was then let into the secret, a Detective Sergeant had been suspended for letting his wife into the Abbey by using his pass, the Duke had stopped her and the Serg. was removed from duty. That's how strict the man was. Jock told about the party he had trouble with and the reason that his report was simple. Just after they had been let under the ropes and most of the group were clustered like kids around the back of the chair, they were examining the woodworm and repairs and one of them must have been feeling tired for she decided to take a seat. Rather unfortunate for her, she wasn't allowed to sit in the Coronation Chair for that was where she decided to rest her posterior. She hadn't time to feel that she was being crowned before she was gripped tightly by both arms and she couldn't get up.

The commotion she kicked up attracted the attention of the guide who was in charge of the party. He decided to demand what on earth Jock and his colleague were doing. He wanted to know what was wrong when he saw the woman sitting in the chair. He was advised to read his pass, with its directions, and after he had consumed the contents Jock then suggested that the orders be obeyed. He was told to collect his group together and leave the Abbey. If he did this quietly, knowledge of the incident wouldn't be known to the passing crowds.

"And if we don't?" he asked.

"As you see by the pass, Sir, any refusal will be met with any amount of force required to arrest and eject you, so please go quietly," Jock answered.

The friends of the Duke left with a lot of subdued muttering, leaving Jock and his colleague in peace with a lengthy report to write.

HUMAN NATURE

"Well, I'll leave the decision to you. Please yourself," said the Dean after the lengthy discussion. He had just informed Jock and his friends that they were going to have a Service in the Abbey but none of the chairs or the jewels would be moved. As they had the responsibility for the articles, naturally they would have to be in a position to keep their eyes on them, for protection.

The expected audience were to be high officials of the country, Foreign Ambassadors, High Ranking Officers of the Armed Forces, High Ranking Civil Servants and the Deity etc. Jock and his pals were not unduly worried about the positions held by these people, all they were interested in was the positions they themselves would occupy in order to guard the precious articles that they were responsible for.

"I think the television box would be the best place, if that's alright with you" said Jock, making his decision known to the Dean. "I don't want to seem as though as I'm not interested in the religious way of life but I'll be able to concentrate on the job in hand."

His mate agreed with him and so it was decided that they would take up their seats in the television box and as this place looked across the front of the altar, straight onto the Crown Jewels and over the Chair, it was certainly the best place. Their other colleague could cover the rear of the Abbey by the Air Force Chapel.

"In this way we can get out and move around without disturbing the service" said his colleague.

The Dean was fully in agreement, after all he didn't want the group of coppers sitting with his audience of High Ranking personnel, he wanted the upper class left in peace.

The day of the Service came and they all took up their positions and made themselves comfortable. Jock started to smile as the line of old Bishops took their places on seats which were placed in front of the Crown jewels. Obviously they couldn't have a better bodyguard, they were right in the line of vision of Jock and his pal so they couldn't avoid noticing the obvious.

It was quite apparent that age was telling on some of the Deity for when the sermon started that was the signal for sleep. Slowly, papers slipped from lifeless hands onto the floor as one after the other the old men went to sleep and eventually one of them lost his grip on his walking stick as it fell to the floor.

The snores were occasionally heard over the droning voice of the Clergy delegated to speak to the flock. Once he had stopped speaking, however, and all the audience stood up to sing the Bishop slept, in the arms of Morpheus, whilst they were being read texts from the Bible. Their neighbours shook them awake and helped them to their feet until they came back to the land of reality. Then, with quaking voices, they joined in the singing. 'Oh, if only your flocks could have seen you' thought Jock.

They were not going to get any peace while their tour of duty lasted because the day after the service, they were informed that a play was to be held in the Abbey. Workmen were all over the place putting up screens etc. across the end of the aisle, in front of the Coronation Chair. A door was placed at each side and a stage in the centre, and spotlights were also fitted. The stage was small and most of the play was about the Royalty of England through the ages, various Kings and Queens were to be represented, hence the dialogue. The spotlights would be centred on the people speaking, and slowly extinguished leaving the Abbey in total darkness.

The two leading ladies were to use the Queen's Dressing Room and her Ladies-in-Waiting who were situated alongside each other just behind the altar and facing the three Dukes' Chairs which had been covered by sheets. The rest of the cast were to use the Air Force Chapel as a dressing room, at the rear of the Abbey.

This meant that a lot of people were coming and going through the area where the valuable articles were placed and consequently everyone had to be stopped and asked to show their passes. It wasn't that they didn't trust the actors, but anyone could have slipped in and moved around. A lot of their friends did try to gain access to get a close view of the Coronation Chair and the Crown Jewels.

For instance, the leading lady had a habit of greeting everyone with the typified stage greeting of 'Good Evening Darling'. Everyone got it, including Jock, and not once but several times as she passed - he lost count of the number of times she said it.

"You don't want to see my pass again do you?" Jock accepted the fact that he knew her face and the fact that she had a pass and let her pass through. However, in the line of people waiting in the queue behind her, he saw a female he didn't know. He guessed what had happened. He looked closely at the pass that the woman produced for examination. He checked the name and turned his head.

"Miss Compton, you have dropped your pass, this lady is trying to catch you up to return it." The pass was snatched from his hand and two red faced ladies walked off in different directions, with not even a 'Thank You Darling'.

After the first night show was over the crowd of well-wishers knew it was impossible to go through the front doors which were guarded, so they headed round the back and tried to go to the Dressing Room via the Air Force Chapel. However, Jock was there and met them and the invasion was stopped. He pointed out that this was a place of worship, not a theatre. Not even the mention of well-known people made him change his mind.

One night, the place was in darkness, all lights were out except one small spotlight and as he slowly made his rounds past the Crown Jewels and behind the altar, he saw a figure in armour with a blood-stained bandage round his head and his left arm in a sling, resting in one of the Duke's chairs!

"Who are you?" he whispered.

"I'm King Henry VI," was the dull reply.

"Well move yourself laddie, you're sitting in the wrong chair, that's the Duke of Edinburgh's seat you're in."

His orders were simple - none of the cast were allowed to use the Royal Chair, nor any of the seats allocated to the Bishops.

CHURCH SERVICE

After the play was finished it was decided to hold a Service for all the Big Parts to attend. The Dean had a discussion with Jock and his colleagues.

"I know you will want to be as close as possible," he said, "Would you like a seat in the front or in the sides where you can move; or have you any other idea?"

The problem was considered for some time. If they were in the audience they could hardly move without causing a disturbance, and apart from that they would be stuck amongst all the Royal personages etc. So Jock eventually suggested using the TV Box that was situated alongside the Coronation Chair and from here they could see all the Crown Jewels. Two men were to go in there and one was to cover the back of the Alter and dressing rooms. They were all agreed.

The day they took up their positions in the Box Jock noted, with amusement, that the line of Bishops would be facing them whilst the Service was taking place and it was during the Service that he noticed it was not only the public who occasionally doze off because apparently sermons had the same affect on elderly Bishops!

FAMILY PROBLEMS

Although work was endless, normal family life still carried on. Every individual has his own problems and Jock was no exception. During his stay in the 'Big City' most of his family, and that of his wife's, had died. Only recently his brother had been killed at work and his wife was dying of cancer; the neighbours were good and had looked after her while his husband was at work.

"What would happen down here under similar circumstances?" asked Puggle. She was obviously worried and Jock had often thought about the same thing, without getting a satisfactory answer. This was due to the Big City being so big and lonely. Friends were just not made and neighbours tended to ignore one another, Puggle was worried and her health began to suffer. Jock thought of all aspects, one of which was the children's education plus his work prospects. If their future was to be considered and a move was necessary, then he must do it soon. Most of his wife's family were still alive so if they had to move home, at least they would be company. Although he enjoyed his job and the position he held, he was prepared to leave the Department because his family came first.

He mentioned the subject to his boss, who became seriously concerned.

"We don't want to lose you Jock, you know you're in line for promotion shortly?" The man persisted in his attempt to change Jock's mind and later, he told Jock he had been making enquiries for him due to the fact he was insistent about leaving the Branch. He had arranged for him to have a Chief Security Officer's job at a Scientific Research Laboratory. This was a job normally kept for men leaving and was a 'cushy' job for retirement. Jock thanked him.

"No, I've been away from my family too much and that job wouldn't be any different and that he would still be away from the wife and family."

The boss told him about all the 'perks' that went with the job, paid holidays abroad and family fares. Holidays, then he could think of another job that had been offered, to check up on senior Civil Servants, MPs and other people in authority - again with all the holidays and pay, which was far in excess to anything that Jock could ever hope to earn in a lifetime.

"Thank you Sir, but I've made my mind up," Jock answered. "I have to go, for my wife's sake."

Whilst on holiday he made tentative enquiries regarding a transfer to the local constabulary. At the local Police Office he dropped in lucky for the Inspector informed him that an interview board was actually taking place that very day. He directed Jock to the County Headquarters where all the hopefuls were gathered for interview. He made his way to the given location and after a few delicate questions and suggestions he jumped the queue.

The Chief Constable and his Assistant Chief Constable sat in harmony at a long desk. He looked with curiosity at the tall, well-built man, mature, and obviously much older than the other applicants.

"Name?"

"I know my name is not on your list," Jock replied. "I'm a member of Special Branch, New Scotland Yard. I'm on holiday and I called in to make enquiries regarding the possibility of a transfer to this Force and somehow I have finished off in here."

"Rather a coincidence and ideal for a transfer applicant receiving full treatment of a rookie, this has never been known before. We have no record from your Department regarding a transfer."

"That would be correct Sir, I have spoken to my Superintendent about moving but, as yet, I have not submitted a report," Jock said.

"You have not yet asked for a transfer, yet you come here for an interview, why?" asked the Chief Constable.

"I needed to know that my application would be favourably considered when I submitted it,' Jock answered.

"Well, you certainly believe in crossing your bridges before you reach them. I like a man to be sure of his ground," the Chief Constable told him. "Now you're here, we may as well obtain a few details."

So the interview began but it was only a matter of form obtaining Jock's particulars, and was soon over. With smiles all round, they wished him 'Good Day' and the Chief said, 'Enjoy your holidays'.

Upon his return to his office, Jock typed out his application for a transfer and handed it to the Inspector for approval. After noting it, he said

"Why, Mr MacGregor, why, you're an experienced officer in the Department, your education is all one could ask for in this field of work and your knowledge of languages and the contacts you have made will all be wasted up there. Have you considered all the points? Are you discontent with anything? Your promotion is also guaranteed shortly - is it extra cash you need, or is it family matters?" asked the Inspector

"I'm sorry Sir, I do enjoy doing my job and much as I would like to stay, I must consider my family, who you have just mentioned. I have considered all points over a long time before making this decision. I know that I will also be worse off financially," Jock replied.

"Well, if you have made up you mind I will put your application through for you but I'm sorry to see you go Jock." Jock had already spoken to his Superintendent and the Commander about the move.

"I've already spoken to the boss about it, he knows how I feel and the reasons for it," he said.

"Right Mr MacGregor we'll see how it goes and all I can say is Good Luck to you." The Inspector was quite despondent.

A week later Jock received a letter informing him that a transfer had been approved and had been accepted by the local Constabulary. A house had been provided for him, as well as the day and time that he should report at a small Police Office, from where he would operate.

He began making arrangements for the sale of his house and the removal of his family and goods to his new home.

A million and one things had to be done in a short space of time and when the removal van arrived, they were ready. The van was loaded and packed, the house was cleared and locked up and the keys were left with the house agents. Good-byes had already been said to their acquaintances and now they were on their way to a new life.

As Jock looked back at the empty house his feelings were mixed. 'What will happen next?' he wondered.

Printed in the United Kingdom
by Lightning Source UK Ltd.
123175UK00002B/133-152/A